DARING TO DATE DR CELEBRITY

BY
EMILY FORBES

RESISTING THE NEW DOC IN TOWN

BY
LUCY CLARK

MILLS & BOON

Emily Forbes began her writing life as a partnership between two sisters who are both passionate bibliophiles. As a team, 'Emily' had ten books published, and one of her proudest moments was when her tenth book was nominated for the 2010 Australian Romantic Book of the Year Award.

While Emily's love of writing remains as strong as ever, the demands of life with young families have recently made it difficult to work on stories together. But rather than give up her dream Emily now writes solo. The challenges may be different, but the reward of having a book published is still as sweet as ever.

Whether as a team or as an individual Emily hopes to keep bringing stories to her readers. Her inspiration comes from everywhere, and stories she hears while travelling, at mothers' lunches, in the media and in her other career as a physiotherapist all get embellished with a large dose of imagination until they develop a life of their own.

If you would like to get in touch with Emily you can e-mail her at emilyforbes@internode.on.net

Lucy Clark is actually a husband-and-wife writing team. They enjoy taking holidays with their children, during which they discuss and develop new ideas for their books using the fantastic Australian scenery. They use their daily walks to talk over characterisation and fine details of the wonderful stories they produce, and are avid movie buffs. They live on the edge of a popular wine district in South Australia with their two children, and enjoy spending family time together at weekends.

DARING TO DATE DR CELEBRITY

BY
EMILY FORBES

First published in Great Britain 2013
by Mills & Boon, an imprint of Harlequin (UK) Limited.
Harlequin (UK) Limited, Eton House, 18-24 Paradise Road,
Richmond, Surrey TW9 1SR

© Emily Forbes 2013

ISBN: 978 0 263 89910 8

Harlequin (UK) policy is to use papers that are natural, renewable and recyclable products and made from wood grown in sustainable forests. The logging and manufacturing process conform to the legal environmental regulations of the country of origin.

Printed and bound in Spain
by Blackprint CPI, Barcelona

Dear Reader

I'd like to introduce you to Caspar St Claire, Paediatrician and the star of a reality medical television series. This story began with the idea of Caspar, with his curly, dark hair and mesmerising green eyes he took up residence in my head and refused to leave until I gave him a voice.

Things fell into place from there as he created his story. Despite his celebrity status he was first and foremost a doctor with a very gentle nature so I decided he would suit paediatrics. He also struck me very much as a white knight and therefore he needed a woman. Annie Simpson is that woman.

Their story is ultimately quite different to what I had initially imagined, my characters do seem to like taking over, but in this case I was happy to let them take the lead as they seemed to know what they were doing ☺.

I hope you enjoy a glimpse of country South Australia as Caspar and Annie find their Happily Ever After.

Love, Emily

For my gorgeous Goddaughter, Kate,
I am enjoying watching you grow into a beautiful woman.
Your constant smile brings happiness to everyone around
you and that is a gift I hope you never lose.

With love and best wishes for a happy life,

Your Godmother.

CHAPTER ONE

'ARE YOU TELLING us or asking us?' Annie demanded.

The rest of the staff who were assembled around the boardroom table seemed to be sitting in quiet acceptance but Annie Simpson wasn't having a bar of that. She stared at Patrick Hammond. Was he serious? Was the hospital director really telling her, telling them all, that Blue Lake Hospital was going to be the setting for a reality television show? That there were plans to film a hospital drama featuring real patients and real doctors, *their* patients and *their* doctors, in *their* hospital, and he expected the staff to get on board?

'I'm telling you what's happening and asking if you're prepared to be part of it.' For a large man Patrick was very softly spoken and today was no exception. If Annie's question had irritated him he showed no signs of annoyance.

Annie knew Patrick didn't run his hospital like a dictatorship—most decisions were discussed with senior staff to some degree. Most *medical* decisions, she qualified. The day-to-day running of the hospital was not something Patrick would normally converse with them about. Annie wondered exactly where a reality television show fitted into the scheme of things.

'Do we have a choice?' she asked.

Patrick rubbed one hand over his closely cropped hair. 'Of course you do. But I would like you to consider what this means for the hospital—money going into the coffers, good publicity, *free* publicity. With so many country hospitals struggling to stay open, having this sort of media buzz can only be a good thing.'

'Are you sure?' Annie argued. 'What if something goes wrong? What if there's a disaster and the hospital gets sued? That won't garner good publicity. And it's not likely the government would close this hospital. We may be rural but we're not a small six-bed outfit. We are a specialist facility in the state's second-biggest town. There would be an outcry if they even mentioned shutting us down.'

'We may be a large hospital but we're still government funded and that means we have the same funding issues as everyone else,' Patrick countered. 'Do you have any idea how many people watched the last series of *RPE*?'

Annie had thought his question was rhetorical but when Patrick paused, obviously waiting for her answer, she shook her head. She didn't have a clue.

'Two million. Every night.'

That was a huge audience for Australian television. Annie had known *RPE*, the series filmed at the Royal Prince Edward Hospital in Melbourne, was popular, but she hadn't realised how popular.

'And Caspar St Claire is one of the stars,' Patrick continued. 'This spin-off series is a big deal. He's a local boy made good. There will be big interest in what he does, not just locally but around the country. And the television network is compensating us nicely for the opportunity to film here.'

'So it's all about the money?'

Patrick shook his head. 'Don't be too quick to criticise, there's a long list of things the hospital needs and the money from the network will go a long way towards providing those things, including refitting a birthing unit for your department. And you do realise Caspar is a paediatrician?' he queried. 'As an obstetrician, I thought you'd be pleased to know that I've found someone to cover Paediatrics while Phil is on long service leave.'

Annie wasn't ready to let Patrick have the last word. She'd been the subject of media interest before and it hadn't been a positive experience. She'd moved to this quiet, regional centre to rebuild her life and she wasn't happy to find that she might be cast back into the public eye whether she liked it or not. Not happy at all. 'I would be pleased if I thought you'd found a replacement who has come to work but it seems to me you've just found one who is coming accompanied by his own circus. I'm not interested in being a part of that.'

'I have never worked with a circus. Children, yes, animals, no, and definitely not circuses.'

Annie jumped as a deep masculine voice spoke up behind her and ran like molten lava down her spine. From the seat beside her she heard Tori Williams, one of the anaesthetists, catch her breath and then sigh, and Annie didn't need to turn her head to know that Caspar St Claire was standing behind her and had obviously heard her every word. She could feel his scrutiny just as she could feel the eyes of everyone else in the room. They were watching her, waiting with interest to see what she was going to do.

She had no idea what Caspar St Claire was thinking and she didn't want to turn round to read the expression on his face, but he had addressed her and she couldn't sit there pretending to be deaf. She turned in her seat to find the devil himself watching her. A rather handsome devil, she had to admit, but that didn't change the fact that she didn't want him here.

Of course, she recognised him immediately. No introduction was necessary, at least from her side. Patrick was right, *RPE* was a huge ratings winner and, even if Annie hadn't actually been glued to her television like everyone else for the last season, she'd certainly caught a few episodes and knew who Caspar St Claire was. But why did he have to turn up here?

'Let me assure you,' he said in his ridiculously rich, made-for-radio voice, 'that my patients always come first and the crew are exceptionally good at being as unobtrusive as possible.'

She wanted to laugh at him. If he thought she believed that for one second he was in for a surprise, but the force of his gaze made the laughter catch in her throat. His green eyes held hers, challenging her to argue with him, but she was temporarily struck dumb. She wished the floor would open up beneath her feet, but of course she wouldn't have the good fortune for that to happen.

Every medical television show had a resident heart-throb doctor and even though *RPE* was a reality show they'd still managed to find some attractive stars, and Dr St Claire was the pick of the bunch. But she hadn't expected him to be even better looking in real life. His dark hair was probably an inch longer than it needed to be but that extra inch gave enough length to let his hair curl, lending him a youthful look. A just-tumbled-out-of-bed look.

As she pictured him tangled up in his sheets, running his fingers through his hair to try to tame it ready for the day, she could feel the heat of his gaze burn into her as he continued to watch her, waiting for her reply. She felt her cheeks begin to flush as her temperature rose but she couldn't think of anything to say.

'Do you have any other objections, Dr Simpson?'

He knew who she was? That shocked her out of her imaginings and back into the real world. Back to reality. She frowned. How the hell did he know her name?

But she'd have to worry about that later. The rest of the staff was sitting mutely around the table, all watching the interaction, one-sided though it was at present, and there were more important things to worry about than how he knew her name. Far more important things.

'I'm sure I have a lot more objections, Dr St Claire, and without more information, a lot more information,' she stressed, 'I won't make a decision about my involvement. When do you begin filming?'

'Tomorrow.'

Annie's eyebrows shot skywards. She needed more time. She wasn't ready for her department to be invaded by cameras. She wasn't ready for that exposure. Not again. Not by a long way.

The easiest thing would be to say no immediately. To tell him she *didn't* want to be part of this. Then she wouldn't have to worry about anything further. She wouldn't need to wait for more information. There was no way she was going to agree to a media circus in her delivery suites and she should tell him that right now.

She opened her mouth but before she could speak Caspar interrupted.

'Don't say no just yet.'

Annie stared at him. Was she that easy to read? Although she supposed it was a reasonable guess, given her reaction so far. She was tempted to deny her intentions, though, just to prove him wrong. But what if that was his game? She wasn't ready for this. She didn't want to play games, she didn't want to play at all.

'Let me introduce the show's producer, Gail Cameron. She will run through the details, answer any questions and take care of the legalities. You don't have to make a decision today,' he said as he continued to hold her in his sights, 'but filming starts tomorrow and it would be great if some of you are on board by then.'

He broke eye contact with her as he looked around the table at the other staff members and Annie felt some of the heat leaving her body as he looked away, almost as though a cloud had passed across the sun, casting a shadow over her.

'We're not here to sensationalise things,' he continued. 'We're here to tell stories, to raise awareness and, as I'm sure Patrick has told you, Blue Lake Hospital, and therefore your departments, will benefit financially.'

Annie decided she didn't want anyone accusing her of being difficult or obstructive and she was well aware the hospital could always use extra funds. She'd pretend to give the situation due consideration.

And then she'd say no.

Patrick stood up and moved chairs around, making room for Caspar and Gail to sit at the table. Annie couldn't help but notice that Caspar waited for Gail to sit first and his manners earned him a brownie point, but he still had a long way to go in her opinion.

Annie studied him as he stood beside the table, waiting for Gail to get settled.

He was wearing a single-breasted suit, pale grey in colour, with a plain white shirt and a striped tie. His shoulders were broad and square and filled the suit jacket out very nicely. His shirt was crisply ironed but the suit was a little crumpled. Perhaps, despite being Australia's latest celebrity pin-up, appearances weren't at the top of his list of priorities. Annie decided she could like that about the man, even if she didn't have to like him being here.

He undid the buttons on his jacket and held his tie against his stomach, keeping it out of the way, as he sat in his own chair. His stomach was flat and lean and Caspar was slimmer in real life than he'd appeared on television, but then she remembered that the camera supposedly added pounds. Did, in fact, add pounds. She knew that from her own limited experience.

Gail was speaking, saying something about the types of medical cases they were interested in, and Annie knew she should be listening but her attention kept wandering. Caspar was rolling a pen through his fingers and the movement caught her eye. His fingers were long and slender and his hands were large. Annie could imagine him cradling the newborn babies in his care, holding them nestled safely in the palms of his hands.

Now that he was sitting down, diagonally opposite her, Annie had less of him to peruse. His head was turned to his left, slightly away from her, leaving her looking at his profile. Leaving her free to study him. There were flecks of grey at his temples, a touch of salt and pepper in his black curls, and his olive skin was darkened by the shadow of designer stubble on his jaw. His nose was perfectly straight but maybe a touch longer than it needed to be, which was a good thing, Annie thought, as it stopped him from being too good looking.

Was there such a thing as too good looking? She'd never wondered about that before.

His green eyes were scanning the room, working his way around the table in a clockwise direction as he studied each person present in the meeting, and Annie wondered what he was thinking.

He was looking at Colin, one of the orthopaedic surgeons, and Annie knew it was only a matter of time before his gaze landed on her. She felt her heart rate increase with that thought. For some reason this made her nervous. Her palms felt sweaty and she wiped them on her trousers.

Caspar was watching Tori now but Tori seemed oblivious to his inspection. She had her head down and was furiously taking notes. That was good. She and Tori had formed a close friendship in the six months since she herself had moved to Mount Gambier and she could use Tori's notes to catch up later on everything she hadn't heard Gail say.

And then it was her turn. She'd meant to look away before his gaze reached her but she hadn't and now he was looking straight at her, his green eyes locked with hers. Annie could feel herself begin to blush again under his scrutiny. The heat started over her sternum and she knew it was only a matter of time before it spread to her face, but she was unable to break the connection.

Until Tori nudged her with her elbow.

'Ow,' Annie complained. But it was enough to get her to glance to her right.

'Are you paying attention?' Tori asked. 'You need to listen to this.'

'I'll read your notes later,' Annie told her, but as she turned her head away from Tori she deliberately sought out Gail's face as she pretended to listen and tried to keep Caspar St Claire out of her line of sight. She'd expected his attention to have moved on to the next person at the table but from the corner of her eye she could see that he was still watching her and she couldn't help but move her head, ever so slightly, to look back at him.

He appeared to be concentrating and she wondered again what he was thinking. What he thought about her. His expression seemed to be challenging her but she wasn't sure what his challenge was. Did he want her to question him or back down? If he wanted her to give in on the very first day he was going to be sorely disappointed. She had no intention of giving in, not today and not tomorrow.

She met his gaze as she thought about all the ways she could say no but then his intense expression gave way to a smile and his seriousness dissolved into something else altogether. Something slightly carnal and iniquitous, and Annie forgot all about reality television, all about the cameras invading the hospital, all about saying no as his smile raced through her.

It lit a fire in her belly that poured through her, warming everything from her face to her toes and everything in between, until she felt as though her insides might melt together in a big pool of lust. She'd thought his serious, brooding expression had been handsome but his smile transformed his face completely and now his expression was cheeky and playful and made her think of sex. Something she hadn't thought about for a long time.

Sex wasn't something that had ever been high on her list of priorities. She enjoyed it but she didn't really see what all the fuss was about. She was quite happy being celibate. But Caspar St Claire made her think of sex. And not the type of sex she was used to. He made her think of hot, sweaty, take-no-prisoners sex. Tangled bedsheets and late-afternoon sex. The weight of a hard, firm, male body. He made her think of multiple orgasms and sex that was so all-consuming she'd be too exhausted to be able to move afterwards. The kind of sex she'd read about in novels and seen in movies but had never experienced.

The temperature in the room felt as though it had increased by several degrees and Annie could feel her nipples harden as her imagination worked overtime. That was enough to make her break eye contact. She looked away hurriedly, almost guiltily, afraid he would be able to see her shameless thoughts.

Her ill-fated marriage had been based on lots of things but desire hadn't been one of them. She'd been a young, inexperienced bride and her marriage had been more about companionship and less about physical attraction or raging hormones. At the time she'd thought she was making a sensible choice. She had seen her parents' relationship self-combust repeatedly and theirs had definitely been a physical thing. As a teenager she'd decided she wouldn't make the same mistake. The trouble was she just made a different one.

But she'd never felt such a strong, unexpected stirring of desire before and to have it triggered by a complete stranger disturbed her. She didn't want to be affected by him. She didn't want to be affected by anybody. As far as she was concerned, that was asking for trouble.

She was going to put Caspar St Claire and everything he was associated with into a mental box marked 'Do not open'. She didn't need to worry about him or his business. It was going to be nothing to do with her.

CHAPTER TWO

CASPAR LOOKED AROUND the table, watching the people, reading their faces, trying to guess their thoughts. Some of them were harder than others. He'd done his research so he knew who they were. He'd found it paid to be prepared—life was challenging enough often enough that he didn't want to deal with unnecessary surprises.

Most looked receptive to Gail's spiel; she made the show sound exciting and new, something people would want to be a part of. Most people. The reality was that it was the editing that would make the show exciting. It was in post-production that the tears and the drama, the heartache, the relief and joy would be enhanced. That was when the emotions would be increased and amplified. For the hospital staff it would really be business as usual. But with cameras.

Gail would make a good salesperson, Caspar thought as his gaze travelled around the group. He didn't have a clear view of the hospital director, Patrick, as Gail was blocking his line of sight, but that didn't matter. He knew he was on board. Ravi Patel, general surgeon, was sitting beside Patrick. He was watching Gail intently and nodding his head in all the right places. Caspar would bet his precious sports car that Ravi would sign the paperwork before the day was finished.

The RMOs from the emergency department were next. They were shooting glances at Colin Young, one of the hospital's two orthopaedic surgeons. They would take their cues from him and the fact that he was in this meeting led Caspar to believe that he was agreeable to the project. The director of nursing was to Caspar's right. He already knew that Maxine, and therefore her nursing staff, was ready to go. Which left only two—Dr Tori Williams, anaesthetist, and Dr Annie Simpson, obstetrician.

They were seated diagonally opposite him around the oval table. Dr Williams was hunched over the table, furiously taking notes, but he couldn't see her face and he didn't know whether her note-taking was a positive sign or not. He watched her scribbling for a few more moments but his mind had already moved on to the next person at the table.

Dr Annie Simpson. Patrick Hammond had sent him a short biography of each of the department heads and he recalled what little he'd read about Dr Simpson. Obstetrician, aged twenty-nine, single, trained in Adelaide and started work at Blue Lake Hospital six months ago.

Obviously intelligent and attractive, his mind added a few more adjectives for good measure and he decided he'd have to find out whether 'single' meant unmarried or not in a relationship at all.

If he was honest he'd admit he'd been looking forward to meeting her since he'd seen the photo Patrick had included. He'd specifically asked for photos so he'd be able to identify everyone but he had to admit that Annie's photo hadn't done her justice.

It was a good photo, she was an attractive woman, but it hadn't done justice to the glossy shine of her brown hair or the creaminess of her skin. It hadn't highlighted her sharply defined cheekbones that gave structure to her elfin face neither had it captured her scent.

Standing behind her as he'd entered the room, he'd caught a soft scent of jasmine, which could have come from any one of the women in the space but somehow he'd known it belonged to Annie. The fire in her dark brown eyes had been another surprise. Her eyes had burned with barely contained disapproval, which she hadn't attempted to hide.

He'd expected a lot of things but her passionate objection was something he hadn't anticipated. But he wasn't one to back down from a challenge and he suspected that was just as well.

He'd found it interesting that when Dr Simpson had voiced her concerns no one else had spoken up. Did that mean that she was the only one with concerns or just that she was the only one forthright enough to voice them?

He could see her now in the corner of his eye. A petite woman, she was sitting with perfect posture, her spine stiff and straight, self-control evident. Whatever she might be lacking in size she'd certainly made up for in spirit, but he wondered if she would have been so forthright if she'd known he and Gail could hear every word.

He turned his head to look at her properly. Her shiny curtain of hair fell smoothly down each side of her face, framing it perfectly. Dark chocolate-brown eyes, the colour of which contrasted sharply with her creamy complexion, looked back at him and as he watched he could see two crimson patches of heat appearing over her chiselled cheekbones.

The only other contrasting colour on her face was the soft, plump swell of her pink lips. She held his gaze and he could see the challenge in her brown eyes demanding he convince her of the merits of this project.

Yep, he reckoned, she would have told him straight to his face if she'd known he was standing behind her within earshot. He got the impression she wasn't one to hold back.

Well, challenge accepted, he thought. He needed her on side and he wouldn't rest until she came on board.

Along with the television project he had his own reasons for coming to Mount Gambier. He'd suggested Blue Lake Hospital as a potential location because it suited him and he wasn't about to sit here and see the project fall apart now. It needed to go ahead and in order to work it really needed the support of the existing hospital staff. And not just one or two of them, he needed them all.

The television network hadn't brought anyone other than him across from the previous series. The budget, with the hospital board's permission, was being used to bolster the hospital coffers, and there wasn't any money to pay extra doctors. The project needed to use the doctors and nurses that were to hand.

He would do whatever it took to convince Dr Simpson of that. He just needed to find out what she wanted. And work out how to give it to her.

He smiled at her, giving her the smile he'd always used on his older sisters when he'd wanted to get his own way, but this time there was no answering smile. No response at all from Dr Simpson, unless he counted the turning of her head to look away. Not the outcome he'd wanted, he had to admit, but there was still time. This had to work.

Annie couldn't get out of the meeting room fast enough once Gail wrapped up the session. She had no desire to hang around under Caspar's inspection. No desire to be coerced into signing consent forms. And she wasn't prepared for further discussions about why she was so against the idea of appearing on television. Her reasons were none of his business. All he needed to know was that she wasn't interested. In any of it.

She dragged Tori to the staff cafeteria, desperate for a coffee fix after the stress and strain of the meeting. She couldn't think straight while he was watching her with his heavy-eyed green gaze. Her mental picture of him tangled in his sheets was proving hard to shift and even though she knew it was entirely a product of her imagination she was mortified that her mind had taken her there, and she knew she had to put some distance between them if she was going to be able to keep those lustful thoughts out of her head.

She needed some distance if she was going to be able to focus on her job. But if she'd thought she was going to escape discussing the hottest topic in the hospital, she was mistaken.

The cafeteria was buzzing with the news and even Tori, despite bringing Annie to task for staring at Caspar earlier when she should have been listening to Gail, couldn't resist bringing him into their conversation now. 'What have you got against him?' she wanted to know.

'It's not him per se,' Annie tried to explain. 'I just don't want cameras following my every move. I'm here to do a job. I owe it to my patients to give them my best. I don't want people in my way. And that includes him.'

The idea of cameras watching her terrified her. Twice in her life she had been the subject of media attention and neither time had the experience been pleasant, but the thought of working in close proximity to Caspar St Claire, of having him watch her with his bedroom eyes, was even more terrifying. She didn't know if she'd be able to concentrate under his gaze and that made her feel vulnerable. And feeling vulnerable was not something she enjoyed.

'Well, I think he's here to stay,' Tori told her. 'At least for the next eight weeks. And you'll probably be working quite closely with him. He'll be responsible for the care of all those little newborns you deliver. I don't see how you can avoid him. Or why you'd want to.'

Annie sighed. Tori was right. She was going to have to come up with a solution. She was going to have to work out how to cope with the situation, as unpleasant as it seemed. 'I suppose I can't avoid him,' she agreed, 'but I should be able to avoid being on camera. They'll soon get sick of taking footage of the back of my head and then hopefully they can leave me alone to get on with my job.'

Tori was laughing. 'You're amazing. You'd have to be the only female in the entire hospital who would complain about having to spend time with Dr Tall, Dark and Handsome. Enjoy it. You'll be the envy of all the women in town.'

Annie couldn't imagine being able to enjoy one single minute of it and she'd happily swap places with Tori. With anyone, for that matter. 'I'm sure you'll get your turn, he's bound to need your services while he's here,' she replied. 'You can make sure you have yourself on the roster when they're filming. You can show your face on camera and then they won't need me.'

'I'll be in Theatre with a mask over my face,' Tori grumbled, as she picked up her coffee and moved away from the counter. 'Hey, maybe you could just start wearing a mask for your consults—that would solve your problem.'

Annie didn't bother to respond to that comment. She just glared at Tori as she stirred milk into her coffee but Tori wasn't finished.

'Caspar St Claire.' She sighed. 'He even sounds like a movie star.'

Annie snorted. 'He probably changed his name for television. I mean, really, who has a name like that?'

'You don't like my name, Dr Simpson?'

Damn it. Annie closed her eyes and groaned silently. He'd sneaked up on her and caught her out again. She was going to have to be more careful. She opened her eyes to find Tori trying to stifle a smile. Great. She turned round and came face to face with Dr Tall, Dark and Handsome.

He wasn't trying to stifle a smile. In fact, he was smirking. At her expense. How she'd love to wipe that look off his face but the only way she could think of doing that was by telling him she didn't like his name. And that wasn't true. It was a name that rolled smoothly off the tongue, a name that wouldn't be easily forgotten. Smooth and unforgettable. Much like the man himself, she guessed. Real or not, his name suited him.

'You have a very nice name,' she admitted grudgingly, 'but it's unusual enough to make me wonder if you made it up.' She had to tilt her head back to look up into his face. He was several inches taller than her, an inch or two over six feet, she guessed, and from her viewpoint the strong angles of his jaw, darkened by the shadow of his beard, were even more obvious.

'I admit it's unusual but I assure you it's the name my parents gave me. I can't practise medicine under any other,' he replied.

Annie shrugged. He'd made a fair point.

'I seem to be needing to assure you of a lot of things,

Dr Simpson.' He was standing close enough that Annie could see where his day's growth of beard was beginning to darken his jaw and she could feel his breath on her face as he spoke. She looked down, away from his inquisitive green eyes, but she was still aware of the little puffs of soft, warm air that smelt of peppermint and brushed her cheekbones when he spoke to her.

'Is there anything else that's bothering you?' he asked. 'I'd really like you to be on board with this project. As the hospital's obstetrician and paediatrician our paths will cross often, and if we can find a way to work together I think it will be to everyone's advantage. Should we clear the air some more while we have time?'

She looked up again, dragging her eyes away from the broad expanse of his chest to meet his eyes. At this distance she could see they were flecked with brown. Annoyed with herself for noticing, she retorted, 'You may have the time, Dr St Claire, but I'm very busy so if you'll excuse me I have patients to see.'

She knew she sounded snippy but he was standing too close. She was too aware of him. Of his green eyes, of his broad shoulders, of his breath on her skin, and his proximity was playing havoc with her senses, making it impossible for her to think. She couldn't cope with him in her personal space. She hadn't worked out how she was going to deal with him yet. Not in her hospital or in her life. She needed distance. It was the only thing that was going to work for her. She needed to leave. Now.

She picked up her coffee, gripping the cardboard cup so tightly it was in danger of being crushed, and stalked off, glaring at Tori to make sure her friend followed her. She didn't want to leave her consorting with the enemy.

'That was rude,' Tori admonished as she hurried to

keep pace with Annie. 'You'll need to play nicely. He could arrange to make you look bad on camera.'

'He wouldn't!' Annie's stride faltered. She hadn't stopped to consider the consequences of her behaviour.

'No, probably not,' Tori admitted. 'If you'd been listening to Gail you would have heard that their intention isn't to paint any of us in a bad light but to give people an insight into what goes on inside a hospital. But I'm sure they're not averse to showing any sparks that might be flying between patients and their families or families and staff or even just between the staff. And where those sparks come from is probably irrelevant—antagonistic or friendly, they all make for good television. But don't forget, Gail's first priority will be to Caspar. She has no loyalty to you so my advice is to play nicely.'

Annie cursed her bad luck. Why had the television network decided to film here? All she wanted was to be left in peace, to be left alone to do her work. Working under the scrutiny of cameras wasn't part of her agenda. She didn't want to be in the spotlight and she had no intention of being a celebrity doctor.

If she didn't give permission to include her in the series then Caspar St Claire wouldn't have the opportunity to make her look bad. But she supposed it wouldn't hurt to play nicely just in case. But it would be even better if she could avoid him altogether.

That plan worked for the rest of the afternoon. Almost.

Annie was heading home, exiting through the main lobby, when the front page of the local paper caught her eye. Caspar was smiling up at her from the centre of the page, looking just as handsome in black and white as he did in the flesh. Curiosity got the better of her and she stopped and picked up the paper, noticing that it was a couple of days old already.

She flicked it open and as she unfolded it Caspar's photographed companion came into view. A tall, attractive blonde woman, Annie recognised her as the host of a popular light entertainment show. Her curiosity piqued further, she began to read the article. Naturally it started by espousing Caspar's talents as the local boy who was returning to his home town as a celebrity doctor and went on to talk about the success of the television series. Annie opened the paper, turning to page four to continue reading, interested to see what the journalist had to say about the woman on Caspar's arm.

'Anything interesting in there?'

Annie jumped as Caspar's warm-treacle tones broke her concentration, interrupting her before she got to the gossip. She looked up, taking in his narrow hips, grey suit and broad shoulders almost as a reflex before her eyes came to rest on his face. One corner of his mouth lifted in the beginning of a smile and she could see the humour in his eyes as he waited for her to deny that she'd been reading about him. But there was no use pretending she hadn't been hunting for information.

'You interrupted me before I got to the good bit,' she replied.

The smile that had been threatening to begin now broke across his face as he laughed. 'If there's anything you need to know, why don't you ask me? I'll trade you a question for a question.'

She tried to ignore the way his smile made his eyes sparkle, triggering the tremble in her stomach. 'Mount Gambier is a long way from the bright lights of Melbourne. How did the network convince you to come here?' she asked.

Annie herself had moved to Mount Gambier happily, hoping the regional location and the job opportunity would give her a chance to rebuild her life, but in her mind the country town seemed a strange choice not only for the television series but also for Caspar St Claire. Regardless of the fact he'd been raised here, she knew he hadn't lived in the Mount for a long time and she wondered what had made him agree to return. With his confident manner and his high profile he seemed far more suited to a big city hospital and to the perks his celebrity status would bring him in a city like Melbourne.

'I wanted to come.'

'Why?' she asked.

'That's two questions,' he said, as he shook his head at her. 'I believe it's my turn now. What are you doing after work?'

His question surprised her. She opened her mouth to say 'Nothing' but quickly realised that, depending on his motives, she might be opening herself up for an unwanted invitation. She closed her mouth, biting back her reply as she tried to think of a different answer.

'Going to the gym,' she told him. That was sort of true. It was what she should be doing, although it wasn't what she felt like and she knew she'd probably skip it altogether, but he didn't need to know that. Just like he didn't need to know her stomach was fluttering with nerves. She told herself it was because she found his presence irritating but she knew she was also bothered because she found him attractive and there was no way she wanted him to know that either.

She wished she could ignore his good looks but she suspected she was going to find that difficult. She'd just have to ignore him instead, she thought as she made a show of checking her watch.

'I'll see you tomorrow, then,' he replied, leaving her wondering why he'd asked in the first place, but his answer served to remind her that it was going to be impossible to ignore him completely. Whether she liked it or not, they would be working together.

Annie hung back as Caspar headed for the exit. She stuck with her pretence of being busy as she didn't want to walk out with him. From the hospital foyer she watched as he climbed into his car. He drove a silver Audi TT, which was definitely a car for a big-city doctor, and she wondered how much the television network was paying him, before reminding herself that he, and therefore his circumstances, was none of her business.

Annie briefly considered skipping her after-work gym class but she knew Tori would expect a decent reason before she'd allow her to opt out. They'd made a commitment to exercise together, hoping that would make them take it more seriously, and 'Can't be bothered' wasn't going to get her off the hook. She changed into her gym gear at the hospital so she could avoid going home first. She knew that if she went home the temptation to pour a glass of wine and sit on the couch and think about how her day had gone pear-shaped would be too much. In retrospect she decided that going to the gym might help keep her mind off her day.

'So, did you decide to sign the network's consent form?' Tori asked when they met before their gym class.

'Not yet. Have you?'

Tori nodded. 'I'm really excited about the project. Not to mention working with Caspar. Phil is a terrific paediatrician but he's old enough to be my father. I think we've got a pretty good deal having Caspar take over while Phil is on leave. I can't think of many better ways to spend my theatre time than watching Caspar St Claire.'

Tori had a point but Annie didn't agree wholeheartedly. 'I would have preferred him to be here minus the cameras, though,' she replied. She had been on television before and both occasions had been unpleasant, to say the least. Traumatic would be a better way to describe it. She didn't relish the idea of being exposed to the cameras.

And she knew that was how she was feeling—exposed and vulnerable. Annie had found Tori's support and friendship invaluable since she'd moved to the Mount but Tori still only knew half the story as far as Annie's history went. She thought about telling Tori the whole truth but now wasn't the time or the place.

'Unfortunately it doesn't work that way,' Tori said. 'The cameras are part of the package. Look at it this way—you want your contract renewed, don't you? I think taking part in this series would be a very good way of getting support for an extension of your contract.'

The instructor called them all to order and the class began putting an end to their conversation. Annie wasn't fit enough to talk and exercise at the same time but she was co-ordinated enough to be able to exercise and think about Tori's comment.

Her contract with the hospital was for twelve months. She needed it to be extended. She needed the job and needed the money. As much as she hated the idea of being on television, she knew Tori was right. She didn't have a choice. She couldn't afford to be choosy or create waves. She would have to sign the agreement and she would have to work with Caspar St Claire.

* * *

Avoiding Caspar for one afternoon had been a good start but she couldn't avoid him for ever and, in case she'd forgotten the fact, she had an early reminder when she arrived at the hospital the following morning. Parked almost outside the front doors was a large van emblazoned with the television network logo.

Filming was due to start today and it appeared they were ready and raring to go. Just thinking about it made her insides tremble. She actually felt nauseous at the thought of the camera crew dogging her steps.

Annie sighed as she made her way into the hospital and upstairs to the maternity ward. She had little doubt her path would cross with Caspar's at some point today.

She still hadn't signed the agreement, but she planned to do it later that day. She was hoping to delay it just a little longer to buy herself one more day, one more day when she would be safe from observation.

She kept her head down as she hurried past the nursery, too afraid to look through the large glass door in case she saw him—she was keen to avoid an inevitable meeting for as long as possible. She stopped briefly at the nurses' station to check for any updates before rushing to begin her rounds, rushing to hide behind the sanctuary of ward room curtains and doors.

Once she was among her patients she slowed her pace, ambling through her rounds. She wasn't consulting until the afternoon so she took her time, hoping that Caspar would be long gone from the floor before she emerged again. When she eventually finished she returned to the nurses' station to sign case notes but she made sure she kept her back to the wall, not wanting to give Caspar another opportunity to sneak up on her and overhear any conversations. She had no idea where he was but she wasn't taking any chances.

However, within a few minutes she realised he must be on the floor. Nurses started appearing from all corners of the wing, from patients' bedsides, the tearoom and even the pan room, as if there had been a silent announcement about events unfolding. And the only thing Annie could think of that would have the nurses all heading into the corridors would be if word had got around that Caspar St Claire was coming their way.

She glanced up from the notes and wasn't surprised to see him walking towards the desk with nurses trailing in his wake, almost falling over themselves as they rushed to offer their help. One of the nurses, whose name Annie thought was Tiffany, almost knocked down another in her desperate hurry to get to Caspar first.

The scene was rather amusing and Annie found she was smiling to herself and feeling positive for the first time since Caspar had arrived at Blue Lake Hospital. But that didn't mean she wanted to deal with him this morning. She thought about pretending she hadn't seen him and making her escape, running away and hiding again. But it was too late. He was heading her way. And smiling. At her.

Did he think her smile was for him? She supposed he would. He had no reason to think she was smiling to herself about the unfolding tableau.

She had to admit he had a really lovely smile. A crease appeared on either side of his mouth, running down to his jaw. They framed his lips and accentuated his square jaw, and the brooding expression in his eyes was replaced with laughter. It was all too easy to keep smiling back at him in return but she needed to remember that she wasn't one of the young, impressionable nurses and she had to remember that he wasn't Dr Tall, Dark and Handsome to her. He was Dr Disturbing-her-peaceful-life.

Annie wiped the smile from her face as he drew nearer but she hadn't completely forgotten Tori's warning to play nicely.

'Good morning,' she greeted him. 'Are you finding your way around all right?'

'Yes. Everyone's being very helpful,' he replied, but he looked at her for a moment longer than he needed to and Annie could almost hear the unspoken words. *Except for you.*

Well, that was too bad for him. She imagined he was used to getting his own way but that didn't mean he deserved to. And if Tiffany and the other nurses on this ward were the yardsticks then she didn't doubt the females on staff were being extremely helpful.

'Where is the crew?' she asked, choosing to ignore his unspoken implication.

'They're busy doing their own checks. They need to do some run-throughs before we start—lighting, sound, that sort of thing.'

She'd expected to see him with an entourage. 'How many of them are there?'

'Only a few,' he answered. 'Liam, the cameraman, Keegan for sound and lighting, and you met Gail, the producer.'

'No make-up?'

'No make-up.'

That would explain why he looked so good in the flesh. Dr Tall, Dark and Handsome wasn't made up for the cameras. The thought didn't make her feel any better. She still wasn't sure how she felt about men who were so good looking.

She'd thought his nose was slightly too long but standing directly in front of him now even that looked perfect and she knew she'd just been searching for flaws. It was hard to fault him physically.

'Apparently our production budget is very modest, which is why the network can afford to be generous towards the hospital. We don't have a lot of expenses.'

'What about your fee? They must pay you?' She remembered his sleek silver sports car and the words were out of her mouth before she realised how rude she sounded. 'Sorry, ignore that, it's none of my business.' She was desperate to change the subject and she looked around quickly, searching for another topic of conversation.

The nurses, having all come out of the woodwork, were now milling around, pretending to look busy, but Annie could see they were all there to check Caspar out. She remembered how he'd known everyone in the meeting yesterday and wondered if his extensive knowledge included the nurses.

'Do I need to introduce you or have you memorised everyone's names?' she asked as she gestured towards the nurses.

'I didn't have time to learn everybody's name, just the most important ones,' he replied as he zeroed in on her with his green eyes. He was watching her intently and she felt as though he was putting her under the microscope.

'So what was that little party trick all about?' Annie was vaguely aware of the ward phone ringing as she tried to concentrate under the force of Caspar's gaze.

'Which one?'

'That stunt yesterday, knowing who we were?'

'It wasn't a stunt. I figured I was going to be at a

disadvantage. You know each other already but I'm going to be working with you all and the quicker I get everyone straight in my head the faster I'll settle in. I like to be prepared.'

'Dr Simpson?' Ellen, one of the more experienced midwives, interrupted them. She had answered the phone and she covered the mouthpiece with her hand as she spoke to Annie. 'I have one of your patients on the phone, Kylie Jones. She says her waters have broken. Do you need me to pull up her file?'

Annie shook her head. 'No, that's all right.' She knew Kylie. 'Is her husband home?'

'I'll check,' Ellen replied, but within a few seconds she was shaking her head. 'He's not due back until next week.'

Annie knew that Paul Jones worked in mining, which meant he worked away for two weeks before coming home for two. 'Tell her we'll send an ambulance for her. She needs to be in here. If she's up to it she can contact Paul while she's waiting so he can organise to get home as soon as possible.'

Annie turned to Caspar. She couldn't believe she was about to ask this of him.

'Kylie is thirty-three weeks pregnant with twins. I'm going to need your help.'

'Of course.' He grinned at her and the sparkle returned to his eyes. Annie felt that funny warmth rush through her, as though his smile was the match and her belly was full of dry tinder. 'I thought you'd never ask,' he said as he pulled his phone from his pocket.

'What are you doing?'

'Calling the camera crew.'

'What? No!' she protested.

'What do you mean, "no"? This is what we're here for.'

Annie disagreed. 'Why do you want to film Kylie? What's the point? You have no back story, no history with her.' *And I don't want a camera crew in my delivery suite.*

But Caspar wasn't going to back down easily.

'We can do all that afterwards,' he said, unperturbed. 'We can follow her story and follow the babies' progress.'

Somehow she'd known he wouldn't give in. 'These babies are premature,' she argued. 'They have to survive first.'

As she debated the situation she realised that from the television perspective it probably didn't matter if the babies survived or not. Either way it would be high drama. But to his credit Caspar didn't point that depressing fact out to her. In fact, he seemed to try to make an effort to reassure her.

'I am a paediatrician, this is what I do. You have to trust me, I am very good at my job and just like you I swore an oath to do no harm.' His brooding expression was back, his green eyes darker now, his jaw set. 'This is a perfect story for the show—a premature delivery of twins with the father not able to make it for the birth. It's in my best interests to make sure it has a happy ending and then we'll be able to film an emotional reunion scene as well.'

'You're forgetting something,' Annie argued. 'I'll be in the delivery suite and I haven't given my permission to be filmed.'

Caspar shrugged. 'We'll keep you out of the shot. It's Kylie and the babies we want. We can use voiceovers, music, whatever we need to eliminate anything you say as well if you prefer. The wonders of modern technology.'

'Are you telling me you'll film without my permission?'

'Are you always this argumentative?' he asked as a broad grin broke across his face and his eyes sparkled again.

Was he smiling at her? Did he find her amusing? Did he think she didn't mean business?

She didn't know where to look as she tried to ignore the funny tumbling sensation in her stomach. All she knew was that he was responsible for the feeling and that frightened her. She didn't want to be attracted to him. She couldn't imagine dealing with that on top of working with him. The stress made her belligerent. 'Only when I think people are wrong,' she snapped.

'But I'm not wrong. We can edit you out but you can't stop us from filming. I have the hospital's permission and all I need is Kylie's. If you like, I promise to show you the edited version before it goes to air.'

By God, the man was irritating. 'I have no idea whether I can trust you to keep your promises, though, do I?' Annie had learned through bitter experience that some people lied, cheated, made promises they had no intention of keeping and let others down on a regular basis. And to trust someone she barely knew didn't sit comfortably with her.

'This discussion could well be moot anyway,' Caspar said. 'It all depends on Kylie now.'

He pressed a button on his phone and made the call while Annie stood by, fuming silently. If he thought he could win every time by being stubborn she had news for him, but she knew that his chances of getting his own way were better than hers. Kylie's babies would need Caspar St Claire. Annie couldn't do this without him.

She could hope that Kylie would choose not to invite the cameras into the delivery suite but if that didn't happen Annie knew she'd have to relent. She hated feeling powerless. She had sworn an oath to herself to take charge of her life, not to let other people dictate things to her, but ever since Caspar had walked into the hospital she could feel control being wrested from her.

She'd thought she would be able to avoid him and his cameras but she realised now that it wasn't going to be her decision and, what was even worse, she realised that there would be times when she'd need him and she'd have to acquiesce.

'Now, why don't we agree to put our differences aside and you can tell me about Kylie,' Caspar said as he ended his phone call. 'Regardless of whether or not we film this delivery, I will be taking care of the babies, so is there anything I need to know? Has she had any medical complications? Have there been any issues with the pregnancy?'

Before Annie could answer any of his questions they were interrupted by Ellen. 'The ambulance is nearly here.'

'I want to meet the paramedics,' Annie told him as she resigned herself to the fact that she was going to have to work with him. 'If you come with me I'll fill you in on the way, but her pregnancy has been pretty straightforward. She's young, twenty-three, first pregnancy, fraternal twins. I'm not expecting any problems aside from the usual premmie issues.'

They arrived at the ambulance bay as the paramedics were opening the ambulance doors. Caspar was on the phone again and Annie could hear him instructing the crew to meet them in Emergency. She hoped Cas-

par was able to focus on more than one thing at a time.
He needed to. Time would tell.

'You know this patient?' the paramedic checked as
Annie introduced herself, and when she nodded, he
continued. 'Her waters have broken for at least one
twin. Her blood pressure is elevated, one-sixty-five
over ninety-five, and foetal heart rates are both around
one-forty.'

'Any contractions?'

'A couple of mild ones. Several minutes apart.'

Annie spoke to one of the nurses who had followed
them out to the ambulance. 'Can you page Dr Williams
and get her down here?' she asked. Kylie's blood pressure was much higher than she'd like and an epidural
might help, but she'd let Tori decide.

The paramedics retrieved the stretcher with her patient and Annie bent over her, talking quietly. 'Kylie,
welcome. I wasn't expecting you quite so soon. We're
going to take you into the emergency department and
see what your babies are up to.' Annie needed to determine how far along Kylie was. She didn't need her
wanting to push as they were on their way to Maternity.

She was aware of Caspar hovering at her right shoulder. She had to introduce him to Kylie as, like it or not,
he was going to be part of this. But he wasn't waiting
for her. He stepped around her and spoke to Kylie.

'Hello, Kylie, I'm—'

'Caspar St Claire,' Kylie gasped. 'I've seen you on
telly. What are you doing here?'

Of course, Annie thought, Caspar's fame would have
preceded him. Annie wasn't quite sure how Kylie had
found the energy to gush over Caspar. Surely if she
was in labour she should have more pressing things to
think about.

'We're filming the next series of *RPE* here at Blue Lake Hospital. Would you like to be a part of it?' Caspar asked as Kylie was wheeled through the hospital doors.

'You'll deliver my babies? On telly?'

Annie felt her temper rising but Caspar shook his head and quickly put Kylie straight.

'No, Dr Simpson will deliver your babies but I'll be right here, ready to look after them as soon as they are born. We'll get it all on camera and you'll have a perfect recording of the whole experience to show your husband when he gets back to town.'

And with those words Annie knew Caspar would win the argument. Kylie was already looking at him as if he could give her the moon—knowing that her husband was going to miss the birth of their babies had to be bothering her. If Caspar could solve that problem by taping the birth, not only for national television but for Kylie's husband, then there was no way Kylie would kick him out of the delivery suite.

'I'll feel better if you are here, Dr St Claire.' Kylie turned her head to look at Annie. 'Can you imagine, Dr Simpson? My family on national telly.'

And just like that Annie found herself overruled. She knew she had to be a gracious loser and she didn't have time to argue anyway. Her patient was her first priority, her only priority, and she had more pressing concerns—Kylie's blood pressure for one—than whether or not her patient wanted her fifteen minutes of fame.

Annie forced herself to smile as she said, 'Okay, then, let's get you inside.'

CHAPTER THREE

THE CAMERA CREW arrived as Kylie was being shifted across onto a hospital bed. Caspar spoke to them quickly as they began to pull equipment from an assortment of bags and trolleys. Annie was relieved to see that there were only two men, as Caspar had told her, but she had no time to pay them any attention as she started to pull the curtains around the cubicle to give Kylie some privacy as they got her changed into a hospital gown.

'Can you give us a minute?' she asked Caspar as she closed the curtains, barely waiting for his nod in reply before she shut him and his crew out. Albeit temporarily. They'd barely got Kylie sorted before Caspar was back in the cubicle. He didn't ask for permission, he simply got on with the job of attaching the foetal heart monitors to Kylie's abdomen.

Annie was about to tell him she could manage but she bit back her sharp retort when she realised that if Phil had been the paediatrician in the cubicle instead of Caspar, she would have been grateful for his assistance. It wasn't Caspar's fault she didn't know how to handle him. She was going to have to find a way though. For her patient's sake.

People were bustling around Kylie and Annie shifted her attention away from Caspar's long fingers, as he stuck electrodes onto their patient, and over to the monitor, which was now displaying Kylie's BP. It had dropped since the paramedic's report. It was now one-fifty over ninety. Still high but not dangerously so. Had Kylie just been apprehensive?

Annie knew that was possible. Going into early labour when your husband was thousands of miles away would be nerve-racking for most people, and looking at her patient now she certainly appeared more relaxed than when she'd arrived. Kylie was lying calmly, staring at Caspar as he finished attaching the electrodes and hooked her up to another monitor.

Maybe Kylie's improved blood pressure had less to do with apprehension and more to do with the visiting specialist, Annie thought, and she just managed to stop herself from rolling her eyes. It seemed Caspar St Claire had this effect on all women, herself included, she admitted grudgingly, but if he was aware of the scrutiny he didn't show any sign of discomfort.

The monitor was displaying two distinct foetal heartbeats. Caspar turned to Annie and gave her a thumbs-up accompanied by a big smile. He was the epitome of someone who was completely in control. He was composed and relaxed and Annie knew his demeanour would help Kylie.

It was time for Annie to take a leaf out of his book and get to work. She straightened her back as she finished drying her hands. She could do cool, calm and collected just as well as he could.

'All right, Kylie,' she said, as she took up her position at the foot of the bed. 'I'll need to do an internal exam to see what's happening. Are you okay with that?'

Annie wondered if she'd need to tell the camera crew what was appropriate for them to film but at the moment they were concentrating on Kylie's face and no doubt were including shots of Caspar's handsome face too, just for good measure. Probably just as well. She supposed they knew what the viewers wanted to see and she'd bet they'd be happier looking at Caspar St Claire than anything she might be able to offer them.

Annie was surprised to find that, despite not reporting much discomfort, Kylie was already several centimetres dilated. She could see Kylie's abdominal muscles ripple as a contraction ran through her. She checked that the nurse had recorded the time as she asked, 'Have you been having contractions for a while?'

'No. They only started after I called the hospital,' Kylie answered.

'Any other aches and pains?'

'My back's been a bit sore today but I spent the past couple of days cleaning the house so I think I just over-did it.'

'Well, it seems that twin one is determined to arrive today. He's in a good position and I'd say you're well into the first stage of labour.'

'Are you telling me I'm too late?'

Annie turned as Tori came into the room. 'I actually wanted your opinion on giving Kylie an epidural to bring her blood pressure down, not for pain relief as such.'

Tori's eyes flicked to the monitor, which showed one-forty over eighty-five. 'Her BP looks okay.'

Annie nodded in agreement. 'It's lowered considerably since she arrived. Kylie is thirty-three weeks, in established labour with twins and coping well with discomfort.'

'I'll hang around for a bit if it's a multiple birth, just

in case,' Tori said. 'I assume you've got a theatre on standby?'

Annie nodded. She had a theatre reserved but she hoped she wouldn't need it. She also hoped to avoid delivering the twins in the emergency department. She spoke to Caspar. 'Where would you like me to deliver the twins—here or in a delivery suite in Maternity?'

'I think the environment in Maternity is far more conducive to a relaxed birth,' Caspar replied. 'And it's closer to the paediatric unit and the nursery. That gets my vote.'

'It is much nicer in Maternity,' Annie said to Kylie. 'More space, windows, music. So if you're okay with it I'll just give you an injection that will help the babies' lungs and then we'll get this show on the road.' She drew up a syringe of corticosteroids and injected it into Kylie before instructing the medical team, 'All right, people, let's get ready to move.'

It took less than ten minutes to get Kylie to Maternity but her labour had progressed rapidly and by the time they reached the delivery suite she was ready to push.

Annie managed to position herself so that Liam and his camera were behind her. That served a dual purpose—she could pretend he wasn't there and the camera could only get pictures of the back of her head. But as she coached Kylie through the birth of the first baby she realised that Liam wasn't interested in her anyway. Just as he'd done in Emergency, he concentrated on Kylie and Caspar.

Even though Annie had talked about the first twin in a masculine form, something she had a habit of doing unless she knew the sex, the first baby was a girl. She was small, with the familiar premmie appearance of too much skin and not enough padding, but perfectly proportioned with the right number of fingers and toes.

Caspar was standing by Annie's shoulder as she delivered the baby. She couldn't see him but she knew he was there. She could feel him. She turned slightly to give him the baby. He was ready and waiting, his hands reaching for the tiny newborn.

As he lifted the baby from Annie's palms, the backs of his hands slid against her skin and Annie had the strangest sensation of heat exploding inside her. She'd noticed his smile had the ability to make her feel as though she was melting but his touch made her feel like she was combusting. How was that possible? Thank goodness she was already sitting down. She knew her legs wouldn't have been able to support her. It felt as though her bones had turned to jelly, as though her limbs were liquid.

And then, as suddenly as she'd been aware of the heat, it was replaced by cold, empty air as he took the baby from her hands.

Annie followed his movements with her eyes. The tiny baby appeared even more diminutive cradled in his large hands. She swallowed and rubbed her hands together, encouraging the warmth back into them, but she couldn't reproduce that intense heat and now she wondered if she'd just imagined it.

To have her body react on such a level, seemingly uncontrolled by her brain, was a strange concept. She wasn't completely inexperienced, she was a twenty-nine-year-old divorcee, but she'd never felt this sort of visceral, impulsive attraction before. Were other people constantly aware of these feelings? Maybe she was the odd one out.

Surely this sensation must be an extraordinary one

because how anyone could get anything done if they were trying to focus while dealing with these feelings was a mystery to her. She needed to get a grip. She couldn't let herself be distracted by Caspar St Claire.

She returned her attention to her patient, annoyed with herself for losing focus. She waited to hear the baby's first cry before she clamped and cut the umbilical cord and began to check the progress of twin number two.

Caspar finished his one-minute Apgar check, pronounced a birth weight of two thousand five hundred grams and handed the baby to a tearful but happy Kylie. Ellen, the midwife, loosened Kylie's gown so she could expose her shoulder and have some skin-to-skin contact with her baby. With the new mum comfortably occupied with her newborn daughter, Caspar's focus returned to Annie. She could sense his attention.

'The amniotic sac is still intact,' Annie told him. The second twin wasn't in such a hurry to be born. 'But the baby is breech.'

'Can you turn it?' he asked, even as Annie was positioning herself to try.

'I think so.' She hoped she could manage. She didn't want Kylie to go through a Caesarean section, not after delivering the first twin so successfully. Managing premature twins was going to be enough for Kylie to deal with without having to recover from major surgery as well.

Annie was relieved when she was able to turn the baby without much difficulty. She checked the monitors, pleased to see that Kylie's blood pressure was within normal limits and so were the unborn twin's vital signs. He wasn't distressed. Annie couldn't stop Kylie's labour now but they could afford to wait for this delivery to happen at its own pace. She sat back and relaxed.

'Good job.'

Caspar's words, delivered in his rich, deep voice, sent a warm glow through her. She glanced up to find he was smiling at her. She smiled back and was aware of that slow burning heat in her stomach again but it was nothing like the roaring fire she'd felt when he'd touched her. The slow burn she could handle but she wasn't so sure how to deal with the rest of it.

She was pleased he was there with her and that was unexpected. They worked well together and she allowed herself to feel an affinity with him. It was good to know they would be able to manage professionally.

'Once Kylie's contractions pick up again I'll do an amniotomy and hopefully we can have another smooth, intervention-free delivery,' she said.

It didn't take long for Kylie's contractions to build up. By the time Caspar had done his second lot of Apgar scores on the little girl and given her some more bonding time with her mum before placing her into the humidicrib to keep her warm, Kylie's contractions were strong and frequent.

As Annie ruptured the membranes she made a mental note to remind Kylie that she'd have to get to the hospital quickly with her next pregnancy because once she went into labour things happened rapidly.

Annie delivered the baby's anterior shoulder and in between contractions administered an injection of oxytocin into Kylie's thigh before completing the delivery. At two thousand six hundred grams the baby boy was slightly heavier than his older sister.

Caspar waited for Annie to pass the baby to him and even though Annie was prepared for the contact this time, the sensation still made her catch her breath. She concentrated on delivering the placenta while Caspar took care of the second baby. Once he was out of her space it was business as usual. Everyone had a job to do and Annie's focus was on Kylie, yet she was still aware of Caspar.

Annie was inserting a drip into Kylie's arm when the twins were taken off to the nursery. The little boy needed additional oxygen but otherwise Caspar pronounced them healthy. Annie had completely forgotten about Liam and his camera until she noticed him trailing behind Caspar as they headed for the nursery. She couldn't believe she'd been so immersed in the delivery that she had been able to forget they were being filmed.

Ellen had taken Kylie into the en suite bathroom and Annie's job was finished. Caspar and the twins were gone and in a minute Ellen would take Kylie to the nursery as well. Normally Annie would call in at the nursery too if she wasn't needed elsewhere, but she was reluctant to do that today as she didn't want to follow Caspar or the camera. She was due in her office shortly to start her outpatient clinic but she didn't feel like rushing off. She actually felt at a bit of a loose end.

The spark of attraction she felt for Caspar had opened up old wounds. She couldn't deny he was a good-looking man and she knew it was simple chemistry that had her feeling as though she was on fire. But the trouble was, she knew it wasn't simple. In her experience, chemistry rarely was.

She'd seen how complicated things could become when chemistry was part of the equation. She'd seen it with her own parents and she always swore she would never succumb to it. She wanted so badly to be different from her mother. She might find Caspar attractive but she wasn't going to do anything about it. Unlike her mother, she could, and would, resist temptation.

For years she'd listened to her mother talk about how she'd fallen in love with her father at first sight. They hadn't been able to get enough of each other physically, even though they'd been a disaster emotionally. Their tempestuous relationships had come at the expense of all other relationship in their lives, their daughter's most of all.

Her parents spent more time apart than together but when they reunited, initially at least, they had no awareness of anything around them, including their daughter. Nothing existed beyond the two of them. Inevitably, though, when they had satisfied their physical desire to the point where they were able to notice their surroundings again, they began to irritate each other.

Beyond their chemistry they had nothing in common and Annie had promised herself that when she was old enough she wouldn't get caught up in such a physical relationship. She would make sure she chose someone with whom she had could share something beyond the physical. At the age of twenty-one that was exactly what she had done and yet, by the age of twenty-nine, she found herself divorced, childless and homeless.

Since her divorce, delivering other people's babies had always been a bittersweet experience. She loved the whole new-life thing but currently it just reminded her that she was not only divorced she was also not a mother, and as her thirtieth birthday approached she couldn't imagine her situation changing. Along with her house, her marriage and her job, her divorce might have also cost her the chance of having her own family.

But sitting in the delivery suite feeling sorry for herself wasn't achieving anything. She had work to do.

* * *

Caspar had no time to reflect on his first official day at Blue Lake Hospital until he was in his car on the way to dinner. As usual he was running late. He'd organised for the camera crew to film Kylie and her babies in the nursery and of course it had taken longer than planned. But overall the day had been a success. Along with Kylie's story there had been another good case requiring the services of Colin Young, the orthopaedic surgeon. Caspar hadn't been involved in that story but the crew was pleased with the footage they'd taken so they were off to an encouraging start.

But in his mind the biggest success had been getting Annie Simpson to agree to allow filming during the delivery. He had kept his promise and instructed the crew not to focus on her. After all, it was Kylie's story they were telling, but as a paediatrician he knew he would more than likely be spending a large chunk of his time working with Annie, and if they could come to a compatible arrangement that would be ideal.

He'd been impressed with her skills and her unflappable nature. Once again she hadn't held back when it came time to expressing her opinion but he decided that he liked that about her. She wasn't tiptoeing around him or the television network. Her patients came first, as they should, and when they were in her delivery suites she made sure everyone knew she was in charge.

But something told him she'd look great on camera and he was still keen for her agree to that. But for now he was happy just to have her permission to film her with her patients.

As he pulled to a stop at the traffic light outside the Royal Hotel he couldn't resist looking inside and he knew he was looking for Annie. Sitting in the car, he fancied he could still smell her. The sweet, subtle hint of jasmine had stayed with him even though he'd showered and changed, and the scent had him searching for her.

Tiffany, one of the many very friendly and helpful nurses, had invited him to join in for Friday drinks at the hotel but he was already committed to, and now late for, dinner at his sister's. But what if Annie was in there? What if Annie had invited him? Would he have delayed his plans? She was an attractive woman, that hadn't escaped his attention, but she was also intriguing. But no matter how alluring he found her, he couldn't let his sister down. He knew he hadn't been pulling his weight as far as family responsibilities went and he was in Mount Gambier now to share the load. That was why he'd pushed for *RPE* to be filmed here. It suited him.

The light turned green and he drove on down the road, choosing to behave responsibly and resist temptation.

He pulled his car into his sister's driveway, scattering his teenage niece and nephew, who were taking shots at the basketball ring over the garage door.

'You're late,' his niece chastised him as he hugged her.

'Occupational hazard, I'm afraid,' he replied.

'Enough talk. Let's get inside and eat,' his nephew said as he had one last shot at the ring before ushering them along the front path.

'How's Grandpa doing?' Caspar asked as they headed into the house.

'He knows who we are today so that's pretty good,' they told him.

His dad unfolded his lanky frame from the lounge and stood up as Caspar came into the room. He was a tall man and was perhaps a little more stooped than when Caspar had last seen him a few months ago, but other than that he was unchanged.

The old man in front of him was the reason Caspar had pushed for *RPE* to be filmed in Mount Gambier. Basing this series at Blue Lake Hospital had brought him back to his family and would give him time to help sort through the issues involving his father. Dementia was a difficult illness to manage, not least for the families of the sufferers, and Caspar's sisters had been coping for quite a while without any help from him.

Until a couple of weeks ago Joseph St Claire had been staying with his middle child, Kristin, but she had her hands full with two children and a third one due very soon, on top of which she worked with her husband in their winery and lived half an hour from town. Caring for her father as well had become too much to deal with and Joe had moved in with Brigitte.

Joe's grey eyes lit up when he saw Caspar walk through the door. 'Caspar, my boy, how are you?'

Caspar hadn't stopped to consider how he would feel if his father didn't recognise him. He supposed it was ultimately inevitable but he was glad he didn't have to confront that fact today. However, his relief was short-lived.

'How were your final exams?' his father asked.

He'd done his final exams five years ago at the age of twenty-eight.

Brigitte, older than Caspar by eight years, heard the exchange as she came out of the kitchen. 'Hi, baby brother,' she said, as she hugged him, before she expertly changed the subject by announcing, loud enough for everyone else to hear, 'Let's eat.'

'We'll talk later,' she whispered to Caspar, as her family assembled in the dining room.

'Aren't we waiting for your mother?' Joe asked as Brigitte's husband began to carve the roast.

'She's not here tonight, Dad. Do you remember what I told you?'

Caspar watched as his father frowned, obviously concentrating and trying to recall what Brigitte had said to him.

'It's her bridge night,' Brigitte said.

Now it was Caspar's turn to frown. Their mother had died three years ago. What was Brigitte doing?

'I'll explain later.' Brigitte mouthed the words silently across the table.

Caspar attempted to put the exchange to the back of his mind while he tried to enjoy his dinner. Brigitte was a good cook and he couldn't remember the last time he'd had a roast dinner with all the trimmings, but the dramatic decline in his father's condition since he'd last seen him a few months ago concerned him greatly and took the pleasure out of the meal.

He knew it was tinged by guilt. Guilt that he hadn't visited as often as he should and guilt that he'd left his sisters with the burden of caring for their father.

At the end of the meal Brigitte's children helped settle their grandfather for the night while Caspar helped Brigitte in the kitchen. Their father had asked no more questions about their mother's whereabouts during the remainder of the meal and Caspar figured he'd either forgotten she was out, forgotten he'd asked the question or had remembered she'd died. Caspar didn't know which one of those was right but he was relieved not to have to deal with more questions.

He'd never thought he'd back away from a challenge but this situation was not something he'd had any experience with and he didn't know how to deal with it.

Their mother had died from a stroke. Her death had been sudden and traumatic for all of them but at least they hadn't had to watch as she'd slowly declined. Caspar had no experience with treating the elderly and no experience with treating dementia yet he felt as though he should have something to contribute. He felt as though he was letting his family down.

'Dad's forgotten that Mum died?' he asked Brigitte as he scraped plates before stacking them into the dishwasher.

'Sometimes he remembers and sometimes he doesn't. It's too difficult to go through it with him every time. Can you imagine what it would be like to hear for the first time that Mum has died and to have to hear that every few days? It's distressing for him and for us. It's better to say she's out and usually he forgets to ask when she'll be back or he goes to bed and forgets. Tomorrow he might remember again that she's dead and if he does that's okay, but it's better if it's something he can recall rather than reliving the grief over and over again.'

'I didn't realise he'd gone downhill quite so fast.'

'I think moving here from Kristin's has unsettled him a bit,' Brigitte said as she filled the sink with water for the pots and pans. 'But it really hasn't been that quick a decline, Caspar, it's just that you haven't seen him for months.'

There was no criticism in his elder sister's tone, she was just stating facts, but it all added to his guilt. He didn't really have a good excuse. Mount Gambier was only a few hours' drive from his home in Melbourne. His work and filming the last series of *RPE* had kept him busy but filming had wrapped up several months ago and both his sisters worked too yet they had managed to care for their father.

'Tell me what you've been up to. Have you got any juicy bits of celebrity gossip? Are you dating anyone? Is there a story behind that photo I saw of you with the host from that talent show that was on the front page of the paper?'

It seemed Brigitte had developed quite a knack for changing the subject. Caspar went with the new topic. He knew he'd find out soon enough exactly how his father was faring.

'We went out a couple of times but we had nothing in common,' he replied. They'd been quite compatible in the bedroom but his sister didn't need to hear about that, and they'd had absolutely nothing to talk about.

Brigitte laughed. 'Other than both being in reality television shows.'

'Other than that.' Caspar grinned. 'But you know I don't think of myself as a celebrity and I don't really want to date one either.'

'No, you're far too high-brow,' his sister teased.

Despite being on television, he wasn't interested in the television business, but that wasn't because he thought it was beneath him, it was because his focus lay elsewhere.

His interest lay solely with doing as good a job as he could with the show from a medical perspective. He wasn't really interested in the politics of show business, of being seen at the right parties and with the right people. He wasn't planning on having a career in the media. He had a career he loved already, a career that was vastly different from the entertainment business.

He had agreed to be on *RPE* because he wanted to raise awareness of medical conditions and he'd hoped to raise funds for particular causes, but he hadn't really counted on becoming a celebrity himself, however minor.

'No, I just don't want to have a high-profile relationship that's played out in front of the media. I didn't think this series would be as big a success as it is and I would prefer to be able to have a private life that is actually private.'

'You never know, you might be able to date quietly here. No one ever pays any attention to what's happening in the country. Maybe Kristin and I can find you a nice country girl and then you'd have a reason to stay in town. I know exactly the type you need.'

Caspar knew he shouldn't ask but he was intrigued. 'And what type of woman do I need?'

'One with a bit of substance. One who won't always let you get your own way or rule the roost.'

'You make me sound like a bully,' he protested.

'Not at all, but you've always done things on your terms. You like to be in control. You need a girl with enough attitude to stand up to you. One who can hold her own in an argument.'

His thoughts went immediately to a petite brunette with a ballerina's physique and exquisite cheekbones who certainly didn't hold back her opinions. One who was happy to tell him exactly what she thought of him and his ideas. He wondered what his sisters would make of Annie.

He almost laughed out loud at the idea of asking Annie on a date. He could just imagine what she'd say to that.

And what would she make of being splashed across the front of the local paper or in the magazine social pages? He knew she'd be less than impressed. He imagined her aversion to cameras would extend to all types of media and there would be nowhere to hide in a town the size of Mount Gambier, despite what Brigitte thought, and he knew anyone he dated would be of interest to the media.

It was a ridiculous idea. Why was he even thinking about it?

He didn't have time to date. He had other priorities at present. 'Between work and this television show I haven't had time to help you with Dad, so where would I find the time for dating? The PR team for the television show found my last half-dozen dates for me when I needed one.'

That had suited him as it had meant good publicity for the show without requiring too much input from him.

'Well, maybe we could do a better job than the PR department,' Brigitte replied.

'Thanks, but I really don't have time.'

He wasn't interested in a serious relationship. He told himself it was because he didn't have time but he knew that his reluctance stemmed mainly from a belief that happy endings were few and far between. He didn't want to start searching for the perfect woman; he was convinced she didn't exist, and he didn't want to waste time or energy looking for someone who didn't exist. He didn't want the disappointment.

He'd learnt the hard way that he couldn't control other people's actions so he concentrated on what he could control—his own actions. There was never any shortage of eager women to keep him company when he wanted it so there was no reason to look for anything more. Short, casual relationships meant he could retain control and that suited him perfectly.

He didn't believe in fairy-tales. If fairy-tales came

true, he wouldn't have been abandoned as a baby. His story had had a happy ending but that had been thanks to the two people who had rescued him and given him a family. Love had a big part to play but he didn't think he could be that lucky a second time. Getting two fairy-tale endings in one lifetime just didn't happen. He didn't want a serious relationship. He didn't need it. He wanted to stay in control.

'And despite what you think,' he added, 'I know that anyone I dated would be fodder for the media, even in the Mount.'

'If you're worried about privacy, why don't you stay here instead of at the apartment block, then?' Brigitte offered.

'You'd be surprised at the number of fans of the show who would track me down wherever I stayed. I don't think your family, or Dad, needs people camped out the front of your house and I think you have enough on your plate without having a lodger who comes and goes at erratic hours.'

Brigitte shrugged. 'Dad wanders in the night. You could keep him company if you get in late from the hospital.'

A thought occurred to him. 'Do you need me to stay? Do you need an extra pair of eyes or hands?'

His sister shook her head. 'No, it's all right. It's enough that you're in town. This will give us time to make some decisions.'

'I'm sorry. I haven't been much help, have I? You and Kristin have shouldered the burden.'

'Kristin more than me,' Brigitte said. 'We've managed but it's getting harder. Dad is deteriorating and the timing is terrible with Kristin's baby due and my overseas study leave coinciding. We've got a few weeks up our sleeves but not much more than that. And unless you're planning on taking time off, we have to hope we get a bed for him somewhere soon. Anything else will just be a short-term fix.'

'How many options have we got?'

'Kristin and I have put his name on a couple of waiting lists but the trouble is we don't need just an ordinary bed, we need one in a dementia unit and we need a male bed. There aren't many beds allocated for men in nursing homes. Do you think you could pull any strings?' Brigitte asked.

'You'd have more luck than me, I reckon,' Caspar said. 'You're a local. I'm not one any longer.'

'But you're a celebrity and a medico—surely that counts for something.'

'I'll find out the names of the doctors who visit the nursing homes and maybe if they have visiting rights at the hospital too, I can have a word, but it's probably the nurse manager I need to sweet-talk. Why don't you give me the names of the nursing homes you've chosen and I'll see what I can do?'

Caspar knew he'd have to make an effort to find a solution. It was time he did his share. This was something that had to be fixed, and soon.

Annie's weekend was dragging by. She'd done her ward rounds, been to a gym class with Tori, cleaned and done her grocery shopping. But buying meals for one didn't take long and now she was restless. Sunday afternoon stretched before her, she had the rest of the day to fill and no plans.

For the past few months she'd been content with her own company and going to work each day had been enough activity for her, but today she was bored. She checked her phone for the umpteenth time but she hadn't missed any calls. There wasn't one woman in labour who needed her help.

She pulled on her running shoes and decided to walk to the store. Surely a good movie could fill up a couple of hours. She shoved her phone, keys and wallet into a small bag and slung it across her body before heading out the door.

Of course, deciding to get out of the house was all it took to make her phone ring. She was halfway between home and the hospital when she took a call from Emergency. There had been a motor vehicle accident on Millicent Road. One of the victims was a pregnant woman and Tang, the RMO on duty, wanted Annie's expertise. The woman was being brought in by ambulance, they were still several minutes away, but all other details were sketchy. Annie could jog home and get her car but instead she turned and headed for the hospital.

Caspar heard the automatic doors of the emergency department slide open behind him. A hint of jasmine surrounded him and he knew Annie had arrived. He'd been keeping an eye out for her all weekend and had been surprised not to see her earlier, but there had been no babies born this weekend. He knew, he'd been checking.

Blue Lake Hospital served a large rural community but it still wasn't as busy as a city hospital and, on average, there were only two births a week.

He turned now, seeking her out, not doubting that she was there.

Annie was just inside the doors, her cheeks were flushed and she seemed out of breath. She was dressed in exercise gear, skintight Lycra leggings and a fitted tank top. Her legs were incredible and for a slightly built woman Caspar noticed she had curves in all the right places.

He saw her push her hair off her face and lean forward, placing her hands on her hips to catch her breath, giving him an unexpected glimpse of cleavage and a not totally unexpected stirring of desire.

But this was not the time or place. He knew she wasn't keen on having him in her hospital but he'd been pleased to learn she had finally signed the television network's consent forms. He hoped that working together the other day had started to create the foundations for a harmonious professional relationship, but he didn't want to jeopardise a promising start by complicating matters, and satisfying any physical needs he might have were a long way down his list of priorities at present. He knew he still had to win her trust.

'Are you all right?' he asked.

Annie straightened up when she heard his voice. She nodded. 'Just unfit,' she replied. Running to the hospital had required more effort than her regular gym class.

Over Caspar's shoulder she could see the camera crew and she realised that Caspar hadn't been called in; more than likely he had been here already. Just because she'd had a quiet weekend it didn't mean he had. She looked from the cameraman back to Caspar. His jaw was darkened by weekend stubble, accentuating both his square jaw and his masculinity and making him even more attractive. Annie forced herself to concentrate. She didn't need distractions.

'Have you been working?' She hadn't actually thought they would work on weekends.

'There have been a few interesting cases and we filmed Kylie and Paul's reunion yesterday. We had their permission to film Paul meeting his babies for the first time.'

Annie thought that would have been rather special and despite her misgivings about the television series being filmed in her hospital, she realised she hoped that the stories would cast the hospital in a positive light. Although she still wished she could ignore the fact that Caspar and his team were there. But before she felt obligated to say something nice she was interrupted by Tang, the RMO on duty. She latched onto his presence, relieved to have someone else to talk to.

'Tang, what can you tell me?' Annie asked as the young resident approached her.

'A car misjudged overtaking a logging truck. He clipped the back of the truck, flipped and rolled down an embankment.'

Annie winced. Accidents involving logging trucks weren't uncommon in this area and they were often nasty, with the occupants of the cars always coming off second best. Annie hated dealing with car-accident victims. It brought back memories of her marriage. Her husband's drink-driving conviction had been the final nail in the coffin of their relationship and now car accidents brought back old memories that she'd rather forget.

'The male driver is being airlifted to Adelaide with spinal injuries,' Tang continued, 'and his wife is on her way here. The driver of the truck is being treated for shock.'

'So, only one patient for us,' Annie remarked as they heard the sound of the ambulance siren approaching.

'Or maybe two,' Caspar said, 'depending on what's happening with the baby.'

'Let's hope we can keep it to one, then,' Annie replied, as the ambulance pulled into the bay.

The paramedics wasted no time in removing their patient from the ambulance. 'Unconscious female, eighteen weeks pregnant, BP eighty over fifty, possible pelvic fracture, but no other serious visible injuries.' The paramedics recited the information they knew.

'Her name is Suzanne.' Annie was aware of the camera hovering behind her but she had no time to worry about that now. She looked at the paramedic, querying how he had so much information from an unconscious patient. 'Her husband was conscious at the scene,' he explained.

Annie and Tang jogged beside the stretcher as Suzanne was wheeled into Emergency.

'We're going to need a CT scan,' Annie told Tang as she pulled a gown over her gym clothes. 'Her hypotension could be indicative of internal bleeding and we need to check for pelvic fractures.'

Suzanne was wheeled into an examination room, swiftly transferred to a hospital bed and connected to various monitors.

'Run a unit of blood and cross-match blood type,' Tang instructed the nurses as they attached electrodes and hung the drip bag on the stand.

The room was crowded but the team worked smoothly, everyone knowing their job and their place. They needed to get Suzanne as stable as possible before moving her for the CT scan. There was no time or space to deal with the television cameras.

'You can't follow us,' Annie told Liam as they prepared to move Suzanne. 'You don't have the patient's permission to film her.' Annie had accepted the inevitable and had signed the consent forms for the network yesterday, but she knew her signature was only part of the necessary paperwork.

'You know we can get permission later.' Caspar didn't even bother to discuss it with her and she had neither the time nor the energy to debate the facts with him. She had to trust that they wouldn't use footage already taken without obtaining permission.

'If your crew get in our way I'm kicking them out,' she said, keen to have the last word for once as she turned her back, preparing to take Suzanne to X-Ray. Liam and Keegan would have to work around the medical staff.

The CT scan results weren't good. The pictures showed significant abdominal haemorrhaging and a fracture of the right acetabulum.

Suzanne was rushed to the operating theatre where Annie would have to do her best to stop the bleeding before the orthopod would take over. Tori was the anaesthetist on call, which Annie was pleased about, as she knew she didn't have to worry about that end of things. The theatre team continued to pump blood into their patient to counteract the haemorrhaging while Annie, Caspar and Tang all scrubbed, preparing for surgery.

Annie stood side by side with Caspar, both with soap suds up to their elbows as they prepared to go into Theatre. She took a deep breath. Caspar was ready and willing to assist. If they were going to have any chance of saving Suzanne and the baby, she needed all the help she could get. Tang was capable but she doubted he'd had the experience needed for this scenario. She barely knew Caspar but they had worked together smoothly to deliver Kylie's twins just forty-eight hours ago and there was something about him that evoked a sense of capability.

An air of assuredness, confidence and calmness that made her feel she could trust him. She didn't like the feeling, that she was so willing to trust a man she barely knew, but she would have to. In this situation she had to believe he wouldn't let her down.

Annie backed through the door into the theatre. Tori had anaesthetised Suzanne and she was prepped, her body draped in sterile sheets, with the exception of her abdomen, which was stained orange by the antiseptic liquid. Her abdomen was distended but Annie knew that distension probably wasn't due to her pregnancy but was more than likely a result of intra-abdominal bleeding. She couldn't waste time. Gloved and gowned, with Caspar beside her and the camera crew forgotten in the background, Annie got to work.

But what she found when she opened Suzanne up wasn't what she'd expected.

It was worse. Much worse.

CHAPTER FOUR

'OH, MY GOD.' Annie could scarcely believe what she was seeing. The CT scan had shown a massive amount of blood in the abdominal cavity but it had been difficult to see where it was coming from. Now that Annie had opened Suzanne up they were able to see the extent of the damage.

Suzanne's uterus had ruptured too. Annie could see a large tear in the upper quadrant. The baby, a tiny boy, was lying outside the womb, marooned in Suzanne's abdomen. Annie's fingers ran along the umbilical cord, praying that her eyes were deceiving her. But she wasn't that lucky. The umbilical cord had ruptured.

Annie looked up at Caspar. Wanting him to tell her that it wasn't as bad as it looked. Wanting him to tell her it would be all right.

But of course he couldn't do that.

His green eyes locked onto hers. Annie could see compassion in their depths but she could also see despair.

The baby was blue and lifeless.

'We can't save the baby.' Caspar told her what she already knew. His deep voice was husky and Annie knew this was affecting him as much as it was her. 'We have to try to save Suzanne.'

Caspar checked for vital signs but they both knew it was too late. He gently lifted the baby out of Suzanne. He was perfectly formed in miniature. Only about fourteen centimetres long, he was slightly bigger than the palm of Caspar's hand and his little head rested against Caspar's fingers. Caspar wrapped him in a small surgical drape before handing him to one of the nurses as Annie swallowed, trying in vain to dislodge the lump that had formed in her throat.

'Can you organise a heat lamp? I want to keep him warm and nearby.' Caspar spoke to the nurse. 'Suzanne may want to hold him when she wakes up but I don't want him placed where she can see him without asking. That might be too big a shock.'

The nurse nodded and Annie blinked back tears. She had no idea what Suzanne would want but she was sure she wouldn't want to hear that her baby had died. At least Caspar had thought about what might come next.

The baby was so tiny. Annie knew he wouldn't weigh more than a couple of hundred grams and at eighteen weeks gestation he was too young to be considered a stillbirth, too young to legally require a name, too young to legally require registering. It was heartbreaking but she couldn't afford to waste time. She had to try and save Suzanne. The nurses were running another unit of blood as Suzanne continued to bleed heavily.

Annie continued to work, blocking out thoughts of the baby as she tried to stem the blood flow. She was almost on autopilot, her hands moving swiftly to cauterise damaged blood vessels. She could smell the burning tissue as she worked and she was aware of the constantly replaced bags of blood. She felt like she was fighting a losing battle but eventually the bleeding slowed as she sealed and repaired the vessels, and then she had to turn her attention to the torn uterine wall.

That took several more minutes but finally she was able to stitch Suzanne's abdominal wound. The surgery would leave a scar that would resemble that of a Caesarean section but Suzanne would have no happy ending and Annie dreaded having to impart the news. She'd been able to save Suzanne's uterus, which she hoped might at least give her the chance of having children in the future, but Annie knew that wasn't going to lessen the pain right now.

And it wasn't over yet. Once Annie had finished, Suzanne was left in Tori's care as they waited for the orthopod to see what he could do about her fractured pelvis. But Annie didn't doubt that Suzanne would recover faster from her fractured pelvis than she would from her fractured heart.

A bassinette with a heat lamp had been brought into the theatre. The baby would be moved with Suzanne but kept out of sight, as Caspar had instructed. Annie wished the baby was out of sight now. She tried not to look at Suzanne's son as she left the OR but, of course, that was impossible. Her eyes were drawn to the tiny bundle and tears blurred her vision again. It was such a tragic situation.

She put her head down and headed for the scrub room, vaguely aware of Colin as he came into Theatre to take care of Suzanne's fractures. Annie couldn't imagine how Suzanne was going to bear the news that her husband was in another hospital hundreds of kilometres away and her baby was dead.

Annie flung open the door to the scrub room, pulled off her mask, gloves and cap and tossed them into the bin, before removing her gown. She leant against the sink, keeping her back turned to the window that looked into the OR. She closed her eyes and let the tears run down her face. She had a few moments of peace before she heard the door open as someone joined her. The air around her stirred and she smelt a faint scent of peppermint and she knew it was Caspar.

'Hey, what's the matter?'

She kept her eyes closed as his voice wrapped around her, calm and deep and soothing, and then she felt his arms wrap around her too, pulling her against his chest. He was warm and solid and smelt wonderful. Annie knew she should resist but she didn't have the energy. It was a comforting place to be. She felt safe and shielded from her troubled thoughts.

Caspar didn't hesitate when he found Annie in the scrub room, in tears and alone. Taking her in his arms felt natural. It was what he would do for his sisters if he found them upset.

Annie fitted perfectly against his chest and into the curve of his shoulder. She'd removed her cap and her hair fell down her back, forming a soft, smooth cushion for his hand as he pulled her into him.

But holding her in his arms felt nothing like hugging his sisters.

He tried to block that thought from his mind. Tried to convince himself that he was only doing what he'd do for anyone else. That Annie was no different to anyone else.

But she felt and smelt different. He couldn't deny that.

He felt her sobs begin to subside as he rubbed her back in a slow, circular rhythm to try and relax her. Her tears were soaking through his scrubs, turning the fabric damp and cool against his skin.

He knew how she felt. He hated it when he couldn't save a life. Losing a baby was devastating for everyone involved and he always found it difficult as it made him think of his own circumstances. Always made him wonder if his own birth mother had struggled with the decision to give him up. Made him wonder if she ever thought about what had happened to him. But he'd learnt not to dwell on that. It was all in the past. What mattered now was the present. What mattered now were Annie and Suzanne.

The door from Theatre opened and Caspar saw Liam, his camera propped on his shoulder, about to come into the room. He shook his head, shooing him away before Annie noticed his presence. She needed privacy and despite the fact that she'd consented to filming he knew she wouldn't thank him for this intrusion. He didn't want to bear the brunt of her ire if he let Liam film this scene.

Annie took her hands away from her face and let them fall to his chest. Two small, warm palms pressed against him and sent a surge of heat straight through his rib cage to his heart. His heart went into overdrive and heat flooded through his body, warming everything from his fingers to his toes. He could feel the warmth flowing in his bloodstream. He could feel a stirring of desire in the pit of his belly and a tightening in his groin. He had to remind himself to breathe. Focus.

He had to move her away. He couldn't let her feel the effect she had on him. He couldn't let her notice his reaction.

He stepped back, just half a pace, far enough for distance but still close enough that he could hold her as he wasn't willing to lose touch with her completely. 'Are you going to tell me what's wrong?'

She looked up at him. Her face was tear-stained and her eyes were shiny with unshed tears that were trapped against her lashes like dewdrops, threatening to spill over. The tip of her nose was red but somehow she still managed to look beautiful. It was incredible—he'd never known anyone who could look good while crying.

And then he knew he was in trouble. He had priorities: his dad; his job; the television series. He didn't have time for anything more. And Annie Simpson was definitely more.

The cold crept in as Caspar stepped away. Except for two warm spots on her upper arms where his hands still held her she felt as though her temperature had dropped several degrees. She looked up at him. Tall, dark and handsome, and just moments before she'd been in his embrace.

She couldn't believe she'd been in his arms. What had she been thinking? She needed to put him back into the box marked 'Do not open'. She couldn't believe she'd let him out. Let him close.

She was silently berating herself until she realised that *she* hadn't let him out. He'd taken himself out. He'd crossed her boundaries and entered her personal space.

But you welcomed him in, said the voice in her head. The voice she thought of as the voice of reason, only this time it wasn't being very reasonable. But it was right. Being in his arms had felt good. And she hadn't resisted. Even now her hands were still pressed against his chest, still touching him. She had to move away.

With great effort she removed her hands from his chest and, in order to try to make the movement seem natural, wiped her face, attempting to remove all traces of her tears. She rubbed her damp hands on her pants as she took a deep breath. That was a mistake. Another hit of peppermint assaulted her senses but it was enough to force her to concentrate.

She might not have resisted but she hadn't asked him for comfort. She hadn't asked him for empathy. Embarrassment and confusion made her angry. She was annoyed with herself and cross with him. She didn't care if they were both to blame. His gesture had taken her by surprise and, while she wasn't denying she felt better for it, she wasn't sure that his actions had been completely innocent.

Maybe his comfort had been genuine but perhaps he'd simply seen this as an opportunity to get past her defences, a chance to ingratiate himself into her good graces and make her more amenable to the idea of the television series.

She had no real idea but she decided she had enough to deal with without trying to second-guess Caspar's motives. The situation with Suzanne had left her emotionally spent and, given her lack of resistance, letting Caspar out of the box could only make matters worse. She'd have to be stronger. She'd have to make sure it didn't happen again. She needed to rebuild her barriers.

'You can't use that footage,' she snapped in response to his question.

A shadow darkened his eyes. He didn't answer immediately, just watched her.

Eventually he spoke. 'That's what's bothering you?'

Was that disappointment in his expression or was it just her imagination? She almost apologised for her mood. Almost.

'No one should have to watch that. It's too sad. Please

tell me it's not something you would want to show your viewers?'

'I doubt very much we'd get permission from Suzanne to show that, and we won't ask.' He spoke slowly, his tone calm and measured, but Annie could hear the sadness in it too. 'I agree, it's not something people will want to watch. If we screen Suzanne's story, Gail will focus on the fact that we saved her life, *you* saved her life, she won't focus on the tragic loss of the baby.'

Annie may not have apologised but she did temper her irritation. It was difficult to stay angry when he was agreeing with her for once. It was difficult to stay angry while he was still holding her. His touch made it hard to concentrate. And she needed to concentrate. She needed to work out if she could trust him.

She had decided he could be trusted in the operating theatre but could he be trusted away from there? Could she trust him to put her patient before his viewers?

She really had no choice. She couldn't condemn him for something he hadn't yet done. She believed in people being innocent until proven guilty.

She would give him the benefit of the doubt.

Her tone was softer when she next spoke. 'Did you know Suzanne and her husband were driving here from Robe? They had an appointment tomorrow for her eighteen-week antenatal ultrasound?'

He shook his head and she remembered he hadn't been in the room when that information had been passed onto her.

'She was coming here full of anticipation and expectation and now all I have to give her is bad news. Her husband is seriously injured, in a hospital hundreds of miles away, and she's lost the baby.'

'You saved her life.'

'I'm not sure she'll thank me for that.'

'You did everything you could. I'm not denying it's going to be tough on her but she can't blame you for anything.' He spoke softly, his voice gentle and reassuring. 'If she's going to blame anyone, she'll blame me. I'm the baby doctor. Suzanne was your patient and you did everything right for her. I couldn't save the baby, I don't think anyone could have. Do you want someone else to give her the news?'

Annie shook her head. 'No. It'll be okay.'

'Are you sure you're up to it? If you're this upset you might not be the best person to have this conversation with her. Do you want me to do it? I'll have to speak to her at some point.'

The thought of having that conversation with Suzanne made her feel sick but it was her job. A job she'd managed to do perfectly well before he'd arrived in town so why was she now letting him take her into his arms, letting him offer support? She didn't need it. She didn't need him. She needed to show him she could manage.

She was still sandwiched between him and the sink, his hands were still holding her arms and she'd made no effort to move away. She stepped around him, forcing him to let her go. She lifted her head. 'It's my job. I'll handle it.'

'She's going to be a while in Theatre yet so you'll have a long wait in front of you. Do you want me to give you a lift home?' He was still offering help. 'I can bring you back later when she wakes up.'

Annie shook her head. 'No, I'll wait in my office.'

She didn't want him to be nice to her. She felt like she'd let Suzanne down and she didn't want someone to make excuses for her. She straightened her shoulders and headed for the door before she was tempted to seek solace in his arms again. Before she was tempted to hide her face against his chest and let her sad thoughts float away. She couldn't depend on him. She didn't *want* to depend on him. She had no intention of depending on anyone except herself.

Annie might think she could cope with the situation but Caspar had no plans to let her deal with this alone. Not after finding her in tears. She hadn't asked him to go with her to talk to Suzanne but she couldn't keep him away altogether. He was worried about her. Since he'd met her he'd been trying to figure out what she wanted. Now it was obvious. She wanted a happy ending.

He almost smiled to himself. He should have been able to guess that. He'd had enough experience with women, and wasn't that what they all wanted? He knew he couldn't deliver the fairy-tale ending but surely he could think of a way to make her feel better. He couldn't fix the situation but surely he could improve it.

He needed a bit of luck and he got it when his producer called and handed him a solution.

Caspar swung into action. He felt much better now that he had a plan. He asked the nurses to call him as well when Suzanne woke up. He wasn't planning on seeing Suzanne but he didn't want to miss Annie.

He was waiting for her when she emerged from Recovery. It was a moment or two before she noticed him and he used that time to observe her unseen. Purple smudges under her eyes contrasted sharply with her pale skin and made her brown eyes look even darker than normal. Her pink lips were pressed together, drawn and pinched. She looked tired.

He saw her scan the corridor, saw her register his

presence, and when her eyes met his he realised that the expression in her eyes wasn't tiredness, it was sadness. Caspar's heart felt like a lead weight in his chest. He longed to take her in his arms again, longed to offer comfort, but he knew it was unwise.

She hesitated and he wondered if she would approach him or not.

'How are you?' he asked. As far as questions went it was highly inadequate but it was all he could come up with. And he knew that if he didn't say something quickly he wouldn't be able to resist closing the distance between them and offering physical comfort.

Annie almost wasn't surprised to see Caspar standing in the corridor. She was beginning to get used to him popping up when she least expected it. For a moment she thought she might even have been glad to see him until she stopped to wonder why he was there. She hoped it wasn't because he wanted to film something. She wasn't in the mood for that. Not in the slightest.

But his question hadn't been about work. It had been about her. And he hadn't bothered asking how things had gone with Suzanne, which was a blessing. He must know how difficult that conversation would have been.

She was standing several feet from him, forcing herself to keep some distance. She shrugged in response to his question. She was exhausted, physically and emotionally, and she didn't have the energy to construct a sentence.

He didn't seem to expect an answer. 'We got the best outcome we could have,' he told her. 'You saved her life. There was nothing either of us could do for her son. Some days it's important to try to focus on what you did achieve, not on what you didn't.'

She knew he was right but it didn't make her feel

any better. She felt as though she had the weight of the world on her shoulders.

'If you're up to it I think I have something that might cheer you up,' he said.

That surprised her. 'How could you? You barely know me and even I can't think of anything that would help.'

He wasn't going to be shut down. 'Gail called. She's got the first edit ready from filming on Friday. What we taped with Kylie and Paul and the twins, the delivery and their reunion in the nursery. I thought that might be something you'd like to see,' he persisted.

'Watching footage that I didn't want taken, you think that's going to cheer me up?'

He smiled at her. 'You're feeling better already, I see.'

'What do you mean?'

'You're arguing with me again.'

He was right, she realised, she did feel better. Having him there, someone who had gone through the drama with her, someone who understood what the day had been like, had lightened the burden of responsibility. And it didn't hurt that he was still smiling at her and he'd changed out of his scrubs into jeans that hugged his hips and an aqua T-shirt that moulded to his chest and made his eyes look more blue than green. Just looking at him was enough to lighten her mood.

'Please,' he said.

She hesitated.

'I'll drive you and drop you home afterwards,' he added, attempting to sweeten the deal, but that made her more hesitant. Not because she didn't want to go with him but because she did. But surely being in his tiny sports car would only complicate matters. He would be far too close for comfort. The memory of being in his arms was still so fresh.

She couldn't deny how good it had felt but it had left her feeling very confused. No, not confused, she knew exactly what she'd felt. Conflicted would be a better description, she thought. She didn't want to get close to Caspar, she didn't want to get close to anyone, but yet she'd let him close, she'd let him hold her, offer comfort—and she'd accepted. Without argument.

She could count on one hand the number of friends she'd made since moving to Mount Gambier. All right, she could count on one finger—Tori—and she knew it wasn't because the locals hadn't been welcoming. It was because she had shut them out. She hadn't made an effort.

She had promised herself she would keep away from Caspar but she'd fallen at the first hurdle. Found herself trusting him when other people had to earn her trust the hard way.

Her life had been nothing but complicated, her history messy, and trusting people didn't come easily to her. In her experience people almost always had an ulterior motive. Very few people really did things out of the goodness of their hearts without any thought for themselves.

'You don't have a car here, remember,' he said, still trying to convince her.

She could have postponed the invitation, delayed it until she had her own transport, but her misgivings weren't enough to overrule her hormones. She didn't feel like going home to an empty house. Going with Caspar was a far more appealing option.

CHAPTER FIVE

AN APPEALING OPTION, certainly, but not the most sensible one, she thought as she strapped herself into the seat beside him. The car smelt of leather. Caspar smelt of peppermint.

The car was tiny. Caspar was not.

The seats were soft, plump and comfortable. Caspar was masculine, lean and made her feel decidedly uncomfortable.

But it was too late now, she thought as he put the car into gear and pulled away from the hospital. She tried to blend into the upholstery, not sure if she wanted to be seen in his car as she tried to regain control of her nerves. She kept her face turned away from the window, not wanting to make eye contact with anyone on the street, but her plan wasn't a good one. The interior of the car was small, which meant there wasn't a lot to look at besides Caspar.

His posture was relaxed, making him seem at one with the car, as though the car was an extension of him, sleek and powerful. The engine noise was deep and rich and the car throbbed beneath her like a living thing, exacerbating the tension she was experiencing.

The lines of his jaw were darkened by his weekend stubble and Annie closed her eyes and imagined the contrast between the roughness of his beard and the softness of the leather seats under her hand.

She opened her eyes; after all, reality might be easier to handle than fantasy. Her gaze landed on the steering wheel; Caspar's fingers were looped casually around the curve, caressing the leather. Annie could remember how his fingers had felt on her arms, how his touch had warmed her skin, and her earlier nervousness doubled, churning through her stomach. She dragged her gaze away from Caspar, away from his long fingers, green eyes and designer stubble, and forced herself to look around the car. But, short of opening the glove box and searching through its contents, there wasn't an awful lot to hold her interest. Not when Caspar sat mere inches away.

'It's a very nice car,' she said, attempting to make conversation. 'The television network must pay you well.' She'd been trying desperately to find something to say and she could have kicked herself for the words that had popped out of her mouth, but it was too late.

'That's the second time you've mentioned my salary. Does it bother you, the idea that the network would pay me?' His eyes didn't leave the road and Annie couldn't tell if she'd annoyed him or not.

She remembered when she'd asked him how much he got paid. She remembered that he hadn't answered because she'd apologised and stopped him.

Did it bother her? She supposed it must do.

'It's the idea that people will do things differently if they're getting paid,' she admitted. 'People have been known to do strange things for money.'

Herself included. She had signed the consent forms for the television series because she needed to keep her job. Because she needed the money. If her divorce hadn't left her almost bankrupt she would have behaved very differently, she wouldn't even be in Mount Gambier. She knew exactly how money, or the lack of it, made people behave out of character.

Money was a big consideration for her but she hoped she wouldn't, or couldn't, be persuaded to do things she felt uncomfortable about just because she was being financially rewarded. And while she knew other people were often tempted by monetary gain, she hoped Caspar wasn't among them. She wanted him to be motivated by something other than money.

She realised that was unfair of her. After all, her move to Mount Gambier had been partly motivated by the lower cost of living in the country, which meant she'd be able to rebuild her life more quickly. But she was providing a necessary service, she wasn't using other people's situations to build up her bank account, and she hoped Caspar's reasons for doing the show weren't purely mercenary. He'd shown her such compassion today that she didn't want to be disappointed in him.

She shouldn't care. But she did.

'I couldn't agree with you more,' Caspar replied.

'What?'

'I think you're right. Money can do strange things to people. But I'm not doing this for the money. The network doesn't pay me, they're just filming me doing my job. If they paid me they would have to pay all of you. They do, however, make a generous donation to a children's charity on my behalf.'

'So you do the series for nothing?' Annie didn't know what to make of that information. On one hand she was pleased to hear that money wasn't his driving force but why would he choose to work under the watchful eye of television cameras? He must have something to gain from it.

'I agreed to be part of series one because I thought it was a chance to raise awareness of different medical conditions and ultimately I hoped to get the government to fund more health care programmes and initiatives. There are still so many underfunded areas.

'And,' he said as he pulled into the car park at the rear of the building that housed the local television station, 'if it makes you feel any better, I'm off the clock right now.'

It did make her feel a little better, Annie thought as she shut the car door. His offer to spend this time with her had come from him. It didn't mean that his reasons were necessarily purely unselfish but it was nice to know it had been his idea.

The television station was a small, unimaginative building painted an unattractive grey with lots of television aerials and satellite dishes on the roof. Caspar held the door open for her as they entered, and stopped to sign them in as Annie glanced around. There was a short corridor lined by several closed doors but she didn't see another soul.

'Where is everyone?' she asked. She hadn't stopped to consider that they'd be alone once they reached their destination. She'd thought there'd be safety in numbers.

Caspar gestured for her to follow him as he replied. 'Gail has gone, but she left everything set up for me. The local team will be preparing for the evening news broadcast so we're not in anyone's way.'

That wasn't what she'd been worried about. But she was being silly. Just because her hormones had gone into overdrive and she was nervous about being alone with him, it didn't mean anything would happen. After all, he couldn't possibly be attracted to her. Why on earth would he be? She was sure he had his pick of beautiful women, she'd seen plenty of them photographed with him, so why would he look twice at her?

He led her to a small viewing room. A desk, its surface covered with various hi-tech boxes and monitors, ran along one wall. Several screens were fixed to the wall above it and three chairs were crammed together in front.

Caspar pulled out a chair for her, before sitting down himself. He flicked some switches and pressed a few buttons and the overhead lights dimmed and one of the screens came to life. It wasn't a large one and Caspar pulled his chair closer to hers so they were both sitting in front of it. They were separated by only a few centimetres.

Annie tucked her feet under her chair so that their knees didn't touch but she could feel the heat coming off his body. She was still wearing her exercise gear and her arms were bare, the hairs standing to attention. The air felt charged, full of static, and while it could have come from all the electrical equipment in the room, Annie knew it didn't. It was coming from Caspar, almost as though he was positively charged and was seeking out her negative one.

Her nipples hardened, pushing against the Lycra of her tank top, obvious to anyone who cared to look. She crossed her arms over her chest and made herself concentrate on the screen.

A shot of Kylie came into focus, with the back of Annie's head in the foreground. The scene began with the discussion about where to deliver the babies—in Emergency or Maternity—before cutting to footage of Kylie being wheeled along the corridors.

Annie would swear that the footage had been speeded up, making everyone appear as though they were hurrying, and then suddenly the first twin was being delivered. Everything looked far more urgent and exciting than it had actually been. Annie was riveted to the screen. If Gail had managed to capture her attention like this through clever editing then Annie knew the audience would be even more entranced. Which was the whole idea.

Annie almost forgot about Caspar sitting beside her as she waited to see what happened next.

Liam had captured a lot of close-ups. Kylie cuddling the first twin and looking contented. Caspar holding the second twin and looking drop-dead gorgeous. The camera devoured Caspar, his colouring and the angles of his face were made to be photographed.

There was some footage of Annie but mostly it was of the back of her head, as she'd requested, except for a few frames where Liam had captured shots of her in profile when she had been handing the first twin to Caspar. She had a dreamy, slightly vacant expression on her face and she knew the shot had been taken just after she and Caspar had touched for the first time and she'd had been completely disoriented by the powerful charge his touch had sent through her.

Fortunately it looked like Annie was focussed on the baby when she knew the reality was that she hadn't been able to drag her gaze away from Caspar. She wanted to ask for that scene to be cut but she realised that would be ridiculous, That shot needed to be there. It was part of the story and the story was about Kylie's experience, not about her.

The actual delivery of the twins was only a small part of the edited version. Most of the scenes concentrated on Kylie and Paul's reunion and on Paul meeting his babies for the first time. Caspar featured prominently while she only appeared as an extra.

'What do you think?' Caspar asked as the screen went black.

'It's been really well edited,' she admitted. And it had certainly managed to distract her from the events that occurred earlier in the day. Which had been his intention.

Caspar pressed a button and the overhead lights came back on. 'And not too much footage of you?' He was smiling at her, looking his usual confident, handsome self. Assured of the answer.

'Not too much,' she agreed.

'Can we leave you in?'

Annie nodded.

'And future episodes? Are you still willing to be a part of those too?'

'I don't want to feature,' she told him, 'but if they're going to be presented like that then I'm happy to co-operate.'

She didn't want the camera's focus to be on her but she realised now, after seeing the footage, that it wasn't going to be about her. The hospital could do with the money the network had promised and she needed to be a team player.

'Excellent. Shall we go and grab a drink to celebrate our agreement?'

He wanted to go out? In public? She couldn't do that. That would be crossing more boundaries than she was prepared for. No matter how well intentioned his invitation was, anything more than a working relationship wasn't something she was going to encourage or accept.

Being a team player didn't extend to social activities. Caspar had to stay in that box marked 'Do not open'.

'I'm not really dressed for it,' she replied, gesturing at her outfit. A flicker of what she took for disappointment in his eyes had her lifting the lid on the imaginary box. Just a tiny bit. After all his efforts today she felt she probably owed him something more than a refusal. 'You did offer to drop me home. I can make you a coffee there if you like,' she offered.

Caspar thought Annie looked perfectly fine in her gym gear, better than fine actually, but he happily accepted her alternative invitation. He'd won round one. He'd got her to agree to be part of the series and she seemed to have lowered her guard a little. She hadn't argued with him for the best part of fifteen minutes and had even invited him for coffee. Progress had been made.

Annie directed him to an old house on the outskirts of town. It sat squarely in the middle of a large block and was surrounded by aging fruit and citrus trees. It looked much too big for one person yet he had the impression she lived alone. The back of the house was almost smothered by a jasmine creeper and Caspar knew he'd never be able to smell the scent of jasmine without thinking of her.

She entered the house via the back door, which led directly into the kitchen, which appeared to be in almost original condition. Narrow cupboards with laminated bench tops lined two walls, the stove was tucked into the old fireplace and a large kitchen dresser took up most of the fourth wall. In the centre of the room was a laminated table, the type usually seen in institutions, and four vinyl chairs.

A shiny, modern, state-of-the-art coffee machine sat on the bench, looking completely out of place.

The 1950s décor was not at all what he had expected and was vastly different from what he was used to. Home for him was a stylish penthouse in an exclusive apartment block. Walking into Annie's kitchen was like stepping back in time, back to his boarding-school dining-hall days.

'Is this your house?' he asked.

'No, I'm renting,' she told him as she pushed a pile of paint colour charts to one end of the Formica kitchen table, dumping her bag on top of the mess. 'It came furnished,' she added, as she saw him taking it all in.

'With everything bar the coffee machine, I'm guessing.'

Annie nodded. 'And my bed. My landlord has been modernising the house.'

'While you're living in it?' He knew he'd never have the patience to live in the midst of renovations, no matter how minor.

'It's a little bit inconvenient but because of work I'm not here during the day so the tradesmen and I don't really get in each other's way. And it's kept the rent low. The kitchen is the last room on the list. The rest of the house isn't stuck in the same time warp any more,' she said, as she scooped freshly ground coffee into the machine. 'Have a seat, I'm just going to ring the hospital to check on Suzanne.'

'All good?' Caspar asked when she finished the call. He knew neither of them expected any more bad news. The hospital would have called Annie if necessary.

'She's sedated,' she replied, 'and her vitals are stable so it appears as though we stopped the bleeding.'

'So are you feeling better about things now?'

'I feel better about the television series and about Suzanne, but I don't feel so good about her baby,' she said, as she passed him his coffee and set milk and sugar on the table.

She picked up an old, faded, pink sloppy joe that was hanging on the back of the chair and shrugged into it before she sat down. The neck had stretched, allowing one shoulder to slip down, revealing her collarbone and the curve of her deltoid muscle at the top of her arm.

She was wearing more than she had been a moment before yet Caspar had a sense that he was glimpsing forbidden skin. The idea was tantalising and caused him to lose his train of thought. He forced himself to stir his coffee, which was unnecessary as he took it plain and black but it gave him a chance to recover his equilibrium. He was careful with his words.

'Losing a patient is always difficult. Are there any support networks in town for family and staff to access if they need to?'

'I would imagine so but I'm not sure.'

He was a little surprised that Annie didn't know the answer. 'What have you done in the past?'

'I haven't lost a patient, mother or baby, in the six months I've been here,' she explained. 'High-risk pregnancies are sent to Adelaide or Melbourne in plenty of time, and after today I'm going to make sure that practice continues. Today was not something I'm keen to repeat in a hurry.'

It wasn't something she *ever* wanted to repeat. Caspar had told her to focus on what she had been able to achieve but she knew it would be a long time before she could forget the sight of that tiny baby, still and lifeless, cradled in Caspar's palm.

She had no idea how she was going to get to sleep

tonight and if there hadn't been the chance she'd be
called back to the hospital she would have suggested
they drink something stronger than coffee. But coffee
it was, she thought as she drained her cup.

She placed it on the table at the same moment as
Caspar. The table was so small that her fingers brushed
the backs of his knuckles as he put his cup beside hers.
Annie froze, paralysed by the surge of awareness that
made her stomach tremble and her heart race. She felt
a stirring in the air as the heat left Caspar's body and
rushed through hers.

She lifted her head to find him watching her. His
eyes were dark green, darker than she'd ever seen them,
and she could see herself reflected in their depths. Neither of them moved a muscle. Annie wasn't sure she
was even breathing.

Movement in the corner of the kitchen caught her
eye, startling her, and it was enough to break the bubble of attraction in which she found herself. She pulled
her hand back and exhaled through slightly parted
lips, turning to face the very pregnant cat that had just
sneaked in through the open back door.

'Aggie, have you come for a feed?' she said.

'Yours?' Caspar queried. 'Are you constantly surrounded by pregnant females?'

Annie laughed as she stood up and closed the back
door. Aggie had provided her with the perfect reason to
move out of Caspar's force field and she was relieved to
find she could still walk and talk and breathe.

'She's not mine. She belongs to Bert, my landlord.
He lives next door but Aggie knows I'm a soft touch.
I'm thinking of keeping one of her kittens when they're
ready for a new home.'

Speaking of Bert made her realise that aside from

her octogenarian landlord and neighbour, Caspar was the only man she had invited into her house. While Bert had almost blended into the furnishings Caspar was a complete contrast. He was too big, too vibrant, too virile to be contained within these four walls. It had been a mistake to invite him here. She wasn't keeping her distance at all. She had well and truly opened the box. She hoped it wasn't too late to stuff him back inside.

'Are you planning on staying in Mount Gambier?' he asked.

'I might. I'm only on contract but it would be nice to settle down somewhere for a while,' she said as she poured some cat food into a small bowl and placed it on the floor.

'Have you moved a lot?'

She nodded but didn't volunteer any further information.

'Well?'

'Well, what?'

'Why have you moved so much? Was it work? It sounds interesting.'

'It's not,' she replied, as she decided what to tell him. She figured she could give him an edited version. 'I moved a lot as a child.'

'Because of your parents' work?'

'Not exactly. My mother was a nurse and my father was a carpenter with a rather erratic employment record. My parents had a rather volatile relationship, not helped by my father's inconsistent employment. He worked on construction sites, sometimes for the mining companies, sometimes in small towns, wherever he could find a job.

'My mother would follow him around the country for periods of time, dragging me with her, but we never

seemed to stay permanently. Inevitably things would
play out the same way over and over again. Construction
work would dry up or finish and my father would
be "between jobs". He'd then spend his spare time at
the pub, which led to fighting, which would lead to my
mother saying she wasn't going to put up with it any
more and she'd pack our bags and we'd leave.'

'Where did you go?'

'Back to my gran's, my mum's mum. But that would
only be temporary too. Dad would eventually get a job
and beg Mum to come back. She was never able to resist him. I never understood what was happening. I
still can't figure it out, but Mum always said that even
though most of the time she was miserable with him,
she was more miserable without him.'

'How often did you move?'

'Sometimes every few months. I don't think we ever
stayed in one place for more than a year,' she said, as
she closed up the bag of cat food and put it back under
the sink. 'It's not the way I'd want anyone to grow up,
never knowing where you were going to be from one
minute to the next. Being taken away from people without notice. Never having anywhere to call home.'

'And you did this until you started university?'

'No, only until I was twelve.'

'What happened then?'

'My parents died in a house fire.'

She heard his intake of breath. She'd shocked him.
She hadn't meant to but she wasn't sure why she'd been
so blunt. If she ever shared that information with anyone, she was usually a little more subtle.

'Annie, I'm so sorry. Were you there?'

She hadn't meant to pause, she hadn't wanted to give
him an opportunity to offer any sympathy or to ask

questions. She hadn't meant to do a lot of things but Caspar seemed to have the ability to throw her off kilter.

She nodded. 'I'd been asleep but something woke me and our neighbour said he found me in the hall. He managed to get me out but he couldn't get into my parents' room. The fire had started there and by the time the fire brigade got to us it was too late. I was the only survivor.'

'Were you the only other person in the house? No siblings?'

'I'm an only child. Whenever we were going to or from Dad's place Mum always said she couldn't imagine dragging more kids around.'

'Were you hurt?'

'Not physically. I suffered from PTSD and lost my capacity for speech for about three months. There was an investigation into the fire and the media became fascinated with the case and with me because I wasn't speaking. That was my first experience with the media.'

'As a twelve-year-old after a traumatic event?'

She nodded.

'I can see why you don't like to be followed by cameras.'

She didn't tell him that for a long time she hadn't actually been able to remember the events of that night and had been placed into foster-care for three nights because her gran, her only other relative, was living interstate and, because she herself hadn't been talking, it had taken some time to track her down.

Annie wasn't volunteering any more information and Caspar didn't ask more questions about the fire. His thoughts had moved ahead. 'Where did you live after the fire?'

'With my gran. Her house was the only place I've

ever felt at home.' It was the only place where Annie had felt truly safe and loved, and she knew she longed to re-create that feeling in a house of her own one day.

'What happened to her?'

He was watching her closely and she knew he was wondering how she could have left the only place she truly loved.

'Gran died and I had to sell the house.' She phrased her words carefully, deliberately making it sound as though her gran had died recently and that selling the house was linked to her gran's death when, in fact, her gran had died nine years ago while she had still been at university, before Annie had embarked on her ill-fated marriage. The marriage that had cost her the house.

He didn't need to know she'd had to sell the house to pay her husband's fines. That his drink-driving conviction had meant his insurance had been null and void and that the consequences of his actions had cost her her home. When her gran had died she had lost the person who had loved her most in the world. She had tried to replace her with a husband and then to lose her home as well had almost been the end for her.

But that was a whole different story and not one she was prepared to tell Caspar. She was trying to move on from there and her move to the country was part of the healing process. She was seeking a new start.

'Do you have other family? Aunts, uncles, cousins?'

Annie shook her head. 'No, there's only me.' It was time to change the topic of conversation. She didn't want to sound depressed or maudlin. 'We'll have to talk about your family instead. Do they all still live around here?'

Caspar nodded. 'Dad and my sisters are here.'

'Do you visit often?'

'No. That was one reason I pushed for the show to be filmed here when the network was looking for alternative hospitals.'

'Filming here was your idea?' Annie was surprised. Along with the box marked 'Do not open', she'd also put him in a box labelled 'Hotshot, big-city doctor'. She knew she was being unfair. She'd judged him on his celebrity status, his car and his impeccably tailored suits, even though his behaviour had been anything but flashy.

'Dad suffers from dementia,' he explained. 'I've been letting my sisters handle it for too long. I thought it was time I did my bit. Filming the series here meant I could help out.'

'Is your dad in care?'

'No.' Caspar shook his head. 'He's living with one of my sisters but we need to look at other options. He's declining rapidly.'

'Why didn't you just take holidays? Surely you didn't have to move the whole series here?' she asked.

Caspar shrugged. 'I prefer to be busy.'

Annie imagined that looking for a suitable nursing-home bed would have kept him very busy but that was just her opinion. It didn't make her right. 'Are you staying with one of your sisters?'

'No. The network has put us into apartments near the lake. But my sister, Brigitte, feeds me most nights.' Caspar paused and Annie could see in his eyes as his thoughts took a different direction. He checked his watch. 'Which reminds me, I'm late for dinner. Again,' he said as he stood up. 'I should go. If I don't mend my ways, she'll stop offering to feed me.'

For a split second Annie thought about inviting him to stay for dinner with her. But then common sense prevailed. She could stretch her dinner for one to feed a second female but she doubted she'd have enough to satisfy a male appetite.

And why would he want to stay anyway? Thinking about her gran made her realise how often she was lonely and how much she missed company, but Caspar wasn't the answer. He should go.

'Thanks for the coffee.' He'd crossed the kitchen floor and was standing in front of her now. Annie had the kitchen sink behind her and she thought back to the last time they'd been in this same position only a few hours earlier. It seemed a lifetime ago.

Her eyes were level with his chest and she watched it rise and fall as he breathed. If she lifted her hand she'd be able to place it over his heart, she'd be able to feel him breathe. The pull of attraction was back. Annie could feel herself fixed within his force field and she made herself keep her hands by her sides. Out of danger's way.

He reached towards her and Annie held her breath, waiting to see what he was going to do. He bent his head and she lifted her face up and met his eyes.

CHAPTER SIX

'ARE YOU GOING to be all right by yourself?' he asked.

His hand was past her shoulder now. He wasn't reaching for her, she realised, he was reaching for the doorknob. Disappointment flooded through her, dousing the warm glow in her belly with cold reality. 'Yes, of course,' she answered. She was used to being on her own. She didn't always like it but she was used to it.

He paused and for a moment Annie thought he had something more to say. But then he turned the doorknob and let himself out into the night.

Annie shut the door and leant against it. She closed her eyes as she tried to make sense of the myriad emotions swamping her. Desire, disappointment, relief and loneliness all competed for space in her head.

Loneliness won, shrouding her in its icy grip, emphasising the emptiness of the room. The warmth that had come from having someone to share a drink with, a conversation with, had gone with Caspar.

Loneliness was an ache in the pit of her stomach.

But she knew the cure. She'd had plenty of practice. Keep busy.

She took their coffee cups to the sink to rinse them. The cat wound her plump, furry body between Annie's calves as if she sympathised with Annie's predicament. The phone rang as she dried the second cup.

'Would you like to tell me what's going on? I've been trying to reach you all afternoon.' Tori's voice came down the line.

'I've been busy.'

They both knew Annie was never busy except when she was at work.

'I could see that.' Down the line Annie could hear the smile in Tori's voice. As the anaesthetist Tori would have had a bird's-eye view of Annie being wrapped in Caspar's arms. 'What I want to know is just what is it the two of you have been busy doing. If you've been ignoring me because you've been having wild sex all afternoon, that's okay, but I'm not interested in any other excuse.'

Annie had ignored several calls from Tori. She knew she wasn't ignoring anything urgent because important calls regarding patients would come through the hospital switchboard, not through Tori's mobile.

'Sorry to disappoint you,' she replied. 'He took me to see the first edit of the footage they've taken so far. That's it.' Annie wasn't ready to share anything more than that. Besides, what was there to share? Nothing had happened.

'So he's not with you now?'

'No.'

'I'm coming over. I'll pick up a movie and you can make up a story about your afternoon of steamy sex to keep me entertained.'

Annie knew there was no point in trying to put Tori off. She'd be around regardless, but at least that would take care of the loneliness.

Annie didn't know whether to be relieved or disappointed when a few days passed with very little contact with Caspar. Tori kept checking for updates but there was absolutely nothing to report. No babies had been born and she'd had no cases that had been considered interesting enough for the cameras and nothing exciting was happening with Kylie or Suzanne to warrant any further screen time.

She had bumped into Caspar during ward rounds but there had been nothing they'd needed to discuss and there had been no need to call for his services. She'd seen him being interviewed by the one of the entertainment channels outside the hospital and his photo had been in the local newspaper *again*, but that just served to remind her of their differences. He was happy being in the public eye while she would do anything to avoid the attention.

On top of all that she was a little embarrassed that she'd confided her family history to him *and* then had thought he had been going to kiss her. And that she'd wanted him to. She decided she couldn't blame him if he was avoiding her.

But just as she was aware that their paths weren't crossing so she was aware of her days passing slowly. Whereas she'd been happy with the routine days and lack of drama that she'd experienced since moving to the country, she now found herself wishing for a little more excitement. And Caspar St Claire had the potential to give her excitement in spades.

But, she reminded herself, Caspar St Claire wasn't for her. She was managing just fine on her own.

Annie had one more patient to see before lunch and then she'd be free to think about any topic she chose, but for now she owed it to her patient to concentrate. She picked up the referral letter on her desk. As she re-

read the letter she remembered a phone call she'd had in regard to this patient earlier in the week.

Taylor Cartwright was a sixteen-year-old schoolgirl who thought she was pregnant by her teenage boyfriend. She was coming to the appointment with her high-school principal, Mrs Brigitte Lucas, who had organised the referral through a medical contact and had phoned Annie to give her some background. According to Mrs Lucas, Taylor was from a very religious family and Taylor didn't want to say anything to her parents until she knew for sure what her situation was.

Annie thought it strange that she would confide in her school principal and not her own family, but she would reserve her judgement until she met them both and got a feel for the case.

Annie finished getting the background straight in her head before calling them through to her office.

Taylor was a reasonably tall girl with a healthy, solid build. Because of her larger frame Annie knew Taylor could be many weeks pregnant before anyone would notice major physical changes.

'I assume you've missed a period or two or had some very light spotting?' Annie asked the teenager. 'Have you done a home pregnancy test?'

'Yes. Mrs Lucas gave me one. I couldn't get one from the pharmacy because someone might have seen me and told my mum.'

This seemed a bit above and beyond her idea of the job description of a high-school principal. Annie looked enquiringly at the headmistress.

'We run a programme at my high school for teenage mums. It allows them to finish their schooling around the demands of a baby. The girls know they can come to me for support,' Brigitte explained.

'The test was positive?'

Taylor nodded.

'I'll do another test, just to confirm that, and once we know for sure we can talk about your options,' Annie said. 'Do you remember when your last menstrual cycle started?'

'Mrs Lucas told me you'd ask that,' Taylor said, and told Annie the date.

Annie sent Taylor into the bathroom to give a urine sample while she calculated dates and asked Brigitte some more questions.

'Do you have many teenage mothers finishing their schooling?' In the six months Annie had been working at the hospital she hadn't, to her knowledge, encountered any pregnant girls who were still at school and neither had she met Brigitte Lucas.

'Fortunately, not too many,' Brigitte replied. 'There are four who have had their babies and are trying to finish their schooling and only Taylor, as far as I know, who is pregnant now. Not all of the girls need my input to the same degree as Taylor. Most have family support eventually, but I think it's important for them to know that there is help and that completing their education is an option. It might take a year or two longer than they'd planned but in my experience it can make all the difference to their futures.'

Annie couldn't imagine trying to juggle the demands of motherhood with finishing high school but she guessed she was way past having to worry about that. She was more worried that she'd never have a family of her own. She didn't want to be a single mother. She wanted the fairy-tale, she wanted to meet Mr Right and then have a family. With her family history there was no way she'd contemplate trying to do it alone. But

the closer she got to thirty the more she thought it might
not happen for her.

However, she couldn't worry about that now, she
thought as Taylor finished in the bathroom.

'Positive,' Annie said as she tested Taylor's sample.
'You're having a baby.'

Taylor blanched and Annie was glad she'd waited
until the teenager was sitting down. Despite her earlier positive test, it was clear that Taylor had been hoping that perhaps it had been wrong, and she clearly had
misgivings.

Annie watched as Brigitte reached across and held
Taylor's hand. 'Two positives tests. It looks like this is
really happening for you.'

Taylor met Brigitte's eyes and Annie was relieved to
see her straighten her shoulders. She might have wished
the news were different but she at least appeared to have
some strength of character.

'What's next?' Brigitte asked Annie, as Taylor's gaze
swung over to her.

Annie smiled at the girl. 'There are lots of decisions
to make and things to discuss, but first I think we should
have a look at your baby.'

'I can see it?' Taylor's voice wobbled slightly but
she wasn't denying the truth and Annie took that as a
positive sign.

'I can do an ultrasound scan. It's a non-invasive tech-
nique that uses sound waves to give us a picture of your
baby. It will help me to determine or confirm dates too,'
Annie replied. The scan would also allow her to check
that everything was as it should be at this stage.

When Taylor was comfortable on the examination
bed Annie quickly checked her blood pressure before
squeezing the conducting gel onto her stomach and

sweeping the transducer head backwards and forwards to build up a picture of the baby.

She found the amniotic sac and inside it was a tiny foetus. There was no mistaking the little jellybean shape.

'There's your baby,' Annie said. 'Two arms, two legs,' she said as she pointed to the screen. 'It all looks about right for ten weeks gestation. See the little flicker, like an anemone opening and closing? That's your baby's heart.'

'Wow, that is so cool. It's a little person already.'

'So, this is good news?' Brigitte asked the teenager.

'I don't know about good but I do know that I am going to keep it. I can't believe I have a little person inside me.'

'What about the baby's father?' Annie asked, as she printed off a picture for Taylor and cleaned up the gel. 'Does he know?'

Taylor shook her head as she stared at the black and white photo of her baby. 'Not yet. But I'll have to tell him.' She hesitated slightly before adding, 'And my parents.'

Annie hoped Taylor would be supported through this, at least by her parents and hopefully her boyfriend too, but she knew there was little she could do about that.

'You have some important decisions to make,' Annie said, as Taylor hopped up from the examination table. 'And when you've had time to tell the baby's father and your parents the news, I'd like you to make an appointment to see me and bring anyone who would like to support you. I'm sure everyone will have questions.

'There's no hurry to come back to me. Everything is perfectly natural and normal and healthy, but if you have any concerns at any stage, let me know. And at some point we will have to have a conversation about safe sex. Not just to prevent pregnancy but to protect against sexually transmitted diseases too.'

Taylor went bright red when Annie broached that topic. Annie was always amazed that teenagers were embarrassed about having that discussion yet weren't embarrassed about the fact that they'd clearly been having unprotected sex. But she wasn't going to lecture Taylor today. Instead, she spent several more minutes answering Taylor's immediate questions before she gathered a pile of brochures and handed them to the teenager.

'There's some useful information here, plus a number for a good social worker if you would like someone else to talk to.'

Annie expected to find an empty waiting room as she escorted Brigitte and Taylor to the door of her office so she was surprised to find someone standing there, and even more surprised to see it was Caspar. She was definitely not expecting him.

Automatically she put a hand to her head, checking to see if her hair was a mess or whether she looked presentable. As she chastised herself for being so vain she noticed Taylor doing a double-take when she spied Caspar.

Despite the fact that Caspar was old enough to be Taylor's father, Annie noticed that even teenagers weren't immune to his good looks. She smiled to herself. The poor girl was being swamped with hormones. Was it any wonder she was affected by Caspar? Annie didn't imagine many women would be completely unaffected. The only one who didn't seem fazed was Brigitte.

She walked straight up to him and hugged him, and Annie was surprised to feel a surge of jealousy.

'Hey, little brother, are you looking for me?'

Brigitte was Caspar's sister? Annie looked closely at the two of them, searching for a family resemblance, but apart from a similar determination about them they were like chalk and cheese to look at. Brigitte was fair while Caspar was dark. She had blue eyes, not green, and she had none of his height.

'If I were, I wouldn't be looking here,' Caspar replied, smiling. 'I'm looking for Annie.'

He fixed his eyes on her. 'I know you've a lunch break scheduled—have you got time to grab a bite to eat? There's something I'd like to discuss with you.'

Annie felt herself flush. Even though she knew it would be work related, just the idea of Caspar inviting her to lunch made her heart pound and her colour rise. She seriously needed to get a grip.

She nodded, before saying goodbye to Brigitte and Taylor and reminding Taylor about her follow-up appointment.

'You had something you wanted to discuss with me?' Annie asked the moment they had chosen their lunch and a seat.

Caspar had purposely chosen a semi-secluded table in the corner of the cafeteria. He knew people would assume they were discussing work and, while that was his intention, he didn't want to be overheard if their discussion took a change in direction. But it seemed Annie was treating this lunchtime break purely as a professional one.

He nodded. 'I saw Kylie Jones this morning when I

was checking the twins. She says you are planning on discharging her.'

'Tomorrow,' Annie agreed. 'There's no medical reason to keep her in hospital.'

'I realise that but I thought you might want an update on the twins. They need to gain another hundred grams each and preferably do that without any losses in between before I'll be happy to send them home.'

'Kylie can come into the hospital each day to be with the twins until they are ready for discharge. I can't justify a bed for her,' Annie replied. She took a sip of her coffee before she added, 'You didn't need to have lunch with me to discuss this.'

Her comment made him smile. He wondered if she was always so prickly or whether he brought out her defensive streak.

'Maybe I wanted to have lunch with you,' he said, surprising himself with his honesty and hoping it didn't make her run for shelter.

He had deliberately kept his distance for the past few days as he'd tried to work out how he felt about her. Annie Simpson unsettled him. She fascinated him. She excited him. Her forceful opinions intrigued him and it wasn't often that people disagreed with him so vehemently or so delightfully. He wasn't used to being amused when people disagreed with him yet her unexpected comments constantly made him smile.

But despite her strong opinions he sensed a fragility about her. Initially he'd thought her delicate appearance had created that feeling but now he realised it was probably something innate, stemming from her childhood. That was no surprise really. Her childhood had hardly been a stable, peaceful one.

While his own life had begun on rather shaky

ground, he'd had the good fortune to have been given a solid, happy childhood. Annie's situation had been somewhat different and, he suspected, far more complicated. He didn't do complicated.

While Annie intrigued him, he didn't really want to become involved. Becoming involved meant giving up some control and that was something he preferred not to do so he'd tried his best to avoid her. But he'd only lasted a couple of days before he'd begun looking for excuses to see her. Searching for cases they had in common, reasons why he'd need to seek her out.

Kylie Jones had been his best option, although not a very good one. Annie didn't need his input and, as she'd said, they didn't need to have lunch to discuss her situation. Anything Caspar had to say could have been said in a sentence or two as they passed in the corridor. He'd known that but it hadn't been enough for him. He'd wanted to see Annie.

He had tried to ignore the stirrings of desire that had been present ever since he'd watched her bending over to feed the cat, the Lycra of her exercise pants moulding to her bottom. He had tried to keep busy with work and filming the series and in any spare moments going with Brigitte to visit nursing homes, albeit without success at this stage.

He could still recall when the shoulder of Annie's sloppy joe had slipped to reveal her collarbone and the little hollow at the base of her throat, just the spot he always thought begged to be kissed, and ever since he'd had difficulty keeping thoughts of Annie Simpson out of his head.

He'd tried to tell himself that lust and desire were just chemistry, that physical attraction didn't necessarily make them compatible, but it was a difficult thing to ignore, particularly when he didn't really believe it.

Although he did suspect that, beyond their chemistry, they were unlikely to have much else in common. She wasn't his type. She was the type to feed other people's cats, the type who lived in a house that was too big for her and spent her spare time looking at paint charts and redecorating rooms as she made a home for herself. She wanted to settle down. He wasn't guessing. She'd said as much. She wanted a home and he suspected she'd want a family to go along with that home.

He lived in an apartment he didn't own and had never bothered decorating beyond new bed linen and matching towels. He hadn't lived in one place since he'd been thirteen, first boarding school for five years then university colleges, share houses and a couple of years overseas before returning to Melbourne. He had never missed having a place to call home and he'd never thought about putting down roots.

Annie was the type who would want happy endings and romance. Hearing about her childhood convinced him that she would want the fairy-tale ending and he couldn't blame her for that. But he didn't believe in fairy-tales.

He'd be a fool to pursue her. She wasn't the type of woman he could discard after a few dates. He should stay away.

But chemistry was a hard thing for him to ignore and he was finding her irresistible.

He needed to find a reason for her to spend more time with him. He needed to create an opportunity or a reason. But his mind was blank. He decided to make small talk while he racked his brain for a legitimate project. 'What did you think of my big sister?' he asked.

'I liked her.'

Caspar laughed. 'You sound surprised,' he said. 'She didn't remind you of me, then?'

'Actually, she did. A little. I got the feeling she could be as stubborn as you.'

'Is that good or bad?' He couldn't resist asking the question.

'You don't want to know.' She smiled and he felt as though the sun had come out. It was a ridiculous expression and not one he'd ever understood before, but now it made perfect sense. 'I thought her programme for teenage mothers was amazing. I'm really keen to work with her on that some more if I can.'

Unwittingly Annie had handed him a perfect idea. He could be the common link between them and maybe he could even find a way of featuring the project in the television series, which would give him a legitimate reason to be involved.

'What did you have in mind?' he asked.

'I'm not sure. It depends what's under way already. How did she become so involved in it? It seems above and beyond what I imagine is the job description of a school principal.'

'We were all brought up to have a social conscience and encouraged to support a cause. Brigitte's cause is teenage pregnancy.'

'And what is yours?' she asked, and Caspar gave himself a mental high five. She was interested enough to ask more. Surely that was a good sign?

'It's a long story. Why don't you meet me for a drink after work and I'll tell you then?' He felt marginally guilty about using her curiosity to his advantage but not guilty enough to stop.

Annie wasn't sure if she'd heard him correctly. Was he was asking her out for a drink for a second time?

'Don't you take no for an answer?'

'I don't often get knocked back.' He grinned and Annie knew he wasn't being arrogant, just honest.

She wished she'd met him under different circumstances. She was beginning to think she could really grow to like him, in a purely platonic sense, of course. She wasn't interested in anything else. Not any more. She sucked at relationships.

'I can't,' she told him.

'Can't or won't?'

'Won't,' she admitted. 'You do realise you've been here for two weeks and you've been on the front page of the local paper twice and on the evening news as well. I'm not interested in being fodder for the local gossip columnist, and even if it's an innocent drink I'm sure it won't be portrayed that way. I don't want to invite the media into my life.'

'Can't blame a man for trying,' he said. 'What about tomorrow night?' he asked, obviously unwilling to give up just yet. 'You are coming to the pub to watch the screening of the first episode of the series, aren't you? Can I buy you a drink then?'

The senior hospital staff and several of the nurses and admin personnel had received invitations earlier in the week to attend a function at the Royal Hotel to watch the first episode of *RPE at Blue Lake*. Annie was sure the television network was hosting the event. 'I thought the network was paying for it?'

'They are,' he admitted. 'I was just making sure you had accepted the invite. Brigitte is coming, you'll be able to chat to her about your ideas then. There will be a crowd of people but no cameras.'

She nodded as she stood and stacked her lunch tray. 'I'll be there.'

'Good, it's a date.'

She looked up from her tray and opened her mouth, ready to protest, but before she could say anything he winked at her and she realised she'd be making a fuss over what was essentially a throw-away line. He didn't mean anything by it.

But despite knowing it was a throw-away line and despite telling herself she wasn't interested in dating, she found herself racing home from work the following day and spending a ridiculous amount of time deliberating over what to wear to the pub.

In the end she figured that to wear anything unusual would invite questions so she stuck with a casual outfit of jeans and wedge heels. The only concession she made was to choose a camisole top in a pale yellow silk that she knew suited her colouring.

She was deliberately late, not late enough to miss the start of the show, just late enough to make sure she would have other people there to act as buffers between her and Caspar. Of course, it made no difference. He came across to her as soon as she arrived.

She watched him as he crossed the room, weaving through the crowd. He was wearing soft, faded jeans that moulded to his thighs and a black polo shirt. He had a casual, tossed-together look, as though five minutes ago he'd been naked and had just quickly thrown on the first clothes that had been to hand. Yet the result wasn't untidy, as she might have expected, but effortlessly sexy.

Her breathing quickened, keeping time with her heart as heat flooded through her belly. Caspar continued walking towards her. He was wickedly handsome, potently male and dangerously hot. He had a devilish gleam in his eye and Annie could imagine him holding out his hand in a silent invitation and she knew she would follow. She wouldn't be able to resist.

He held out his hand and smiled. 'Hello. I believe I owe you a drink,' he said, as he offered her a glass of champagne.

Her fantasy bubble burst but it was just as well. She was falling for something that wasn't even real, something that was a product of her hyperactive imagination. She focussed on reality. 'If I accept it, will you tell me about your story?'

'My story?'

'About your cause. You did promise.'

'And I am a man of my word.' He took a sip of his beer. 'Paediatrics is my cause.'

'Isn't that your career?' she protested. 'You can't fob me off with a made-up cause, otherwise I'll accuse you of getting me here under false pretences.'

He grinned and her stomach did a lazy somersault.

'I swear to tell the whole truth and nothing but the truth,' he said, as he made the sign of a cross over his heart. 'Medicine is my career but I chose paediatrics in particular. I guess, more correctly, I should say that children are my cause.'

'What does that mean exactly?'

'Remember I said it was a long story?' he said with a raised eyebrow. 'Are you sure you're ready for this?'

When Annie nodded he continued. 'Paediatrics was my favourite rotation but it all started long before that. It starts with my mother. She was born in Australia during World War Two to parents who were German immigrants. Because of their heritage they were classed as enemy aliens and interned in a camp for the duration of the war.'

'A camp in Australia?'

Annie was surprised when Caspar nodded. She'd had no idea that such things had existed in Australia.

'My mother was born in the camp,' Caspar continued. 'Her parents were Australian citizens but because they had been born in Germany they were detained against their wishes. My mother grew up being taught to speak up against injustice and she passed that on to us. She thought it was important that those of us who had a voice spoke up for those who didn't.

'Whenever we thought someone wasn't being given a fair hearing we were encouraged to actively do something about it. Brigitte has taken on pregnant teenagers, Krissy is a foster-mum and I studied medicine, and that led me to paediatrics.

'I want to protect children from harm. So many children don't have a voice either because they are too young or they are abused or disadvantaged or just ignored or unwanted. They need someone to listen to their story or ask questions on their behalf or fight for them. That's what I do.'

Annie had barely heard Caspar's last sentences. She hadn't heard much after 'foster-mum'. Those words always put her into a bit of a spin. She'd had first-hand experience with foster situations and hadn't much cared for it. When Caspar stopped speaking she quickly tried to think of something to say that wouldn't let him guess she hadn't been paying attention.

'Your mum must have been very proud of you,' she said.

'I'd like to think so but I also know she expected

nothing less from us. Sometimes I think our efforts are only a drop in the ocean but at least we're trying.'

'I think it's amazing that you're all so committed. Is Brigitte here? I'd like to talk to her about her work.' Annie didn't want to spend too long talking to Caspar, she didn't want to monopolise his time. She was worried that people would notice and start to comment. Talking to Brigitte instead was a good alternative. But it wasn't to be.

'No. She can't make it. Dad's having a bad day and Brig didn't want to leave him. He's not recognising her husband or kids today and she didn't want to leave him with people he thinks are strangers,' he explained. 'I've told her you are keen to be involved in her project and she'll call you. I hope that's okay.'

'Yes, that's fine,' Annie said, as she tried to think of another way to excuse herself, but she was saved by Tori's arrival. In Annie's mind, adding a third person to their conversation would attract less attention.

'Hi, what have I missed?' Tori asked. She was looking carefully from Annie to Caspar, but Annie wasn't about to divulge anything.

'Nothing,' she told her. 'We were just talking about work.' That wasn't quite true but Tori didn't have time to question her further as Gail commandeered a microphone to make a short speech before the show began.

Tori, Annie and Caspar were at the back of the room. 'Shouldn't you be up at the front?' Annie asked Caspar as the lights were dimmed and the opening credits rolled. She was all too aware of his proximity.

'No, I'm fine here,' he replied.

His voice was a whisper in her ear. It sent a tingle through her and she could feel her nipples harden. God, she was ridiculous. She needed to get a grip. She should move but there was nowhere to go without drawing more attention to herself. She tried to relax as the show began. Tried to ignore Caspar sitting beside her.

The show opened with an aerial scene shot from a helicopter as it flew across Blue Lake, before heading over the town and out to the farms, vineyards and pine plantations that surrounded the regional centre. The landscape was green and extremely picturesque but the voiceover was talking about the dangers lurking beneath the beauty.

The scene changed to a low-angle shot taken by the roadside, showing the huge logging trucks racing along the highways before the camera angle changed yet again, and now the audience could watch as the camera followed a truck. From the angle of the shot it was clear that it was being filmed from a car, a car that was dwarfed by the enormous tree trunks that were strapped to the trailer and towered above the car.

Annie knew exactly where Gail was heading with these pictures: the show was going to begin with Suzanne's accident. The husband suffering spinal injuries, the wife eighteen weeks pregnant, who had sustained terrible abdominal injuries. Annie held her breath, not sure she was ready to watch this on screen.

The screen went black but the audio continued. There were several seconds of metal shrieking, glass shattering and people screaming and then silence before the picture returned. The camera was now focussed on an ambulance parked in front of Blue Lake Hospital.

Annie kept watching—she didn't want to but she found herself unable to look away. She heard the paramedics telling her and Tang that Suzanne was pregnant. She could hear orders being yelled and could see people running to and fro.

She was only vaguely aware of her own role. There were so many people involved it was difficult to make out who was who, and she knew the audience would have an even harder time keeping track of all the people. No doubt they would be focussed on the drama rather than the doctors and nurses.

The voiceover was telling the audience that Suzanne was going for scans and the picture cut to a different patient, an orthopaedic case, before going to the birth of Kylie's twins, establishing the three cases that were obviously going to feature in the first episode.

Annie relaxed as the orthopaedic story was told. This case had nothing to do with her, and she remained relaxed as the show returned to Kylie Jones's segment, but her composure was short-lived. Liam had captured Kylie batting her eyelashes at Caspar but Annie hadn't expected him to include her as well. The scene in which she'd handed Caspar the first twin had been included and Annie was intensely aware that she was gazing at Caspar. She hoped no one else would notice but she could feel Tori watching her. The next ad break couldn't come soon enough.

After the ad break the show returned to Suzanne's case. The CT scan had been done and Suzanne was now in Theatre. The camera panned around the theatre, taking in the beeping machines, the bags of blood, the gowned and masked theatre staff, the scans on the light box and the patient on the table.

The camera focussed on Annie. She wasn't mentioned by name and she knew it would be difficult to recognise her underneath the cap and mask and shapeless gown, but she knew it was her. The scene showed her making an incision into Suzanne's abdomen. The camera was focussed on the wound. There was an awful lot of blood, which would make it difficult for the audience to see what was going on. Annie's hands were also in the shot, partially blocking the view, but she didn't need to watch to know what was happening. She knew what she'd found.

The shot cut away from Suzanne's abdomen and onto bloodied drapes. Annie squeezed her eyes closed, afraid to watch what came next.

She heard her own voice say, 'Oh, my God.' She couldn't believe this was happening. She couldn't believe they were going to show Suzanne's dead baby.

Annie opened her eyes and stood up. Other people might be willing to watch that, although they probably wouldn't have a choice as they wouldn't have any warning, but she couldn't sit there, knowing what was coming next. To her relief the show cut to another ad break, which gave her time to hurry from the room. She needed to get out of there.

Caspar had lied to her. He'd agreed that people wouldn't want to see this and yet it looked as though they were going to. Maybe Gail had persuaded him that it should be included, but if that was the case Annie was still disappointed in him. She paused in the passage while she thought about what she should do. She wasn't sure if she could go back into the room. She was relieved that the function room was upstairs and the hallway was empty as it gave her time to gather her thoughts. Or it would have except that Caspar had followed her out.

'Are you all right?' he asked.

'Of course not.' Annie put her hands on her hips as she prepared to give Caspar a piece of her mind. Not that he should need to hear her opinion, he should have a fair idea about what she had to say. 'I can't believe you're going to show that scene.'

'We're—'

'How could you?'

'I—'

'You can't tell me the audience will want to see that.'

'Will—?'

'It's far too confronting. Do you want people to change the channel? I can't believe I listened to you. I trusted you—'

Caspar took one step towards her, closing the small gap that separated them. In an instant his head dipped down and he pressed his lips to hers. The rest of her sentence disappeared into his kiss.

Caspar St Claire was kissing her!

Involuntarily, Annie closed her eyes as his mouth covered hers. His lips were warm and soft but his kiss was far from gentle. It was demanding and insistent and powerful and made her insides tremble. It was firm enough to take her breath away and make her swallow her words. His five-o'clock shadow was rough against her cheek but even that sensation was pleasant. She should protest, she should resist, but he wasn't giving her a chance and she didn't really want him to stop. For a moment she even thought about kissing him back.

CHAPTER SEVEN

THE KISS ENDED almost as quickly as it had begun. Within seconds her lips were free and she felt them spring back into shape as he lifted his mouth from hers.

She opened her eyes. She knew she should be angry. What exactly did he think he was doing? But the overwhelming emotion she felt was desire.

His kiss had been forceful and demanding and she'd felt it reverberate through her entire body, but he hadn't given her time to respond and she realised, as he freed her mouth, that she wanted to respond, she *would* have responded.

Perhaps it was just as well the kiss had been brief and unexpected, otherwise she might very well have made a fool of herself.

'What was that for?' she asked, once she'd recovered her equilibrium.

'You weren't giving me a chance to defend myself. I had to shut you up so I could get a word in.'

'You could have asked,' she argued.

'Asked to kiss you? What would you have said?' He was smiling at her, enjoying himself.

She couldn't be angry. Moments before she'd been enjoying herself too.

'No, asked me to be quiet,' she clarified.

'I tried—'

'Well—'

Caspar reached out and put one finger on her lips. 'Are you going to let me speak now or do I need to kiss you again? Believe me, I'd be happy to.'

She blushed and folded her arms across her chest. 'Be my guest.'

He leant towards her and Annie realised he'd taken her words as an invitation to kiss her a second time. She put a hand out against his chest, stopping him from leaning any closer. As much as she would enjoy another chance, now was not the time or place. 'I *meant* have your say.'

'Oh.' He was grinning widely now, one eyebrow cocked in amusement, and it was enough to make Annie feel as though she could melt into a warm pool of desire at his feet.

'We don't show Suzanne's baby,' he told her. 'Gail wouldn't dream of it and if she had wanted to, I would have demanded that the scene be cut. I think losing a child is the worst thing in the world and, as I told you before, no one needs to see that. When the show comes back to Suzanne's story it cuts to a shot of me handing the baby to the nurse. He's wrapped, the audience don't see him, they see my back, and the theatre staff's tears and then Colin arrives to start the orthopaedic surgery. Come back and watch the rest. You'll see I'm telling you the truth.'

Annie shook her head. She couldn't go back into the room. Not because she didn't want to watch the show but because she couldn't return to the crowd after being kissed. She wanted to savour that for a little longer. She wanted to keep it to herself, she didn't want to be distracted by the show or her colleagues.

'No. I think I'll go home.'

He didn't try to kiss her again, neither did he try to persuade her to stay. He just looked at her carefully, before nodding his head and returning to the room.

Annie barely remembered the drive home. All she could think was that he'd kissed her and it had been every bit as lovely as she'd imagined it would be. But it couldn't happen again.

She wasn't ready for a relationship or any sort of tryst, for want of a better word. She had made a promise to herself that she would steer clear of any romantic involvement. She had a terrible track record and she had other things to focus on. And no matter how handsome Caspar St Claire was, or how well he kissed, he wasn't right for her.

But that wasn't enough to stop her from turning on the television when she got home. Aggie, the very pregnant cat, was waiting for her and she let her up beside her as she got comfortable on the couch and found the right channel. She told herself she wanted to see what unfolded in the rest of the programme and she was glad to see that when the show returned to Suzanne's story, Caspar had told her the truth. There was no footage of the baby. Instead, the camera panned to the faces of the staff, who were all in tears, and the outcome was self-explanatory.

But while Annie was glad Caspar had been honest, she knew her real motivation for watching the show was so she could watch him. The camera loved him. The strong contours of his face caught the light, casting shadows in just the right places, and his olive skin was a lovely foil for his dark hair and green eyes. His presence on screen drew one's attention. It was no wonder the viewers couldn't get enough of him.

She'd seen for herself the effect he'd had on her patients. And she imagined plenty of women would have liked to have been in her shoes just a short time ago. And then she wondered just how many had been in her shoes. She'd seen plenty of photos of him with different women on his arm and there were probably many more whose photos she hadn't seen.

Had he meant anything at all by the kiss? She was reliving it and getting herself all worked up about it while he'd probably meant it as nothing more than what he'd said it was, a way to shut her up. He'd probably already forgotten all about it. She should do the same.

'Where's Annie?' Tori asked Caspar when he returned to his seat.

'She went home,' he said, as he tried to ignore the empty chair between them. While Tori didn't know what had transpired, the vacant chair was a reminder to him of his spontaneous indiscretion.

Tori frowned. 'Is she okay?'

'She thinks we're going to show Suzanne's baby.' That was only part of the problem but it was all he was prepared to divulge to Tori and it was enough of a reason to explain Annie's absence. Tori had been the anaesthetist and would know what had happened next.

'I hope she's wrong.'

'Of course she is. I tried to tell her but she doesn't want to watch.'

'Okay.' Tori nodded. 'I'll call past her house later.'

'It's all right, I told her I would,' he fibbed, hoping Tori wouldn't argue with him. He knew he should let Tori check on Annie. He knew he should leave Annie alone. But he couldn't do it. Someone needed to make sure she was okay and he'd rather it was him.

The programme ended on a happier note with footage of Kylie and Paul in the nursery holding their twins. He wondered if Annie was watching.

The minute he thought he could escape without anyone noticing, he headed for his car. Annie had tasted as good as he'd expected. Her lips had been warm and forgiving under his and she hadn't resisted, even though she must have been taken by surprise. He had surprised himself.

He didn't stop to consider if Annie would mind him calling at her home. He couldn't think straight after that kiss—all he could think about was getting a chance to do it again.

He knocked on her kitchen door. The scent of jasmine engulfed him as he waited, evoking memories of her, but he knew the smell came from the plant that clung to the back veranda. The creeper was heavy with flowers, their perfume thick in the warm, still night air. He knocked a second time and the door opened.

The pregnant cat was winding herself around Annie's ankles, drawing Caspar's attention to her legs. She had changed out of her jeans into soft shorts that displayed her sensational legs to full effect. She was barefoot now and from his height advantage he could see the swell of her cleavage under her shirt. On the drive between the pub and Annie's house he had thought about what he wanted to say but the moment he saw her standing in the doorway all he could think of was how she tasted.

He wanted to kiss her again but not without an invitation this time. One spontaneous kiss was possibly all he would be able to get away with.

'What are you doing here?'

He could hardly class that sentence as an invitation.

'I wanted to know if you saw the end of the show,' he said. 'Whether you've forgiven me.'

'Forgiven you?' she asked. 'I saw the end. You were right about the footage. I should be asking you to forgive me for jumping to conclusions.'

'I was talking about forgiving me for kissing you.'

'Oh.'

'I shouldn't have done that,' he said, as his gaze drifted to her soft, pink lips. 'But…' His words drifted off into silence as he let himself be distracted by her mouth.

'But what?' Annie's voice was whisper quiet.

'But, so help me, I'd like to do it again.'

She didn't say anything in reply. She just stood there looking up at him with her enormous brown eyes and pouty pink lips, and it was all Caspar could do not to scoop her up in his arms and carry her into the house.

And then she stepped back, out of the doorway, making room for him to move inside. That was all the invitation he needed.

He stepped into the kitchen and kicked the door closed behind him.

The door slammed shut. Caspar was in her kitchen, inches from her.

She shouldn't have let him in but she had been powerless to resist. Her body continued to betray her, operating independently of her mind. She could feel herself being drawn to him. Her breaths were shallow and she could feel her nipples harden as he looked at her with his green eyes almost daring her to close the gap between them.

She never knew if she reached for him or if he

reached for her, but in an instant she was in his arms with her hands wound behind his neck.

He bent his head.

She lifted her face and his lips met hers. They were warm and soft but the pressure was firm. He was taking control, taking what he wanted, and she was letting him. She wanted it too and this time there was no reason to stop.

His tongue teased her lips and she parted them in response to his pressure. She tasted him, minty, sweet and warm.

She wanted him, badly, inexplicably. She'd never felt like this before. She had an overwhelming, overpowering need to taste and touch and hold another person and to have them hold her.

For the first time she thought maybe she could understand why her mother had been unable to resist her father. If their chemistry was anything like this, it would be almost impossible to resist.

But she had to resist, she had to be stronger than her mother had been.

She took her hands from behind his head, removing her fingers from the dark curls at the nape of his neck and dropping her arms to her sides. She stepped back. She was breathing loudly, panting, her breaths coming in short, shallow bursts. She needed to tell him to stop but she couldn't speak.

'Which way is your bedroom?' It seemed he still had the power of speech.

She should stop him now. But she couldn't.

'Front of the house, on the right.' Somehow she found the strength to answer.

Before she'd even finished the sentence Caspar had picked her up and was carrying her down the hall. Her reply had obviously been taken as consent. A fair assumption, she supposed. She could have said no. But that was unlikely to happen. She didn't have the willpower to resist.

She didn't bother to protest. She didn't want to. She wanted this. Maybe more than she'd wanted anything ever before.

Her legs were wrapped around his waist, his hands, warm and large, cupped her buttocks, holding her close. The heat of his palms seared through the thin fabric of her shorts. He dropped little kisses on her mouth and throat as he carried her the short distance down the hall. He paused in the doorway of her room, Annie nodded her head and he stepped inside, and for the second time that night he kicked a door closed with his foot.

Annie lay on her back, her head turned to the side as she watched Caspar propped on one elbow, watching her. She didn't have the words to describe how she was feeling, which was just as well as she didn't have the energy to speak. She didn't have the energy to move.

They were both naked, the bed sheet covering them from the waist down leaving Annie's breasts exposed. Caspar reached out and brushed her breast with his fingertips and her nipple peaked instantly, her body responding instinctively and involuntarily to his touch, ready for more.

Until tonight she'd only ever slept with one man, her husband, and in the beginning sex had been interesting, enjoyable even, but it had never been like this. It had never been the all-consuming, passionate, amazing experience that she'd read about. Until now.

She couldn't believe she was twenty-nine years old and was only just finding out what she'd been missing all these years. Her resolution to stay away from men was looking a little flimsy. Sex like that would be enough to make her change her mind about a lot of things. She didn't think she was strong enough to resist. Perhaps she was more like her mother than she wanted to be.

She was glad they hadn't taken it slowly. Glad she hadn't had time to think about what she was doing. She might have found the willpower to stop and then she would have missed out on the best sex she'd ever had.

'Are you okay?' Caspar asked, before he bent his head and covered her breast with his mouth. He flicked his tongue over her erect nipple, making her moan with pleasure. He lifted his head and replaced his tongue with his fingers. He was smiling at her. 'You're very quiet. Have I just discovered the secret to stop you from arguing with me?'

Annie laughed as she arched her back towards him, pushing her breast further into his hand as if she was afraid he might stop. She couldn't believe how good she felt. 'I just realised what all the fuss is about,' she said.

'So no regrets?'

'Not regrets as such.'

'But...?'

'I didn't mean to get myself in this situation. I moved down here to have a fresh start. Not to jump into bed with the first man who crosses my doorstep.'

'Really? I'm the first man to be in your house?' He sounded pleased and a little surprised.

'Not exactly, but Bert, my landlord, is an octogenarian. I think he's safe from any advances on my part but I certainly wasn't planning on having sex with you.'

'Why not?'

'Oh. Let's see.' Annie fought hard to concentrate but

it was extremely difficult while Caspar continued to tease her nipple with his tongue. 'I barely know you,' she said, as he moved his mouth to her other breast. 'We work together,' she moaned, as he ran his tongue from her breast to her belly button. 'This is completely out of character for me and I've only been divorced for six months.'

That was enough to break his concentration. He lifted his head. 'You were married?'

'Yes.' Annie gave a half-smile. It would almost be funny if it wasn't true. But on this occasion she was pleased she was divorced as if she were still married she would have missed out on tonight. On him. 'The last man I slept with had to marry me first.'

He grinned at her. 'I didn't realise a precedent had been set. I wasn't planning on proposing.'

'That's good, because I never want to get married again. I just meant I don't usually sleep with strangers.'

'I'm not a stranger,' he said, as he slid his hand under the sheet and between her thighs. Annie's knees fell apart, proving his point.

'Maybe you're not a total stranger,' she admitted, 'but you don't really know anything about me.'

'I know you smell like jasmine and you moan in a very sexy way when you orgasm.'

Annie felt herself blush. 'That doesn't count.'

'All right, then. Tell me something you think I should know.'

Annie struggled to think of something while Caspar's fingers were busy under the sheet, distracting her. 'I've never had a one-night stand,' she said.

'And I vote we keep it that way. I'm more than happy to repeat tonight's events,' he replied, before pausing slightly. He was frowning. 'Have you slept with *anyone* since your divorce?'

Annie wondered if she should tell him she hadn't slept with anyone since long *before* her divorce. She couldn't actually remember the last time she'd had sex. She hadn't really missed it. Now she wondered how she'd ever survive without it.

She shook her head.

Caspar removed his hand from between her thighs and slid it around her hips to cup her bottom. He pulled her towards him and she could feel his erection pressing against her stomach, but he seemed unaware of it. He was focussing on her. 'If I'd known, I would have done things differently. Taken it slowly.'

'It's fine. Better than fine. It was just what I needed.'

Caspar doubted that. Annie should have had some romance. She was right. They were virtually strangers. He should have spent more time getting to know her. Not knowing a person was fine if it was only a one-time thing but he didn't want this to be a one-night stand. She deserved better.

'Do you think we could start again tomorrow?' he asked as he nuzzled her neck. 'I'll take you to dinner first, do things properly. We could even try having a conversation first.'

But Annie shook her head.

'Okay, we'll skip the conversation but you have to eat,' he teased, and to his relief she laughed.

'I don't mind the conversation but I don't really want to go out to eat. I don't want to draw attention to myself or invite questions, and I think that's unavoidable if I'm with you. You're a celebrity around here.'

'Only a minor one,' he retorted.

'Enough to make it impossible to have a quiet dinner, I'd imagine.'

'Why don't I pick up some dinner and bring it here, then? Would that be okay?'

He wanted a chance to make it something more than a frenzied, albeit passionate and thoroughly enjoyable experience. He wanted to make it special. He knew what to do. She just had to agree.

Annie nodded and he felt a surge of satisfaction. He'd been worried she would find more excuses.

Annie dragged herself to the gym the following day. She ached in strange places. Muscles she'd forgotten she had complained every time she moved but the ache wasn't unpleasant. Tori was waiting for her and Annie tried to be enthusiastic, even though she didn't want to be there.

She wanted to be back in her bed with Caspar. Her legs were only just strong enough to hold her up and she hadn't quite recovered her focus or strength after last night. Her mind kept wandering and her body kept threatening to collapse with exhaustion.

'Were you okay last night?' Tori asked. 'You left early.'

Annie could scarcely believe so much had happened in the past twelve hours. So much had changed.

'Did Caspar call at your place?' Tori added, when Annie didn't reply.

'Mmm-hmm.'

'So what happened?'

'What do you mean?'

'Did he stay for a drink? Did you let him take you to bed for that steamy sex I've been waiting to hear about?'

'What?' Annie immediately wanted to run and hide.

What had made Tori ask that question? Had Caspar said something?

'There was enough heat between you both to fry an egg,' Tori said. 'I thought, hoped, you might get carried away.'

Annie breathed a sigh of relief. Tori was only fishing for information but her description was enough to make Annie blush, despite the sense of relief. She could feel heat suffusing her cheeks and cursed her tendency to turn scarlet. Of course Tori noticed.

'You did, didn't you? Well done,' she cheered. 'Was it fantastic?'

Annie opened and closed her mouth without divulging anything. She had no idea how to respond to that question.

Tori held up a hand. 'No, that's okay. You don't need to tell me, but are you seeing him again?'

'He's coming over tonight,' Annie admitted, knowing Tori would get that information out of her eventually anyway. 'But I don't know what to do.'

'What do you mean? You sleep with him again. It's not a difficult decision.'

'It is, considering I've only ever slept with one other man.'

Tori's eyebrows almost disappeared into her hairline. 'You're kidding.'

Annie shook her head. 'I wish I was.'

'Well, in that case I suggest that you don't think about it, don't analyse it. Just use him for sex.' Tori laughed. 'He can be your post-divorce gift to yourself.'

'That doesn't seem like much of a relationship,' Annie said.

'But you don't want a relationship, do you?' Tori argued. 'He's only here for a few weeks. Why don't you have some fun? You can have mind-blowing sex without the relationship. In fact, in your current situation I'd recommend it. But it's your choice.'

Annie's body was still humming with a post-coital glow and she knew she didn't *have* a choice. She couldn't give him up. Not yet.

Annie heard Caspar's car pull to a stop out the front of her house. She'd been listening for the sound of his Audi for the past thirty minutes. She had planned on being cool, calm and collected but her body seemed to have a different idea and she found herself waiting at the back door to let him in.

He was wearing his soft jeans again and a casual green and white striped cotton shirt. He had the sleeves rolled up to his elbows and in his arms he held a box filled with containers of Indian takeaway. She could smell cumin, coriander and jasmine rice.

He put the box down on the kitchen table and Annie could see that in his hand he held a bunch of flowers. 'For you,' he said as he handed them to her. It was a colourful assortment of sweet peas and she had the perfect vase. An old ceramic milk jug sat on the mantelpiece above the stove. She pulled it down and filled it with water, pleased to have something to keep her busy. Pleased to have something to stop her from throwing herself straight into his arms.

A little bit of control wouldn't go astray, she thought, if only she could summon some. As part of her intended cool, calm and collected approach she had planned on trying to eat first but now all she could think of was ripping Caspar's clothes off—starting with unbuttoning his shirt.

The mental image of sliding his shirt from his shoulders to reveal his broad chest underneath distracted her from the task at hand and by the time she had eventually arranged the flowers he had pulled several take-away containers from the box. The containers were stacked in two piles and there was enough food to feed four.

Annie frowned. 'Are we expecting more people?' She hadn't intended on sharing him.

'Making love builds an appetite,' he said as he winked at her, and Annie was tempted to start getting rid of his shirt right then and there, but she forced herself to slow things down as much as she was capable of doing.

She smiled as she lifted the lid on one container to peek inside. 'You're getting a little ahead of yourself, don't you think? I thought we'd eat first.'

'Well, that's disappointing,' he replied, as he reached out and ran a finger down her bare arm. A surge of desire shot through her and it was so powerful she nearly gave in on the spot.

She looked at the foil containers stacked on the table and then she looked at Caspar. 'Maybe we could put the containers into the oven,' she suggested.

'Now, there's a good idea.' He grinned and Annie's insides wobbled.

He picked up the containers and slid them into the oven. Annie followed him across the kitchen and bent over to turn the oven on. Caspar was behind her now and she felt him push her hair off her neck and then his lips were on her skin, kissing the back of her neck where it sloped down to her shoulder, setting her nerves on fire.

Her dress zipped at the back and as she straightened up, his fingers slid the zip down, exposing her spine. His hand was inside her dress and his fingers skimmed her waist as he slid his hand around over her rib cage and cupped her breast. Annie moaned with longing as his fingers brushed her nipple.

'You're not playing fair,' she said, as she turned round to face him.

'You'll have to teach me the rules then,' he said before his head dipped down and he claimed her mouth with his.

Annie closed her eyes as she kissed him back while she let her fingers work blindly, furiously, to undo the buttons on his shirt. She slid it from his shoulders and ran her hands down his chest, over the ridge of his abdominals and lower still until she could feel his erection under her palm, and it was his turn to moan.

He shrugged his hands out of his sleeves and dropped his shirt on the kitchen floor as they left a trail of clothes strewn behind them on their way to her bedroom.

CHAPTER EIGHT

For the second time in as many nights they lay, naked and spent, beneath her sheets.

'I don't seem to be doing this right,' Caspar said.

Annie couldn't see how it could get any better but she wasn't brave enough to say so, scared she would highlight her own naivety. 'You don't hear me complaining,' she said.

'No, but I believe I promised you dinner and conversation.'

She sighed and rolled onto her side, facing him, pulling the sheet up and tucking it under her arm. He was smiling, his green eyes dark and gleaming.

'I don't have the energy to get up.' She couldn't be bothered moving.

'Shall we eat in here? I'll bring you something,' he offered. 'What do you fancy?'

You. But she was too shy to say it. 'You choose.'

He dropped a kiss on her bare shoulder before he swung his legs out of bed. He stood stark naked without a hint of timidity while Annie lay in bed and admired his butt as he walked from the room. She wished she had his self-confidence. When he touched her there was no room in her head for anything other than desire, but now that he was gone from her sight she worried that he might not return. What if he just kept on walking?

Now that their sexual appetite had been sated, all her self-doubt crept back again. What did he see in her? Why would he want her? What would he want *from* her?

To her relief, he returned. He'd found his underwear somewhere between her bedroom and the kitchen so he was no longer completely naked, which was a pity, she thought. His shirt was hanging over his arm and in that hand he held he held two wine glasses and a bottle of sauvignon blanc. Along the other arm he held two bowls, heaped with steaming food. She was impressed with his multi-tasking.

'Something smells good.'

'I aim to please,' he said, as he laid the wine and glasses on the bed, along with the bowls, before passing her his shirt. 'I thought you might want to wear this. The food is still hot and I'd hate you to spill something and burn yourself.'

Annie took his shirt, breathing deeply as she slid her arms into the sleeves. The shirt smelt of him. She did up a couple of buttons, just enough to preserve her modesty, as he poured her a glass of wine.

'Here's to us,' he said, as he raised his glass in a toast.

'Us?'

'Yes. A new beginning. Didn't we agree to start over again tonight?'

'I'm not sure we agreed exactly. I'm not sure about anything, I'm completely out of my depth,' she admitted. 'This is all new territory for me.'

'What is?'

She waved one hand vaguely in his direction, not quite sure how to phrase her feelings. Surely she couldn't tell him how inexperienced she was, how he had opened her eyes to sex? It might frighten him away and while she still wasn't sure exactly what she wanted, she was pretty sure it wasn't that.

'All of this. I've only ever had one physical relationship and that was with my husband.'

Caspar almost choked on his wine. 'How long were you married?

'Seven years.'

'And you've been divorced, what, six months?' She could see him trying to do the calculations. 'How old were you when you got married?'

'Twenty-one.'

'Why so young?' He was frowning as though she'd done something quite incomprehensible.

Annie supposed that amongst medical students getting married early was unusual but in the general population it wasn't that strange. Annie had spent many hours in the latter stages of her marriage analysing what had convinced her that marrying young was a good idea. She understood why she'd done it but she wasn't certain it would make sense to anyone else.

'My gran died when I was twenty. After my parents' death she was all I had and when she died she left a gaping hole in my life. Most people marry for love. Or money. I told myself I was in love but I wasn't. I was scared of being alone. I married for companionship.'

'What about him?'

'If I had to pick one of my two options I'd say "money" but I didn't realise it at the time. I thought we both wanted the same thing, needed the same thing, but my marriage cost me everything I had left.'

'Everything?'

She nodded. 'My home, my privacy, my job offer in Adelaide.' *My confidence too,* she thought.

'You moved down here to start again?'

'Yes. And I intend to do just that. I'm not going to make the same mistakes again. I have no intention of having a relationship with anyone, of getting involved.'

'By the look of us, I'd say we're already involved.'

'Yes, but I'm not sure how involved we should be.'

'What does that mean?'

'I'm no good at relationships. I'm complicated.'

'I already figured out the complicated part but I think it's time you had some fun.'

There was that word again. Fun. First Tori and now Caspar. But Annie wasn't sure she knew how to have fun, although, if it meant repeating last night, she reckoned she could be persuaded.

'I know you said you wanted to avoid the spotlight but we could keep it low-key. Private. Just like this,' he said.

'And what is this like exactly—a clandestine affair?' she asked.

'You've got to admit it's not a bad idea. There's no downside. We can have sex as much as we like and no one has to know.' He was smiling again, his green eyes had lightened in colour and she could see the brown flecks again. 'You can avoid attention and I don't have to share you.'

As an idea it did have some merit. She could have her cake and eat it too. But Annie wasn't going to be like her mother. She wasn't prepared to schedule her time around a man and needed to be able to keep the few commitments she had. Caspar would have to fit in with her too.

'I guess if we can find time that suits us both it could work,' she said, trying to play it low-key. 'And we have to keep things professional at work.'

Caspar agreed without argument and Annie was left wondering if she'd just made a terrible mistake. Caspar St Claire was well and truly out of the box and she hoped she wasn't going to regret it.

Annie wanted to keep their relationship discreet but it was impossible to avoid him at work, especially as Caspar seemed to find ways of being where she was. When Annie needed to speak to Suzanne about her future and whether she would be able to have more children, the film crew asked if they could film this meeting and Caspar, in his role as paediatrician, was there too. When it was time to film Kylie and Paul taking their twins home from the hospital they asked Annie to see them off and again Caspar was there.

No matter where Annie turned, Caspar materialised and that made her nervous. She was worried she wouldn't be able to hide her thoughts and reactions to him and that their relationship would become obvious to everyone, but Caspar, to his credit, played the game perfectly.

He didn't avoid physical contact but somehow he managed to disguise any contact at work, but her nerves made her abrupt and she looked forward to the evenings when they could be alone and she could relax and stop worrying about trying to keep their relationship a secret.

Tori, who had been sworn to secrecy over the affair, assured her that no one would guess there was anything going on and Annie found that, despite her reservations, a pattern very quickly emerged where they would spend several nights a week together. Annie insisted on continuing with her normal schedule, which included her gym classes with Tori, and on those nights

Caspar would have dinner at Brigitte's and then come to her house.

On other nights they ate together but always at Annie's. Caspar continued to educate and excite Annie in the bedroom but she always made him leave before morning. She wasn't ready to let him stay the whole night.

At least once a week Caspar would be invited to a function, often a charity event, sometimes a social event, sometimes as a celebrity guest, sometimes as a guest speaker, and he always invited Annie to accompany him and she always refused. Tori badgered her about going but Annie couldn't bring herself to take the relationship public. She still had reservations, she still wasn't sure exactly what they were doing.

But Caspar was not so secretive. He wasn't used to sneaking around and, while he respected Annie's wish to avoid the media, after a couple of weeks he began to feel as though he was now leading a double or even triple life.

His work life had been split into two and now his personal life was going the same way. He had his normal work persona, his on-camera work persona and his private life, which was now divided into more pieces than he was used to—the life he shared with his family, the part he shared in public and then a third part he shared with Annie. He didn't know how long he could keep juggling all the different parts but he couldn't work out which one he could give up.

Cutting Annie from his life was really the only possibility, but he wasn't prepared to do that. Being in this situation was a novelty for him. He had never been the one to want more out of a relationship before and he wasn't sure if he liked the feeling. He wasn't sure if it equated to losing control but he wasn't ready to give her up. He enjoyed spending time with her and he wasn't prepared to deny himself that.

Instead, he tried to combine Annie with his social life, inviting her to several of the various and varied functions he found himself invited to, but she wasn't at all interested.

But one night when Annie was waylaid at the hospital with a delivery and had to cancel their plans, a different opportunity presented itself and Caspar grabbed it. In what he hoped she would take as a magnanimous gesture he met her at her house with leftovers from his dinner at Brigitte's. His sister was an excellent cook and he didn't think Annie would be able to refuse Brigitte's schnitzels with herbed potatoes. But Annie was more concerned about their privacy.

'She knows about us?'

'She won't say anything,' Caspar argued, before he played his trump card. 'I figured it's only fair that I could tell one person since you've told Tori.'

'You know about that?'

He nodded. 'I don't have a problem with people knowing about our relationship. You obviously trust Tori. I trust Brigitte and she's instructed me to invite you to dinner tomorrow night—she says it will give the two of you a chance to talk more about her teenage mothers project.' He appealed to her sense of duty, knowing she would then feel slightly obligated. He knew he was being sneaky but if it worked to his advantage he wasn't going to feel guilty. 'I'll be there too,' he added.

Annie nodded slowly, clearly thinking through the prospect before agreeing. 'Okay.'

She may be hesitant but at least she had agreed.

He thought it would be nice to have somewhere non-threatening where they could meet, rather than always being cooped up in Annie's house. He would really like to take her away for a weekend, he wanted to wake up with her in the bed beside him, but to date she hadn't let him stay overnight and this secretive behaviour was beginning to wear thin. He was starting to feel as though she was ashamed of their relationship and he didn't like that feeling.

When Annie arrived at Brigitte's house she was pleased to see Caspar's car already parked outside, she felt better knowing Caspar would be there to break the ice. Annie and Brigitte had met once to discuss the project but that had been in Annie's office, a completely different environment from tonight's meeting, and Annie had to admit she would feel far more comfortable if their meetings were held in a more formal setting.

She was okay with meeting new people, she'd had plenty of experience, but she wasn't great at making friends. She'd learnt not to do that as eventually it would lead to learning about each other's lives, which always made her uneasy. Colleagues and patients were different, she wasn't expected to be sociable, but this was Caspar's family, and she realised, with some surprise, she wanted them to like her.

Caspar met her at the front door. He kissed her, which made her forget her nerves, took her hand and led her to the kitchen. To Annie's relief Brigitte was as relaxed and friendly as she'd been the last time they'd met, and her husband, Tom, was just as nice.

'Where's Dad?' Caspar asked Brigitte, as Tom poured everyone a glass of wine.

'He had an early dinner and has taken himself off to bed,' Brigitte replied. 'He's very tired at the end of the day, probably a result of his night-time wanderings. The number of times I get up during the night, it's like having a newborn again.'

'No news on an aged care bed for him yet?' Annie asked. She'd been curious to meet Caspar's father but it was probably better she didn't. It might just confuse him and there was really no need to meet him as she wasn't going to be a permanent part of Caspar's life.

Brigitte shook her head. 'No. I found out today that he is top of the list for the next available male bed at our preferred home, but who knows when that will be? I feel bad wishing it would happen soon 'cos that means another family will have lost someone in order for the bed to be vacated.'

'It's never easy, is it?' Annie agreed. She could imagine how difficult the whole situation must be. She'd been fortunate that her grandmother had been able to stay in her own home. Families came with a lot of additional worries and while she wished her life had been different, she wasn't sure the alternatives were necessarily always easier.

She was just about to offer to help Brigitte in the kitchen when they were interrupted by a new arrival. A heavily pregnant woman with fine, dead-straight, strawberry-blonde hair appeared in the family room.

Caspar went to greet her. 'Krissy, good to see you.' He kissed her on the cheek before turning to introduce her to Annie. 'Annie, this is my other sister, Kristin Scott.'

'We've met,' the woman said to Caspar as she extended her hand to Annie. 'Hello, Dr Simpson.'

Annie was confused. The woman was obviously pregnant, and Annie assumed she was a patient but she didn't recognise her straight away. She racked her brain. Kristin Scott, it wasn't ringing any bells. It was also hard to believe she was Caspar's other sister. She looked nothing like either Caspar or Brigitte.

'You've met?' Caspar asked.

'Hello?' Kristin laughed and waved a hand over her swollen belly. 'I'm a pregnant woman, how many obstetricians do you think there are around here?'

So it seemed they had met at an antenatal visit. 'I haven't seen you for a while,' Annie said, hoping her assumption was correct. 'How many weeks are you now?'

'Thirty-seven,' Kristin replied. 'I saw one of the midwives last week.'

Kristin's wrists and arms were thin but her face was quite puffy and she looked tired and strained. That wasn't unusual at this stage of pregnancy, especially if she had other children at home, which Annie thought Caspar had said she did, but there was something about her that set alarm bells ringing for Annie.

She quickly swept her gaze over Kristin as she'd been trained to do. Kristin's calves and ankles seemed swollen and quite disproportionate to her upper limbs. She appeared to be retaining a lot of fluid.

'How are you feeling? Are things going well?' Annie questioned her carefully, not wanting to panic her if she was feeling good, but something made her doubt that.

'I've been fine, until today. That's why I called in. I came into town to do my grocery shopping but I'm really not feeling up to it. I have a splitting headache and I wondered, Brig,' she said, as she turned to her sister, 'if I could borrow Nikki or Sam? I could use their help with carrying the bags.'

Brigitte glanced from Kristin to Annie, a question in her eyes. She'd obviously picked up some of the subtle signs too. Annie shook her head, very slightly, enough to give Brigitte the answer she was looking for.

'Why don't you give me your list?' Brigitte replied. 'The kids can go and do your shopping for you. You look like you'd be better off putting your feet up for a bit.'

'I think that's a good idea,' Annie added. 'I have my medical bag in my car. If you like, I can check your blood pressure.'

Kristin didn't argue, lending weight to Annie's initial theory that she was feeling far from well. Annie fetched her bag. As she'd expected, Kristin's blood pressure was high, and she also noted pitting oedema in her lower calves. 'I think we should take you into the hospital and do a urine test,' she told Kristin.

'Why?'

'Your BP is high, your ankles are swollen more than I think is acceptable and you're not feeling well. I need to check for pre-eclampsia. Do you have any family history of it?' Annie couldn't remember what they'd discussed in her initial antenatal visit.

'I didn't have any problems with my other two pregnancies,' Kristin replied. 'I can't tell you about any family history.'

That made no sense to Annie. Why wouldn't she have any details on her family history? Kristin didn't sound confused but perhaps her headache was interfering with her concentration. Annie glanced at Brigitte, hoping she could fill her in.

'Kristin is our foster-sister,' Brigitte explained. 'She doesn't have any details about her birth mother's medical history.'

Annie tried to keep the surprise from showing on her face but she knew it would be evident to anyone who was watching her. Any time fostering was mentioned Annie knew it always came as a shock to her.

'Right.' She struggled to keep her tone neutral. 'Then I think it's best that we check this properly. In hospital. Are you happy for me to drive you?'

Kristin nodded while Brigitte began organising everyone. 'Caspar, why don't you go with Annie? That way you can call me from the hospital when you know what's happening. I'll send the kids to the supermarket to do the shopping and if necessary I'll drive out to Kristin's place and look after the kids so John can come into town.'

Brigitte seemed perfectly in tune with the role of eldest sibling and everyone else fell into line, including Caspar. Annie briefly wondered if she was the only one who seemed to butt heads with him, although she had to admit their arguments had decreased in intensity of late—they had been too busy expending their energy in other ways.

Within minutes Annie and Caspar had Kristin in the car and were en route to the hospital.

'Aren't you going to ring your camera crew?' Annie couldn't resist asking.

'No,' he replied.

'Why not? Is it because it involves your family?' she asked.

'No. I just don't think this is exciting enough for the programme. There's no real emergency, no drama. If the crew were already at the hospital I might think about it but I know they're not. I won't call them in for something that more than likely would get cut.'

Annie couldn't argue. She'd been prepared to be annoyed if he was avoiding filming because it was personal but she knew in this case he was probably right. Even if tests showed that Kristin did have pre-eclampsia, she was unlikely to require emergency intervention tonight.

Annie was quiet, lost in her own thoughts, for the remainder of the short drive.

When they arrived at the hospital Annie took Kristin straight into the emergency department, explaining it was quicker than admitting her. They could do that later if necessary.

'You'll need to give a urine sample,' she told her as she left her with Tang, the RMO on duty.

'That's one thing I have no problem with,' Kristin said.

When Annie returned, Kristin's BP was still high and the protein reading in her urine was more than she liked. 'You said you came into town to do your grocery shopping. Do you live far away?' she asked.

'We're on a vineyard, about thirty minutes away.'

'In that case, I'm going to admit you overnight,' Annie told her. 'I want to do a twenty-four-hour urine analysis and it's a lot easier to do it in hospital. I'm pretty sure you have pre-eclampsia but I want to do more investigations. Can your husband manage with the kids?'

'Of course. Caspar, can you ring John and tell him what's going on?' Kristin asked, and Caspar pulled out his mobile phone and left the room.

'I've heard of pre-eclampsia but I've never paid much attention. What is it exactly?'

'It's due to constriction of your blood vessels, which can cause high blood pressure and the swelling in your tissues, you can see that in your ankles, and it can cause your kidneys to leak protein,' Annie explained. 'It's normal to see some protein in your urine but your first reading was higher than I'd like.'

'Is it harmful to the baby?'

Annie knew that pre-eclampsia could lead to seizures or restriction of blood flow to the uterus or, in serious cases, organ failure, but considering she hadn't officially diagnosed the condition yet she didn't want to mention the worst-case scenarios. She informed Kristen that they would keep her in hospital for close monitoring and discuss other problems if and when it became necessary.

'How do you treat it?'

'For now, bed rest and monitoring. Bed rest is just to try to lower your blood pressure and we'll do the twenty-four-hour urine test and I'll order some blood tests as well. *Then*, if we confirm pre-eclampsia, the only cure is to deliver your baby. Once we deliver the placenta the condition will resolve. Your baby is old enough to be induced if necessary but, remember, everything may settle spontaneously.' Annie doubted that but it was better to leave Kristin feeling calm.

'I'll organise an ultrasound tomorrow to check your baby's development if I need to. For now, we'll take some blood and then admit you and transfer you to Maternity. You just have to try and rest in between going to the toilet and having your obs checked constantly.' She smiled, knowing how little rest Kristin would probably get.

'Easier said than done,' Kristin replied, 'but at least I won't have to get up to two other kids during the night.'

Annie admitted Kristin while she waited for Caspar and once Kristin had been transferred to Maternity it was just the two of them again.

'Is she going to be okay?' Caspar wanted to know.

Annie nodded.

'She must be feeling pretty crook, considering she didn't give any of us the third degree about why you were at Brigitte's. I initially thought she'd dropped in on purpose to check you out.'

'She knows about us too?'

'I didn't tell her but don't be surprised if Brigitte has. They're thick as thieves, those two.'

Terrific, Annie thought as she unlocked her car and wondered just how many other people were going to hear about their relationship through the grape vine.

'Shall we see if Brigitte has saved us some dinner?' Caspar suggested as they turned into her street.

'It's too late now, isn't it?'

'Brigitte will be up, she'll want to know how Kristin is.'

Annie didn't want to stay, she had too many questions competing for space in her head and not enough answers. 'Do you mind if I don't come in?' she said as she parked outside. 'I'll go home and get some rest in case I get a call about Kristin.'

'You don't want company?'

Annie shook her head.

'Are you okay? You've been quiet. I always worry when you're quiet.'

Annie knew that she was still feeling a bit thrown since hearing that Kristin had been a foster-child. It always made her cast her mind back and while she'd managed to concentrate on Kristin's needs while they had been at the hospital, now that her attention wasn't needed elsewhere she found herself distracted. She thought of a believable excuse. 'I don't want to intrude. I'm not used to family dynamics any more,' she said.

'Is that what's bothering you, my family?' he asked.

'I know we can be a bit overwhelming but it's not always that bad.' He smiled at her, his green eyes shining. 'We don't always have such major crises, at least not at dinnertime.'

'Your family is lovely. Kristin is very lucky…'

'We all are. Our lives would be very different if Mum and Dad hadn't made us a family.'

'What do you mean?'

'We're not biological siblings. Brig and I are adopted and Krissy is our foster-sister. Mum and Dad created our family in an unorthodox way, I suppose, but it was Mum's way of making a difference. Her way of taking care of those who didn't have a voice. We had lots of foster-kids living with us over the years but Kristin was the one who never left. She's just another sister to us, even though she wasn't adopted.'

'Why wasn't she?'

'Her mother refused to give her up, even though she wasn't interested in caring for her.'

'She was lucky to get your family. Not every child is so fortunate.' Annie was pensive as their conversation returned to the heart of the problem.

Caspar was frowning. 'You sound as though you know what you're talking about.' Annie realised he'd become very adept at reading her moods. Perhaps it was a legacy of growing up with two sisters, but Annie had learned that not much escaped him.

'In a way I do. I was put into foster-care after the house fire.' She didn't usually talk about that short period in her life but she suspected Caspar might understand better than most, given his own experience.

'I thought you went to your grandmother's?'

'I did, eventually. But remember I wasn't talking because of the PTSD and no one knew my gran existed so they couldn't track her down. She was living interstate so it took a few days for her to even hear about the fire and for her to come forward. By then I'd had several nights in foster-care. It was horrible.'

'What happened?'

'It was just a dreadful time. My parents had just died and I was sent to stay with strangers. It wasn't their fault. I was traumatised, I wasn't speaking and no one had the time or energy, and probably not the training back then, to deal with me. I was just thinking how lucky Kristin was to have a very different experience.'

'Yes, she was. But she also had a mother who was a drug addict who turned to prostitution and left her. Kristin was lucky but don't be fooled, she has her own demons. You were lucky in different ways. You had a mother and a grandmother who loved you.'

He was right. Annie's mother had loved her, in her own way. She may have loved Annie's father more but Annie's family had never given her up.

Annie smiled. 'It's okay, I know all that. I've had counselling. Having a few nights in foster-care hasn't scarred me for life and probably hasn't even impacted on who I am today, it's just an experience I had that I would never want to repeat, but it's nice to hear that some children have a better time of it.'

'I think Kristin would agree with you. She and her husband are foster-parents now too. That's her cause, as you call it, so I guess it wasn't all bad for her.'

'Have you all chosen causes that resonant with each of you?'

Caspar smiled. 'I guess we have. Brig was born to an unmarried mother, although I think she was just out of her teens, and I was adopted after I was abandoned as a baby.'

'You were abandoned?' Caspar's casual tone shocked Annie. She couldn't believe he'd never mentioned this to her. They'd spent hours discussing her family yet he hadn't mentioned the fact that he was adopted as a baby. Why hadn't he said anything?

Caspar nodded.

Annie knew very well how much she had struggled to overcome feelings of abandonment after her parents' deaths, even though it had been a tragic accident. She couldn't imagine how someone dealt with being abandoned as a child.

'Have you ever had any contact with your birth parents?'

He shook his head. 'No. I have no desire to either. I have a family I love, I don't need anything more.'

'You're remarkably matter-of-fact about it.'

'I have no reason to be otherwise. I was adopted as a baby, I've only known one family. One life. My life. Although I admit I did go through a stage of wondering what my birth mother was like when I was quite young. I went through the stage of wishing I had a different family, like I think most kids do at some point, and I used to imagine what it would be like for her to come and get me, but when it dawned on me that she was probably never coming back I decided to focus on what I could control.

'Mum explained all the reasons why my birth mother might have needed to give me up without ever condemning her. I'm very grateful to my parents for the life I've had and if I can help other children and families in some way then I think I'm making an important contribution. I do feel the need to give something back.'

'And now, if you're not coming in with me, I'd better go and give Brig an update.' He leant over and kissed her softly on the lips. 'Thanks for looking after Krissy for me. I'll see you tomorrow.'

Annie watched him walking up to Brigitte's front door. If she had thought she'd had a lot of questions running through her mind before, she had twice as many now. She needed to go home and try to make sense of what she'd just learned. Did any of it matter? Did it have any impact on her? On them? She really didn't know but she needed to find out.

She'd never been through what Caspar, Brigitte and Kristin had, and it was amazing to see the people they had become thanks to the love and support they had been given. Chemistry wasn't the answer, neither was biology, but it seemed as though love could be.

Caspar's strength, resilience and humour and his willingness to help others was encouraging. He had taken control and had shaped himself into the person he was today. He hadn't let history decide his fate. If he could do it, she could too. She was making a new life for herself and it could be anything she wanted.

Annie saw just how close Caspar's family was two days later when she made the decision to induce Kristin's baby. Kristin's blood pressure and protein levels had remained high and when the ultrasound scans of the baby looked good, Annie decided it was time to introduce the baby to the world.

The delivery was a family affair. Naturally Kristin's husband, John, was there, as was Caspar in his role as paediatrician. Brigitte had Kristin's two older children and once the baby, a little girl, was born, Brigitte brought the entire family to the hospital, including Caspar's dad.

It was such a joyful occasion and Annie knew it was

going to become one of her favourite deliveries. It was a moment to be celebrated and the St Claire family was making the most of the opportunity.

'That's one thing we do well. Celebrate,' Caspar told her. 'Mum was big on celebrations. She loved celebrating anything from losing a first tooth to winning a prize at school to birthdays.'

Kristin and John named their daughter Gabriele, in memory of Kristin's foster-mother, and that gave them all cause for further celebrations. Annie liked how they talked about their mother and it was obvious she'd had a big impact on their lives. Just like the St Claire family was impacting on her life now. She now had ties, not only to Caspar but also to Brigitte through the teenage mothers' programme and to Kristin as her ob-gyn.

That concerned her a little. She could feel herself getting drawn in by his family, a little like an insect in a spiderweb, and she wondered how she was going to feel when Caspar left Mount Gambier and she lost not only him but his family too.

She wondered if she should be starting to think about how to extricate herself from Caspar's family before it was too late. But over the following week she found she had more contact with them than ever.

Whenever she popped in to see Kristin for her postnatal follow-ups there was always someone visiting her and then Caspar's father got a bed in the nursing home, which meant, because Brigitte had her hands full with minding Kristin's and John's older children, it fell to Caspar to move his father into the nursing home so he had less time for Annie. At times it felt like she was seeing more of Caspar's family then she was of him.

As she left the gym on Saturday she had a phone call from Caspar. His words echoed her thoughts.

'I feel like I've barely seen you. I'm at my dad's house. I've been going through some of his papers in his study but I need a break. You don't fancy coming over, do you? I have wine.'

Annie didn't need bribes to persuade her. She got the address and made her way to Bay Road. Caspar's father's house was towards the top of the road on the hill up to Blue Lake, not far from the Courts where he would have spent time as a lawyer. It was a magnificent house, built from local limestone with an elegant bay-windowed facade shaded by an enormous oak tree. It was obviously the St Claire family home.

Annie found Caspar sitting in the back garden, nursing a glass of red wine. She'd never known him to drink on his own and she wondered nervously if this was something he did often, but when she saw his expression she knew it was out of character. Something was bothering him.

This was her chance to listen to him. It always seemed to be her issues they were discussing and if he had a problem she wanted to be able to offer comfort for a change. A bottle of wine and an extra glass were sitting on a table beside him. She poured herself a glass, noting it was John and Kristin's label. John had already given her a dozen bottles of the same wine as a thank-you for delivering Gabriele.

Annie took her glass and perched herself on Caspar's lap. She brushed his dark hair from his forehead and kissed him gently. He put his glass down, wrapped his arms around her waist and rested his head against her shoulder.

'Thanks for coming.'

His voice was sombre and Annie hoped that whatever it was that was bothering him wouldn't be too difficult to fix.

'What's happened?' she asked.

'Nothing. The house just feels too empty. I know Dad hasn't lived here for a couple of months so nothing's really changed but it felt too lonely and sad. I needed a break and a glass of wine but I didn't want to drink alone.'

Annie suspected Caspar was also feeling bereft. Sad, like the house.

'What's going to happen to the house?'

'We're going to put it on the market. None of us need to live in it.'

'Is that what's bothering you? Selling your family home?'

'I don't know.' Caspar looked around the garden. 'This place holds a lot of happy memories for me, for all of us. I guess it is going to be hard to let it go.'

'Do you have to sell it right away? You've all got a lot to cope with at the moment.'

'What do you mean?'

'I think you're mourning. It's the end of an era. Your dad has gone into a nursing home, his condition is not going to improve and I think you need time to come to terms with that. The father you knew has changed and perhaps now isn't the time to deal with selling the house as well. Why don't you rent it out while you get used to the changes? That might be a gentler transition. It'll give you a bit of time to get used to the idea that your father won't be coming home.'

'I guess we could look at that as an option, although it might be simpler to sell it than to get it ready to rent.'

'Can I see the house?' she asked, keen to see where he'd grown up.

'Of course.' He topped up their glasses and they wandered through the house. The rooms were large and spacious, the kitchen and bathrooms had been modernised, but there were relics of Caspar and his siblings' teenage years throughout. Annie knew he'd gone to boarding school so his strongest memories were probably all formed before the age of thirteen, and being the last house his mother had lived in would make it even harder to let go.

The house was fully furnished, which begged the question. 'Why didn't you stay here instead of in the apartment?' Annie thought he would have preferred to be in his childhood home.

'I felt a bit strange about sleeping in my parents' bed.'

'What about your own room? Or did that get turned into an en suite the minute you left for boarding school?'

'Not quite.' Caspar had one hand on a door handle. 'This was my room,' he said as he opened one of the last doors off the hallway.

Annie stepped inside, curious to see what traces of the teenage Caspar remained.

'I'm a bit too big now for a single bed,' he said.

'It looks comfy enough,' she said as she bent over and leant both hands on the mattress, giving it a couple of gentle pushes to test its firmness. 'I don't suppose this bed has ever seen any action?' she asked as she glanced back over her shoulder, thinking that perhaps she could distract him from his sombre thoughts.

Caspar shook his head.

Annie straightened up. 'It would be a shame to let a good bed go to waste, don't you think?' she said as she stepped out of her canvas sneakers and started to unbutton her shorts.

She didn't get a chance to finish undressing. Caspar did it for her.

His old bed was narrow but they didn't need a lot of room.

CHAPTER NINE

ANNIE LAY CURLED into Caspar's side. She had one leg thrown over the top of his thigh her foot tucked against his knee as she ran her fingers in lazy circles over his bare chest. 'This is nice,' she said. 'It's like we're hidden from the world and no one would be able to find us.'

'Maybe I should keep the house and we could meet here for dirty weekends once I'm back in Melbourne,' he suggested, his earlier sombre mood dispatched by their lovemaking.

Caspar only had two weeks left but it was the first time he had mentioned leaving. She knew he was going, they both did, but that didn't mean she wanted to talk about it. They'd had enough serious discussion for one day.

'You'd have to get a bigger bed,' she said, trying to lighten the mood.

'If I did, would you stay the night?'

'Maybe.' Staying the night would make their relationship seem more serious. She'd already breached her own rules by getting involved with him, she'd well and truly let him out of the box, but while she could get him to leave her bed before morning, while she didn't wake up with him beside her, she could tell herself it was still all just a harmless bit of fun.

'I've been invited to a film premiere in Sydney next week,' he told her. 'The Park Hyatt has big beds. Would you come with me?'

He'd been trying to get her away for a weekend for a while but so far she'd managed to avoid agreeing to his suggestion. She smiled. 'Did you think you could get me in a moment of weakness?'

'It might be my only chance.'

'I can't have a weekend off. What if one of my patients goes into labour and needs me?' She rolled out one of her favoured excuses but this time he was ready with an answer.

'It's one weekend. Have you got any expectant mothers due in the next few days? Can't the local GPs cover you?' he asked. 'You're allowed to take holidays. We could leave Friday night and be back on Sunday. I want to be able to wake up beside you in the morning. I want to be able to take you out.'

'Out?'

'Yes, in public. It's Sydney, no one will take any notice of us.'

Was this her opportunity? She hated making him leave before daybreak but she couldn't risk someone seeing him leave her house in the morning or, worse, seeing them arrive together at the hospital. In Sydney, in a hotel, they could have a whole night together without compromising their privacy. But staying together overnight wasn't the only issue.

'What about at the film premiere?' she wanted to know.

'I'm only invited to make up numbers. Do you think anyone will be interested in me when it's Hugh Jackman's new movie?'

'Hugh Jackman!' Annie sat up in bed. 'Will he be there?'

'Apparently.'

'I love him.'

'So you'll come?' He was laughing now, his good humour well and truly restored.

Annie nodded. She couldn't resist. She'd get to spend the weekend with Caspar, pretending they had a proper relationship, *and* she'd get to see her favourite movie star. She couldn't say favourite celebrity any more as Caspar had that mantle. As long as they could preserve some anonymity she didn't think it could get much better.

'You have no qualms about invading his privacy, then?' Caspar asked.

'If I ran into him at the supermarket I'd leave him alone, but if he's promoting his movie, that's work for him and he would be fair game.'

Annie and Caspar woke up to a glorious Sydney morning. From their bed, which was as big as Caspar had promised, they could look across the harbour to the Opera House, where the iconic building's white sails contrasted sharply with the brilliant blue sky.

They had brunch at Bondi Beach and spent the early afternoon lying on the warm golden sand. Caspar was incognito in board shorts, a hat and sunglasses, and despite being shirtless and tanned and gorgeous nobody seemed to recognise him and nobody bothered them.

Annie tensed when she noticed a film crew setting up on the beach a short distance from where they lay until Caspar pointed out that it was a rival network preparing to film an episode for their reality TV series about lifeguards.

'I told you people don't always recognise me,' he said.

'I bet you they do in Melbourne and I know for a fact they do in Mount Gambier. No one expects to see you here, that's the difference.'

Caspar shrugged. 'My turn in the spotlight won't last long. There are always new celebrities being created in this day of reality television. You only need to look over there to see that I'm right.'

Annie glanced across to where a crowd of locals and tourists had gathered around the cameras. She laughed and relaxed, the irony of the situation not lost on either of them.

'Maybe,' she agreed, too lethargic and comfortable to argue or even think about what he was saying. The heat of the sun was soporific and she closed her eyes and caught up on some of the sleep she'd lost the night before when she and Caspar had made the most of their luxurious bed.

They returned to the hotel in time for an early dinner, before changing for the premiere. Annie had borrowed a red evening gown of Tori's and the hotel had arranged for a hairdresser to come to their room. By the time she had finished attending to Annie, Caspar was ready. He looked impossibly handsome in his black suit, crisp white shirt and bow-tie and part of Annie wished the evening was already over so she could have him to herself. But the real world waited.

Annie's stomach was churning with nerves as the limousine pulled away from the hotel and headed to the premiere. Apprehension and excitement fought for attention. She was equally apprehensive about being on public display—she knew Caspar would not go unnoticed when they arrived at the premiere, he was far too gorgeous to be unobtrusive, but she was also excited to think that she was about to experience a proper night out. But her apprehension increased disproportionately as they drew nearer to the theatre.

Camera flashes lit the night sky like fireworks and Annie's heart was racing as she saw the crush of photographers and journalists standing behind the barriers, waiting to capture a photo or grab thirty seconds to speak to a celebrity.

Caspar stepped from the limousine at the end of the red carpet and reached for her hand to help her out. Her mouth was dry and her hands were clammy.

'Are you okay?'

'Can I sneak in a back entrance?' she asked. She felt faint and a little nauseous and she wasn't certain she was going to make it anywhere.

Caspar bent his head until his lips were millimetres from her ear. 'No way. I want you with me. You look gorgeous,' he said, as his eyes travelled down the length of her gown. 'Let me show you off. Come on, it'll be fun.'

Annie wasn't so sure.

'I'll take care of you,' he said. 'I promise. It's only a few steps and we'll be inside. No one will take any notice of us.'

Despite his assurances that no one would be interested in him, she could already hear journalists clamouring for Caspar's attention and the noise and jostling reminded her of the last time she'd had the press hounding her. That time she'd been standing on the steps of a courthouse knowing she was about to lose everything. It wasn't one of her best memories.

She longed to find another way into the theatre. She desperately wanted to avoid the media, but she knew it would be next to impossible to get away now and she didn't really want to leave Caspar's side. He made her feel safe. She'd seen how he cared for his sisters and his father and his patients and she knew he would do the same for her. It was time to trust him.

She took a deep breath and gripped his hand a little more firmly, taking comfort from his strength as she stepped forward in her strappy sandals. She could hardly believe this was happening. A month ago she would never have dreamed she could brave such an event.

They'd taken three steps along the red carpet when Caspar was asked to stop for a photo. Annie tried to step out of the shot but he pulled her in close to his side as he smiled for the camera.

'And who is your date tonight, Dr St Claire?' the photographer asked as his flash temporarily blinded Annie.

'Dr Annie Simpson.'

The photographer was asking more questions but Caspar turned and kept walking. Annie was vaguely aware that the questions related to her and to their relationship but Caspar ignored him as he led Annie inside. She was glad Caspar had answered on her behalf, glad he had given just the right amount of information. She knew she would have made a mess of any reply.

Her mouth was so dry her tongue was stuck to the roof of her mouth and she was in desperate need of a glass of water. If Caspar hadn't been holding her hand she didn't think she would have made it inside. Her knees were like jelly. She couldn't believe she'd let Caspar talk her into this but if it wasn't for his strength she knew she wouldn't have made it.

He waited until they made it into the sanctuary of the theatre and away from the prying eyes of the media before he gave her a quick kiss and a wink. 'Well done,' he said, and his praise gave her enough courage to make it through the rest of the evening.

The movie was fabulous but the best was yet to come. They were invited to attend the after-party. Annie had an amazing night. She got to meet the star of the movie and his wife, who were both lovely, but the highlight was spending quality time with Caspar. It was such a pity that this wasn't anything like their real life, she thought on more than one occasion.

The only moment of concern was when they were asked to pose for another photo, this time with Gail, Caspar's producer and her partner. Annie was sure it was the same photographer who had taken their photo earlier in the evening and she couldn't understand why he would need another. But Caspar assured her that the photo would probably never be used, surely there would be plenty of other more newsworthy celebrities, and he eventually convinced her to relax by taking her onto the dance floor, where she managed to forget all about inquisitive newshounds.

She didn't notice the photographer taking a few more candid shots of her and Caspar during the evening. Neither did she notice him in deep conversation with a newspaper reporter. She wasn't aware of anything other than what a good time she was having.

She felt like Cinderella at the ball and she wished the night could last for ever. She floated around the room and at times felt that the only thing anchoring her to the floor was Caspar. It was like a dream, a glorious, colourful, delightful dream. She wanted to absorb everything about it—the music, the food, the people—and store the memories away. She was glad she'd agreed to spend the weekend with him.

It was an experience she'd never forget and she secretly wondered, if she relaxed and let go of her past and embraced the future, whether things could always be like this. While she was with Caspar she almost believed she could do it. What was the worst that could happen?

Her positive frame of mind lasted until Monday morning when they were back in Mount Gambier and she was getting ready for work when Caspar arrived at her house unexpectedly, and very early, carrying an armful of papers.

She greeted him at the kitchen door. 'Hi, what are you doing here?'

She was pleased to see him, although he didn't look quite as happy and relaxed as she was used to. Perhaps, like her, he was wishing they were back in Sydney.

'There's something you need to see,' he said as he dumped the newspapers on her kitchen table. His green eyes were dark, a sure sign that he was distracted. Either something was bothering him or he was thinking about sex. Annie doubted it was the latter, judging by his expression.

'There's no easy way to tell you this,' he continued. 'You're in the papers.'

'Me? Why?' Annie's heart plummeted, sinking like a rock to collide with her stomach. Was something she'd done to blame for Caspar's expression? He definitely looked far from happy and relaxed. Annie thought he looked ill.

'One of the journalists at the film premiere must have gone looking for a story. He found yours.'

'What?'

Annie separated the papers. Caspar had brought the

Sydney, Melbourne and local papers and had folded all of them to the entertainment sections.

Annie read the first headline.

Reality TV doc's heartbreaking surprise.

Beneath that, in smaller type, it said: *'The tragic past of Caspar St Claire's girlfriend.'*

'Girlfriend!' she exclaimed.

'That's not the worst bit.'

Annie read on.

Caspar St Claire has a reputation as both a compassionate doctor and a Casanova. Never short of attractive female company, Dr St Claire has been photographed with several high-profile personalities but his latest companion, Dr Annie Simpson, seen with him in Sydney last weekend, is supposedly just a colleague...

The story was punctuated with photos of them. The photo in the centre of the page was of the two of them on the red carpet but also included was the one taken with Gail and her partner. But there were more photos too, photos Annie couldn't recall being taken, photos that showed them sharing a drink and dancing, rather intimately, and it was obvious they were more than just colleagues.

Things look to be more serious than most but Dr Simpson, an obstetrician, has a complicated history. Is she the reality TV heartthrob's latest project or has he got more than he bargained for...?

Annie continued to read.

Dr Simpson first hit the headlines seventeen years ago as a twelve-year-old when she was the sole survivor of a house fire that took the lives of both her parents. Although initially under suspicion of starting the blaze, she was later cleared of any involvement when the origin of the fire was attributed to a burning cigarette in her parents' bedroom. More recently she was in the spotlight again when her husband was gaoled for involuntary manslaughter. Which brings me to the question—what has Caspar St Claire got himself into?

Annie felt sick. She collapsed onto one of the kitchen chairs. 'I don't believe this. Why would they print this?'

'Is it true?'

Annie shook her head. 'It's all true, but why would someone dig this up? This is exactly what I wanted to get away from.'

'You were accused of starting the fire that killed your parents?'

Annie nodded.

'Who made the accusations? The authorities?'

'No. The media.'

'Why would they do that?'

Annie took comfort from the fact that Caspar sounded prepared to come to her defence. It wasn't something she was used to. 'They jumped to their usual sensationalistic conclusions. Because I was the only occupant who survived, they supposed that I started it. And because I wasn't talking, couldn't talk because of the PTSD, they didn't bother to get my story, they just decided that made me more guilty. Once the fire department cleared me they had to retract their accusations but once those things are out in public they never really go away, hence the reason for my dislike of the media.'

Caspar nodded and moved behind her. He stood close enough that she could feel his body heat warming her back. His arm brushed against hers as he leant over her and pointed at a paragraph in the paper. 'What about this part about your husband?'

The sense she had that he was on her side evaporated with his question. Was he going to attack her over her husband's drink-driving conviction? That hadn't been her fault.

'It's true,' she admitted. 'He had, has, a drinking problem. If he drank around me I would take the car keys to make sure he couldn't drive but one night, after we had separated, he got in the car and drove and that's when he had the accident. He hit a pedestrian. She was killed and he was gaoled for six months.'

'I meant was it true that he is your husband? I thought you were divorced.'

'Oh.' Annie wasn't surprised she'd misconstrued his question. She was so overwhelmed she couldn't think straight. 'We're divorced now but at the time of the accident we were separated so legally he was still my husband. The journalist hasn't printed anything that isn't correct.'

'Did you know he was an alcoholic?'

'He didn't have a drinking problem when we met. Or I should say he didn't seem to drink more than any other uni student. But his drinking escalated when I got accepted into my specialty and he didn't.'

'He's a doctor too?'

Annie nodded. 'We met at medical school. His parents had cut off his funds after he failed his second-year exams. He needed somewhere to live so he moved in with me after my grandmother died. I thought we were bonding over our loss of family, our loneliness, but in hindsight he was using me for free accommodation. I didn't realise at the time that he was taking advantage of me. I was too naïve. I thought we were in love and getting married seemed like a good idea. It meant I wasn't alone and it entitled us to better student subsidies, something he was keen on.

'I actually thought things were okay until he started drinking. It turns out I'd picked someone just like my father. Someone who turned to the bottle when things got tough.

'Eventually, when I realised I couldn't change things if he wasn't prepared to seek help, we separated. I couldn't let my life be dictated by his addiction. My childhood had been dictated by my mother's addiction to my father and by my father's dependence on alcohol. I couldn't spend my adult years like that too. Our marriage was already over in all but name but the accident was the final straw.

'Because I'd put my grandmother's house into our joint names when we got married I had to sell it to pay his fines and legal fees. That accident changed everything but I've been trying to move on, trying to get past it. To have it brought up all over again is exactly what I didn't want.'

Annie turned the paper over, not surprised to see that her hand was shaking. She felt nauseous and she'd seen enough. She didn't need to read what the other papers had printed.

'I'm sorry,' Caspar said. 'I had no idea about any of this.'

'No. This is my fault.' She couldn't blame Caspar.

She'd put herself in this situation and she'd deliberately avoided telling him her whole sordid history. She hadn't wanted anyone in her new life to know the details but that was now a moot point. She could just imagine how quickly this information would spread around the hospital and the town.

As much as she wanted to bury her head in the sand and hide, she knew the only way to deal with it was to confront it. She pushed her chair back and stood up.

'Where are you going?'

'To work.'

'Are you sure that's wise?'

'What would you suggest?' she asked. 'I have to do my job.'

'I thought you might want to let things die down a bit first. There's bound to be someone waiting for a comment from you at the hospital.'

'Well, the sooner I start setting the record straight the better, wouldn't you agree?'

Annie picked up her bag and headed for the door.

'Can I drive you?' he asked.

'No.' She shook her head. 'If the media is waiting and we arrive together, that will only fuel the fire. I can handle this.'

She didn't want to handle it but there was nothing she could do about that now. She didn't have a choice.

Caspar was only a few moments behind her as she turned into the hospital parking. Liam had parked the television network's van in its usual spot but there was an additional van parked near the ambulance bay. The extra van belonged to the local news channel and Annie knew they were there for her. Had Liam given Caspar a heads-up? Was that why Caspar had suggested she wait? Was that why he was shadowing her?

She straightened her shoulders and marched towards the entrance. She was three paces from the doors when a microphone was thrust at her.

'Dr Simpson, can you tell us how long you've been involved with Dr St Claire and did he know about your background?'

Annie stopped and turned to face the journalist. She gave him her best cold stare. 'I am not in a relationship with Dr St Claire. That is my only comment.' She turned and let the hospital swallow her. She hoped she would be left alone to do her job.

Thwarted by Annie, the reporter turned his attention to Caspar. 'Dr St Claire, do you have anything to say?'

'No comment.'

He could think of plenty to say but not to a reporter. What he wanted to say was for Annie's ears only. He had heard her answer. What he couldn't figure out was why she was denying their relationship. It wasn't going to change the facts that had been written about her in the paper. Why wouldn't she admit they were involved? At least then he'd legitimately be able to watch her back. At least then he could tell the world he knew everything he needed to know about Annie.

He could tell the media to leave her alone. But she'd deliberately shut him out. To hear her deny their relationship upset him more than the fact she'd kept secrets from him.

He caught up to her just as she stepped into the lift. The smell of jasmine enveloped him as the doors slid closed. He shut his eyes and breathed deeply, letting her scent seep into him and calm him before he spoke. He needed to count to ten, needed to phrase his question carefully. Being frustrated wasn't going to help matters.

'Why did you deny we are involved?' he asked, hoping he sounded curious, not furious.

She looked at him as if he'd gone completely mad. 'If there's no relationship, there's no story. If they think we're together, they'll keep chasing a story.' She'd been a fool to think she could escape her past while she was involved with Caspar. A fool to think the media would leave her alone. Caspar was news and so she was news, and the only way to defuse the situation was to end their relationship.

'But I can help sort this out,' he said.

'I think you've done enough already.' The lift doors opened and Annie stepped out. Her office was a few paces along the corridor. He followed her and she kept talking but didn't break stride. 'I should never have gone with you. I should have trusted my instincts. I should never have let you out of the box.'

'Pardon?'

Annie ushered him into her office and closed the door before she answered. 'From the moment you first smiled at me all I could think about was sharing your bed. You made me think about sex, which was something I hadn't thought about in a long time. But I had other priorities. Sex wasn't a big part of my life, I didn't need it, I didn't think I wanted it. But after I met you I couldn't think of anything else. In order to focus on my priorities I thought I'd better put you into a box in my head.

'But I couldn't stop thinking about you and once I let you hold me it became even harder. Once you kissed me it became impossible. I couldn't resist you. I let you out of the box and then I couldn't stay away.'

He took a step towards her, closing the gap that separated them, but Annie stepped back. She held up one hand, raising a virtual barrier between them. 'I never wanted to be like my mother but it seems I am. I let myself get swept away by chemistry and that is no excuse. I saw how chemistry got my mother into trouble and I swore I would never repeat her mistakes. I can't do this any more.'

'Can't do what?' Caspar was having trouble following the conversation. He was stuck on the part where Annie had admitted she couldn't resist him.

'Us. I told you, I suck at relationships. I should have learnt my lesson. We are never going to work.'

That brought him back down to earth with a bang. Was she about to walk away? He'd never been in this kind of situation before. He was always the one who walked.

He wasn't entirely sure what he should do but he didn't want to give her up and he wasn't prepared to let her give up so easily either.

'A lot of things don't work out exactly as we'd like. That doesn't mean you stop trying. Not if you want something badly enough,' he argued. Was she going to let the media dictate their relationship? He'd thought she was tougher than that.

'Caspar, please, what is the point? You leave at the end of the week. We always knew it was going to end some time, I'm choosing to end it now.'

She was normally serious but still quick to smile, but she wasn't smiling now. Surely there had to be more to it than the media interest. She must know it would settle eventually. The media would find something more sensational to focus on and would forget all about them.

This was all his fault. It didn't matter what she said.

He'd badgered her to go away for the weekend. He'd chased her when he'd known he shouldn't, but together they could get through this. If only she would let him help.

He didn't want it to be the end. He couldn't imagine it being over. Somehow, despite himself, he had found the woman he wanted to spend the rest of his life with. His perfect woman did exist and she was standing right in front of him. He couldn't let her go now. He didn't want to be without her.

He loved her.

'No,' he said. 'We can make this work. I'm not going to let you walk away.' If he didn't tell her how he felt now, he might not get another chance. This was it. She needed to know. 'I love you.'

'You can't.'

That wasn't the response he had been expecting. 'What do you mean, I can't? I do.'

She was shaking her head. 'Everyone who loves me leaves me. My mother, my grandmother.'

'Neither of them left you intentionally. I don't think anyone has ever loved you like I do.'

'But you're leaving too, aren't you? You're going back to Melbourne.'

Was that what this was about? She didn't want to be left again? Was she planning on leaving him before he left her?

'You could come with me.'

'You're not listening to me. I am not going to repeat my mother's mistakes. She was never able to just let my father go. She followed him endlessly and I am not going to do that. I will not do that.'

'I am not your father and you are not your mother. I promise I won't let you down.'

'You can't know that. I'm trying to put my life together again. I had to do that when I was twelve and I'm doing it again now. That's enough. I don't want to do it a third time when things go wrong again.'

'You can't live your life expecting the worst. You can't hide from love.'

'I'm better on my own.'

He disagreed but he tried in vain to convince her. 'You told me once your mother loved your father. She couldn't live without him. Do you love me?'

For the first time he actually wanted to make a relationship work but Annie was resolute.

'I don't know,' she said. 'I'm not sure I know what love is.'

CHAPTER TEN

CASPAR HAD BEEN gone for three weeks, four days and fifteen hours and Annie wondered how long it would be before she would stop counting.

His last week in Mount Gambier had been horrible. The media had camped outside her house and she'd had to stay with Tori, hiding from the world. But that hadn't been the worst part. The worst part had been seeing him every day but not being with him. She'd been missing him before he'd even left. She wondered when she would stop.

Losing her mother and her grandmother had been hard but this was worse. Much worse.

Maybe it was because his absence was still so new. She felt as though he'd been taken from her life before she was ready. Perhaps if they'd had more time together she would have discovered things about him that had irritated her. Perhaps then she would have been glad to say goodbye.

She tried making a mental list of the things that had annoyed her. Maybe that would ease the pain.

He always had an answer for everything and he was usually right.

He had a terrible habit of laughing at her when she was mad.

He was stubborn.

He ignored boundaries.

She had to admit, as far as lists went, it wasn't very good. If it wasn't for those things they would never have got together. If he'd taken no for an answer or respected boundaries she would never have ended up in his arms or in his bed, and no matter how much she was hurting now she knew she didn't regret the experience. She just wished it hadn't ended so soon.

But she'd recover. Given time. It was just going to take longer than three weeks, four days and fifteen hours.

After three weeks, four days and eighteen hours Kristin arrived for her six-week postnatal check-up. Annie went through the formalities of the appointment, which included admiring the baby and asking after the rest of Kristin's family. Kristin proceeded to fill her in on the activities of her offspring but that wasn't who Annie wanted to hear about. However, as she didn't want to be the one to bring up the topic of Caspar she had to wait patiently until Kristin, hopefully, got around to it.

'You haven't forgotten about Gabriele's baptism, have you?' Kristin asked. 'This Sunday, at St Paul's.'

Annie had been pleased to be invited to the baby's baptism and she hadn't forgotten. She was looking forward to having a reason to go out. 'Eleven o'clock, right?'

Kristin nodded. 'Caspar is coming home for it. Did you know?'

Annie felt the colour drain from her face. She shook her head. 'I haven't heard from him.' Hearing that he was coming to the Mount and hadn't bothered to let her know was almost more than she could bear. Did he know she had been invited to the baptism? Was he going to turn up and act as if nothing had happened? Annie knew she had called off their relationship, there had been no other option, but she hadn't realised how much it was going to hurt.

'Not at all?'

'Judging by the papers and magazines, he's been far too busy to stay in touch with me.' On more than one occasion over the past few weeks Annie had seen photographs of Caspar out with different women. At times it seemed like he had a different companion every night.

Kristin didn't ask for clarification, she seemed to know exactly what Annie was talking about. 'It's not serious with any of them.'

'Not yet.'

Kristin was watching her carefully. 'You could put an end to it, you know.'

'How?'

'You could go to Melbourne.'

That wasn't an option. She wasn't going to be like her mother. She wasn't going to run after any man, no matter how much she loved him.

The colour flooded back into Annie's cheeks. No. She couldn't love him. She loved things about him but that didn't mean she loved him. She was confusing chemistry with love. Just like her mother. She was a fool.

'He's a good man, Annie, he'd look after you if you'd let him.'

She didn't know if Kristin was right.

She didn't know what to do.

She'd never been in love before.

Throughout Friday Annie had one eye on the door and one hand on her phone. She had no idea when Caspar was arriving in town or, for that matter, whether he'd get in touch, but she hated to think she might miss him. By Saturday afternoon she was a wreck, filled with nervous anticipation. In an attempt to calm her nerves she went straight to the gym after her morning rounds, showering before she left for home just in case she ran into him. She wanted to see him, she wanted to see if she could make sense of her feelings.

As she turned into her street, she spied a silver Audi sports car parked outside her house.

He was here. Really here.

Her hands were shaking as she negotiated the driveway and parked under the carport at the rear of the house. Caspar was sitting on her back veranda. He stood as she switched off the engine and crossed the back lawn. Her heart hammered in her chest as she watched him in her rear-vision mirror. Her breath came in shallow spurts and she was afraid to take a deep breath, afraid if she concentrated on anything except him he might disappear.

He was divine.

She stepped out of her car on wobbly legs. She had to hold onto the door for support.

He'd had his hair cut. His dark curls were shorter but his green eyes were just the same, hypnotic, mesmerising. She was scared to ask what he was doing there. Why he'd come. She was afraid the answer might not be the one she wanted to hear.

He'd almost reached her. She waited for him to speak first. She didn't trust her voice.

'I was beginning to think I was waiting at the wrong house.'

A sense of relief flooded through her. Nothing had changed. He still managed to surprise her.

She laughed and her nervousness eased. 'Of all the things I thought you might say, that wasn't on my list.'

'What was?' he asked.

'I thought you might tell me you've missed me. That you've been miserable without me.'

'Would you like me to be miserable?' He smiled, looking far from despondent, and Annie's stomach flip-flopped at the sight of his familiar grin.

'A bit,' she admitted. 'Just so you'd know how I've been feeling.'

'Oh, Annie, of course I've missed you.' He closed the gap between them and Annie stepped towards him, meeting him halfway. He wrapped his arms around her and she rested her head over his heart, letting its rhythm calm her nerves further as she breathed in his peppermint scent. 'Why do you think I'm here?'

'For Gabriele's baptism.'

'No, not in the Mount, *here* here.' He kept one arm wrapped around her as he stroked her hair with his other hand. 'I wanted to see you.'

That was the answer she'd been hoping for but it wasn't enough information. 'How long are you staying?' Her voice was muffled against his chest. How long would they have before he left again? An hour, a night, two?

'That depends.'

'On?'

He took her hand and led her to the chair on the veranda. He sat in the chair and pulled her onto his knee. She didn't resist. She was right where she wanted to be.

'On whether I can get a job here.'

Annie frowned. 'Here? But what about your job in Melbourne? What about the television series?'

'I've resigned,' he told her. 'From the hospital and from the show. You know that Phil has decided, after his long-service leave, to resign from his position as paediatrician.' Annie nodded, she'd heard the news. 'I've applied for his job. I don't want to be in Melbourne. I want to be here.'

He was returning to the Mount? 'Why?'

'This is my home, but it wasn't until we put my parents' house on the market that I realised what I was about to lose. You understand that, you experienced it when you sold your grandmother's house, but until now I've never missed a place to call home because home was always here, even if I chose to live elsewhere. But now I've realised I don't want to give it up.'

'The house?'

He nodded. 'I had a meeting with Dad, his lawyers and the real estate agent this morning. I've spoken to my sisters and I've bought the house. I'm coming home.'

He'd bought the house. He was coming back to live. Annie wasn't sure exactly what that meant. Could they start again? Did he want to?

'I did a lot of thinking about our situation and I realised it was unfair of me to expect you to move for me when I wasn't offering you what you wanted. I know you want security and I want to give that to you. Despite the fact that I am currently unemployed and temporarily homeless…' he grinned '…I want to share my life with you. I want to give you the house as a wedding present.'

'What?' Annie wasn't sure she was following the conversation.

'A wedding present,' he repeated. 'I want to put the house in your name. It's your security,' he said as he lifted her off his lap and put her on the chair. He got down on one knee and held her hands in his.

'People talk about soul mates, about their other halves, but I never really expected to be lucky enough to find the person I wanted to spend the rest of my life with until I met you.' He looked up at her, his green eyes luminous.

'Until I met you I couldn't imagine believing in, trusting enough in another person to make that commitment. But I know you are my other half. I know I won't find anyone else like you. I don't even want to look. I love you, Annie. Will you marry me?'

'You want to marry me?'

He nodded. 'I thought I'd had my happy ending. I thought I was lucky to have been given the family I have, the family who chose me, but now I'm getting greedy. I want you to choose me too. I want another happy ending. With you. I want you to marry me.'

Annie couldn't think straight. He wanted to marry her. He'd bought her a house. He loved her. 'I feel like I should have some objections.'

Caspar laughed. 'I'd be disappointed if you didn't— you've never agreed with me without some sort of debate first. But I have known you to change your mind before and fortunately I know how to convince you. Just give me a minute,' he said as he stood up, 'I'm too old to stay down on my knees, waiting for you to come to a decision.'

He pulled her up off the chair and took her place, putting her back on his lap. He wrapped an arm around her waist, sliding his hand under the hem of her top and resting it against her hip. His hand was warm and his touch lit a fire in her belly. 'Okay, let's hear your objections.'

'I'm no good at relationships.' That was the first one.

'We have the rest of our lives to get it right,' he said as he kissed the side of her neck. 'Next.'

'I've been married before and it didn't work out so well.'

'What can I say? You married the wrong guy.' His lips moved up her neck and he kissed her just below her ear. The fire in her belly spread to her groin and she struggled to remember what she'd been about to say.

'I'm afraid of being like my mother. She would have been better off on her own.'

'I think we're better off together than apart and you don't need to chase me, I'm not running anywhere. I'm right here. From what you've told me, your parents' relationship was nothing like ours. Your mother talked about being less miserable when she was with your father. Did she ever talk about being happy?'

Annie shook her head.

'Do I make you happy?' he asked, as his hand slid up inside her shirt and found her breast.

'Yes.' Her voice was breathless with longing.

'Well, then, are you going to make me ask twice? As usual?' His fingers were caressing her nipple. Annie could feel it peaking under his touch. 'Will you please marry me?'

'I'm afraid of making a bad decision,' she said, although she didn't think she was actually capable of making any decision, good or bad, right at that moment.

'I promise that marrying me will be the best decision of your life. We belong together. We are going to have a long and happy life together. With our own family.'

'You want children?'

'Of course. But only if you are their mother. We should be parents, don't you think—an ob-gyn and a baby doctor? We're meant to be parents. So, you see, you can have as many objections as you like and I will find a way around them. For every objection you have I will have a dozen reasons why we should get married, but there are only two that really matter. One—I love you. Two—I think you love me. Am I right?'

Could he be right? He seemed so sure, so confident. She wanted to believe him.

It all depended on love. Could she do this? Could she depend on love?

It was up to her.

He was offering her everything she wanted. It was up to her to take it.

Chemistry wasn't the answer. Biology wasn't the answer. Was love the answer?

She could put the past behind her and have a new beginning with the man she loved.

It was up to her.

She nodded and his smile was enough to convince her she was making the right choice. 'Yes. I do love you. Even unemployed and homeless, I still love you. I will always love you.'

'And you will marry me?'

She was grinning like an idiot too now. 'Yes, I will marry you.'

'And have my babies?'

'Yes to that too,' she said. 'Should we go inside and practise?'

'That sounds like a very good idea to me.'

Annie put her hands up to his face and turned it towards her. She kissed him, a deep, searching kiss that was filled with love. She took him into her heart and then she took him to her bed.

* * * * *

RESISTING THE
NEW DOC IN TOWN

BY
LUCY CLARK

MILLS &
BOON

First published in Great Britain 2013
by Mills & Boon, an imprint of Harlequin (UK) Limited.
Harlequin (UK) Limited, Eton House, 18-24 Paradise Road,
Richmond, Surrey TW9 1SR

© Anne Clark & Peter Clark 2013

ISBN: 978 0 263 89910 8

Harlequin (UK) policy is to use papers that are natural, renewable and recyclable products and made from wood grown in sustainable forests. The logging and manufacturing process conform to the legal environmental regulations of the country of origin.

Printed and bound in Spain
by Blackprint CPI, Barcelona

Dear Reader

Welcome to the second book in my *Sunshine General Hospital* series. I love writing stories about friends, and these four women—Mackenzie, Bergan, Sunainah and Reggie—are all interesting and unique in their own ways.

Bergan was probably the most closed-off out of the four women, and it has been both a pleasure and a challenge to help her to open up, to learn how to trust and to accept that there is a man out there who is perfect for her, who doesn't care about her past and who is willing to share a beautiful future with her.

Richard... Oh, what can I say about Richard other than I was completely besotted by him from the moment he entered my imagination? I had a much clearer picture of him than I had of Bergan, when most of the time it's the other way around. I loved his quiet strength, his acceptance of Bergan's past and the realisation that even after heartbreak there can still be a happily-ever-after.

I do hope you enjoy Bergan's and Richard's story—don't forget to find me online and tell me what you think. Go to www.lucyclark.net, where you can find the links to connect with me on both Facebook and Twitter.

Warmest regards

Lucy

Dedication:

To my big sister Kate.

From the moment I was born you have been there
for me, a never-failing tower of strength.

Thanks, sis.

Psalm 91:2-4

CHAPTER ONE

THIS WAS ONE of the many times Richard Allington was pleased he was six feet five inches tall. In an effort to stay awake and combat jet lag, he'd taken up his mother's suggestion and come to Maroochydore's annual Moon Lantern festival, but now, as he stood in a crowd of thousands upon thousands of people, he wondered if he'd made the right decision.

There were so many people, jostling to get here or there, calling out to their friends, waving or just shoving past without a care. Many different languages were spoken, but thanks to his travels he found himself able to understand the odd word in Mandarin or Japanese as people continued to shove past him. Up on the huge open stage, with its large flat screens on either side, was the last dance act, a group of young Indian women, dancing in colourful saris.

Richard clapped with the rest of the crowd as the women finished and left the stage, and the master of ceremonies came on to announce that with the full moon now rising in the night sky, the extensive lantern festival would soon begin.

Smothering a yawn, Richard moved through the crowd towards the stage, interested to see just what some of these 'lanterns' actually looked like. He could well imagine they'd be nothing like the lanterns Miss Florence Nightingale would have carried around hospital wards.

From what he could see, the lanterns were all at least over two metres high. So far, he'd seen one in the shape of a tiger, one in the form of a bee buzzing around a honey pot and another made to resemble an old yellow taxi. He'd read a sign earlier explaining that the lanterns were all made with balsa wood frames then covered with tissue paper and decorated. It certainly sounded like a skilled operation and Richard could well appreciate the time and effort people had put into making these lanterns.

'I don't want to do it!' The loud, vehement words cut through the crowd and a few people turned to see what the commotion was all about. Richard was one of them, and as he shifted closer to where the young male voice had come from, he saw a heavily tattooed and pierced teenager, dressed from head to toe in black clothing, glaring fiercely at the woman before him.

He was standing in a group with about twenty other young teens, all dressed similarly in dark clothes, congregating in the lantern marshalling area, waiting to take their turn in carrying the amazingly structured lantern next to them. The young man, who Richard guessed to be about sixteen or seventeen years old, had his arms crossed defiantly over his chest, towering by a few inches over the woman who was talking to him with assured calmness.

Richard couldn't help but stare at her, captivated not only with the way she was handling the teenage tantrum with amazing alacrity but also by her beauty. She couldn't be more than about five foot six, slim with a long auburn plait swishing down her back as she moved her head. She was dressed in flat, black boots, denim jeans and a white top. Neat, casual, classic.

Although he had no idea what had initially caused the young man to flip out, Richard couldn't help but admire the way the woman had instantly taken charge of the situation, defusing what might have resulted in a teenage, ticking time bomb.

Some of the other kids were trying their best not to listen, but others were clearly supporting the woman, agreeing with her. A few of them pointed to the two-metre-high lantern they were about to carry along the snaking path that wound its way through the large crowd. Richard looked away from the woman for a moment to look at the lantern. The words 'Maroochydore Drop-In Centre' had been printed carefully on the side. He instantly looked back to the woman. Was she a social worker of some kind?

He couldn't help but edge closer, not necessarily wanting to hear what the woman was saying to the young man, more intrigued to know what her voice sounded like. Was it as beautiful as her face? As calm as her attitude? He shuffled his way through the crowd and was soon closer than before.

'You've put so much work into this lantern, Drak.' Her smooth, clear tones floated through the air towards him. 'I think it's important for you to carry it in the parade.' There was no sarcasm or censure in her tone, but there was a lot of pride. 'It's not a bad thing to take pride in something you've made. And I'll tell you another thing...' Her smile was small but earnest. 'Now that I know just how talented you really are, I'm not going to let you hide this gift anymore. I have big plans for you, my friend.' Her encouraging smile grew bigger as Drak groaned and shook his head, but Richard could see that he was almost puffing out his chest with pride at her words, and his arms weren't folded nearly as tightly as before.

'I knew this lantern thing was a mistake.' Drak's tone was gruff but not stern. 'It's going to be embarrassing, carrying it.'

'Nah. You can do it, Drak. You're awesome,' a teenage girl about the same age as Drak said encouragingly.

'Jammo's right, Drak. You see an embarrassment. I see brilliance. It's all just a matter of perspective. Also, I'll bet there are oodles of people here tonight who would love to have your gift of being able to create such a thing of beauty.'

'You think it's beautiful?' Drak asked, looking quizzically at the lantern.

'Undoubtedly. And so will many other people. They won't think it's sissy or girly to be able to create something like this. They'll think it's clever, skilful and... magical.'

He gave her a sceptical glance. 'Magical?'

The woman smiled. 'So you'll help carry it? Please?' She didn't break eye contact with Drak, the glow of the drop-in centre's lantern giving her a sort of angelic halo as she waited for his answer.

'Fine, Bergan. I'll carry it.'

'Thank you.'

'Bergan.' Richard found himself whispering her unusual name. Then he frowned for a moment, realising he'd heard that name somewhere else, somewhere before tonight, but right now his brain was still too jet-lagged to figure it out. As though she'd heard him whisper her name, as though he was almost willing her to look his way, Bergan patted Drak on the shoulder, then actually glanced his way, staring directly at him, her honey-brown eyes still bright from her triumph.

Their gazes locked for what seemed an eternity, yet in reality was only about five seconds. She raised an eyebrow, as though asking him what he thought of the situation. But that couldn't possibly have been what that look had meant. They didn't even know each other— why would she be interested in his opinion? And why, as he continued to watch her encouraging Drak, had his mouth gone dry and his gut feel as though it had been tied in knots? Who *was* this woman?

Just then, Richard saw one of the organisers come up to Bergan and speak to her. She listened, nodded, then turned to face the group of teenagers.

'All right. We're up next. Get ready to go,' she called. Richard continued to be amazed at the way she expertly organised everyone, talking to a few of the other adults who were no doubt her colleagues at the drop-in centre. Within another three minutes the people of the Maroochydore Drop-In Centre were ready to show their lantern to the thousands of people gathered for the festival.

Richard watched for as long as he could as Bergan and her crew snaked their way up the hill, with Drak and his mates carrying the lantern, which was shaped like a house with its doors wide open. The young man was indeed very talented to have made such a thing. Finally, when they had delivered their lantern to the top of the hill, where it was placed with the other lanterns on display, the members of the drop-in centre disappeared into the crowd. Where had Bergan gone?

Even once the festivities were finished and people began to disperse and head home, Richard found himself loitering, unable to admit to himself he was waiting for just one more glimpse of Bergan, the gorgeous brown-eyed redhead who had clearly made a difference in a young man's life tonight. He took photographs of all the lanterns on display. He continued to hang around, waiting for the owners of the lanterns to come and remove them, unable to quell his disappointment when a group of teenagers came to collect the drop-in centre's lantern. There was no sign of the beautiful Bergan.

Calling himself foolish, Richard spun on his heel and struck out with the rest of the dwindling crowd, heading towards his car, which he'd had to park at least five blocks away. It had been many, many years since just the sight of a woman had captivated him in such a way. As he pulled into the cul-de-sac where his parents lived, garaged the car and walked into the dark and empty townhouse, he couldn't help but be a little puzzled as to why he'd been so intrigued by a beautiful stranger.

He noticed the light was flashing on his parents' answering machine and listened to the message. It was from his mother, telling him they'd arrived safely in Paris and were now installed in his apartment on Rue de Valance. Richard was glad he'd finally been able to persuade his parents to travel, especially as he was now busy travelling around on an international fellowship, meaning his apartment was sitting empty.

The fellowship not only enabled him to travel, spending time at various accident and emergency departments around the world, but also to gather information on the latest technological and biomedical advancements each country had to offer. Ten countries had been included in the terms of the fellowship, and when Australia had been offered, Richard had requested to do his four-week placement at Sunshine General hospital, mainly because that was the hospital where he'd done his medical training so many years ago.

After Australia, he would return to the northern hemisphere and write up an extensive report of his findings, which would be shared with all the countries he'd visited. After that, he'd return to his job in Paris, working in the public hospital's ER.

Deciding he should probably make himself a late snack, he yawned, hating the fact that he was still jetlagged from his flight two days ago. He'd forgotten how travelling to the other side of the world could mess with a person's body clock. It was imperative he get a good night's sleep as he was due to start work at Sunshine General tomorrow morning and he doubted the A and E director, who he would be working closely with throughout the duration of his placement, would take kindly to him falling asleep whilst on duty.

Twenty minutes later, at nine-thirty in the evening, he laid his head on the pillow and closed his eyes thankfully, only to be awoken moments later by one of his neighbours coming home, obviously with a carload of happy revellers. It was a Sunday evening, for heaven's sake. Why were they revelling?

He pulled the spare pillow over his head in an attempt to drown out the noise of car doors being closed and friends laughing and chatting with each other. It appeared his neighbours on either side had gone out together, one of them with a very excited child. After ten minutes of chatting and laughing, they called goodnight to one another, and within another few moments the cul-de-sac was quiet once more.

Exhaling with relief, Richard shifted the pillows into a more comfortable position and gratefully drifted off into a deep, deep sleep.

* * *

'He's late!' Bergan wasn't happy. As director of the A and E department, she was a stickler for punctuality, and for her new international emergency travelling fellow to be late for his first shift didn't make for a good impression at all. She knew his name. Richard Allington. She knew his parents, Helen and Thomas, as they'd been her neighbours for the past few years in the small cul-de-sac of four townhouses. Now his parents had headed overseas and Richard was staying at his parents' house, or at least that's what Helen had told her. That meant Richard was her new neighbour.

She frowned. Having been raised in a foster-home environment, Bergan had learned the hard way the importance of compartmentalising her life. She'd learned how to get along with people she didn't necessarily like, and she'd learned how to ensure the government system, supporting fostered children, worked in her favour.

She'd worked hard, transforming herself from a desperate, abandoned child to an educated woman who now ran a busy A and E department—but one of the rules she'd worked hard to follow was to keep her personal and professional lives as separate as possible. There were exceptions to the rule, of course, especially with her three closest friends, Mackenzie, Reggie and Sunainah, but even then those relationships had taken years to forge.

Bergan checked her watch, her frown deepening as she realised it displayed exactly the same time as the A and E clock on the wall.

'Perhaps you should have knocked on his door this morning and woken him up yourself,' Mackenzie offered as she wrote in a set of case notes.

Bergan stepped closer to Mackenzie, not wanting the

A and E nurses working nearby at the desk to overhear their conversation. 'I don't even like it that this new fellow lives next door to me, so why on earth should I assume responsibility for him arriving on time? You know I don't like interacting with my colleagues in a social setting.'

'I live next door to you,' Mackenzie offered, and received a bored stare from Bergan.

'You're different and you know it. You're the closest person I have to family, you nutter.' A small smile teased at Bergan's lips, but only for a moment. 'You know I'd be lost without you and Sunainah and Reggie. I freely admit it. But neither do I work hand in hand with any of you every single day.' The frown returned as she checked her watch once more, clicking her tongue in annoyance.

'True, but at least Richard's only here for four weeks. Then he moves on to the next port of call for his travelling fellowship.' Mackenzie closed the set of case notes and checked her watch, the wedding ring on her left hand gleaming brightly. Married only three months, Bergan had never seen her friend this happy. 'And speaking of moving on, I'm due to start my orthopaedic clinic in exactly three minutes so I'd best get my butt upstairs.'

'Especially before your husband starts calling you to find out where you are,' Bergan added, a small smile on her lips.

Mackenzie shrugged one shoulder, her own smile incredibly bright and happy. 'It's not so bad being married to the boss.' She winked at Bergan and turned to walk out the nurses' station when a loud commotion came from the front doors leading into the A and E department. Together, Bergan and Mackenzie stared as a tall man came bursting through the doors, trying to shove his arms into a white coat, holding the tube of his stethoscope in his mouth as he narrowly avoided a barouche coming the opposite way.

'Sorry,' he mumbled, finally shoving his arm into the right sleeve and shrugging the coat onto his broad shoulders. Next, he looped the stethoscope around his shoulders, fixed his shirt collar and straightened his striped tie. He paused for a split second, taking in his surroundings, before heading with purposeful strides towards the nurses' station.

It wasn't until he was three steps away from where Bergan stood that he saw her. He stopped stock still and openly gaped, his eyebrows raised in astonishment. 'It's you!'

'What's that supposed to mean?' she retorted, glaring at him with impatience. 'Of course it's me, Dr Allington.'

He blinked one long blink, then stared at her in disbelief. 'You know who I am?'

Bergan shot Mackenzie a look as if to say, 'can you believe this guy?' Mackenzie instantly smiled before holding out her hand.

'Hi. I'm Mackenzie. I live in number two.' She briefly shook hands with him before jerking her thumb over her shoulder. 'Bergan's in number four and while I'd love to hang around and chat, I'm late for clinic. Look forward to catching up with you later, Richard.' And with that, Mackenzie headed off towards the orthopaedic department, leaving Bergan and Richard just standing there, staring at each other.

'What did she mean?' Completely puzzled, Richard eventually found his voice, desperately trying to clear his still jet-lagged mind in order to try and make some sense of what was happening. 'You live in number four?'

Bergan rolled her eyes and clenched her jaw, not wanting to have this discussion in the middle of the nurses' station where she knew several of the staff were sneaking interested glances their way. She couldn't blame them. Richard Allington had arrived at Sunshine General Hospital's A and E department with a crash, boom, bang. Add to that the fact that he was extremely good looking with his tall, dark and handsome stature and eyes of the bluest blue, and she could well imagine why the female staff were willing to stand around ogling their new colleague instead of tending to their duties.

She also had no idea why she'd mentally catalogued his features. Usually, she thought of her colleagues in terms of their abilities rather than their looks, but as she continued to stare at Richard for another moment, recalling the photographs she'd seen of him hanging on the walls at his parents' place, she realised those pictures hadn't done justice to those incredible eyes of his. Was he wearing contacts? Was that why they were so perfectly blue?

She gave her head a little shake, desperate to clear it of such thoughts. She couldn't remember the last time she'd stood and stared at a man like this, feeling a flurry of excitement churning in her belly. He was a colleague, for heaven's sake! How could she be so unprofessional? Forcing herself to look away, she cleared her throat and made sure her tone was crisp and impersonal. 'Dr Allington. If you'd be so kind as to step into my office, we'll tidy up the remaining paperwork so you can legally start your first shift.'

The words had been polite enough, but they'd been

said through gritted teeth and as Bergan stalked out of the nurses' station, an intrigued Richard followed closely behind. How was it possible that the one woman he'd noticed at the Moon Lantern festival, that one woman out of hundreds of thousands of people, was now leading him down a small corridor in the A and E department towards her office?

He'd even dreamed of her last night, dreamed he was back at the festival and that after she'd finished talking to her teenage charge, she'd lifted her gaze to meet his once more and had smiled sweetly at him. He'd returned her smile and, after a long moment, she'd quickly excused herself from the throng of teenagers and made her way over to where he was standing, looking as though she had every intention of striking up a conversation.

'You handled that very well,' he'd complimented her. 'Very diplomatic.'

'Thanks. Listen, I have a…thing to do,' she'd said, jerking a perfectly manicured thumb over her shoulder towards the group of teens waiting to take part in the festival. 'But afterwards how about we meet up right back here and, well…?' She'd shrugged a perfectly elegant shoulder and then smiled a perfectly suggestive smile at him. 'Have a cup of coffee or something?'

Richard shook his head, bringing his thoughts back to the present. The dream had been nothing more than a dream. This was reality, and Bergan had stopped in front of an office door. The problem was that he'd been so caught up in his reverie that he'd almost collided with her. He stopped short and quickly took a step back, just as she glanced at him over her shoulder and gave him a perfectly annoyed look. Shaking her head, she used the pass card hanging around her neck on a hospital lanyard to unlock the door, then headed inside the brightly lit office.

As Richard entered the room, he read the name plate: *'Bergan Moncrief. Director'*.

'Bergan Moncrief?' He spoke out loud. 'That's your name?'

She walked behind her desk and waved a hand towards the door. 'That's what it says. Why? Who did you think I was?' She waited for him to speak, but when he didn't say anything immediately, she spread her hands wide. 'Didn't it state my name on your paperwork? I'm not really sure how your travelling fellowship works, but I would have thought you at least have a contact person at each different hospital. Right?'

'Bergan Moncrief.' He stated her name again, the penny finally starting to drop. He *had* heard that name before and it had been his mother who had mentioned it. Bergan Moncrief. Yes. He remembered now. 'You live next door to my paren—' He stopped and nodded as realisation dawned. 'So *that's* what Mackenzie meant. She's at number two, you're at number four and my parents live at number three.'

It was Bergan's turn to show her puzzlement. 'I thought your mother told you.'

'Told me what?'

'That you'd be working with me here at the hospital.' She spread her hands wide, her smile polite, official. 'She certainly mentioned it to me, on more than one occasion, and asked me to make you feel welcome. So…I guess…welcome.'

'I do remember her saying something about knowing some of the people I'd be working with, but she told me that before my fellowship started, which was almost a year ago.' Richard came farther into the room and dropped comfortably into the chair opposite her desk, glad to finally be on the same page as the beautiful Bergan. 'I'm still rather jet-lagged. Even after all the travelling I've done, and even though I try to sleep on the planes and keep myself hydrated and all the other things you're supposed to do to combat jet lag, they haven't worked.'

He watched as Bergan slowly lowered herself into her chair, back still straight, mind on alert, as though she didn't trust him one little bit. And why should she? They knew next to nothing about each other, and yet Richard couldn't help but feel that the brief glance they'd shared at the festival had penetrated them both deeper than they'd like to admit.

'I hope that's not going to interfere with your work today.' Her words were brisk. 'You've already turned up late.'

'I'd like to apologise for that. For some reason, my alarm didn't go off or else I slept right through it.' He scratched his head, as though completely baffled by the situation. There was a small, lopsided smile tugging at the corner of his mouth and as he held her gaze, she once more found herself staring into his gorgeous eyes. He *was* cute. That wasn't up for debate, but her reaction to him was, and once more she had to force herself to look away.

'Hmm.' Bergan continued to frown as she shuffled some papers around on her desk until she found the manila folder she was looking for. She sounded completely uninterested in what he was saying. Richard wasn't sure whether to be happy she wasn't going to belabour the point or sad because she'd dismissed his explanation so easily. He didn't know why he wanted more of her attention. For some reason, this woman intrigued him and right now he wanted to see the same smile on her lips as she'd had last night at the lantern festival.

'Not only did I sleep through my alarm,' he continued, while she prepared the papers in front of her, 'but I was plagued last night with some very noisy neighbours, chatting not too far from my open bedroom window at some ridiculous hour.' There was a teasing note in his tone, but instead of getting her to smile, he watched as she glared at him, bristling with annoyance.

'It wasn't *that* late. And as I saw you at the festival, you can't possibly have been in bed all that long by the time we arrived home. And, yes, we probably shouldn't have chatted so loudly, but Ruthie was excited as she's never been to a Moon Lantern festival before and—'

'Whoa. Whoa.' He held up his hands in a defensive manner, chuckling lightly. 'I was only teasing.'

Bergan closed her open mouth and frowned, desperate to ignore the glorious sound of his deep laughter, which had momentarily filled her office. The only way she knew how to deal with this situation was to be blunt with him. Perhaps, once he knew where she stood, they could begin their professional relationship and put an end to his silly teasing.

'Then don't. I think I should let you know right from the start that I don't particularly like mixing business with pleasure. In other words, I don't like the people I work with on a daily basis knowing too much about my private life. I am the director of a very busy department and as such demand a certain level of respect from my colleagues and staff. The fact that you are my neighbour means I'll be asking you to respect those boundaries. If we happen to see each other around the cul-de-sac, that's one thing, but I will not have you chatting or gossiping about my private life with anyone here at the hospital. Is that clear?'

'Crystal.' He nodded then paused, a thoughtful look on his face, but when he spoke, that same teasing note was still evident in his tone. 'What about Mackenzie? She's your neighbour and now she's my neighbour, so am I allowed to discuss cul-de-sac goings-on with her within hospital grounds?'

Bergan sighed heavily and rolled her eyes, shaking her head. 'Does your mother know how annoying you can be? Because she never said anything about it to me.'

Where she'd intended her words to be a bit of chastisement, to help bring him back into line, she was surprised when Richard stared at her for a split second before throwing his head back and laughing. The warm, rich sound washed over her like a comforting memory and Bergan was slightly confused to how she could be both annoyed and attracted to him at the same time.

There was no denying he was a good-looking man. The phrase tall, dark and handsome fit Richard Allington to perfection, but she'd never been the type of person to judge someone simply on looks. His relaxed, teasing demeanour, on the other hand, was certainly reason enough for her to remember to keep a professional distance from him at all times.

'I'm fairly sure Mum knows. So do my sisters. That's what big brothers do, they annoy their sisters.'

Forcing herself to look away from his dazzling blue eyes, especially as they were twinkling with mirth, Bergan decided it was better not to give him any more reasons to tease her and pushed the manila folder towards him, along with a pen.

'Well, as I am not your sister, would you kindly refrain and concentrate on your job? Now, if you would read these documents and sign them, I can issue you with your pass card. Then you'll need to head down to Personnel to have your photograph taken for your identification badge. Once that's done, report back to me and we'll sign the last lot of papers. Then you'll be all cleared to work at Sunshine General for the next four weeks of your travelling fellowship.'

'You say those words with such disdain.' Richard leaned forward in his chair, that infuriating smile still in place. 'You don't want me here, do you?' he asked.

'What I want, Dr Allington—'

'Richard, please,' he interrupted. 'After all, we *are* neighbours.'

Bergan gritted her teeth. Had he heard nothing of what she'd said? Was he intent on thwarting her by not adhering to her wishes to keep her professional and private lives separate?

'As I was saying, *Richard*,' she replied pointedly, 'what I want is to keep my department functioning as smoothly and as efficiently as it always has. Whether you're going to be a help or a hindrance is yet to be seen, and with the way you all but burst through the front doors this morning, and have hardly been serious since your arrival, I'm inclined to believe it's the latter.'

Richard chuckled at her words as he took the folder and started scanning the pages. 'Fair point. Looks as though I'll have my work cut out for me in changing your mind.'

She hoped he wouldn't, but instead of prolonging the conversation, Bergan nodded towards the documents he was holding, clearly wanting to be done with this interview. When the phone on her desk shrilled to life, she picked it up instantly. 'Dr Moncrief.' She listened for a

moment before saying, 'I'll be right there,' and returning the receiver to its cradle.

'Problem?' Richard asked as he finished signing the
documents, watching as Bergan rose from her chair
with poise and grace. She flicked the long auburn braid
from her shoulder and lifted her chin just a touch. The
action caused something to tighten deep within his gut
and Richard couldn't help but accept the fact that he was
indeed attracted to this woman who appeared to want
as little to do with him as possible.

'Multiple MVA.'

'Ambulance ETA?'

'Five minutes.'

'Right.' He quickly rose to his feet, his entire demeanour changing so quickly that Bergan was momentarily stunned. 'Let's go, then.' Within two of his long
strides he was at her door and holding it open for her
to precede him.

'But the paperwork—' She came round her desk.
She'd hoped to send him off to Personnel while she
went to deal with the emergency, but with the way he'd
changed from being all teasing and jovial to the stern
medical professional now standing by her open door,
she wasn't sure how to react.

'The important forms have all been signed, so the
hospital's public liability and my personal insurance
are all in order.' He followed her out of her office and
checked the door was locked behind them, before heading down the corridor. 'How would you like to handle
this? You take trauma room one and I'll take trauma
room two, or would you prefer to assess my capabilities
and confirm I really do have the extensive qualifications
listed on my curriculum vitae?'

As they re-entered the bustling accident and emergency department, they found a hive of activity. Nurses, registrars and interns were all ensuring stock and treatment rooms were ready and waiting for when the first lot of patients started arriving.

'Bergan?'

She glanced up at Richard, who was clearly waiting for her response. She had read his CV and his qualifications were indeed extensive, more so than her own. Initially she had planned to monitor him, to reassure herself of his abilities, but now, with no other qualified A and E consultants presently on the floor, it would be beneficial to have him running one trauma room while she ran the other. Trust. That's what it came down to and Bergan was not the type of woman to trust easily. Not at all.

'I'm happy either way,' he said, prompting her a little. 'It's your call.'

The sound of ambulance sirens was drawing nearer, almost at the hospital gates, and some of the staff were heading out to meet the ambulances. She glanced around at the registrars on duty, the experienced nurses, and knew that a wise director would use the resources presently available to her.

Swallowing, she returned her gaze to meet Richard's and nodded. 'As you said, I'll take trauma room one, you take trauma room two.'

'Thanks for the trust.' He nodded, a small, knowing smile touching his lips as though he'd enjoyed watching her thought processes at work. 'See you on the other side.' And with that he spun on his heel and headed off in the direction of trauma room two, but not before turning to look at her over his shoulder and giving her a cheeky wink.

It was the wink that did it. Bergan had been fine until

then, holding herself under control in the presence of
the man who not only riled her but also had the ability to set her entire body tingling with one of his infuriating smiles and warm laughter. The cheeky wink
was worse, as she felt her knees weaken, her mouth go
dry and her head spin. Why would such a handsome,
intelligent man choose *her* to flirt with? And at such
a moment as this! She reached out a hand towards the
wall in an effort to steady herself, hating the feeling of
being so unbalanced.

When she'd seen him at the Moon Lantern festival,
she'd instantly recognised him from the family photographs his mother, Helen, had on display around on the
walls of her home. Bergan had been surprised, first, at
just how tall he was in the flesh and, second, that from
one brief, momentary glance she'd been hit with the
same sensations she was experiencing now.

Never before had a man been able to make her almost
swoon with just a look, or a smile, or a wink. No one…
except, it appeared, Richard Allington. And the most
annoying thing was that he'd done it twice.

As she dragged in a breath and stood up straight,
squaring her shoulders and preparing her mind for
the busy task ahead, Bergan was determined that although her new colleague may have cause havoc with
her equilibrium, she would force herself to be immune
to him. She was a strong, independent woman who had
worked hard for many years to gain control over her
silly, schoolgirl emotions.

Yes, she would be immune to him, she thought as
she pushed away the emotions he'd evoked. And that
was most definitely that.

CHAPTER TWO

In A and E, Bergan remained the focused and consummate professional that she'd worked so hard to become. It certainly wasn't every day that a man could enter her well-ordered, neat and controlled world and make her knees weaken with a single smile, and for that reason alone she knew she needed to keep her distance from Richard Allington.

The fact that she was friends with his parents, and that for the next four weeks he would be her neighbour as well as working alongside her at the hospital, meant that it was going to be difficult to maintain her composure, but she'd lived through much tougher situations than this and she'd always come out on top.

It's only four weeks, she'd thought over and over again, every time she'd caught a glimpse of him roaming around *her* A and E, tending to patients, chatting with staff, flirting with every available female. He was just the same as every other man, interested in only one thing—conquering and controlling a woman. Well, she certainly wasn't going to fall for his charm and charisma.

Having been raised in foster homes since she'd been small, her parents both drug addicts, Bergan had grown up with a skin much tougher than that of the average little girl. Bad things had happened to her and she'd forged her own way through them, coming out stronger and more determined than ever. Now, after many years of hard work, she was the director of a busy A and E department, running it effectively and efficiently, respected by her colleagues and peers. Four weeks wasn't long. She could and *would* survive the onslaught to her life that *was* Richard Allington.

Squaring her shoulders, she headed to the nurses' station, where he was leaning comfortably against the desk, chatting with Katrina, one of the best retrieval and triage nurses Bergan had ever worked with. 'All done?' Bergan asked, barely glancing in his direction as she sat down to write up a set of case notes.

'Basically.' There was a hint of relief combined with satisfaction in Richard's voice. 'Just waiting for two patients to return from Radiology, but the most serious cases are off and away to Theatres.'

'Off and away?' Bergan looked up at him, unable to stop the small smile tugging at the corners of her mouth. 'You do realise you said those words with a hint of an Irish accent?' she pointed out.

'No, I didn't.' Richard shifted from the desk and shoved one hand into the pocket of his trousers. 'Did I?'

'You did,' Katrina confirmed for him, smiling brightly at the handsome doctor. 'Have you worked in Ireland?'

'A few months ago, yes, but I hadn't realised I'd picked up any of the accent.' He shrugged one shoulder, his smile brightening. 'One problem I have had during this fellowship has been to control my French—and I mean that literally. Having lived and worked in France for the past six years, for the first few months of the fellowship, when I was in emergency situations, as we were just now, I'd often break into rapid French when giving instructions to staff. It was only when they all stopped and stared at me as though I'd grown an extra head that I even realised I'd done it.' He chuckled and Katrina joined in.

Bergan's smile increased as she pictured the stunned looks on people's faces at an Australian doctor, working in somewhere like Spain, giving out instructions in French. Then, as though realising she was enjoying his company, she quickly frowned and returned her attention to the case notes open in front of her.

'What led you to settle in France in the first place?' It was Katrina who had asked the question, but Bergan was very interested in the answer. Although she'd known Richard's parents for quite a few years now, it wasn't as though they all sat around listening to Helen's anecdotes about her children's accomplishments. And at any rate Bergan preferred not to engage in deeply personal conversations with people, except for her three closest friends, who had definitely proved themselves worthy of her friendship over the many years they'd been together.

Would Richard prove himself worthy? The question jumped into her head unbidden and she quickly shook it away. Her friendships with Sunainah and Reggie had been forged well over a decade ago and Mackenzie was the closest thing she had to a sibling, as they had both been raised in the foster system. Richard was here for one month and she doubted if that was long enough for any man, no matter how ambitious, to break through the barriers she'd spent almost a lifetime putting carefully in place.

Even though she was writing in the case notes, Bergan couldn't help but listen to his reply to Katrina's question.

'It was one of those strange things that happened. I was working in the UK, my contract about to expire, and a friend who worked at the public hospital in Paris told me of a job going there. Well, I spoke the language so I thought—why not?' He shrugged nonchalantly and yet… Bergan could have sworn she heard something in his tone that suggested there was much more to the story than he was telling.

She glanced up at him, quickly noting that his previously jovial blue eyes now reflected a hint of sadness.

'And one year morphed into two years then three, and before I knew it I'd been working at the hospital for six years.'

'And then you were offered the fellowship?' Katrina asked.

'That's right. My first two years in Paris…I actually worked part time and did some further study, which meant I was qualified for the fellowship.'

There it was again, Bergan thought. That little pause in his words, as though he was choosing them carefully. Was he avoiding saying something too personal? Perhaps the cheeky, arrogant man she'd met earlier that morning wasn't all there was to Richard Allington.

'Well,' he said a moment later, drawing in a long breath and slowly exhaling, 'I don't know about you, but three hours of dealing with emergencies has left me with an appetite. Care to join me?'

Bergan kept writing up the notes, thinking he was talking to Katrina, but it wasn't until the nurse cleared her throat that Bergan looked at her. Katrina nodded pointedly in Richard's direction and it was only then Bergan realised he'd been talking to *her*. 'Oh!'

She stared at him for a moment, his words sinking in. 'You're asking me to join you for a late lunch?'

Richard watched her closely for several seconds before replying. 'I'm asking if you wouldn't mind accompanying me to the hospital cafeteria so we can continue our debriefing.' He spread his hands wide. 'I'm hungry. You've got to be hungry, too, and it just seems to make sense if we eat and get some work accomplished at the same time.'

'Go, Bergan,' Katrina encouraged. 'I can follow up with the patients who are in Radiology if they come back before you return.'

Bergan looked at the clock and then, as if on cue, felt her stomach grumble. Her eyes widened and she looked up at Richard, wondering if he'd heard that. His answer was to wink at her again and the same flood of tingles spread through her at the action. At least this time she was sitting down. Why did he have to be so... personable?

She shook her head and forced herself to look back at the case notes before her. Knowing it would probably raise more questions if she declined his polite offer, and as she was clearly hungry, it seemed easier to accept, but still, something held her back from saying so. Probably her strong self-preservation instinct. Already, in just a few short hours, he'd somehow managed to get under her skin and she didn't like it one little bit.

'Is that a no?' he asked, as she signed the case notes and handed them to Katrina, who instantly took them from her, mumbled an excuse of some sort and left them alone.

'What?'

'You shook your head. Does that mean you don't want us to eat together?'

'I don't really have anything else to debrief you on. There are just a few more forms to sign, but…'

Richard shifted his stance and gave her a look of veiled amusement, as though he could easily read her thoughts and knew she didn't want to spend time with him. 'Well, I'm not up to date with mine. I have several forms that require your signature.' He held out a hand towards her, but Bergan ignored it, rising to her feet and pushing in the chair. 'It's business, Bergan. Two colleagues walking together, eating together. Nothing more sinister than that, I promise.'

Bergan sighed heavily, knowing if she kept refusing him he might end up making a mountain out of a mole-hill. After all, he was an international fellow, and for Sunshine General to host such an accomplished doctor as Richard Allington had been quite a coup. 'Fine,' she said, rolling her eyes. The action, designed to show her impatience and to let him know once and for all that she wasn't happy with this arrangement, brought an unexpected chuckle from him.

'Thank you. You do me a great honour.'

She ignored the way his light laughter washed over her, ignored the delighted prickling down her spine, which heightened her awareness of him. 'You're teasing me,' she murmured as she headed out of A and E, catching Katrina's gaze and mouthing the word 'Lunch'.

He chuckled again as they entered the stairwell, the rich, deep sound echoing around the walls. Bergan tried not to like the way his laughter made her feel. It had been a long time since any man had dared to tease her. Most of the men she knew were colleagues and although her friend Reggie had done her best to set Bergan up on a few dates, none of the men had interested her.

'*Moi?*' Richard feigned ignorance. 'Tease? *Je ne sais pas ce que vous dites.*'

Bergan was glad she was a few steps in front of him so he didn't see the small smile on her lips. 'Teasing *and* rude. Speaking in a language a simple girl like me would have absolutely no hope of understanding. Tut-tut, Dr Allington.' She glanced at him over her shoulder as they rounded the landing, heading up another flight. 'This is not a good beginning for you.'

'And yet,' Richard said as he came up beside her, easily overtaking her in order to hold the door open, 'why do I get the distinct impression you understood every word I said?' He gave her a quizzical smile as she came up the final few steps. 'Do you speak French?'

'As I said, a simple girl.'

Richard gave a hoot of laughter and Bergan had to close her eyes for a split second in order to block out the delightful sound. She'd made him laugh. She'd actually teased him back, had said something that had made him laugh. That wasn't something she did every day. She much preferred to keep her distance from her male colleagues and as she walked past him Bergan met his gaze, holding it briefly and doing her best to ignore the way his spicy scent penetrated her senses. She had to admit she was mildly surprised with the way Richard didn't appear to be kow-towing to her like so many other men did and while she found that refreshing, it also made him even more dangerous.

Impersonal. Businesslike. Professional. That was the only way to handle a man like him.

'This way to the cafeteria,' she said, pointing down the long corridor. Before Richard could say another word she headed off, knowing he would fall into step beside her within an instant. She also hoped he'd drop the whole teasing demeanour so they could get their work done, eat some food and then get back to A and E, where she could be sufficiently distracted by work, *not* by Richard's close proximity.

'So…did you enjoy the Moon Lantern festival last night?' he asked.

'What are you doing?'

'What do you mean? I'm making conversation.'

'Here?' Bergan frowned as she glanced up at him. 'Didn't I say that I don't like discussing my personal life at work?' She turned her attention from him and nodded politely at another colleague, who was walking in the opposite direction.

'No one can hear our conversation, Bergan.' He kept his voice low, leaning a little closer to her as he spoke, and she immediately moved away, trying desperately to keep a decent distance between them.

'Yet when you lean in like that and speak in that stage whisper, they'll get the wrong idea.'

'I disagree. Anyone seeing two doctors talking in such a fashion will no doubt think we're discussing a patient.'

'Which should be done in the privacy of an office.'

'We're busy people. Sometimes we don't have time to sit and discuss things in an office. We need to talk and chat and eat and process information along with digesting our food. It's the way doctors are.'

Bergan sighed loudly. 'Is there a point to all of this, or shouldn't I ask?'

'All I'm saying is that no one's going to know what we're discussing so if I want to discuss the Moon Lantern festival and the way our eyes seemed to meet across a crowded…er…crowd, then why can't I?'

Bergan stopped momentarily and looked at him with

feigned astonishment. 'Oh, gee! Was that you? I hadn't realised.' She raised an eyebrow then continued towards the cafeteria.

'And now you're teasing me!'

Bergan couldn't help the smile that touched her lips. *'Je ne sais pas ce que vous dires.'*

Richard's warm laughter floated over her, but this time it was more than just his deep chuckle. The sound warmed her through and through, but thankfully it was drowned out as they entered the busy and noisy cafeteria. *'Touché, mademoiselle.'*

'And our eyes didn't "meet across the crowded...er... crowd",' she repeated, emphasising the way he'd used the same word twice. 'You make it sound all clandestine and romantic—which it most definitely wasn't.'

'What was it, then?'

'We were just in each other's line of sight. That's all. Nothing more, nothing less.'

She joined the queue, waiting to be served, acutely aware of Richard standing very close behind her. Bergan couldn't believe how aware she was of him and as she licked her dry lips and tried to appear nonchalant and completely unaffected by the man directly behind her, a woman with short, black, feathered hair, tipped with hot pink highlights, sidled up next to her.

'And just *who* is this dishy, dishy man behind you?' Regina Smith asked, placing one hand around Bergan's shoulders and pointing interestedly towards Richard. 'Is this...*him*?'

Bergan sighed and shook her head in bemused astonishment at Reggie's complete lack of inhibition, but then, that was Reggie. 'Reggie Smith, meet Richard Allington.'

'Helen's boy?'

Bergan smothered a smile at the 'boy' part, but nodded as Reggie dropped her arm and shifted closer to Richard, holding out her hand in greeting. *'Enchantée.'*

Richard dutifully grazed his lips across Reggie's knuckles before releasing her hand. Even though it was only a simple action, even though he was only being polite and even though this was hardly unusual behaviour for Reggie, the happiest and bubbliest person Bergan had ever known, she couldn't ignore the thread of jealousy that ripped through her. It was odd, especially as she barely knew anything about Richard, and didn't really want to.

How was it this man, who had been in her world for such a short period of time, had somehow managed to get under her skin? Bergan advanced in the queue as Reggie chatted away, telling Richard all about the latest developments in the general surgical department.

She was positive Richard was smiling brightly and staring at Reggie with his deep, engaging eyes. She couldn't blame him because most men were instantly besotted by Reggie and her bubbly personality, but when it was their turn to be served at the counter, Bergan was surprised to find Richard highly attentive and insisting on paying for both Reggie's lunch and her own.

'You are such a sweetie,' Reggie said, blowing him a kiss. 'But you know this means that both of you simply must eat lunch with me and I won't take no for an answer.' Reggie pointed to the corridor. 'We'll go down the first lot of stairs and then out into the small courtyard. It's such a beautiful, sunshiny day, it seems such a shame to waste it.'

'Every day's a beautiful day in Queensland,' Bergan grumbled, but neither of them took any notice.

Richard readily agreed. 'It *is* rather noisy in here. Bergan and I won't be able to get any work done.'

'Work! Good heavens,' Reggie persisted, shaking a finger at Bergan. Bergan merely shrugged, trying to find a way to wriggle out of this situation. 'Take a break for once, Bergan.'

'Listen to your friend,' Richard said to Bergan pointedly, falling into step beside her once more as they headed to the closest stairwell.

Bergan hadn't wanted to eat lunch with Richard in the first place and now he had Reggie as a playmate, so perhaps he wouldn't insist she stay. At the thought of Reggie and Richard locked together in a whispered conversation, an awful taste came into the back of her throat. Why should she care if Reggie wanted to get to know Richard better—or vice versa, for that matter? True, Richard was only here for a month, but if Reggie didn't mind getting involved with a man who would up and leave her when it was time for him to return to Paris, then so be it. She didn't care. Honestly, she didn't. So why did the thought leave such an uncomfortable sensation in the pit of her stomach?

Bergan didn't say a word until they were outside, the early afternoon sunlight shining brightly into her eyes. She followed Reggie to the courtyard, where one or two people were just finishing their lunches before departing. They sat at the picnic table, Bergan ensuring she didn't end up sitting next to Richard. At least, with the table between them, it afforded her a bit of distance.

Reggie sat next to Richard, keeping up a steady stream of easy chatter for the first five minutes before her phone rang. Reggie quickly excused herself and took the call. 'Uh…duty calls,' she said, rewrapping her sandwich and shifting out of the bench seat. 'Looks as though my afternoon surgical list *is* going to start on time after all. Morning Theatre was running late,' she stated by way of explanation. 'You two stay here and enjoy the sunshine. Bye-ee.'

'And there goes Reggie,' Bergan stated as her friend disappeared.

'Is she always that bright and bubbly?'

'Always.' Bergan nodded for emphasis, a small smile on her lips. 'Even when she's upset, she's still more bubbly than I am on a good day!'

'And she's one of your closest friends?'

'Why does that surprise you?' Bergan straightened her shoulders. Richard was still chewing and hadn't yet swallowed his mouthful so she took the opportunity to keep on talking. 'Do you think that because we're so different that we wouldn't be friends?'

Richard swallowed. 'That's not what I meant.'

'Then what did you mean? Reggie and I are incredibly similar. We just show our feelings in different ways.'

He looked up at the sky as though hoping the answer to the question might just fall down and hit him on the head. 'I only meant that, as you've already told me, you don't like mixing business with pleasure and, well…Reggie seems to be the epitome of someone who does the opposite. I find it…interesting that you're good friends. That's all.' He held his hands up, indicating he had no other secret agenda.

Bergan started rewrapping her salad roll, as though intending to leave. 'You're not the first person to be surprised that someone as nice as Reggie should be friends with someone like me, who is far too often closed off and brusque.'

'That's not what I meant, Bergan.'

'Reggie is loyal, trustworthy and filled with determination to spread sunshine among everyone she meets, and a lot of the time people take advantage of her generous nature. She's had a tough life, and yet she's still happy and nice, wanting everyone to be as happy as she is. And, yes, that can be exhausting to be around all the time, but there is nothing I wouldn't do for her and vice versa.' When she went to stand, Richard instantly reached out a hand and caught hers in his.

'Wait. Don't go. Please?'

'Richard?' She looked pointedly at her hand, but he didn't let her go.

'We've got off on the wrong foot, Bergan. I apologise if you thought I was insulting your friend or even questioning your friendship with Reggie. It's clear you're very loyal to her and I can also see how people might take advantage of her, but I am not that sort of person. I admire your loyalty to your friendships, but I truly didn't mean any disrespect with my questions.' He held her gaze and she could see the exasperation in his eyes. He shook his head. 'This whole morning, this whole day…it hasn't gone the way it usually goes when I start at a new hospital.'

As she lowered herself back onto the bench seat, appeased by his words, Richard let go of her hand. The instant warmth from his touch had been enough to send shock waves ricocheting throughout her entire body and her knees actually wobbled. Sitting down had been the best option to get him to stop playing havoc with her senses.

His words also made her feel quite contrite. It couldn't be easy for him, having to change hospitals every month, starting afresh with a new set of people. 'How does it usually go?'

'I introduce myself to the head of department in a

timely and unhurried fashion. We swap paperwork, discuss schedules and then, if time permits, take a tour of the facilities, not only so I can get my bearings in the A and E department and meet a few staff members, but also to see where I'll often be lecturing, as that's part of my fellowship duties.'

'Sounds…ordered, structured. Nice.' She took a sip of her water. 'So why was today's beginning so different?'

'I can make a load of excuses about alarms not going off, jet-lag and noisy neighbours…' He smiled at the last part. 'But I won't because it doesn't change the fact that I was late. Again, I offer my sincerest apologies.'

'Apology accepted.' Bergan swallowed her mouthful. 'So where's this paperwork I need to look at?'

Richard shrugged and gave her a sly smile. 'Actually, I left it at home.'

'But you said we'd be working over lunch,' she protested.

'We are. We're improving public relations.'

'Is that what we're doing?' She didn't sound as though she believed him and took another bite of her roll.

'Actually…' Richard finished his sandwich and balled up the wrapper before tossing it into a nearby bin '…that's not the *only* reason I wanted to have lunch with you.' He spread his arms wide. 'And I couldn't have picked a better setting. Close to the hospital, pretty trees and shrubs, no people. I should thank Reggie for leading us here, although I'm not sorry she had to leave.'

'It was her plan to leave all along.'

Now it was Richard's turn to frown at her. 'What do you mean?'

Bergan swallowed her mouthful and took a sip of her

water. 'Reggie's a born matchmaker. She can't help it. Spreading sunshine to everyone she meets is her mission in life.'

This news also helped Richard to realise why Bergan had been so touchy when Reggie had first left. She would have known that Reggie had dragged them outside simply so the two of them could be alone to talk more freely, and, as he'd already deduced, Bergan didn't seem the type of woman to willingly open herself up to anyone. He nodded, processing these thoughts. 'Is that so? Then I have even more to thank her for.'

'I don't get it.' Bergan ate her last mouthful, frowning at him in confusion. 'I thought you only agreed to come out here so you could spend time with Reggie.'

'No. Not Reggie. You.'

'Me?'

'From the first moment I saw you at the Moon Lantern festival, I've been wanting to ask you out. On a date,' he clarified.

His words so surprised Bergan that she swallowed the wrong way and started to choke. Richard was up from the bench and around to her side of the table like a shot, patting her on the back to ensure nothing was lodged in her windpipe.

Bergan took a sip of water then turned to face him, not too happy when he lowered himself onto the bench seat beside her. 'Sorry, you want to do…what now?'

'Ask you out on a date. Dinner? Tomorrow night?'

Bergan stared at him, unsure what to do or say. Tingles flooded her body and a surprising warmth washed over her. Richard *liked* her? The answer should be instant and of the negative variety, but instead she sat there, actually contemplating what it would be like to go on a date with Richard. He was certainly very handsome so she could well understand the appeal there. He was highly intelligent and that also appealed to her. It wasn't as though she didn't know anything about his past because, thanks to his parents, she did.

'Please say yes,' he whispered, and to her astonishment she found really wanted to.

CHAPTER THREE

BERGAN REACHED FOR her water and took another sip, gently edging back as she needed a bit of distance from his persuasive presence.

'Um...' She swallowed, coughed once, then forced herself to meet his eyes. She'd been turning men down when they asked her on dates for quite some time and her friends had often joked that she was an expert at freezing people with just one look, but for some reason none of that seemed to matter as she looked into Richard's perfectly blue eyes.

They were eyes that reflected his emotions and even though now they looked eager and earnest, she couldn't wipe the memory of earlier when she'd noticed something akin to pain and sadness there. It was clear there was more to Richard than she'd seen so far, but what would happen if she said yes to his question?

He was only here for one month...but perhaps that was a good thing. There was no way she'd ever get attached to any man within such a short space of time. She was the type of woman who liked to take things slowly...*very* slowly...and the average male was far too impatient to spend the time pandering to her whims. Of course, there was a logical reason why she was the way she was, but ordinarily most men couldn't be bothered to take the time to find out what it was.

As Richard's time was clearly limited, surely that meant she could go out with him a few times—just as friends—and then wave him goodbye when it was time for him to return to Paris?

Bergan sighed slowly, continuing to look into his handsome face, knowing she could probably spend the rest of the day sitting here, staring at him. He really was a very attractive man, even though he'd teased her. He'd more than made up for it during the emergency and it was clear that intellectually they were on the same wavelength.

She wanted to go. She wanted to say yes to his question, but as a smidgen of logical thought returned, she remembered she was always busy on Tuesday evenings.

'I…' She licked her lips and gently shook her head. 'I can't.'

'Because you won't date colleagues?'

'There is that.'

'Then think of us as neighbours.'

Bergan couldn't help but smile. 'I don't date neighbours either.'

'Then who do you date?' Richard sat back and spread his arms wide.

'I don't.' Bergan shifted uncomfortably on the seat and capped her water bottle, knowing she should put an end to this type of conversation as it couldn't lead anywhere. 'At least, not in the way that normal people date. Usually, I go out with someone Reggie has set me up with—mainly to stop her nagging me—because she keeps telling me I'm going to grow old by myself and she can't even bear to think about me being alone.'

'So I need to go through Reggie to get you to agree?'

She didn't answer him and stood instead. 'We'd better get back.'

Richard was by her side so fast she barely had time to register he'd moved. He placed a hand on her upper arm and carefully turned her to face him. 'Have you been hurt in the past? Because I've been hurt, too.'

'So you think we should console each other?'

Richard shrugged one shoulder and gave her that cute half smile of his, the one that seemed to always churn the newly acquired butterflies in her stomach. What was it about him that she was having such a difficult time resisting?

'That's one idea to run with.' He paused then shook his head. 'Would it help if I said I don't really know anyone here? That although we might call it a "date", it would really be more like two acquaintances hanging out and getting to know each other a bit better. A friendship date. We don't even have to go out to a restaurant or anything like that. Pizza? My place?'

Bergan smiled, for some reason pleased with his charming insistence. *Friendship date?* He really did want to spend time with her...but why? She decided it was best to tread carefully. 'I don't eat pizza.'

'Chinese take-out? Or a lovely curry?'

She tipped her head to the side, her long auburn plait falling down her back. 'I already have plans tomorrow night and the next night and the one after that.'

Richard dropped his hand and shoved it into the pocket of his trousers. 'Are you just saying that to let me down gently or are you serious?'

'Deadly serious.' She turned and started walking back towards the hospital building, binning her rubbish as she went.

'Busy every night.' His tone was thoughtful as

though she'd just given him a puzzle he needed to unravel. 'You're either here, working late, finishing up
paperwork, or...' He watched her for a moment and
Bergan couldn't help but look at him in expectation to
see what other reasons he might pull from thin air to
guess how she spent her evenings. He snapped his fingers. 'Or you're at the drop-in centre.'

Bergan stopped walking in stunned disbelief. 'How
do you know—?'

'About the drop-in centre? I *was* at the Moon Lantern festival, remember?'

'Of course.' She closed her eyes for a moment, unable to believe he had figured things out, before she
continued walking.

'It isn't common knowledge?'

'It's not a great secret, but neither do I advertise my
involvement.'

'So tomorrow night you'll be at the drop-in centre?'

'Yes.'

'Mind if I tag along?'

That surprised her. 'Do you really want to?'

'I have experience with homeless and troubled teens.
Believe it or not, they have them in Paris, too. A couple
of us help out providing "no-questions-asked" medical
support at a few of the youth centres.'

Bergan looked at him, trying to see whether he was
just saying these things in order to impress her, but
there was sincerity and truth in his face and manner-
isms. 'You can come if you want to. The centre is always looking for volunteers and especially ones who
are trained.' They headed into the hospital and walked
towards A and E.

'OK. Sounds like a plan. What time?'

'I usually get there around eight o'clock.'

'Great. Why don't I get take-out, we can eat and then head in together? It seems silly to take two cars when we're going and returning to the same place. Save petrol and the environment.'

Bergan couldn't help but smile as she glanced at him. 'Sneaky. Don't think I'm unaware of your fake nonchalance, Dr Allington.'

Richard chuckled as she swiped her security card across the sensor, allowing them access to the A and E department. 'Am I that transparent?' His eyes were twinkling with merriment, but he watched as the smile slowly slid from her face.

'I hope you are.'

'Because you don't take kindly to deception.'

'Not at all.'

'Good to know where I stand, Dr Moncrief. Honesty is the only way to proceed.' Then he touched his fingers to his forehead in a salute before turning on his heel, collecting the manila folder with his paperwork from the nurses' station and heading off towards the corridor that led to Personnel.

Bergan watched him go, taking in his long legs, his firm, straight back and very broad shoulders. She stood there until he disappeared from view, not only because she was completely confused by the way she'd reacted to the man but also because, with the way he'd given her that cheeky grin and corny salute, she was fairly sure she was unable to move her legs.

Tomorrow night she had a date...a date with Richard.

'Have you met Bergan and Mackenzie yet?' Richard's mother, Helen, asked him over the phone.

'Yes. In fact, I'm having dinner with Bergan tonight and then we're heading to the drop-in centre.'

There was silence on the other end of the line, and although he was used to the delay that still sometimes happened on international calls, he knew he'd no doubt just shocked his mother.

'Dinner? As in a date? With Bergan?'

'Don't make a big deal out of it, Mum. Besides, it's more like a friendship date. You know I don't know many people here.'

'Friendship date?' Helen sounded as though she didn't believe him. 'Are you forgetting who you're talking to? I'm your mother, Richard. You can't pull the wool over my eyes, even if we are half a world away. I know your tone of voice, my darling.'

Richard closed his eyes, belatedly wishing he hadn't said anything. 'Bergan's nice, even though she does seem…I don't know, to be wound a little tight.'

'She has every right to be, given what she's been through. Look, Richard, I'm not saying don't spend time with her, just…be careful.'

'For her? Or me?' He opened his eyes and walked to the bedroom, crouching down to look under the bed for his shoes. He'd already ordered their dinner but still needed to drive to the restaurant to pick it up.

'Both, but of course I'm worried about you, darling. I'm your mother. I know how difficult it was for you after Chantelle's death, how it was difficult for you to engage with your colleagues on a social level. I know it's the reason why you accepted the fellowship, not only to travel but to force yourself out of that hole you found yourself in.'

'Don't pull any punches, Mum,' he murmured as he sat on the bed and shook his head. 'I have dated since Chantelle's death.'

'Once or twice in how many years?' Helen asked rhetorically.

'I thought you'd be happy,' Richard countered, thinking of the way he'd been captivated by Bergan from the first moment he'd laid eyes on her. He had no idea what it was about the woman that seemed to intrigue him so much, but not even bothering to find out wasn't an option. It was why he'd been a little insistent with her, wanting to discover just why she'd caught his attention.

'I am, darling. Of course I am, but…Bergan…well, just be careful.'

Richard looked at the clock then groaned. 'I've got to go, Mum. I don't want to be late.' After saying their goodbyes, he rang off, tossing his phone onto the bed before pulling on his shoes. He hadn't expected reticence from his mother and it made him wonder what was in Bergan's past that had made his mother hesitate.

'No time like the present for finding out,' he said out loud as he grabbed his phone and walked through the house, picking up his keys and heading to the door. He was taking steps forward. They might be little steps at first, but forward he was moving.

Bergan couldn't believe how flustered she was as she went through yet another change of clothes, checking her reflection in the mirror, worrying that she might be too overdressed or too underdressed.

'Argh!' She stared at her reflection, looking at the casual skirt that came to just above her knees, a plain top and an old cardigan. 'This is stupid.' She turned and stalked to her dresser, picked up her phone and pressed a pre-set number. 'This is stupid,' she said a moment later when Mackenzie answered the call.

'What's stupid?'

'Me. Richard's going to be here in five minutes with dinner and I've changed my outfit seven times.'

Mackenzie couldn't help but chuckle. 'Calm down. You're only having an informal dinner, it's not as though you're out at a five-star restaurant.'

'It would be better if we were because then at least I'd know what to wear. I don't know whether to wear one thing for dinner and then change before we head to the drop-in centre or whether that's too…girly.' Bergan pulled the cardigan off as she spoke. 'You know me. I'm *not* girly. We used to make fun of girls who used to fuss over themselves before dates,' Bergan growled. 'I never thought I'd turn into one of them.'

'You haven't. I'd love to come and help, but Ruthie's in the bath and John's not home from the hospital yet, so instead let me ask you one question.'

'OK.'

'What do you usually wear to the drop-in centre?'

'Jeans, flats, T-shirt, light jacket if it's a coolish evening.'

'So wear that.'

'If I knew what Richard was bringing for dinner, I'd at least be able to gauge the outfit a bit—'

'What does that matter?' Mackenzie interrupted.

'Because he's lived in Paris for so long. When we were travelling after finishing medical school, you didn't spend much time in Paris, but I did, Kenz. I spent three months living there and, believe me, to the French, clothes are an art, along with cuisine. There were certain rules around even the most casual of dinner dates.'

'Ahh…so that's what has you so flustered, the fact that this is a *date*. Now it all makes sense.'

'It's not a date date. It's a friendship date.'

'What's that supposed to mean?'

'I don't know!'

Bergan shook her head and slumped down onto her bed, lying across the large pile of discarded clothes and not caring. 'I haven't been on any sort of date in a very long time, Kenz. You know why.'

'I do, and I think you're incredibly brave, Bergan. In accepting this as a *date*, you're refusing to tar all men with the same brush and that's a big step forward.'

Bergan closed her eyes. 'Even though it was so long ago, it still—'

'I know. You've come so far and you're so brave and you do amazing work at the drop-in centre because you know exactly where those kids are coming from. Focus on that, and the fact that Richard wants to help.'

'He did seem keen.'

'All you're doing is putting food into your stomachs before you go out to help others.'

Bergan opened her eyes and sat up, nodding. 'You're right.'

'Of course I am.'

'What am I fussing about?'

'I have no idea.'

'It's a date…between friends.'

'No reason to stress,' Mackenzie agreed.

'Then why can I hear that smile in your words?' Bergan shook her head. 'You're loving this, aren't you?'

'All I can say is—it happens to the best of us.'

'What does that mea—?' The doorbell downstairs sounded and Bergan jumped up from the bed. 'He's here. *He's here!*'

'Then go.'

'Yes. Good. OK. Love you. 'Bye.' Bergan disconnected the call and quickly reached for her usual jeans and T-shirt combo, pulling them on in a hurried rush, before shoving her feet into a pair of black flats. She glanced once at her reflection, realising her loose hair was a tangled mess, and quickly pulled her fingers through the auburn locks as she raced down the stairs.

'Ow,' she said a moment before opening the front door.

'Are you all right?' Richard asked as he stepped into the house, two brown paper bags filled with containers in his arms. Bergan closed the door behind him.

'Just knots in my hair,' she offered by way of explanation. 'A common problem. Come on through. Something smells good.'

Richard found he was having trouble moving as he stared at the glorious sight of the woman before him. Dressed casually and yet comfortably, she looked so different from the professional woman he'd worked alongside for the past two days, but he had to admit it was her long, glorious auburn locks that had made his mouth go dry and his brain refuse to function.

Now that it was loose, it was far longer than he'd realised, reaching almost to her waist, the colour vibrant and shiny. He wanted nothing more than to reach out his hand and run his fingers through the silky locks, letting them sift through his hand with a tingling delight.

'Richard?'

He forced himself to blink, to move, to do something as he belatedly realised he was just standing there, holding bags of food and staring at her.

'Sorry.' He followed her towards the dining room, where she'd set a basic table. As she walked, he noted the way her hair swished from side to side, a variety of colours—golds, reds and oranges—picked up by the overhead ceiling lights. 'Wow.' The whispered word was ripped from him before he could stop it.

'What?' She looked at the dining table then back at him, her eyes widening as she realised he was staring at *her*.

Richard shook his head. He was behaving like an adolescent schoolboy. He quickly placed the bags of food on the table and crossed his arms over his chest. 'You look…amazing.'

Bergan looked down at the plain and simple clothes she was wearing. 'Really?'

'Uh…' He pointed at her, indicating her hair, feeling more and more like a stunned idiot with each passing second. 'I haven't seen your hair loose before.' Richard cleared his throat. 'It's… Wow.'

'Oh.' She instantly ran her fingers through the tresses, finding a few more knots, but unable to believe how his words had warmed her heart. What a nice thing to say. 'Well, thank you for the compliment.' Feeling self-conscious, she began fussing around with the bags of food, pulling containers out and setting them on the wooden table. 'Asian. Excellent. Do you want to eat with chopsticks?' She turned and began rummaging in a drawer in the sideboard.

'I think there are some disposable ones in the bag,' Richard said, after clearing his throat and giving his brain a bit of a jump-start.

'OK.' Feeling more and more like a deer caught in the headlights of an oncoming car, Bergan tried to think of what else she could do to keep her hands busy and her thoughts off the way Richard was making her feel. She closed the drawer and linked her hands together, hoping that by holding them it would stop them from trembling. 'What would you like to drink? I'm sorry, I don't have any wine. I probably should have thought to buy some for you as actually I don't drink alcohol.'

'At all?' He seemed surprised by that.

'No.'

'There's a reason behind that.'

'Of course there is,' she said, heading into the kitchen to collect a bottle of mineral water from the fridge. Once there, she closed her eyes and took three long and steadying breaths. It was imperative that she stopped behaving like an adolescent and started behaving like the intelligent woman she was. They were just eating food before going to the drop-in centre. That was all.

Feeling calmer, she returned with the bottle of drink and decided to lighten the mood presently surrounding them.

'*Monsieur?*' she asked, holding the bottle out to him as though she were a waiter asking the customer to check the vintage on a nice bottle of red.

'*Oui, mademoiselle. Très bien, merci.*'

With a smile she came round the table, opened the bottle and poured some into the glasses on the table. 'Even if I did drink, I would never drink any alcohol before heading to the drop-in centre. A lot of the kids who come there are battling addictions to alcohol, as well as other substances, and it's hardly fair for them to smell liquor on my breath while I'm talking to them.'

'Fair point.' He picked up his glass and held it out to her. 'A toast?'

Bergan acquiesced and picked up her own glass, waiting for him to speak.

'To being back on home soil—even if it is for a short time—and to making new friends.'

'New friends,' she repeated, and couldn't help but smile as she chinked her glass with his before both of them took a sip.

'Let's eat,' he said, and after sitting down they

opened up the different containers, spooning the delicious food out onto their plates.

'How was your first lecture today? I'm sorry I wasn't able to make it, but I had a meeting with the hospital's CEO and I'd already changed it twice.'

Richard shrugged one shoulder. 'It went OK, I think.'

'Modest, eh? I heard there were people standing around the walls at the back of the lecture hall because there were no seats free.'

'I think everyone's more interested in checking out the new guy rather than what I have to say.'

'There's that modesty again. Do you enjoy lecturing?'

'I do, especially when what I'm relaying is new and exciting information on different techniques or advances in treatment plans.'

'It must be a little discombobulating—travelling all year long, fighting jet lag...' She smiled pointedly at him. 'Not to mention the language difficulties you must have faced.'

'You mean giving instructions in French?' He chuckled. 'Usually, I'm assigned a medical interpreter so that does make things much easier.' He swallowed his mouthful and took a sip of his drink before leaning his elbows on the table. 'OK. My turn to ask a question. Why don't you drink alcohol?'

Bergan had just put some food into her mouth when he asked the question and she simply stared at him as she slowly withdrew the chopsticks from her lips. She chewed slowly, as though considering his question, but she was really wondering just what she felt comfortable telling him. The truth? How would he handle that?

She finally swallowed her mouthful and took a sip from her glass. 'Guess,' she said, as she placed her chopsticks on the side of her plate and crossed her arms over her chest.

'A challenge. OK.' Richard nodded, pleased she hadn't shut him out. He quickly thought back over things she'd said since they'd met, pondering the way she'd been able to connect with Drak at the Moon Lantern festival and how she'd mentioned it wasn't fair for teens to smell alcohol on someone else's breath when they were battling an addiction.

'Teenage drunk?'

'Got it in one. I was a bad one, too.' She looked away from him and toyed with her chopsticks for a moment. Richard remained silent, watching the internal struggle taking place. Would she open up to him? Be honest with him? He'd told her the other day that he believed honesty to be the best policy, but whether or not she'd believed him was another matter. Now he hoped she did, hoped she'd take a chance and continue with what she'd been about to say.

Bergan consciously made herself stop fiddling with the chopsticks and calmly placed her hands in her lap and when she lifted her head, bravely meeting his gaze, her voice was clear and matter-of-fact.

'Three days after I turned fourteen I drank myself unconscious. I'd swiped a bottle of Scotch from my foster-father's liquor cabinet and had a party for one.'

Richard made a point of trying not to change his facial expression at this news. He'd seen first-hand, in many different A and E departments around the world, just how dangerous it could be for young teenagers to have that amount of alcohol in their systems. He listened intently as she continued.

'I drank myself unconscious.' She repeated the words slowly, a sad look in her eyes. 'I must have regained consciousness at some point and left the house. It's little wonder I didn't get hit by a passing car, but in the morning I woke up in some strange boy's bed, without a clue how I'd got there or what had happened.'

Richard swallowed, a bad feeling settling in the pit of his stomach. 'And the foster-father?'

Bergan pulled her loose hair back from her face, holding it suspended in her hands for a moment before allowing the glorious tresses to fall back into place. 'He gave me the beating I deserved for stealing his booze.'

Richard looked away from her then and shook his head. Not at what had happened to her in the past, but that her life had been that miserable that she'd ended up in such a dark place, at such a young and vulnerable age. What else had happened to her? Especially in such an environment? He could hazard a good guess and it wasn't at all pretty. It also explained why she had a problem with dating and trusting men.

'I have a lot of baggage, Richard.' Again her words were matter-of-fact, as though she was trying to be strong and completely detached from her past. Why had he shaken his head? Had she completely turned him off? Wasn't that a good thing? She hadn't really wanted his interest in the first place so now that he knew the truth, he'd no doubt see the rest of the evening through and then their relationship could go back to being nice and professional.

'So I'm beginning to realise.'

Bergan clenched her jaw to stop the sudden pang of pain at his words. To think about scaring him off was one thing, but to actually hear him admit it was gut-wrenching. She knew it was better he left her life sooner rather than later, but deep down, in that small part of her that was still a scared little girl, she had hoped Richard might prove different from the other men she'd known, that he might be the man to help rescue her from the insecurities she'd buried so very deep.

She looked away from him, focusing on her glass, reaching out her hand to touch the inanimate object, focusing on its coolness rather than the fact that Richard might just get up and walk from the room without another word.

Richard put his own chopsticks down and leaned one elbow on the table, resting his chin on his hand as he looked at her. After his mother's words earlier he hadn't been at all sure what he might uncover about Bergan, but now all he could do was gaze at her with awe and admiration. He'd always liked to surround himself with people who were strong, who were able to overcome adversity.

Not only had Bergan managed that, but given her work at the drop-in centre, she was also willing to share her experiences, her thoughts and her emotions with teens who might find themselves in a similar position as she'd once been. That took a hefty amount of inner strength and a tonne of courage.

'And look at you now,' he continued, his rich tones washing over her. She raised her surprised gaze to his.

'What?'

'You're a successful doctor in a busy A and E department, but also spend a lot of your spare time reaching out to help kids who are in similar circumstances.' Richard leaned across the table and took her hand in his, holding it firmly as he continued to look her directly in the eyes, his blue gaze melding with her honey-brown one. 'You are quite an amazing woman, Bergan Moncrief, and I for one relish the challenge of getting to know you better. *Much* better.'

CHAPTER FOUR

BERGAN WASN'T SURE exactly how she managed to keep control of the rioting emotions zipping through her body as she sat near Richard, staring into his hypnotic blue eyes. Where she'd thought he'd high-tail it out of her house as fast as possible, he'd completely surprised her by doing the opposite!

He was so different from every other man she'd met, and where, over the years, she'd thought that no man could ever surprise her again, Richard Allington was proving her wrong. Although she'd only known him a few days, he was definitely intriguing her, making her want to know more about him. The fact that she also found him incredibly handsome was both good and bad.

The way he looked at her, smiled at her, winked at her had the ability to set her body on fire. The fact that he could *do* that so easily brought with it a mountain of confusion and indecision. Should she even risk thinking about the possibility of something other than friendship existing between them in the future? Was that what he wanted or was she just someone to play with, a distraction to fill the hours when he wasn't at the hospital? Had he found a different woman in every country he'd visited?

There were just too many questions, too many unknowns, but even if she pushed them all aside, there was still one question she couldn't figure out—where had her self-control gone? She needed to figure out what it was about Richard that was wreaking such havoc inside her, and to do that she needed to be close to him, to spend time with him.

An experiment, a research project. That's what she needed to make it. She would treat this unwanted attraction towards him with all the same drive and attention she'd given to her medical research projects over the years. Doing research and conducting studies would help her to gain control over her senses and after that she'd be able to treat Richard like any other man of her acquaintance—with indifference.

She knew he would have plenty of flaws. All men did, and the sooner she discovered them, the sooner she could put him out of her mind and get on with her life. Four weeks. He was only here for four weeks and then he would disappear back to where he'd come from. It also meant, if she was determined to get to the bottom of this internal dilemma, that she would need to consciously spend more time with him…all in the name of research, of course.

Therefore, with clarity and logic starting to return, Bergan was able to finish her dinner, finding it was easier to gloss over what he'd said—that he was interested in getting to know her *much* better—and keep up a steady stream of conversation, mainly about the hospital and the drop-in centre. Thankfully, Richard had allowed her to chatter away, releasing her hand from his, leaving it tingling from his smooth, warm touch.

They'd been able to finish their meal and then get ready to head into the drop-in centre, but the moment they entered her car, Bergan once again became incredibly conscious of his closeness as he sat beside her in the passenger seat. *Keep it light, Bergan. It's just an experiment. Nothing more.*

Richard smoothed his hand over the soft leather seats and smiled. 'I had a car just like this, but in black.'

'When?'

'Before I left Paris.'

'You had a car in Paris? I didn't think that was the done thing. Everyone does a lot of walking in Paris, mainly because to drive in the traffic is bedlam.'

'So you *have* been there?'

'To Paris? *Oui, monsieur,*' she teased.

'I thought so. Generally, people can learn to speak French from a tutor, but to really speak French—proper French,' he added, 'it's best to stay in Paris for a while.'

Bergan drove along the darkened streets of Maroochydore, changing down gears as she neared a red light. When she'd stopped, she glanced over at him. 'Agreed.'

Richard's smile was small. 'So you stayed in Paris for a while? Worked there?'

'Oui, monsieur,' she repeated, a small smile playing on her lips, her tone deep, personal, intimate. He swallowed once, not missing the dip of her gaze as she took in the action, watching as his Adam's apple slid up and down his throat.

'I knew it. I knew you'd understood every word I'd said yesterday.'

Her smile increased and Richard once more felt as though she had just delivered a whammy of a punch directly to his solar plexus. She was incredibly alluring and he'd liked hearing her voice dip that extra half octave, as though she was speaking intimately to him, taking him into her confidence. It certainly didn't help that they were in such close proximity in the car. Her fresh, floral scent was enough to drive him to distraction and the fact that it was winding its way about him didn't help one bit.

Keep a clear head? When Bergan was around? It was what he'd promised himself he would do, but now, sitting here, so close to her, he realised it was virtually impossible.

Richard couldn't believe the colour of her eyes. It was different, unique…it was Bergan. The colour of warm, rich honey and combined with her smile, her gorgeous pert little nose, her high cheekbones and smooth neck, it was clear why she'd been a regular feature of his dreams ever since he'd first seen her at the Moon Lantern festival.

And her hair… How his hands had itched to touch it, to run his fingers through the long, free, auburn locks. He'd watched, after they'd finished dinner, as she'd quickly and expertly plaited her hair and for some reason he'd been surprised at how intimate it had felt. It was as though he'd seen her put on a mask, keeping others at arm's length as she'd tossed the long plait carelessly down her back and straightened her shoulders. She'd put on her armour and was ready for action…and she'd allowed him to see it.

Now, as she sat next to him in the car, smiling that cute little smile of hers, he wondered what she'd do if he leaned over and brushed a sweet yet tantalising kiss across her lips.

He was a little surprised at the speed of his thoughts. Yes, he'd managed to go out on the occasional date over the past five years, but he certainly hadn't been captivated by any other woman as completely as he was with Bergan. Was that a good sign? To be moving this fast? It wasn't his usual style. Even with Chantelle things had progressed very slowly, but for some reason he simply couldn't stop thinking about Bergan and right now he couldn't stop thinking about kissing her.

Bergan's eyes widened a little and the smile started to slip from her lips as she stared into Richard's eyes. Was he thinking of kissing her? The question made her heart beat faster. What would she do if he did? Would she let him? Would she slap him across the face? She didn't know and not knowing was the worst.

Beep! The sound of a car horn behind them, alerting Bergan to the fact that the traffic lights had changed colour, made them both snap out of whatever sensations had been pulsing between them and focus on getting to the drop-in centre without further incident.

As she drove, Richard tried to figure out exactly what it was about her that seemed to captivate him so much. He certainly wasn't the type of man to fall in and out of love easily—quite the contrary, especially as it was only five years since Chantelle had passed away. She'd told him to find someone else, that she would be sad to think of him spending the rest of his life living alone, mourning her. She had always been so bright, so cheerful, even during the last days when she'd been terribly weak from pain.

'Here we are,' said Bergan, turning into a driveway and parking next to a building that had certainly seen better days. It was clear people had been doing their best to spruce things up, with a large and colourful mural painted around the building.

'Who did the painting?' he asked as they climbed from the car. The wall was covered with a scene that showed people from diverse nationalities, of all ages and socio-economic situations living together in harmony.

'The kids did it, under the guidance of a seventeen-year-old boy called Drak. He's incredibly gifted when it comes to art.'

'Didn't he do the lantern for the festival?' Richard asked as they headed towards the front door.

'He did.' Bergan looked at him with a hint of surprise. 'How did you know that?'

Richard sheepishly shrugged one shoulder and shoved his hands into his pockets. 'Uh…I sort of eavesdropped on your conversation with him at the festival. You wanted him to be proud of his lantern, to carry it with pride, and he didn't want to.'

Bergan nodded her head. 'He was a little vocal that night, but it wasn't because he was trying to be difficult. He's really quite a sensitive soul, but most of the time all people see are the piercings and tattoos.'

'Never judge a book by its cover.'

'An old cliché, but an apt one in this instance.' Bergan opened the heavy front door and Richard instantly helped her. 'Thanks. Come and I'll introduce you to the director, Stuart. He's amazing with the kids.'

She led the way to where a young man, dressed in dark jeans and dark T-shirt, a piercing or two in his ears and a 'sleeve' of tattoos on one arm, was leaning against a heavy wooden table, chatting with about five teens, discussing a new project the centre was trying to get up and running. If Bergan hadn't told Richard that Stuart was the director, he would have easily mistaken the guy for one of the teens who 'dropped in' here.

'They're all good ideas for how we can practically help the nursing home up the road.' Stuart glanced up and saw them walking towards him. 'And here's Bergan…and she's brought a friend with her.' Stuart instantly held out his hand to Richard as Bergan introduced them. Richard was conscious of the teenagers watching the adults interact and he received the distinct impression that all of them were putting up their barriers, no doubt an inbuilt habit when they met someone new.

'We're discussing the clean-up project at the nursing home,' Stuart explained to Richard. 'Trying to break down some stereotypes. Kids who dress in dark clothes, have a bit of ink and the odd piercing aren't necessarily bad or scary people. They're usually as lonely as half the residents of the nursing home.'

Stuart gestured to a few of the teens gathered around. 'Xenia suggested painting a mural at the front entrance as there's been quite a bit of graffiti on the nursing-home sign in the last month or two.'

'It wasn't us,' Xenia added hotly, draping her arm around the neck of the boy next to her and giving Richard a dirty look.

Richard nodded. 'Understood.'

'Aaron suggested helping with the gardening because, as you know, many of the able-bodied residents are keen gardeners, but aren't actually able to bend down or reach up high or even do too much manual labour, and this way they can also pass on their knowledge of gardening to the younger generation,' Stuart continued.

Aaron, a kid who was as skinny as a beanpole, had no ink or piercings and was dressed from head to toe in brown, nodded enthusiastically, his glasses, which were held together with a piece of sticky tape, almost falling off his nose. 'Old people like to talk and, well... Bergan's always saying we should listen more so...you know.' He shrugged.

A lot of the other kids agreed with Aaron and Richard was pleased to see that in here the breaking down of stereotypes had already begun.

'They're really good ideas,' Bergan agreed, nodding encouragingly at the gathered teens. She looked at Richard. 'What do you think? Any suggestions to add?'

Richard raised an eyebrow at the question then looked around at the group gathered before him. They really did look like a motley crew, but he knew from his work with teens of a similar age and circumstances that beneath all the ink and piercings they were just kids who were making the best of the bad hand they'd been dealt. The fact that they actually came *in* to the drop-in centre and were talking about actively participating in the community was huge.

'I think,' he said after a pause, 'these are excellent suggestions, and as the new guy I'll defer to the group. Although, whatever the final decision, I'd like to help.'

Before anyone else could say anything, a kid came bursting through the doors of the centre, his face red from running, an urgent and wild look in his eyes. Richard recognised him as the teen Bergan had been speaking to at the Moon Lantern festival—Drak. He was clearly out of breath and as he tried to speak, panting and puffing, Richard started to get a bad feeling in his gut.

'Jammo. Passed out. Bergan.' Drak gestured for her to come. 'Medical bag. Overdosed.'

'Not again.' Bergan was rushing towards a cupboard in Stuart's office. She quickly pulled out a set of keys from her pocket and unlocked the doors, taking out a portable medical kit that looked more like a toolbox and then quickly locking the cupboard again. 'This is the second time Jammo's tried something like this,' she muttered, clearly concerned.

'Whatever you ne—' he started to say, but she interrupted him.

'Come with me. Stuart, call the—'

'On it,' Stuart said.

Bergan nodded. 'Good. I'll call you when we have a location. Drak, lead the way.' The three of them raced out of the drop-in centre, running down the footpath, Bergan and Richard following behind Drak, who was sprinting ahead. He continued down the street, the three of them oblivious to their surroundings, the evening traffic starting to pick up in numbers. Car horns honked, engines revved and music blared from stereo speakers.

Bergan was only conscious of following Drak's lead, sensing rather than seeing that Richard was still beside her, his strides slightly longer, which meant he was keeping pace with her, ensuring she wasn't left behind. He also reached down while they were running and took the medical kit from her hand.

'I've got it,' he said, barely seeming out of breath.

'Thanks,' she answered as she noted that Drak had turned the corner. They followed him into an older-style, multi-storey apartment block, one that had certainly seen better days, with a few of the windows boarded up thanks to a few smashed windows here and there.

'She's in here,' Drak panted, as he began taking the stairs two at a time. 'She's in Smitty's old place,' he continued, his eyes still reflecting his fear for the worst.

As Bergan rounded a landing on the stairs, she caught Richard's glance and saw that he looked in control and reflective, as though he was trying to go through a thousand different scenarios, wondering exactly what they might find when they finally reached

Jammo. Bergan knew because she was doing exactly the same thing. She quickly pulled out her cell phone and passed the location information on to Stuart, who informed her the ambulance was on its way.

'Drak,' she called, as he started up another flight of stairs.

'Not much further,' he stated, but kept going.

'Do you know what Jammo took? Was it pills? An injection? Any clues?' Bergan held on to the handrail to ensure she didn't miss her footing on the steps, grateful Richard had thoughtfully taken charge of lugging the medical kit.

'There were pills next to her. I…I was going to bring the bottle with me, but I was just so scared that I forgot and ran to get you,' he panted, still going up the staircase. Thankfully, when they came to the next landing, Drak flung open the door and headed into the corridor.

Within another half a minute they were inside Smitty's old apartment, where Jammo was lying on the floor on an old mattress, seemingly lifeless. The young girl of sixteen wasn't moving, although, as they'd rushed into the room, Bergan thought she'd detected the slight rise and fall of the girl's chest.

Richard instantly dropped to his knees, opened the medical kit and pulled out two pairs of gloves, handing one pair to Bergan. She pulled them on and reached for the bottle Drak was holding out to her. Richard called to Jammo but the girl didn't respond. They shifted her onto her side in case she vomited. They didn't want her to choke. He reached for the penlight and checked her pupils.

'Sluggish but reacting to light.'

'Pulse is slow and weak.'

'What did she take?' Richard asked as he reached for the stethoscope.

'Temazepam. I don't know how many, but the bottle is empty.' As Bergan and Richard continued to treat Jammo, Richard motioned to the girl's wrists, which were both bandaged.

'How long ago did she do that?'

'Two weeks. She ran away from the hospital the day after she was admitted. I managed to check on her a few times and she seemed to be doing OK. Jammo? Can you hear me?' Bergan called, raising her voice. 'Come on. Come round.'

'Cardio is weak. She needs oxygen.'

'She's going to be OK, isn't she?' Drak asked, and Bergan glanced up at the small thread of fear in the words. It wasn't like Drak to show such an intimate emotion and Bergan couldn't help but wonder if there wasn't a deeper connection than she'd thought between the two teens.

'I don't know,' she answered him truthfully. 'You did well to come and get us, but her body's already weak from losing a lot of blood the other week.'

'She's depressed,' Drak offered, by way of explanation.

'I'm not interested in the whys and wherefores at the moment, Drak,' Bergan reassured him calmly, as she took the stethoscope from Richard and listened to Jammo's heartbeat for herself.

'Skin is cold and clammy, lips are blue, fingernails are pale.'

'Prep for possible cardiac arrest,' Bergan said, and he nodded, looking into the medical kit for whatever he might need in case Jammo's heart stopped. 'Drak, why don't you go down and meet the ambulance? Let them know I'm here and get them to bring oxygen on their first trip up those stairs.'

'I don't want to leave her,' Drak said, which only confirmed Bergan's suspicions.

'You can help Jammo by getting those paramedics up here with the oxygen, ASAP. Here…' Bergan held out her cell phone to Drak. 'Take this with you. Richard's number is programmed in, so call him if you need to speak to either one of us.'

Drak hesitated for a moment.

'I promise to take good care of her,' Bergan told him, earnest sincerity in her tone. 'Didn't I take good care of her last time?'

'Yes.'

'Then trust me, Drak. You know you can.' She waved the phone in his direction and after hesitating for a moment longer he took the device from her and headed out of the room. 'Jammo?' Bergan called. 'Can you hear me? Come on. Come round. Do it for Drak.'

'Repeat obs,' Richard stated, and she agreed. Until they had Jammo back at the hospital, where they could at least perform a gastric lavage, all they could do was monitor her and try to make sure she didn't go into cardiac arrest.

No sooner had they started the next set of obs than Bergan shook her head. 'She's slipping.'

Richard listened to Jammo's heartbeat. 'Agreed.'

Bergan pressed her fingers to Jammo's pulse. 'It's stopped,' she said, and Richard nodded in agreement.

Together, they rolled Jammo onto her back before Richard placed a special expired air resuscitation mouth shield over Jammo's mouth and nose. Bergan readied herself to perform cardio-pulmonary resuscitation. Working together as a well-oiled team, they counted out the breaths and beats, determined to get the young teenager's heart started again.

While Richard breathed a few more breaths into Jammo's mouth, Bergan checked the girl's pulse. 'It's there. Just.'

He exhaled heavily with relief. 'Good.' He glanced across at Bergan, who was also smiling, pleased with what they'd just managed to do. 'She's by no means out of the woods,' he continued.

'But at least she's breathing.'

'Let's get her into the coma position while we wait for the paramedics to make their way up all those stairs. Why couldn't Smitty live on the ground floor?'

'Smitty doesn't live here anymore.'

'So where did he move to?' Richard asked, as they made sure Jammo was as comfortable as possible, Bergan hooking the stethoscope into her ears in order to check Jammo's heart again.

She listened intently then removed the stethoscope before looking at Richard. 'He died. Overdose in this very room.'

'Poor kid.'

'Smitty wasn't a kid. He was a druggy that a lot of the foster and street kids came to when the foster-parents beat them or didn't feed them, or life just got too tough. They needed a place to crash. Smitty's—this place, for all its filth—was a safe haven for so many kids. He always offered whatever he had—food, drink and a piece of floor for them to crash on.

'He wasn't a dealer or a pimp and when he wasn't as high as a kite he did a lot of good things for a lot of the kids. He'd tell them they were stupid to take drugs, but then he'd go and shoot up, saying it was too late for him.'

There was a sad, melancholy tone to her words and Richard watched her with increasing confusion. Even though he'd only known Bergan for a few days, he knew her well enough to realise she didn't open up to everyone like this. She kept her hands busy, feeling Jammo's pulse, and not once while she was talking did she make eye contact with him.

'Drugs were Smitty's mistress,' she continued after a moment. 'He told me that once and there was a deep sadness and regret in his eyes. As though he wanted, so much, to go back and live his life again, but knew that was impossible.'

'You sound as though you admired him.' Richard kept his tone quiet as he checked Jammo's eyes.

'I did, in a way.'

'How old was he?'

'He would have been fifty-nine next month, if he'd lived.'

'Wow. I hadn't expected him to be *that* old.' Richard found it difficult to keep the surprise from his voice. 'You sound as though you knew him quite well.'

'Yes. Yes, I did.' It was only then that Bergan raised her gaze, slowly, to meld with his. 'Smitty was my father.'

CHAPTER FIVE

DRAK WAS QUICK in bringing the paramedics up to Jammo and when they arrived Richard and Bergan worked with them to insert an intravenous drip into Jammo's foot, as she'd attempted to slash her wrists only weeks ago. With an oxygen mask over her mouth and nose, the teenage girl's observations began to stabilise.

'I'm going with her,' Drak declared protectively.

'Absolutely.' Bergan placed a reassuring hand on his shoulder.

'They can't make me leave her side when we arrive at the hospital, can they?' His eyes were scared, wild, determined. The last thing either Jammo or Drak needed now was a scene in the A and E department.

Bergan shook her head. 'Tell whoever you see at the hospital that you know me and that I say it's fine for you stay with her—as long as you don't interfere with the treatment. Stay in the room, out of the way, and I'll be along shortly.'

'Thanks, Bergan.' Drak, looking paler than she'd ever seen him, surprised her further by pulling her close for a hug. Tears instantly sprang to her eyes and a lump formed in her throat at the action, and although it was over almost before it had begun, she knew in that one moment that Drak had changed from a troubled teenager into a man with direction. Before she could say a word, he climbed into the back of the ambulance and Richard shut the doors, tapping twice to let the driver know he was clear to leave.

Bergan sniffed and swallowed, blinking away any sign of the emotional tears before she looked at Richard. He was standing beside her, the medical kit from the drop-in centre beside him on the footpath. 'Shall we head back?' she asked, indicating the way back towards the centre.

'Good idea.'

There was no hurry now, and as they walked along, Richard carrying the medical kit, Bergan began to feel highly self-conscious at having revealed so much about her past. The sun had set, the stars were starting to twinkle in the sky, the streetlights had come on and a warm breeze floated around them, almost like some sort of cocoon, keeping them separate from the world.

'Interesting, isn't it?' Richard said after a moment.

'What is?' She almost jumped at the sound of his voice and looked across at him, her defences up in case he said anything personal.

'Watching a boy turn into a man.'

'Oh. Drak. Yes. Yes, it is.' She nodded as they walked along. Her arms were crossed over her chest as though she was giving him a silent signal not to venture into personal matters. 'I can't deny that it makes me feel good. I've known him for quite a few years and it most definitely hasn't been smooth sailing.'

Richard chuckled. 'I can well believe it, but tonight… tonight I think the message you've been trying to get through to him, whatever it might have been, has finally hit its mark.'

'He *hugged* me. Voluntarily!' Bergan couldn't keep

the delight from her voice or the smile from her face. 'It's moments like that that make everything I do, everything I try to teach these kids, worth it.' The smile slowly slid from her face and Richard couldn't help but watch her as they walked out of the glow of one of the streetlights and headed into the comfortable darkness. 'I'm just sorry his realisation came out of Jammo's terrible situation.'

'She has a good chance of recovery, and who knows? Perhaps Drak can get through to her.'

'Hope. There always has to be hope.' Bergan walked past the next lamppost, skirting around the outside of the glow it emitted, but Richard paused, staring at her.

'What did you say?'

Bergan stopped walking and turned to face him, dropping her arms back to her sides. 'Why?' Was that astonishment she heard in his tone?

'Just…please? Repeat what you said.'

Confusion marred her brow. 'There always has to be hope?'

He frowned then gave his head a shake. 'Perhaps it was the tone you said it in.' He closed his eyes and exhaled slowly. 'Never mind.' He started to walk again, stepping out of the light.

'You're confusing me. What did I say that was wrong?' Bergan fell into step beside him.

'Nothing. You said nothing wrong. I…knew someone who used to say that all the time. For a second there you sounded *exactly* like her.'

Her? Bergan's curiosity was definitely piqued. Someone from his past? Someone who was important to him? A girlfriend? An ex-lover? She pushed the thoughts from her mind. If Richard wanted her to know, he'd tell her. She'd learned of old that no good ever came from prying and pushing people when they didn't want to open up. Still, it made him far more intriguing.

They walked in silence for a while then Richard said, 'You're not going to ask me anything? Try and find out more about this woman I mentioned?'

Bergan glanced at him. 'Do you want me to?'

Richard passed another streetlight and Bergan could clearly see the smile tugging at his lips. 'Psych one-oh-one, eh? Answering a question with another question?'

Bergan couldn't help but return his smile. 'Well, you either want to talk about her or you don't. If you do, I'll gladly listen. If not, I'll respect your privacy.' She glanced down at the ground before crossing her arms once more over her chest. 'And...I'd like to thank you for respecting my privacy earlier and not trying to get me to open up more about...well...about what I said about my...father.'

'Hippocratic oath.'

'I'm not your patient.'

'OK. How about the friendship oath?'

'Friendship?'

'Is this not a friendship date? Are we not becoming friends?'

'I guess. Especially as I don't usually blurt out my past to just anyone. In fact, only Mackenzie knows the full truth about my upbringing, mainly because she was a part of it.'

'And your other friends?'

'Reggie and Sunainah,' she supplied, then shrugged. 'They know bits, as do your parents, but they're all more than happy to just accept me for who I am today. It's nice. Refreshing. Rare.'

'Those types of people definitely make the best friends.' Both were silent for a moment before Richard said, 'It hasn't been easy, this past year, on the fellow-ship, to make many new friends.'

'Four weeks here, four weeks there. Different coun-tries, different languages, different traditions.' Bergan nodded. 'I can see that.'

'Hence the recent idea of the friendship date. And I have to say I'm really glad you agreed to let me into your world tonight, Bergan.' They weren't far from the drop-in centre and after they passed another streetlight and entered darkness again, Richard stopped, glad when Bergan followed suit.

'I don't have that many close friendships. A lot of men don't,' he said by way of explanation so she didn't think there was anything wrong with him. 'I have col-leagues spread around the world and I'd classify a lot of them as friends, but *real* friends—people I can rely on at any time, any place, anywhere—are few and far between.'

Bergan nodded, her eyes adjusting to the darkness around them so she could see the lines of confusion creasing his brow and hear the hesitation in his words. He shifted the medical kit to his other hand, removing it as a barrier between them.

'I haven't known you long, Bergan, and yet I feel a connection to you. I think it's important you know that.'

'I sort of guessed when you asked me out.'

He smiled. 'Well, I can't deny that I find you attrac-tive, but that's not entirely what I meant.'

His words warmed her through and through. She wished he wouldn't talk like that, so openly, about this strange attraction that seemed to exist between them, because it made her feel all uncertain and soft and femi-nine. She wasn't used to feeling this way and the inten-sity of her feelings was starting to cloud her thoughts.

'I… It's just…from my point of view, it would be far easier for me to deal with if you *only* found me attractive, on a superficial level, I mean, not…' She stopped and sighed, not sure what she was trying to say.

'Not connected on an intellectual and emotional level as well?' he finished for her.

'Exactly.'

'I can't say I understand what this…thing…is between us, Bergan—'

'Me neither.'

'But it's there and that in itself is a surprise and it's rare.'

'Yes.' The word was a whisper and as he continued to look down into her eyes, he saw a small smile touch her lips. It was the sign he needed, to know that whatever existed between them they were both on the same page. He breathed out slowly, enjoying this moment for what it was.

He stared at her, and she stared at him, yet there was no discomfort. 'Hope,' he said softly. 'There always has to be hope.' Richard spoke slowly, each word enunciated with deep emotion. 'Those were the last words my wife ever spoke to me.'

'Dr Allington?' One of the ward sisters seemed astonished to find him waiting in the nurses' station, especially at almost five o'clock in the morning. He was unsure whether he needed to ask for permission to see a patient.

'At least you know who I am,' Richard stated, smiling at her.

'I…er…was at your lecture yesterday. It was great to learn about the new techniques and equipment being used in emergency medicine.'

'Thank you…' Richard looked at the woman's name badge '…Ayana. It's very nice of you to say so.'

'Oh.' Ayana returned his smile. 'You're welcome. Er…so…um…' She appeared a little flustered in his presence and Richard wondered if he shouldn't have called ahead first. 'What can I help you with?'

'Nothing too bothersome. I only wanted to check on Jammo. We accident and emergency doctors don't usually spend a lot of time on the wards so I wasn't sure of the protocol and decided to just to wander up.'

Ayana reached for Jammo's case notes and handed them to him so he could read the charts for himself. 'She's doing much better. The last time she was in here, which I think was about two weeks ago, she discharged herself within twenty-four hours. At least this time she's stayed a little longer. We might actually be able to do something to help her.'

Richard perused the notes. 'Just over forty-eight hours since we brought her in. It's good to see she's recovering well, and I see she's even seen the social worker?'

Ayana nodded. 'Let's hope we get can through to the poor girl this time.' The sister shook her head. 'Only sixteen. She has her whole life ahead of her.'

Richard nodded and handed the notes back to Ayana. 'Yes. Yes, she does. Is it all right if I just look in on her? I won't wake her up if she's sleeping.'

'That's fine. That bed over there, with the curtain around it. She's very self-conscious and having the curtain drawn seems to help her.'

'Thank you, Ayana.' Richard smiled politely then walked quietly across towards Jammo's bed. Jaime Purcell was the girl's real name, but it stated clearly in her notes that she was to be called Jammo as her first name upset her. Richard could only imagine what the young girl had been through, but all of that was in the past and there was definitely hope, just as Chantelle had always told him. Hope. There always had to be hope.

He slipped carefully and slowly behind the curtain, not wanting to startle the girl if she was indeed awake. Thankfully, he found her sleeping. He wasn't surprised to see Drak sitting in the chair, which had been pulled close by the bed, the two teenagers holding hands. Drak was also sound asleep, resting his head against the edge of the mattress.

'They make a cute couple.'

It was only then that Richard looked over to the other side of the bed, in the shadows near the blind-covered window, and realised that Bergan was standing there.

'I didn't see you,' he whispered, and stepped over to where she stood so their voices didn't carry.

'Drak has barely left her side since she was admitted.'

'Is he also the reason she hasn't tried to discharge herself?'

'He is.' Bergan sighed. 'He's such a good man. He knows Jammo's been through the wringer.' She glanced up at Richard. 'Have you read her file?'

He nodded. 'I had a quick glance.' He also knew exactly what Bergan *wasn't* saying. Back in the earlier section of Jammo's case notes there were several admissions to A and E noted, beginning way back when the girl had been only two or three years old. Admissions for excessive bruising, burns and broken bones. Later, when the girl had been fourteen, she'd been admitted for treatment following a botched abortion attempt.

'Drak won't push her, won't rush her. You were right

the other night when you said he grew up right before our eyes.'

Richard thought back to that night when, after he'd admitted to Bergan that he'd previously been married, they'd made their way back to the drop-in centre and after giving Stuart and the rest of the young people there an update on the situation, Bergan had driven them to Sunshine General's A and E department, where they'd been pleased with the way Jammo had responded to treatment.

Afterwards, Bergan had driven them home and, after thanking him for his help and for the dinner, she'd headed into her house, leaving him wondering if perhaps he shouldn't have said anything about Chantelle at all. Bergan certainly hadn't wanted to talk about it, to ask him questions, like any other woman would have, and that's when it had finally twigged that she *really* wasn't like other women.

She had a calmness about her, a peace that said she accepted people for who they were now, rather than who they might have been before. It was a little odd, but very refreshing and, given the little snippets she'd let slip about her own childhood, it was no wonder she was more than willing to give people a second, third, even fourth chance and probably more.

This revelation only succeeded in making him like her even more and for the next few days after their so-called 'date' Bergan had kept her distance from him. Whether or not she'd been excessively busy or avoiding him, he had no idea. While she might accept people for who they were, he'd also realised it was more than likely that she didn't like being at odds with herself. The fact that both of them could feel and admit there was something...different existing between them was something neither of them had expected.

'Everything still calm in A and E?' she asked a moment later, but before he could answer, Drak shifted and lifted his head. He checked Jammo was all right, placed a soft kiss on the girl's hand then repositioned his head and closed his eyes again.

'Perhaps we should go somewhere else to talk,' he suggested, and she instantly nodded, slipping out through the curtain and holding it open for Richard to do the same.

'Cafeteria?' she asked.

'Sure. I could do with a cup of tea, especially after the night we've just had.'

'I hate multiple motor vehicle accidents,' she said, after they'd stopped and said a brief goodnight to Ayana. 'But I love working in Emergency. I love being there to make a difference, to save a life, to give the patient the best possible chance of recovery.'

'Every day is different,' Richard agreed. 'While I think we all like the quiet days simply from the perspective that no one needs our help, they can make a well-oiled A and E team go stir crazy.' They headed out into the quiet and deserted corridor. 'I've seen it in every hospital I've worked in.'

'Really?'

He nodded. 'There are many cultural differences, but that's the one fact that stays the same. The opposite, of course, is true, that when the emergency room is hectic, that same well-oiled team takes pride in doing everything they can to save a life...and if they're not successful, the next few minutes are the same the world over.

'That moment when everyone pauses, unable to believe they weren't successful. The clock ticks on, the second hand so loud and unnerving, and although you know it's moving, somehow the world seems to stand still. Then someone calls the time of death and everyone's jolted back into action, following the necessary protocols and doing what needs to be done, knowing there will always be the opportunity to grieve at a later stage.'

'It's so true.' She gave him a grim smile. 'Although I don't recall seeing a talk entitled "A global look at intra-professional behaviour during intense medical procedures in the accident and emergency department" on your lecture schedule.'

He grinned. 'No, but now that you've given me such a great title, perhaps it's worth pursuing.'

'Make sure you give me a credit.' She laughed as they entered the cafeteria. Like the corridors, it was mostly deserted, the catering staff having long gone home and the vending machines scattered around the hospital fulfilling their purpose. The hospital, however, did supply staff with free tea and coffee, and Bergan and Richard made a beeline for the urn.

'All you did was give me a title,' he stated, spreading his arms wide, a broad smile on his lips.

'And without it you'd have no paper.' She shrugged as though that ended the debate. They made themselves tea and sat down in the chairs, grateful to finally be off their feet. Bergan slouched forward onto the table, needed its support for her exhausted body. 'It's not until I sit down that I realise how tired I am, but the instant I do, it hits me like a tonne of bricks.'

'I know what you mean.' Richard sipped his tea. They both remained silent for a few minutes, and he was surprised at how comfortable it felt. The other night, after he'd mentioned his wife, their companionable silence had changed into an awkward one.

Thinking about that now caused him to frown. Why *didn't* Bergan want to know about his past? Did she really just see him as someone who was passing through, only in her life for a short period of time so there was no real point in getting to know him any better? It also wasn't like him to be ready to reopen old wounds, to talk about his grief, to open up that one part of his life that he usually kept completely hidden from everyone.

The subject of Chantelle was special, precious and his. A part of him appreciated her not pressuring him to open up; the other part, the one that was now rearing its ugly head, was quite the opposite and for the first time in a long time he realised he *wanted* to talk about his wife, to share her life with someone new.

'Why are you frowning?' Bergan asked, and it was only when she spoke that he realised she'd moved. She was now leaning her arm on the table, her elbow bent, her head propped up on her hand as she held the cup of tea with her other hand and took a sip of the hot liquid.

Richard looked at her for a moment before raising a hand to his forehead, feeling the deep grooves there. 'Am I?' He instantly tried to relax his facial expression, especially as it appeared to be under such close scrutiny. 'Sorry. Didn't realise.'

'Worried about some of the patients we saw tonight? Although A and E is far quieter than it was just a few hours ago, I do feel sorry for the theatre staff because a lot of them still have quite a few more hours of work to get through before they can come and slump into a chair and drink a mediocre cup of tea.'

Richard's smile was instant. 'You're so right.'

'So,' she said, taking another sip of her tea, 'why

were you frowning? Although,' she continued, as quickly as she'd first spoken, 'if you'd rather not tell me, that's fine. I'll respect that, but I will let you know that I'm also quite a good listener.'

He pondered her words for a moment before nodding. 'Fair enough. Well, Dr Freud, I actually do have a question for you.'

'For me?' Bergan eased up from her slouched position, flicking her long auburn plait back over her shoulder.

'Yes.' Richard paused, wondering how to broach the subject delicately, not wanting to put her on the spot but also trying to figure out why she wasn't that curious about his past. He had to admit he was more than a little curious about hers, and while he respected her privacy, he did hope that soon she'd be able to trust him with more. It wasn't that he wanted to gossip, it was simply because...he liked her.

'So what's the question? Do I have to guess?'

He smiled and shook his head. 'No. I was just trying to find the right way to phrase my words.'

Bergan sipped her drink again, watching him closely and making him feel highly self-conscious.

'Well...to answer your question, I was thinking about the other night, with Jammo and what happened after we'd put her in the ambulance.'

'OK.'

'I guess I've been wondering ever since we had our little...chat, on the way back to the drop-in centre, whether or not you were...' He stopped and shook his head. 'I'm afraid this will, no doubt, sound horribly vain, but here goes.' He straightened in his chair before holding her gaze. 'I've been wondering whether or not you're interested in me, in my life. I mentioned my wife and you barely batted an eyelid. Any ordinary woman would have plied me with questions—'

'Indicating you already know what the answers are going to be,' she returned, her tone quite calm and controlled.

'Sorry?'

'If other women have asked you about your wife, then you no doubt have your answers perfectly rehearsed.'

Richard scratched his head. 'I'd never thought of it like that before.'

'And if I were to ask you about her now, would your answers be the same ones you've given to other interested women?'

'Uh... I... Actually, I don't know. You've really thrown me for a loop, Bergan.' He pushed both hands through his hair, leaving it sticking out a little and making him look even cuter. Bergan tried not to smile. 'You do that, you know. From the way you look at me across a crowd of thousands or whether we're sitting quietly in an almost deserted cafeteria at...' He stopped and checked his watch. 'Almost a quarter past five in the morning.'

'And you're not used to such attentions from a woman?'

'That's a loaded question.'

'Is it? Have you dated much since your wife passed away?'

'How do you know she died?' he asked. 'I might have been divorced.'

Bergan instantly shook her head. 'Not with the way you spoke about her the other night. The loss, the grief, the resigned acceptance to continue living your life—it was all there in your tone and body language. And as to why I didn't ask you more about her, I was merely giving you room, as you've clearly been giving me room.'

'What do you mean?'

Bergan looked down at the half empty cup of tepid liquid in front of her. 'I blurted out something about my past, my personal life to you. You know about Smitty and yet you didn't push for all the sordid details.'

'I respect your privacy.'

'As I do yours.'

Richard leaned back in his chair and crossed his legs out in front of him. 'We're both too polite for our own good, is that what you're saying?'

'Got it in one.' She smiled at him.

'I'm curious about you.'

'Ditto.'

'Really?'

Bergan winked at him, feeling a little bolder than usual. Richard was interested in her. She didn't think she was anything special and yet he'd not only admitted to finding her attractive, but he really was interested in *her*. 'I'll share, if you will.'

'Just like that? You'll trust me?'

She shrugged one shoulder. 'You've proved yourself worthy.'

'How did I do that?'

'By checking on Jammo. It shows you really care.' Bergan held his gaze. 'I like that in a person.'

'Oh. So you *do* like me?'

She nodded, slowly and steadily, her expressive honey-brown eyes speaking volumes. 'Far more than I'm comfortable with.'

CHAPTER SIX

RICHARD LOOKED AROUND the cafeteria, noticing the other group of people was getting up to leave. Within another minute it was just the two of them in the large, silent room.

'Why does it bother you so much that you like me?' As he spoke, he edged his chair closer to hers, unable to be that far away from her, especially when she was admitting to their mutual attraction.

'Because I don't like being…tempted. It makes me feel out of control.'

Richard nodded. 'You've had to fight for that control. I understand that.'

'Do you?'

'I may not have had experiences similar to yours, but emotions of helplessness can come from all sorts of directions.'

Bergan nodded then asked the question that had been nestled in the back of her mind for the past two days. 'Will you tell me about your wife?'

Richard shifted in his chair and placed his hands onto the table, lacing his fingers together in a slow and very deliberate way. 'Her name was Chantelle. She was a French nurse and we worked together for many years, first in Australia, then in Paris.'

'Was she the one who told you about the job there?'

He nodded. 'Yes. We were very good friends and then slowly that friendship evolved into more, into love.'

Richard looked down at his hands, his fingers clenched tightly together. 'Then, at the ripe old age of thirty-one, Chantelle was diagnosed with breast cancer.'

Bergan shook her head. 'Oh, Richard. So young.'

'She fought for her life, did everything the doctors prescribed—surgery, chemotherapy—but it was too late. The cancer was…ferocious.' A sad smile came to his face. 'I remember the day we went shopping for her first wig. The French most certainly know the art of wig-making and we found her a beauty. A glorious red and gold, much the same colour as your hair. Beautiful it was, and Chantelle looked very fine in it. She said she didn't want pity, she didn't want sadness, she wanted to enjoy every moment of life.'

When Richard's lower lip wobbled, just for a second, Bergan couldn't help herself and quickly reached out and placed a hand over his. Richard looked at her unseeingly as he looked into the past.

'I loved Chantelle, very much. But sometimes our life together seems more like a dream than a reality. A short dream filled to the brim with every emotion you could imagine. She had days of anger when she'd throw things in frustration. Other days, she'd ask me to hold her close and she'd just…weep. Her sobs were so gut-wrenching, so desperate, so honest.'

He closed his eyes and Bergan could see tears quivering on the ends of his eyelashes. She gave his hand a reassuring squeeze, wanting to let him know she was there for support. He'd been though his own grief, his own personal anguish and she had the sense that, like her, he didn't often talk about those deeper emotions.

Perhaps that was a part of why they'd been drawn together in the first place, the fact that both of them lived a life on the surface, quite happy and content up to a point, because deep down inside was a box of emotions that had been carefully locked away many years ago.

Bergan waited for Richard to collect his strength, simply sitting there quietly, holding his hand, wanting him to feel that she understood how difficult it could be to really open up that secret part of your life to someone else. It wasn't easy. It was often raw—the emotions rising up from the depths below, making a person feel exposed and vulnerable.

The last thing she wanted now was for Richard to feel uncomfortable, to feel as though he'd made a mistake in telling her about Chantelle, but when he finally opened his eyes and looked at her, she had the distinct impression that perhaps this was what he'd needed to do, to talk about his wife once more.

'She was so brave. She had bad days—the ones where she'd cry and rant and rave—but she only allowed herself to do that for twenty-four hours. The next day when she woke up she'd pick up her courage and strength and forge ahead once more.'

'Chantelle sounds like an amazing woman, Richard.' Bergan could clearly see him being married to a strong woman, and Chantelle certainly sounded like an incredible person.

'She was. The chemo, of course, used to take a lot of strength out of her, but she still managed to have a smile on her face, to have patience with those who nursed her.'

'Was she in a hospice?'

He shook his head, a small smile tugging at the side of his mouth. 'Did I mention how stubborn she was?

She didn't want to take up a bed in a hospice when there were people worse off than her.'

'What did you do? I take it she stayed at home, then?'

'Yes.' The smile increased. 'When her mind was made up, that was it. I cut back on my shifts and didn't work nights. Several of Chantelle's friends rallied around, rostering themselves to care for her whenever I was at work or to give me a bit of respite, a few hours when I could go to the shops and pick up groceries. Once, I thought about going to the movies, but it just didn't seem right to go without her.' He shrugged. 'That probably sounds silly.'

'No.' Bergan shook her head. 'Not at all. It can be difficult to try and find some enjoyment in the normal things we do when the person we usually did those normal things with is too sick to join in.'

'Yes. Yes, that's it exactly.' He exhaled slowly.

'How long were you married?'

'Fourteen months. She was diagnosed four months after our wedding.' He looked down at the way Bergan's hand was on his. Firm, understanding, supportive. He shifted his fingers, linking them loosely with hers before he spoke again, his tone dropping to a hushed whisper.

'She was so brave. She'd fought such a good fight. Then one day, with our close friends gathered around her bed, Chantelle looked at me, took my hand in hers and told me to move on with my life. She told me to find someone who'd give me a run for my money, who was stubborn, funny and kind. She urged me to find another true and honest love, filled with passion and power. I promised her, then I kissed her goodbye and it was then she told me never to give up hope.' A lone tear slid down Richard's cheek.

They sat in silence for a while before Bergan sighed and sniffed, unable to believe she was so affected by what Richard had shared. 'She chose how she would die. Not many people get to do that, as we know and see daily proof of.'

'True. I did envy her that. She planned her funeral, the food that would be served at her wake, the music I had to promise to play.'

'On a CD?'

'No. One song on the piano and the other on the guitar.'

'You play both instruments?'

He nodded. 'I do. I've actually found it very cathartic, playing music.'

'Will you play something for me some time?'

He was surprised at this, but instantly smiled and she was glad to see that happy, shining light back in his eyes. 'If you like.'

'Wow.' She wasn't sure why she was so surprised. Perhaps it was because learning a musical instrument was something she'd always wanted to do but had never really had the opportunity, so she admired anyone who could play. 'Are you any good?'

He chuckled. 'Too bad if I'm not. You've already asked me to play something for you so you're going to have to sit there and suffer through my bad renditions of jazz standards.'

'You must have had some talent if Chantelle wanted you to play at her funeral.'

Richard chuckled. 'You would think that. But let me tell you, while Chantelle was a very generous, very giving and kind person, she was also highly mischievous. I always thought she'd wanted me to play so that she could have the last laugh.'

Bergan giggled. 'She sounds like such a wonderful woman.'

'She was. I wish you two could have met.' Richard looked down at their hands, linked loosely together, before meeting her gaze. It had felt right to share with her and now it felt right simply to sit here and hold her hand. 'You're a lot like her, Bergan.'

It was such a very sweet thing for him to say, and combined with the way he was holding her hand and looking into her eyes, Bergan was astonished at the desperate longing winding its way through her, begging her to believe his words. She'd promised herself so many years ago that she would never believe the guff that men, in general, often spouted, but this time she really wanted to.

She swallowed, surprised to find her throat dry, and forced herself to look away from him. She needed to break the intense and intimate atmosphere surrounding them and racked her brain for something different, something mildly humorous to say. 'Apart from her wig,' she added, and was instantly rewarded with one of Richard's smiles.

No. She didn't want to think of it as a reward, she wanted to put distance between them because now that she knew about his past, now that he'd opened up to her and confided in her, he would no doubt expect the same from her.

It was all well and good to say that she trusted him, that she knew he would keep her confidence, but actually *talking* about her past was something she usually avoided at all costs. She looked at where their hands were joined, his thumb rubbing gently over her knuckles, causing little jolts of delight to travel up her arm before bursting forth and flooding her entire being.

'Yes. Before her hair came out, it was jet black, and for years I'd had to listen to her bemoan the fact that even though she'd tried to dye it red, it had never really worked. That's just the sort of person she was. Her hair fell out due to the extensive chemotherapy and she took that as a sign to go and buy a wig in whatever colour she wanted.'

'The glass is half-full, rather than half-empty.' Her words were softer than before.

'Exactly.'

Bergan shook her head. 'I'm not like that, Richard.' She glanced briefly at him as she tried to pull her hand away, but he held it firmly and looked into her eyes.

'I disagree.'

'You barely know me.'

'I know enough. I've seen the way you are with your staff in A and E, firm but fair. I've seen you with patients and with teenagers and with your friends.' He gave her hand a little squeeze, hoping to get his point across, hoping that she'd believe him. 'It doesn't matter to me what may or may not have happened in your past, Bergan, it's who you are *now* I'm interested in.'

She looked at him for one long moment before pulling her hand free and rising to her feet. She shook her head and began pacing up and down, never more pleased that the cafeteria was vacant.

'You shouldn't be.'

'Shouldn't I?' He couldn't help but give her a bemused smile.

'No.' She held out a stern finger towards him. 'Don't look at me like that with those big blue eyes of yours.'

'I didn't realise they caused so much damage.' He chuckled and shifted in his chair, about to stand and walk over to her. Bergan immediately stepped back and raised both hands.

'Don't be cute either.'

'Bergan...I'm—'

'Just stop. Please, Richard?' She took another step away and shook her head. 'I can't...think properly when you're near.'

'Isn't that a good thing?'

She glared at him before turning and pacing towards another table, pushing in a few chairs here and there, needing to do something so she could at least gather her thoughts. Finally, she looked across at him, pleased he was once more sitting down.

'There can never be anything between us. Not of a romantic nature,' she clarified.

'Why?'

The single, soft and totally reasonable question instantly exasperated her. She spread her arms wide. 'Because I'm damaged goods. I've done drugs, I was a teenage drunk. I've done some horrible things and half of them would make your hair turn white right here on the spot if you knew what they were.'

'I very much doubt that.' He stood, but she instantly pointed to the chair.

'Sit.'

With a small smile he did as he was bid.

'Thank you,' she said, trying to inject a little more control into her tone. Dragging in a deep breath, she slowly let it out before closing her eyes. Crossing her arms over her chest, needing to ensure her barriers were up when she spoke, she began.

'I didn't know Smitty was my father. Not for quite some time. Both my parents were druggies. I found my mother dead from an overdose, with the needle still in her arm, when I was only five years old. My father had left when I was a baby and with no other family to claim me, I was put into the foster system.' The words tumbled out of her mouth, clear and matter-of-fact, but Richard realised she needed to say them fast. She'd unlocked a door she'd slammed shut many years ago and now she wanted to deal with this and bolt it all back up as quickly as possible.

'Back then there weren't as many rules as there are now, no background security checks on foster-parents, just too many kids in an already-corrupt system. Thankfully things have improved, but, having been badly treated, I soon realised that the more havoc I created, the less the social workers interfered. I was branded a "difficult case" and left to fend for myself.'

Richard didn't want to interrupt, but when she finally opened her eyes and looked at him, he nodded, to indicate he was still listening. She seemed appeased by that and slowly, as she spoke, she began to pace back and forth.

'I did meet a few people whom I could trust. Poor Mackenzie was one of them. She was ten when we met and she was being picked on by the other kids in the foster-house she lived in. When I arrived, things changed.'

'You protected her.' He hadn't meant to speak, hadn't meant to break her concentration, but the words, filled with admiration and understanding, had left his lips before he could stop them.

Bergan stopped pacing and nodded. 'I was only a year older than her, but I started to realise that the two of us together were stronger against some of the older boys. If we stuck together, it meant protection for *both* of us and the next time the system tried to shift us, they rehomed us together.' Only now did she allow herself the brief glimmer of a smile.

'And Smitty?' Richard asked.

'I'm getting to that bit. Good heavens, you're impatient.'

He shrugged one shoulder but was pleased she wasn't pacing as much as before and had actually uncrossed her arms, shoving her hands into her trouser pockets.

'Like a lot of the other kids, at seventeen I tried my luck living on the street, but it's much harder than I'd thought—surprise, surprise,' she murmured with a hint of sarcasm. 'At any rate, I ended up at Smitty's place and I'd stayed there five nights before I even saw him.' She shook her head, gazing off into nothingness, remembering. 'He was actually quite lucid that first time and the instant he saw me he turned as white as a ghost. Before I could even introduce myself, he grabbed me by the shoulders and demanded I tell him my mother's name. I did, and then this weird man, with long hair and a shaggy beard, hugged me.

'"I'm your dad," he said. Then he told me exactly when my date of birth was, where I was born and how he'd insisted I be called Bergan, after some actress he'd had a crush on when he was a teenager. He also said I looked exactly like my mother and he'd initially thought she'd come back to haunt him.'

'What happened after that?'

'Nothing.' She spread her arms wide for an instant before letting them fall to her sides. 'I went to Smitty's, like every other kid, when I needed a place to crash or some food. I talked to him sometimes, when he wasn't either out of it or jonesing for a hit. There was food, not much but some. Blankets and some old mattresses. There was also running water, so if you could get someone to guard the bathroom door, you could actually have a shower.' She grinned. 'That was bliss. Anyway, in the end Mackenzie and I became regulars, stopping at Smitty's and helping to…er…collect more food.'

Richard's grin was wide as he understood her meaning of the word 'collect'.

'Then one day I came back and found Smitty stone-cold dead. It took me a while, but I finally remembered the name of a social worker who had helped him.' Bergan looked off into the distance. 'This woman was probably only about five or six years older than me, but the instant I looked into her eyes I saw genuine sorrow that Smitty had died. She called the ambulance, and before I left I asked her what would happen with the flat. Could we all still come here and not be hassled?'

'What did she say?' Richard was eager to know.

'She said she would look into ways of keeping it going. More mattresses and blankets miraculously appeared, the cupboards were regularly stocked with non-perishable foods. It wasn't the best system in the world, but it was one that worked.'

'Do you still keep in contact with her?'

Bergan shook her head. 'One night she was admitted to A and E, motor vehicle accident. She was in a bad way and died twenty-four hours later.'

'But…Smitty's. It's still there and the kids still use it, right?' Richard frowned for a moment before he lifted his gaze to Bergan's. 'You pay the rent, don't you?'

She swallowed, knowing she shouldn't be surprised he'd figured it out. 'Mackenzie and I do it together. You've got to understand the importance of that decrepit little flat. The night Smitty died, I realised that if I didn't want to end up like my parents, I'd better make some changes. Just like Drak, I grew up in an instant.

I used Smitty's address as a billing address and managed to get myself a part-time job as a waitress. After a month I had enough to share a small one-bedroom apartment with Mackenzie. I decided that instead of butting heads with the system, I had to learn to make it work for me. By the time I was eighteen I'd completed my higher school certificate and sat the entrance exam for medical school.'

'You're quite a woman, Bergan. But I knew that before you told your story.'

'Thank you, Richard, but the point of my *story* was to let you know that I'm bad news. I'm a train wreck.'

'I disagree.' He stood and shoved his hands into his pockets. 'I see a woman who, against the odds, has managed to not only make good but to help others along the way.'

'You're making it sound more important than it really is.'

'I don't think Mackenzie, or Drak or Jammo would see it that way. Bad things happened to you. I don't deny that, but look at what you've accomplished, Bergan. Look at how you relate to those kids at the drop-in centre.' He took a step towards her. 'How they look up to you. How you gave Drak strength not to be ashamed of his creative abilities.' He took another few steps before she stopped him.

'Stay right there.' She held up her hands. 'It feels like you're stalking me.'

Richard slowly shook his head. 'That wasn't my intention.'

'I can read in your face what your intentions are.'

'They're honourable, if that's what you're implying.'

'I'm not an honourable woman.'

'I beg to differ.' He took another step closer and came

up against her upheld hands. The instant they made contact with his chest, the heat of her touch seemed to scorch him with delight. Bergan dropped her hands back to her sides, but before she could move back, Richard placed two gentle hands on her shoulders.

'You deserve a world of happiness, Bergan. Actually, you deserve more than that,' he said quickly. 'Two worlds. Two worlds filled to the brim with happiness and sunshine.'

Richard moved one hand to cup her cheek, tilting her head up a little, ensuring they were looking at each other as he spoke.

'I promise not to rush you. I promise to let you set the pace, but I won't let you push me away.'

'Richard?' she breathed, wanting to draw him near and push him away at the same time. There was confusion and apprehension in her eyes, and she was unsure what he might do or say next. She was still having difficulty believing he hadn't walked from the room in a fit of revulsion after what she'd told him. The last thing she'd ever expected had been for him to support her, to stand before her, telling her she deserved two worlds filled with happiness and sunshine! She gently shook her head from side to side. 'I don't—'

'Shh.' He placed two gentle fingers momentarily on her lips. 'Believe me, Bergan, when I say that I find you…exquisitely beautiful.'

'I can't.' The words were barely a whisper.

His smile was filled with understanding. 'They say it's easier to believe the bad stuff about ourselves than the good things. The fact of the matter is, though, that you *are* a beautiful woman, both inside and out. You care so much about others and you give and give and keep on giving.'

'But why do you…?' She stopped and closed her eyes, dragging in a breath before slowly letting it out. She looked up at him. 'I come with baggage.'

His smile was instant. 'We all do, but Chantelle showed me how to reach out and grab life with both hands, as well as remember that there's always hope. I thought I was doing that, especially when I agreed to the travelling fellowship, but I'm not sure I've been grabbing life at all.'

'So…' Bergan frowned. 'I'm not sure what you're saying, Richard.'

'I'm saying that I hope you'll allow me to see more of you, to spend time with you while I'm here in Australia.'

'More friendship dates?'

He shrugged. 'It's a good place to start, don't you think?' He stared at Bergan for a moment. 'Perhaps we've both thought we were grabbing life with both hands.'

'When really we weren't?'

'I get the feeling that you know what it's like to be truly lonely, Bergan. I know I do. Standing in a crowd, I can feel alone. By myself, I can feel alone, but that inner, dark loneliness…I think we tend to hide our true selves there.' He spread his arms wide. 'By talking to each other—by feeling *comfortable* to discuss those inner darknesses with each other—surely that's the first step on the road to the hope we both know exists but may not have felt for a very long time?'

Bergan pondered his words for a moment, trying to ignore the lump in her throat. What he'd said had been everything she'd been feeling, especially about the loneliness she'd carried around for most of her life. Surprisingly, she hadn't realised that Richard was also living in that dark, lonely place as well. Eventually, she sighed and lifted her gaze to meet his. 'We spend time together? Friendship dating?'

The slow smile that spread across his face managed to touch her heart as well as cause the butterflies in her stomach to take flight. She'd never been with a man who could make her feel pleasantly and excitedly unsettled with just a look, but Richard seemed to be an expert at it. 'Exclusive friendship dating,' he clarified.

'No—you know—hanky-panky?'

His smile broadened at her term. 'We'll take things as slowly as you like.'

'And when you leave? What then?'

He shrugged. 'Honestly? I don't know. When I leave Australia, I return to Paris where I have a two-week block of writing up and presenting my findings of the fellowship, and after that I'll be back to being just a regular doctor, working in a busy Parisian A and E department.'

'And you'll stay in Paris?'

Richard reached down and took both her hands in his. 'I don't know, Bergan. It's unusual for me *not* to know my next move because ever since Chantelle's death I've immersed myself in routine, in planning ahead, in hiding behind work. Perhaps it's time to make some changes.'

He raised her hands to his lips, pressing a soft kiss to her knuckles. Bergan gasped at the light contact, unable to believe the riotous way her body reacted to his delicate touch. 'All I'm certain of at this point, right now, is that I want to get to know you better.'

'Why?' The question was barely audible, but he heard it.

'Because you're an incredibly intelligent, beautiful and generous woman, Bergan. You're on my wavelength and…' He shook his head. 'I thought I'd *never* find that again. Yes, there are uncertainties, but perhaps, through forging a friendship, we'll be able to find some answers.'

'Help each other to step from the darkness into the light?'

'Yes.' He rubbed his thumbs over the tops of her knuckles, as though massaging in the small kiss.

'Friendship dating.' She spoke the words as though they were finally starting to make sense.

'Think of it like the old-fashioned way a gentleman used to court a lady. No pressure but lots of fun.'

'Court?'

'I said we'd take it slowly. Take it at your pace.'

Bergan angled her head, her eyes twinkling with a touch of repressed humour. 'What if my pace ends up being faster than yours?'

Richard's eyes widened with delight at her teasing words. They really *were* on the same wavelength. 'Then I'd ask you to respect my need to take it slowly.'

Bergan couldn't help but return his smile. Richard wanted to *court* her? As far as Bergan could recall, no man, not any she'd ever been remotely acquainted with, had ever *courted* her. She felt so incredibly out of her depth, but when she looked into Richard's blue eyes she found herself relaxing and sighing and wanting desperately to agree.

He was only here for another three and a half weeks, and it wasn't as though she could fall in love in such a short time. Besides, it would be nice to have some calm and controlled male attention for a change, and although she'd admitted to being attracted to Richard, she knew she was in no danger of falling in love. She didn't *do* love.

She concluded, therefore, that as Richard was allowing her to set the pace of this 'courting' thing, she really was in no danger whatsoever.

Slowly, she met and held his gaze, nodding her head in affirmation. 'OK, then,' she said eventually. 'You can…court me.' Even as she said the words she couldn't help but laugh and as Richard gathered her close, his warm, protective arms about her, she felt lighter than she ever had before.

Hope. She certainly hoped this was the right decision.

CHAPTER SEVEN

'How long have you been dating him now?' Reggie asked as she stirred her coffee.

'We're not dating, per se,' Bergan tried to protest, but even she knew that was exactly what she and Richard were doing, no matter what words they used to describe it.

'Then what would you call it?' Sunainah asked.

Bergan shrugged and sipped her coffee. 'We're... spending time together.'

'Dating,' Sunainah and Reggie said together. Bergan just shook her head and finished her drink.

'Richard calls it "courting",' she told her friends. 'It's cute and old-fashioned and quaint. I get his undivided attention without the stress of always thinking how to fend off groping hands. He's a perfect gentleman and I like it.'

'Break out the blue roses,' Reggie stated.

'Hey!' Bergan growled, frowning at her friend as the others laughed. 'I wish I'd never told you that.'

'What?' Reggie clutched her hands to her chest in a romantic gesture and sighed. 'I think it's a lovely idea, having blue roses at your wedding.'

'Blue roses are rare and hard to find,' Mackenzie added. 'The man who persists in breaking down all your barriers and loving you no matter what is the man who has figuratively searched for the blue rose and found one.'

Bergan shook her head. 'We were young, stupid kids when I said all that and besides…' she levelled a steely glare at her friends '…there's not going to be any wedding. We're just…you know, courting, and besides, he lives on the other side of the world.'

Bergan checked her watch and almost yelped at the time. 'I need to get back.' She jerked her thumb in the direction of Sunshine General Hospital, which was just across the road from the café she and her three friends tried to frequent whenever they could all meet up.

Four busy women with four busy schedules. Some weeks it was nigh on impossible and this week Bergan wouldn't have minded missing their catch-up as, although she loved her friends, she'd rather have spent the time with Richard. She also knew if she told her friends that, they'd read far more into it than was there.

'So do I,' Mackenzie said, and blew kisses to her friends as they stood from the table.

'Go on,' Bergan urged as the two of them walked back towards the hospital. 'Ask.'

'Ask what?'

'Oh, come off it, Kenz. You're dying to find out more information about Richard and me.'

'Am I? Well, OK, then. Has he kissed you yet?'

'No, and it's been two whole weeks since we started this courting thing.'

'Really? That long? That means… Wait a second. Richard leaves at the end of next week? That's gone fast.'

'It really has.'

'So you're…happy?'

'I am...but—'

'Uh-oh. There it is. What's wrong?'

'It's just...Richard has said I can set the pace, but I'm still not sure *how* I'm supposed to do that. I've never been in this type of relationship before.'

'A healthy one?' Mackenzie couldn't resist teasing.

'Exactly. All my life I've been used to being put down by men, or abused in one way or another. Smitty was the first male who didn't seem to want anything from me.'

'Smitty didn't want anything from anyone—except his drug dealer.' Mackenzie's words weren't malicious, merely matter-of-fact.

'True.' Bergan sighed as they entered the hospital, the two women walking side by side, heading towards the A and E department. '*I'm* in a normal, healthy relationship. Who would have thought it?'

'Me.'

'Yes, but that's only because you're a newlywed and you think everyone should be as happy as you.'

'And aren't you?'

Bergan glared at her friend before swiping her pass card over the sensor to open the door leading to A and E. The first person she saw was Richard, standing at the nurses' station, chatting with one of the male registrars. Just at the sight of him her heart rate quickened, her palms seemed to perspire and her mouth went dry.

She stared at him, having not seen him since yesterday evening when he'd left her house after a quiet evening of a relaxing dinner followed by watching some television together. Again, that was something she'd never really done before—just sat and watched television in peace and harmony, Richard's arm around her shoulders, she leaning her head against his chest.

They'd laughed together, discussed different aspects of the show they had been watching and had generally had what most people would call 'a normal night in', but for Bergan it really had been like manna from heaven. When she was with Richard, she felt like a normal girl, in a normal relationship, with a normal boyfriend.

Even the word 'boyfriend' sounded strange when she thought about it, but she guessed that was the term her friends might apply. Before the evening had ended he'd arranged for her to go to his place for dinner where he would make good his threat to play something on the piano and guitar for her.

'Your mother has a piano? I don't remember seeing it.'

He'd nodded. 'In the spare room upstairs. Just a small upright, which I think might be a little out of tune. Must remember to call the tuner before they get back.' He'd made a mental note, but had held her hand firmly as they'd walked from her place to his.

'So…was that *you* playing the other night? I thought you had a CD on.'

'Oh?' He'd looked a little sheepish. 'I didn't think it was that loud. Sorry.'

'Don't be.' Bergan had shaken her head, smiling up at him in delighted surprise. 'I have a feeling that you definitely won't be assaulting my senses with your playing. That piece sounded incredible.'

'Er…thank you.'

'You're not used to people praising your musical ability?'

'I'm not used to *sharing* my musical ability. Playing an instrument is…personal. It's an expression of my inner feelings, my inner self, and as such I've rarely openly played for people, other than for my sisters and parents.'

'And Chantelle.'

'Of course.' They'd stopped outside his front screen door, just shy of the sensor light, and Richard exhaled slowly. 'There were several pieces, mainly Bach, that used to really soothe Chantelle into a nice, relaxed sleep.' His smile had increased. 'Then there were times when she demanded the "1812 Overture" because it gave her the strength to fight on.'

Bergan had sighed and slipped her arms around his waist, delighted that she had the right to do such a thing. 'You truly are a wonderful man, Richard. The more I learn about you, the more I like.'

'I'm going to take that as a huge compliment,' he'd said as he'd dipped his head and brushed a soft and tantalising kiss across her cheek. They'd stood there for a few more minutes, content to simply hold each other, before he'd kissed her cheek again and bidden her goodnight.

And that was the way it had been every time they'd parted at the end of the evening. He was always a perfect gentleman and sometimes she wished he wouldn't be. Was that wrong? After everything she'd been through? It wasn't that their dates weren't romantic because it was clear with the quiet intimacy they shared that Richard certainly took this courting thing very seriously.

Now, as he stood there, chatting with the registrar, his hair slightly messy where she knew he'd pushed his fingers through it, his stance casual but his shoulders back, indicating he was ready to spring into action the second an ambulance arrived, Bergan couldn't take her eyes off him, almost desperate for him to detect her presence.

Mackenzie was chatting away beside her, but Bergan wasn't listening, and when Richard finally turned his head and saw her standing there, that small, intimate smile that she was coming to recognise as being purely Richard touched his lips.

He was rostered on for the afternoon shift and it wasn't until now that she realised she'd been waiting through the long morning for this exact moment. Within a matter of seconds he'd excused himself from the registrar and was heading in her direction.

'Well,' Mackenzie said, sighing, 'I can see I'm superfluous here, so I'll just leave.' She waved to Richard as he came over.

'You're not leaving already, are you, Mackenzie? How was coffee with the girls?' He glanced once at Mackenzie and then at Bergan, where his eyes stayed, as though he needed to drink in every aspect of her. When Bergan didn't answer, Mackenzie chuckled.

'It was good. I've got to run. Clinic,' she said by way of explanation, and headed quickly towards the stairwell.

'So.' Richard crossed his arms over his chest and took a small step closer to her. Bergan couldn't believe the amount of pressure against her chest caused purely by his nearness. She could almost feel the heat radiating from his body, the way the spicy scent she now equated with him seemed to tease at her senses, the way she longed to have his big, strong arms wrapped around her. Why was it that whenever he was within touching distance she wanted to throw herself into his arms and to never let go? Was this a bad urge to have? Was this part of dating? Of what normal people, in normal relationships, did every day?

'I've heard that the morning has been rather quiet, emergency-wise.'

'Yes.'

'Do you want to give me a debrief? In your office perhaps?' he suggested, raising one seductive eyebrow. Bergan's eyes widened with excitement, which she quickly attempted to curb. She opened her mouth to reply, but no sound came out so she nodded instead. As she turned and headed down the side corridor towards her office, her heart rate beginning to increase due to his nearness, she heard Richard's warm, deep chuckle.

It was as though he could see quite clearly the way he affected her and she didn't mind one little bit. She simply couldn't help the thrill of delighted anticipation that pulsed through her at the thought that so very soon she'd be alone with Richard. How was it he could make her feel so pretty and feminine with just one look? His gaze had never been leering in any way, shape or form, but it left her in no doubt whatsoever that he was attracted to her.

As she withdrew her pass card from her pocket to pass it over the scanner, she was astonished to find her hand shaking slightly. That was odd. No man in her life had affected her in such a way. Usually she was able to read them like a book, knowing exactly what they wanted from her, and that way she could choose to provide it or reject the impulse.

She'd made a deal with herself to enjoy the time she had with Richard, to relax, which, for her, wasn't at all easy. Yes, he would be leaving at the end of next week, but she wasn't going to think about what happened next. For the first time in her life she was just going to go with the flow. It had been difficult at first, to really slip into the 'whatever' mode, but now she could definitely see the appeal. It felt as though she was on vacation… a vacation from her usual life. She knew it would end, that Richard would return to Paris and she'd get back to her normal daily routine, looking back on this time they'd spent together as nothing more than the equivalent of a shipboard romance.

The instant they were secure behind her closed door Bergan turned to face him and somehow found herself in his arms in a matter of seconds. She didn't try to pull away, but instead she held him as closely as he was holding her.

'Sorry if I startled you,' he murmured, the vibration from his words passing into her body, causing tingles to flood through her. 'I like it when you're close.'

'Don't apologise,' she whispered near his ear. 'I… like it, too.'

Richard edged back slightly. 'Really?'

'Why should you be so surprised? Can't you tell?'

His smile increased. 'Well, I knew you weren't averse to me holding you close, but I guess I'm pleasantly surprised that you've voiced it.' It meant he was definitely making progress. The fact that Bergan had come to mean a great deal to him in such a short space of time was something he hadn't wanted to fight. It also made him consider what might happen next. She hadn't said anything about his departure in ten days' time and neither had he, not wanting to spoil what they were enjoying right now. He brushed a soft and tender kiss across her cheek before gathering her close once more, breathing her in, closing his eyes and feeling the stress slip from his body.

'I don't understand it,' she said, her tone still a whisper as she wrapped her arms more securely around his neck, her fingers playing with the ends of his hair. He'd be due for a haircut soon, but right now she liked the way his short back-and-sides cut had grown a little, making it less severe.

'I don't know what it is about hugging you, holding you close, Richard,' she murmured softly, sighing into his embrace. 'But it strengthens me, it invigorates me, it lets me know that no matter what else happens in life, there is always somewhere I can feel safe. I've never felt that before and definitely not from just a hug.' She closed her eyes and breathed in his scent once more, relaxing against him, knowing his big, protective arms would never let her fall. 'I like it.'

'Me, too.' And he did. Being close to Bergan, actually having permission to hold her hand or put his arm around her or draw her near to him as he was now, had been an absolutely delight. Spending time with her had been a joy, especially their need to debate and discuss not only medical issues, but world events, too. She was his intellectual equal, as well as being highly compatible with him on the emotional side of things.

She'd become more open about her involvement with the drop-in centre and had listened to a lot of the ideas he'd put forward, the two of them moulding them into a more tangible format that she could then take to Stuart, the director.

Both of them had been delighted with Jammo's progress after her brief stay in hospital. Thanks to Drak, Jammo had agreed to talk to one of the drop-in centre's counsellors, as long as Drak went with her. Bergan had watched the two teens walking along, holding hands and smiling.

'We're taking it real slow,' Drak had told her after he and Jammo had finished the first counselling session. 'Jammo's been through heaps and I really like her. She scared me that night and now I wanna do right by her. So slow is best. You know, like in the olden days. Girls need to be made to feel special and stuff.'

Bergan had smiled. 'You both have plenty of time,' she'd confirmed, encouraging him to continue along this path. It wasn't until she'd arrived home that night to find an envelope taped to her front door, which contained an invitation to dine with Richard at his place, that she'd realised Richard's form of 'courting' was incredibly similar to how Drak was treating Jammo. The fact that she wasn't having to constantly second-guess Richard's motives, or fight off wandering hands, *was* making her feel 'special and stuff', as Drak had termed it.

As he held her now, she couldn't help pulling back a little and looking at him. 'Just out of curiosity, did you speak to Drak about how to take things slowly with Jammo?'

Richard raised an eyebrow at her question, blinking once or twice as though wondering where it had come from, but the cute smile on his lips gave away the answer. 'A few weeks ago. Sure. He wanted to know *how* to slow things down, but still let Jammo know he was interested. Sad that young men nowadays have no idea how to court.' He shook his head as he shifted his hands to her waist.

'I think it's nice.'

'That Drak's taking his time with Jammo or the ethics of courting in general?'

Bergan smiled up at him. 'Both. It's very nice to feel so…secure, but…' She stopped and shook her head.

'But what?'

'It's nothing.'

'Bergan?' There was a hint of amused exasperation in his voice.

'It's just this whole relationship thing. Whether or not we go slowly or speed on through like a freight train. It's still a relationship.'

'Is it the word that bothers you?'

'Perhaps.'

He nodded, his tone still calm and controlled. 'A friendship is a relationship. We enter into a relationship with our patients in a professional and medical capacity. There are many different types of relationships and you're fantastic at all of them.' He fixed her with a pointed look. '*All* of them.'

'Hmm.' She sounded as though she wasn't convinced and when she eased out from his arms he reluctantly released his hold. She walked over to the window.

'We're friends, Bergan. Or at least I'd like to think we are.'

She looked at him over her shoulder and nodded. 'Yes.'

'And friends like to spend time together, correct?'

'Yes.' She turned from the window and crossed her arms in front of her, giving him a studious look. It was one he'd seen plenty of times when she was pondering things. Good. It was good she was asking questions, trying to figure out the whys and wherefores of a healthy, normal courtship.

'Friends can hang out together, watch movies, discuss a variety of topics and sometimes they hug and hold hands, too.'

Her eyes widened a little, veiled fear behind them. 'So you're saying all you feel for me is friendship?' Her voice cracked on the final word and she immediately closed her eyes, not wanting him to see or worry about the internal turmoil that she'd done her best to keep locked up in the back of her mind. She'd tried not to put a definition on what they shared, but it was becoming more and more difficult to ignore it, especially when he didn't seem to want to make any move whatsoever to kiss her properly.

'No. I think you know I feel a lot more than that.'

'I also know that soon you'll be leaving Australia.'

'And returning to Paris.' He nodded, noting that she hadn't said 'leaving *me*'. 'This is a fact we've both been very aware of.' Richard wasn't quite sure what the problem was and as he took a few steps closer towards Bergan, she took one back, coming into contact with the window ledge.

She watched him slowly coming closer, his stance almost predatory but at the same time playful. She liked the combination. There was no anger, no abusive look in his eyes, only intrigue and interest.

'I like you, Bergan. A lot. I think I might have mentioned that once or twice before.'

'Uh-huh.' Where was her brain? Why did she feel the need to rebuild her protective walls when just last night she'd reclined on the lounge while he'd played an acoustic piece on his guitar? Her eyes had been closed, her body relaxed, her defences down as she'd absorbed the beautiful music he'd created with his clever hands. She'd been so open to him and now she wanted nothing more than to shut him out.

'So what's really the problem here?'

Bergan glanced away from him, unable to meet his powerful gaze, knowing sometimes that all it took was one look into his sexy eyes for her to lose all ability of rational thought. 'Noth—'

He stood before her and placed a finger across her lips.

'Don't say "nothing", because we both know it's not true. This is supposed to be an open and honest relationship and it works both ways. If you have anything you need to say to me, please, by all means, say it.'

There was a challenge in his words and she instantly raised her chin, a flash of defiance running through her eyes. 'All right, then. I guess…what's been bothering me has everything to do with why you never seem to want to kiss me. Not just on the cheek, but to…you know…properly… Oh, help.' She stopped, knowing she wasn't explaining succinctly enough.

'*Want* to kiss you?' Richard stared at her in bemusement, momentarily stunned. 'Of course I *want* to kiss you, Bergan. Why wouldn't you think I'd want that?'

'Well…because you haven't even *tried* to kiss me. I mean, I like the long and lingering kisses on my cheek at the end of a night together, but…' She stopped and closed her eyes for a moment.

'You're upset because I won't kiss you?' He gave his head a little shake, wanting to make sure he understood exactly what she was saying.

She looked up at him. 'Yes.' Not wanting to stand there that close to him when she felt this silly, she quickly sidestepped him and headed for the protection of her desk. She pulled back the executive chair but didn't sit down. Instead, she placed her fingertips on her desk and forced herself to slow down her breathing. 'And don't look at me like that.'

'Like what?' He spread both arms wide.

'Like you think I'm insane.'

His smile was immediate. 'I do not think you're insane, Bergan.'

'Yes, you do. I can see it in your eyes.'

Richard shook his head as he made his way towards her. 'It's not insanity you see there but incredulity.' He reached out and took both her hands in his. 'Don't you remember what I said to you when we first started changing our relationship? I said that I would wait for *you* to set the pace. That I would be a perfect gentleman—'

'Until I said otherwise? Letting me take all the responsibility, all the blame when it doesn't work out?' She dropped his hands and moved away, skirting round to the other side of the desk. She knew her actions were probably childish, but right now she didn't care. She was worried, stressed, completely out of her depth with the way this man was making her feel, and that was causing her to behave a little irrationally.

'No. Bergan?' He spread his arms wide again, his gaze imploring. 'Of course we both take responsibility.'

'And yet you're leaving. You're flying back to Paris.'

'Yes.' He still wasn't sure what the problem was.

'And…and you'll be surrounded by all those other French women, and…and…'

'Yes?' He wanted nothing more than to go to her, to pull her close, but he feared that if he moved yet again, chasing her around the office, she'd clam up and not tell him what was *really* wrong. He still wasn't sure where she was going with her little speech, but he wanted to be encouraging, to let her know he hadn't been toying with her emotions, as she was implying.

'And they're far more sophisticated and stunning than I will ever be.'

'*That's* what's bothering you?' Richard was gobsmacked.

Again she lifted her chin, that defiance in her eyes

once more as though she was daring him to say something derogatory, something hurtful, something she could use to push him away. 'Yes.'

Richard closed his eyes for a second, pleased he'd managed to figure things out. She was upset because she was jealous. He never would have guessed, especially when she had no need of the emotion.

'Bergan.' He walked quickly round the desk and came towards her, instantly sliding his arms around her waist and drawing her close. She gasped at the suddenness of his movements but her shock soon turned to delight as she rested her hands against his chest.

'I don't know where this attraction between us might lead. I don't know what's going to happen when I get back to Paris, but I can tell you I'll be focused on my work, not on seeing how many Parisian women I can date.'

'I just thought that now that you've…you know, sort of broken your drought and started enjoying a relationship with me, that when you went back…' She stopped and closed her eyes. 'I sound ridiculous.'

'No. No, you don't,' he replied. 'I'm as much out of my depth as you are, but what I do know is that right here, right now, being with you, I'm happy. I won't make empty promises to you because at the moment my future's in limbo. I don't know what's going to happen once the fellowship's over, once I get back to my apartment, my work, my life in Paris.'

He looked away from her for a moment, but she'd seen the confusion in his eyes.

'I won't bring my uncertainty into your world, Bergan, especially when you've experienced so much uncertainty most of your life. All I am certain of, at the moment, is that being with you makes me happy and I haven't felt truly happy in a very long time.'

Bergan swallowed over the dryness in her throat, his words having affected her far more than she'd realised. Her heart was pounding against her chest, and she wanted him to know that she didn't expect a life plan from him, neither did she want definite answers to her questions, because even the thought of Richard telling her this thing that existed between them, this natural chemistry that had turned their worlds upside down in such a short space of time, wasn't going to last was enough to pierce her heart with pain.

'Is that why you haven't kissed me? Because you can't make any promises?' She forced her words into the room, needing to at least know the answer to that question.

'Oh, Bergan.' He lifted one hand to cup her cheek as he gazed down into her upturned face. 'As I've said before, *you* control how fast this relationship moves.' Gently, tenderly, he brushed his thumb over her plump lips. Bergan gasped, her lips instantly parting at the touch. Richard slid his other arm more firmly around her waist, drawing her close once more.

'If you want me to kiss you, all you have to do is say so.'

Bergan gazed up into his mesmerising blue eyes, knowing that even now, if she didn't say anything, he wouldn't push her. Here was a man who was desperate to continue proving to her that he was trustworthy, that he kept his word.

She still wasn't sure what was going to happen once he left Australia and returned to Paris. Would he forget her? Would he ever return? She shoved the thoughts back into their box, not wanting to deal with them but rather enjoy the man who was holding her close, look-ing at her as though she really was the most precious thing in the world.

'Kissing,' she said softly as she began to slide her hands up towards his neck, 'is very personal. It's pow-erful and it's far more important than people realise.' The instant the words were out of her mouth, the at-mosphere between them seemed to intensify one hun-dred per cent. She continued to push forward, breaking through barriers she'd spent years erecting.

'Yes.' The word was barely a whisper and his parted lips didn't move. He simply continued to drink her in, the way she looked, the touch of her hands on his body, the way she was driving him completely insane.

'When two people touch their lips together, it's not about the pressure, it's not about the need. It's about two worlds melding into one. It's about giving and re-ceiving in equal measure. It's about trust and honesty and belief.'

'Yes,' he repeated, but this time when he swal-lowed, her gaze dipped to watch his Adam's apple slide smoothly up and down his neck, just above his shirt collar and tie. The desire in him increased when he realised he might finally be able to follow through on the one thing he'd wanted to do since the moment he'd first seen her.

'Even with the anticipation of a kiss,' she continued, her soft words winding their way seductively around him, binding them together, 'bodies flood with desire, with longing, with a need so powerful it can make your head spin, make you swoon, wondering if your thirst will ever be quenched.'

'Yes.' The word was more of a soft growl, and al-though he had one hand at her waist and the other cupping her cheek, he still kept all his repressed desire perfectly contained.

'Yes,' she breathed, and stood on tiptoe, sliding her fingers around his neck and urging his head down so that finally, *finally*, their lips could meet.

CHAPTER EIGHT

RICHARD KNEW HE had to remain calm and in control. Even though he was surging with elation at being invited by Bergan to kiss her, something he'd been longing to do for quite some time, the last thing he wanted was to scare her away. Enthusiasm was one thing, but unleashing his—

The phone on Bergan's desk shrilled to life, as did both their pagers. They could perhaps ignore one. They certainly couldn't ignore all three. Richard still kept his arm around her waist, not wanting to let her go but knowing, eventually, he must.

'Hold that thought,' she said, pressing a kiss to her finger and then placing her finger gently on his lips. Smiling, she turned and reached across her desk to answer the phone. 'Dr Moncrief,' she said into the receiver. 'All right. Give me the details.' She shuffled around her desk and quickly picked up a pen to jot down a few notes.

'I'll be right out,' she said a moment later, then paused and looked up at Richard. 'I'm sure Richard's not too far away, especially as his shift has already started.' With that, she rang off.

'Why didn't you say I was in here with you?' he asked as she picked up the piece of paper she'd scribbled notes on and headed for the door. 'It's hardly uncommon for the two of us to talk in private.'

'I just don't like everyone knowing my business.' Her words were sharper than she'd intended but instead of apologising she switched her mind into professional mode. 'Besides, duty calls. A building has collapsed downtown.'

'Good heavens!' Richard was shocked. 'What are the preliminary details?'

'A heritage-listed building, three stories, used as professional rooms.' She looked at the piece of paper in her hand as they headed into A and E. She'd had half a mind to ask him to wait a few minutes so no one saw them heading into A and E together but he'd been right. There was no reason why it would seem odd if the two of them were alone in her office.

She'd overreacted when Katrina, the triage sister, had mentioned being unable to find Dr Allington and had blurted out the first thing that had come to mind. She wasn't used to being flustered about her personal life, primarily because prior to meeting Richard she hadn't really had one.

'There you both are,' Katrina said as they entered the nurses' station. The phones were ringing, several nurses telling the staff who had been called in about the latest emergency requiring the Sunshine General retrieval team to assemble. 'Here's the latest report from the police, who have not long arrived on the scene.'

Bergan scanned the information.

'What's the suspected headcount?' Richard asked.

She looked up at him for a moment, seemingly not having heard him, but after a moment she returned her attention to the sheet. 'In excess of twenty, possibly up to fifty. The building housed the offices of a lawyer, doctor and dentist.'

'Any preliminary conclusions about the cause of the collapse? Burst water mains? Gas explosion? Bad foundations?'

Bergan scanned the report and then nodded. 'Fire crews suspect a gas explosion.' She glanced at him again. 'Have you...been involved in a retrieval like this before?'

'Unfortunately, yes. Buildings may not collapse every day but, yes, I've been involved with this sort of retrieval in the past.'

'Good. Well, if you have any tips,' she said as quite a few of the retrieval team started to gather in the nurses' station, 'don't be afraid to speak up.'

'Oh, I will.' Richard gave her one of those small smiles that never failed to make her heart flip-flop. She wished he wouldn't, especially now when she was trying desperately to concentrate and put what they'd been so close to finally achieving back there in her office completely out of her mind. It wasn't like her to be so unprofessional, but there it was—she was affected by him even in the midst of a crisis. Surely that wasn't right?

Once the majority of the retrieval team had arrived, Bergan accepted the latest updated information from Katrina, who had just finished a phone call from a police officer on the scene, and began the briefing, pleased that her friends, Mackenzie, Reggie and Sunainah, each qualified specialists in their own right, would also make up part of the team heading out to the accident site.

'We've contacted the Red Cross and they'll be setting up a temporary triage station at the local community hall, which is only half a block down from the collapsed building,' Bergan stated. 'Katrina and Sunainah, I'd like you to go there and work with the volunteers to get things set up as quickly as possible. At the moment the count is at least thirty people trapped in the collapsed building, but that doesn't take into account patients or clients who may have been in the waiting rooms of the three different businesses.'

She looked across at Sunainah. 'The dentist's rooms were holding a school clinic today, which is why I'll need you there as lead paediatrician,' she told her friend.

Sunainah nodded in acceptance and Bergan continued. 'The collapse has also affected traffic. Several chunks of the building have fallen onto the footpath and the road so we could be looking at more than sixty possible patients. Some might have scratches and bruises, but others will definitely need more treatment. Extra staff have been called into A and E and both emergency and elective theatres are preparing for the influx.'

'I take it the police have cordoned off the entire block?' Richard asked.

'But we still have access to the community centre?' Mackenzie checked.

'Yes.' As Bergan continued to give out jobs and direct her team, she couldn't help being highly conscious of Richard standing just off to her right. As she looked around at the staff, some already dressed in their bright blue and yellow retrieval overalls, she tried to avoid looking directly at Richard. Just the sight of his bluer-than-blue eyes, eyes that were so expressive they had the ability to make her knees turn to jelly with one simple look, was enough to ruin her concentration.

She'd been about to kiss him. To really kiss him! She'd dreamt of it often enough during the past few weeks, and while she'd been delighted that he hadn't pressured her, that he'd let her set the pace, she honestly hadn't expected him to hold back as much as he had. Had he honestly been waiting for her to give him permission to kiss her? That in itself spoke volumes about his character, about his trustworthiness, about how he was showing her she could rely on him to stay true to his word.

Bergan had given up years ago ever thinking a man like Richard Allington existed. A man who *was* honourable, giving and caring. He often treated her as though she were some sort of queen, his considerate nature showing her that he wanted nothing more than to make her happy. Was it possible? *Could* she allow herself to be happy? Not just for now but for *ever*?

She made the mistake of glancing at him just as she started to wrap up her instructions, and at the serious look of concentration on his face Bergan once again felt her heart melt. He cared. He really cared about his work, about people, about the patients they were about to go and help. And he really cared about her, too.

For so long she'd kept her heart wrapped up tight, locked behind imaginary doors, knowing if she went to great lengths to protect herself, no one could ever hurt her again. And they hadn't. She was a strong, proud and very independent woman, but when she was alone with Richard, especially sharing a quiet night just sitting and chatting, or watching a television show with his arm securely around her as she snuggled into him, Bergan had to admit she felt happy and feminine but also incredibly vulnerable…and it was the last part she didn't like.

'What about me?' Richard asked. 'You haven't given me a job yet. Floating between the site and the community centre?'

'No. You have experience with this type of rescue, so you'll be with me.' She cleared her throat as she said the last words then nodded to everyone else gathered around her. 'That's about it.' As people started to disband, to go and do as she'd instructed, Bergan called out, 'And don't forget to ensure your walkie-talkies are switched to the right frequency.'

She let out a long sigh as she turned to face Richard, who was now leaning against the desk.

'How are you holding up?' he asked.

'OK.'

'Retrievals are never easy—emotionally, I mean. I think that's when we all really need be totally professional in order to deal with the unusual situation we're walking into.'

'Yes.'

'You do very well, preparing the staff, giving everyone jobs. Holding it all together.' He nodded. 'You're an expert at that.'

Bergan frowned. 'Is that a back-handed compliment?'

'What?' Richard looked surprised. 'No. Of course it isn't. I'm saying I admire you, Bergan. I almost envy the way you're able to keep it all together.'

She shifted her weight to the other foot and crossed her arms, looking him directly in the eye. 'Are you saying you can't?'

He stood up straight, giving her a quizzical glance. 'What's wrong? Why are you being so antagonistic towards me?' His words weren't rude, just confused, and Bergan didn't blame him. It wasn't fair of her to snap at him simply because he had the ability to break through her barriers, to get her excited, to make her feel vulnerable.

'Nothing.' She closed her eyes for a second and shook her head. 'I'd better get changed.' Without waiting for a reply, Bergan headed off towards the female change rooms, leaving a very confused Richard watching her walk away.

When they arrived at the accident site, the police waved through the mini-van carrying the staff and the two ambulances that had come to take the first of the injured back to the hospital. The members of the team began to disperse, each one knowing exactly what to do and where he or she was needed.

'Bergan.' A man dressed in a firefighter's rescue uniform came up to her.

'Palmer. I was told you were the man in charge of everything. Good.' She jerked her thumb over her shoulder. 'This is Richard Allington. We'll be working point with you at the site.'

'Terry Palmer,' the man said, and quickly shook hands with Richard, before leading the two of them through the maze of police cars and fire trucks towards the rubble that had previously been a place of business.

'Status update?' Bergan and Richard both carried large medical kits as they followed Palmer, taking in the sight of destruction as well as the smell of despair and devastation.

'You couldn't have timed it better. We're about to pull the first of the survivors from the rubble. There are several pedestrians and motorists who require medical attention, but now that your teams are here, they'll no doubt take care of them.'

'That's what they're trained to do,' Bergan replied as she navigated around a large section of broken sandstone. 'It was reported as a gas explosion.'

'That's the preliminary finding but we won't know for sure until later. At this point we've taken the necessary precautions and shut down all non-essential services to this area.'

'And the community centre?' Richard asked. 'I understand that's close by. Does it have water?'

'Yes. Also, it doesn't have gas pipes, it's all electric, so the medical teams and the Red Cross volunteers should be able to do what needs to be done.'

Bergan continued to look around them as they drew closer to the centre of the blast. 'Oh, my goodness!' she gasped, placing her free hand over her mouth, more from shock at what she was seeing than to protect herself from the dust cloud, which seemed to be suspended in the air.

The actual site looked more like an anthill than a building. Several of Palmer's men, in their bright reflective yellow clothes, were clambering on the mound, carefully moving pieces of rubble with their gloved hands, while others where setting up the heavier machinery that would be required to lift the large sections.

'It doesn't matter how many times you see it, you're never fully prepared for the devastation.' Richard placed his hand on her shoulder, giving it a little reassuring squeeze, showing her he understood exactly how she was feeling. It was strange how alike they were, how they seemed to think the same. It was another thing she wasn't quite used to, having a man actually understand the way she thought.

'Palmer!' one of the firefighters called, and immediately Palmer went over, scrambling over the rubble as easily as a mountain goat. A moment later Palmer was calling them over.

Richard and Bergan made their way towards him and

by the time they arrived, one young girl, about eleven years old with braces on her teeth, was being lifted carefully onto a stretcher.

'Where do you want her?' the firefighter asked.

Bergan quickly looked around, her mind snapping into professional mode, and pointed to a more level part of the rubble. 'Just there. Let me assess her.'

'We've got another one,' one of the men called, and Richard only had to glance at Bergan for them to communicate effectively what needed to be done. She knelt down by the young girl and opened her medical kit as Richard went off to attend to the next patient. They both knew that the sooner people were pulled from the rubble and treated, the better the outcome.

By the time Bergan had dealt with the young girl, calling through on her walkie-talkie to alert Sunainah to the first paediatric case, another patient was waiting for her.

'We've managed to move a large section of the brickwork, which has thankfully given us access to what used to be the dentist's area,' Palmer told her as she dispatched an elderly man back to Sunshine General in an ambulance. 'Once we've sorted out this section, we can start heading downwards, picking our way carefully.'

'How long will it take to clear the whole site?'

'Could be as long as a day or two. It just depends.'

Bergan pursed her lips, but at the call of another person being lifted from the mound of despair she nodded and headed over to do her job. The next woman to be extracted had multiple fractures to her legs and arms and Bergan immediately radioed for Mackenzie's orthopaedic expertise.

'How are things at the community centre?' she asked her friend as the two of them worked together after

Mackenzie had joined her, Bergan inserting an intravenous drip into the woman's arm as Mackenzie splinted the woman's legs.

'Settled.' Mackenzie shrugged. 'Quite a few people being treated for shock, unable to believe something like this could happen in downtown Maroochydore. Where's Richard?' she asked.

Bergan looked around their immediate vicinity, but there was no sign of him. 'I haven't seen him for quite a while. He'll be around somewhere. I'll check with Palmer.'

'Right. I can take it from here. Is there an ambulance due back soon?'

'One is expected in about five minutes.'

'Excellent.'

Bergan left Mackenzie with the patient and headed over to where Palmer was talking to someone on his walkie-talkie. He stood near the edge of one of the large holes that had been excavated. There were also a few abseiling ropes going down into the hole, indicating there were men down there, working their hardest to continue rescuing people from the rubble.

'Status update? Over.' Palmer waited for a moment and Bergan listened in, waiting to ask Palmer if he knew where Richard had gone.

'Slow, but we can hear her and she can hear us. Over.'

'That's Richard!' Bergan stated with incredulity, and pointed to the walkie-talkie in Palmer's hand.

'Yes.'

'What's he doing down there?' And why was there a sudden weight pressing on her chest? Concern for his safety, the need to see with her own eyes that he was indeed OK became paramount. She closed her eyes for a brief moment, trying to get her thoughts under control, to pull on her professionalism, but all she saw was the image of Richard lying in that large hole, covered with dust and rubble. She swallowed convulsively, unable to stop the sensation of dread spreading through her. At a loud noise from down in the hole, her eyes snapped open and she stared worriedly at Palmer.

'Is he all right? Is Richard all right?'

Palmer frowned at her for a second, clearly puzzled by her reaction, before nodding. 'He's fine. There's a woman down there who my men have been talking to while they dig her out. She was complaining of pain and they were hoping that if they could at least get one of her limbs exposed, Richard might be able to put a drip in.' Palmer shrugged. 'Whether or not they'll succeed in time is anybody's guess, but we need to be prepared.'

'I quite agree, but—' She stopped, almost about to ask Palmer why it had to be *Richard* who had gone down, but of course she knew the answer. He was not only a brilliant doctor with experience in such situations, but she also had no doubt that he'd volunteered for the task. It was just like him. Part of her was proud of his courage, the other part was frightened in case something bad happened.

'Is it stable?' she asked Palmer, and to her surprise there was a tremor in her voice. 'The walls, I mean. They won't cave in?'

'It's safe, Bergan. I wouldn't let my men down there if it wasn't. You know what a safety-first type of guy I am.'

She nodded, knowing he spoke the truth. They'd worked together on different retrievals quite a lot over the years, and even though she'd politely refused his suggestions that they perhaps turn their professional relationship into something more, she still knew she could rely on Palmer never to put anyone in danger.

Palmer's walkie-talkie crackled and one of his men spoke.

'We're getting closer but the doc thinks he might need assistance with the medical stuff. Is there anyone free up there to give him a hand? Over.'

'I'll do it,' Bergan volunteered, before Palmer could depress the button to reply. When he looked at her, she shrugged. 'I know how to abseil and I am currently without a patient to care for.'

Palmer nodded. 'Bergan will be down in a few minutes. Over.'

With that, she walked over to where the harnesses were kept and stepped into one, buckling it securely. Palmer hooked her into a D-clamp and attached the ropes, handing her a pair of gloves. 'I don't know if they're a good fit. They might be a bit big.'

She slipped her hands in. 'I'll manage.'

'You always do.' Palmer double-checked her ropes and clamps, before announcing to his men that she was on her way down.

Taking a deep breath, Bergan eased over the edge of the rubble before seating herself more firmly into the harness. Slowly feeding the rope through the clamp, she lowered herself into the hole, looking down towards the shining lights the workers had set up.

'Almost there,' she heard Richard's voice say, and in another few moments she felt his hands clamp around her waist to steady her until her feet met the uneven ground. She turned to face him, their hard hats almost hitting each other. 'Good of you to drop in,' he murmured, and some of the men chuckled.

'She's down. Over.' Richard spoke into the walkie-talkie, then helped to unhook her from the abseiling rope. Bergan pulled off her gloves, her gaze travelling over Richard as though to reassure herself that he was indeed OK. She let out a sigh of relief, her mind beginning to clear of the fog that had surrounded it.

'Status?' she asked, pleased to feel more in control, more like her old self again.

'Female, thirty-one years old. Wendy. Married with one child, who has already been lifted out. She's conscious, quite lucid, can't feel her legs, is having trouble breathing and is very dizzy.' Richard spoke quietly as he led Bergan carefully towards where the men were still excavating.

'Prognosis?'

Richard met her gaze and as her eyes had now had time to adjust to the change from natural to artificial light, she could see the pain reflected there as he slowly shook his head. 'It's not good. I don't know how we're going to sit there, talking to her, waiting patiently for the rescue team to dig her out, but—'

'That's our job,' she finished for him. She could feel his fear for the patient, but was amazed at the way he was able to hold himself together.

She slipped her hand into his and gave it a reassuring squeeze. 'You're not alone, Richard. Whatever it is we need to face, we can face it together.'

As she spoke the words, looking up into his eyes, she realised she truly meant those words, not just in relation to their present situation. She *wanted* to be with Richard. She *wanted* to support him and to have him support her in return. She *wanted* to face whatever life threw at them and she wanted them to face it…together.

CHAPTER NINE

'HELLO? RICHARD? ARE you still there?' a woman's voice asked.

Richard cleared his throat as Wendy's voice floated up through the rubble. He let go of Bergan's hand and with extreme caution sat down on the pile of bricks and mortar near where Wendy's voice had come from. Bergan followed suit.

'I'm still here, Wendy.' To Bergan's surprise, his tone was calm and controlled. 'Just helping my colleague down.'

'Oh. Is that Bergan?' Wendy's voice was interested and Bergan frowned for a moment, feeling a little strange at meeting a woman she couldn't see.

'You told her about me?' Bergan's words were a quiet, perplexed whisper and whether it was the surprised look on her face or the fact that he really was drawing strength from her, Richard nodded his head and smiled.

'How could I not?' he said softly, then angled his head towards the rubble. 'Talk to her. Help me help her.'

Bergan nodded and cleared her throat. 'I'm here, too, Wendy. Can you tell me how you're feeling?'

There was a moment of silence before Wendy's wavering words floated up to them. 'I can't feel my legs.'

The sentence ended with a sob and Bergan raised her gaze to look at Richard, communicating wordlessly that this probably meant there was some sort of spinal damage.

'What about your hands? Can you wriggle your fingers?'

'Yes. I can wriggle my fingers on my left hand, but it really hurts when I try to do it on the right.'

'Possible fractured arm.' Richard spoke softly.

Bergan nodded. 'What about your head?'

'I'm dizzy.'

'That's natural.' Bergan tried to inject a calmness into her tone she didn't really feel. The one thing they had to do at the moment was to keep Wendy as reassured and as stable as possible. 'Talk to her for a moment,' she said to Richard as she held out her free hand for the walkie-talkie. 'I need to give Palmer instructions.' Richard started talking to Wendy while Bergan called up to Palmer.

'I want Reggie and Mackenzie at the top of the hole with a waiting ambulance as soon as we're ready to bring Wendy up. No excuses. Over.' There was determination in her tone. They were going to get Wendy out and she was going to be alive when they did.

With Reggie and Mackenzie waiting at the top, Wendy would be guaranteed two of the best surgeons Sunshine General employed. Bergan pushed aside the small bubble of doubt that entered her thoughts as she glanced at the workers who were carefully and as quickly as possible removing the rubble that had buried Wendy. They *would* get Wendy out—alive.

'I think Mackenzie went back to the hospital with a patient. Over.'

'I said no excuses. You tell them *I* need them. Use

those exact words. That'll be enough. Over.' Bergan placed the walkie-talkie in Richard's top overall pocket. 'Let's get set up.'

'Richard? Bergan?' Wendy's words floated up. 'What's…what's happening?'

There was a smile in Richard's voice as he spoke. 'Bergan's switching into stubborn mode.'

'Is that a good thing?' Wendy wanted to know.

Richard's rich chuckle filled the cavern as he watched Bergan open the medical kit and start preparing what they'd need for an intravenous drip. He noted she had both a bag of saline and a bag of plasma. 'That's a very good thing, Wendy. Never have I met a more stubborn woman than Bergan.'

'Really?' Bergan was surprised at that. 'Never? You've worked all over the world and you've never met a woman more stubborn than me?' She kept her tone light but loud enough for Wendy to hear.

'I speak the truth,' Richard remarked.

'You two sound like you're much closer than just colleagues.' Wendy's words floated up to them and Bergan could hear that she was definitely interested. That was good. If they could keep Wendy's cognitive functions working, keep her lucid until they could reach her, that would be fantastic.

'When you work closely with people, you tend to build closer relationships,' Bergan stated, needing to keep her words matter-of-fact because if she stopped to think about the personal relationship she presently shared with Richard, she might lose her focus altogether. 'Wendy, can you tell me where it hurts most?' she asked.

Bergan was determined to do everything in her power to save Wendy's life. She wasn't sure exactly *how* she was going to accomplish that but she'd learned long ago that if she focused her determination, if she dug her stubborn heels into a situation, she could usually make some sort of difference.

'Wendy? Wendy?' she called when the other woman didn't reply instantly. 'Where does it hurt?'

'Everywhere. My stomach. My heart. My head.'

Bergan closed her eyes, trying to picture Wendy's body, trying to get a clear picture in her mind so that when they had access, she could work more quickly. 'Try and be specific. I know it's not easy, Wendy, but when we get to you—'

'If,' Wendy interrupted.

'*When* we get to you,' Bergan said, stubborn determination in her voice. 'It will make it easier for Richard and I if we know more about where the pain is centred. Just try and focus for me, Wendy. We are going to get you out and you are going to live. I want you to believe that and if you can't believe, I want you to believe in Richard and me. I want you to believe in the crews that are working so incredibly hard up here to make sure we get to you very, very soon.

'I want you to believe that I have two of my best friends, two women who are brilliant surgeons, waiting for you at the top, to give you the treatment you need so you can recover and get back to your family. This *is* possible, Wendy, and as difficult as it is right now to hang on to hope...' Bergan looked across at Richard, who had pulled on a pair of heavy gloves and was helping the crews lift a particularly large section of bricks. He seemed to feel her eyes on him and the instant their gazes met, Bergan said, 'There always has to be hope.'

'She's right,' one of the rescue workers said, and Bergan was amazed to see their weary bodies almost flood with energy, flood with strength, even though they'd already been working so hard for so long.

'Wendy?' Bergan called. 'Where does it hurt?'

'It hurts most near my stomach and I…I keep getting very dizzy and…and tired,' Wendy said, sniffing a little, then coughing and moaning in pain. Bergan closed her eyes, forcing herself to concentrate, drawing a mental picture of Wendy's situation. Opening her eyes, she pulled a few more things to the front of the medical kit, ensuring she would have everything she needed at her fingertips.

'I can see her!' The call came from one of the rescue workers who was lying down on his stomach, peering through a small crack in the rubble. 'Not too far below us is another cavern, similar to this one, so we're going to need to go slowly so we don't cause a cave-in, but I can see her.'

The words were like another burst of energy for the crews, one of them radioing up to Palmer to let him know of this latest development.

Richard and Bergan quickly picked up their equipment and carefully made their way around to where the worker was lying on his stomach.

'Where?' Bergan asked, and as he shifted, she lay down and peered through the hole, surprised that Wendy was indeed much closer than she'd originally thought. She could see the left side of Wendy's body and it was then she realised the woman was lying at an angle, a large wooden beam pinning down the lower half of her body and broken bricks pressing into her back, as well as her abdomen. The woman's face, however, was partly obscured from view.

'Wendy. Wendy, we can see you!' She shifted out

of the way so Richard could look and also assess the situation.

'Really?' Wendy instantly tried to shift at this news. It was a natural human reaction.

'Stay still,' Richard instructed. 'It's natural to want to move but we need you to remain as still and as calm as you have been up until now. You're doing an incredible job, Wendy,' Richard said encouragingly as he straightened. 'How is she breathing?' he asked softly, looking at Bergan.

'There must be a pocket of air around her mouth and nose,' Bergan guessed with a shrug of her shoulders. 'Whatever it is, I'm not going to quibble because it's allowed her enough oxygen to stay alive.'

'Good point.' Richard nodded then angled his words down towards Wendy's body. 'The crews up here are going to do their thing while Bergan and I get ready. Just remember to stay as still as possible.'

'OK.' The hope in her tone was obvious. Until then, it had been difficult to keep the other woman's spirits buoyed, but they'd done it and now they were going to get her out.

As the crews continued to work, Bergan asked Wendy about her family, about her husband and children, because now that Wendy had hope, she was happy to talk about those who would hopefully be seeing her soon.

With crews that were galvanised into action, with Bergan and Richard standing ready and Palmer radioing that both Mackenzie and Reggie, as well as the ambulance, were waiting for them at the top, the rescue seemed to speed up. A stretcher was lowered down via abseiling ropes, ready and waiting for Wendy.

'How much longer until we can get to her?' Bergan

asked, hating that all they could do at the moment was wait. It was the part of being out on retrieval she hated most. She wanted to pace up and down, but that was impossible in their present circumstances. As her impatient agitation increased, Richard placed both hands on her shoulders and forced her to look at him.

'Settle. Calm. Breathe.'

'I can't. I need to be next to Wendy, treating her, making a difference, doing *something*.' She shook her head.

'I know, but it won't be too much longer.' He rubbed his hands up and down her upper arms, wanting to support her. 'The fact that each second feels as long as a minute doesn't help either.'

'No.'

'Bergan? Richard?' one of the rescuers called. 'We've managed to open the cavern a bit.'

'We have access to her?'

'We do. Her left arm is clear, so at least you can start to treat her now.'

'That's marvellous news.'

Richard and Bergan carefully made their way across the rubble to where a new area had been excavated.

'You go first,' Richard said. 'You're much lighter than I am. I can pass you what you need.'

'OK.'

The rescuers were talking to Wendy, keeping her lucid, but when Bergan spoke she could almost hear the relief in Wendy's tone.

'I thought you'd left me,' the woman said, a quiver in her voice.

'Not a chance,' Bergan replied as she followed the instructions given by the crew to sit down and carefully slide and crawl her way closer to Wendy.

'The last thing we want is for that pile to shift.'

'Agreed.'

'Wendy?' Bergan spoke softly once she was in position.

'You're here?' Wendy's tone was filled with excited relief.

'I am. I'm going to touch your free arm now.' Bergan reached out a gloved hand and placed it on Wendy's right arm. 'I know this is going to be very difficult, given we're so close to getting you out, but we still need to take everything very slowly, to take our time, to make sure nothing goes wrong. And to do that I need you to be as still as possible.'

She found the pulse at Wendy's wrist and did a quick count of the beats. 'Sphygmo,' she said to Richard, who instantly nodded and located the portable sphygmomanometer in the medical kit.

Bergan shone the torchlight onto Wendy's arm, hoping to find a decent vein, one that could easily house a needle, which would be connected to a bag of plasma. 'I want to try and talk you through everything I'm doing so you're not startled. The last thing we want right now is to startle you and cause you to move suddenly.'

'Yes.'

'I'm going to wind a cuff around your arm so I can take your blood pressure. All right?'

'Yes,' Wendy replied again.

'After that, from what you've been telling me, with the way you've been feeling dizzy and sometimes zoning in and out, there's a high probability that you're bleeding internally. So what I want to do is first of all give you something for the pain and then I'll put a needle into your arm. That will be attached to a bag of plasma, which will help keep your blood level more stable. The more we can do for you down here, the more stable you'll be when you're ready to go to Theatre.'

'OK.' Wendy was silent for a moment. 'Is Richard near?'

'I'm here, Wendy,' he responded as he accepted the sphygmo back from Bergan. They'd been working alongside each other in the A and E for a couple of weeks now so she wasn't surprised at the way he was able to pre-empt everything she required.

'Of course you want him to talk to you.' Bergan chuckled. 'He has a much sexier voice than mine.'

'I guess he does,' Wendy agreed, and there was a clear hint of embarrassment along with appreciation in her tone. 'But that doesn't mean I don't want to hear yours.'

'Well, I appreciate that,' Bergan said as she drew up an injection of methoxyflurane for pain relief. 'I'm going to swab your arm and give you an injection. You may feel even more light-headed afterwards, but keep trying to talk to us, all right?'

'I'll try.'

'Good.' Bergan administered the injection, then explained to Wendy how she was going to set up the intravenous drip. Throughout it all the crews continued to work, Palmer kept calling down on the walkie-talkie for an update of the situation and little by little more of Wendy's body was exposed.

Finally, they were able to see Wendy's face, although the woman's legs were still trapped beneath the beam.

'We'll need to hook it to the winch to lift it off. Over,' one of the workers was telling Palmer. Things were definitely progressing but Bergan was more focused on Wendy's physical and emotional health. She fitted an oxygen non-rebreather mask over Wendy's mouth and nose, glad she and Richard were able to help the poor woman in whatever way they could. Although conditions were far from ideal, the fact they'd been able to get to Wendy as soon as possible could make a tremendous difference.

'There's a large gash on her abdomen,' Richard said, as one of the workers removed another piece of rubble, allowing him further access to Wendy's battered body. Richard shifted forward, carefully dragging the medical kit with him. He pulled on a fresh pair of gloves and reached for the heavy-duty scissors. He cut away Wendy's bloodstained and filthy clothing before reaching for some gauze. Bergan helped Richard clean the area around the long gash, debriding it carefully.

Richard glanced up at the area where the workers were carefully removing the rubble from near Wendy's face, pleased Bergan had already given her something for pain. 'How are you doing there, Wendy?'

'OK.'

'Let us know if you have any additional pain, OK? That's very important,' Richard said, as he carefully packed a sterile dressing into the wound, soaking up some of the blood so he could take a better look. 'I need someone to hold a torch for me,' he called, and one of the rescue workers was there within a matter of seconds, shining a bright overhead light onto Wendy's wound. 'Bergan, retract and repack,' he said, as she removed the bloodied packing and pulled the skin back with a retractor to afford Richard a better look.

'See anything?' she asked, also having a careful look.

'Aha.' He reached for a set of locking forceps and clamped the artery.

'I'll clean it up a little more,' Bergan said, packing

the wound once more with clean gauze in order to give them the opportunity of a better look. Then she assisted Richard with suturing the offending artery.

'That should hold things for a while,' he stated as he gathered up the rubbish bag they'd been using. Bergan thanked the rescue worker for holding the torch as she put a firm bandage over the gash.

'How are you feeling now?' she asked as Wendy lay there, her eyes closed, her breathing calm beneath the oxygen mask.

'Floaty.'

Bergan smiled. 'Pain level?'

'OK.'

Bergan's tone was clear but firm as she and Richard continued to monitor the intravenous drip as well as regularly performing neurological observations. They began cleaning and debriding other wounds as soon as they could get to them.

Bergan once more checked Wendy's pupils, pleased things were progressing smoothly. Now, though, it was important Wendy understand the reality of her injuries, and while the information wouldn't be easy to hear, Bergan had learnt of old that it was best to deliver bad news as straightforwardly and with as much compassion as possible.

'Wendy, the damage to your legs is quite extensive.' Bergan watched Wendy's eyes and it was clear to see the anguish reflected there at the news. The poor woman. Bergan's heart went out to her.

'Yes,' she responded, her words barely audible behind the oxygen mask.

Bergan glanced over at Richard, their gazes meeting and holding. She could see he was just as affected by the situation as she was and it made her relax a little.

Usually she had no trouble engaging her professional self, keeping her emotional distance from her patients so that she could do her job effectively. This time, with the heightened circumstances, it was little wonder she was feeling more vulnerable.

Richard gave her an encouraging nod, urging her to continue explaining things to Wendy while he continued to monitor her vital signs. The winch was being lowered and soon they'd have the large beam off Wendy's legs. Then things would move fast. They would need to assess, debride and possibly splint and bandage her legs as quickly as possible. It was clear the femoral artery hadn't been severed, otherwise Wendy would have bled out quite a while ago. But the extent of her fractures…? At this stage, it was anyone's guess.

'Mackenzie is the name of the orthopaedic surgeon who will be treating you. She'll discuss all the options with you once she knows what the damage is, but at this stage it doesn't look good. You can trust her, Wendy. She and I have been friends since we were kids.' Bergan shifted closer to Wendy and after removing her glove placed one hand on Wendy's shoulder as the woman closed her eyes and let the tears quietly flow. Bergan had to bite her lip and look away, otherwise she was in grave danger of losing it herself.

'Will I walk again?' Wendy wanted to know.

Bergan shook her head. 'It's too soon to give a firm diagnosis, but that is one possibility.'

'Not much longer now.' Richard's smooth voice was quiet, intimate, and when Bergan looked across at him, she saw he'd shifted closer, too. He removed one of his gloves and placed his hand over hers, the two of them wanting to show Wendy they supported her, but at the same time Bergan knew it was Richard's way of encouraging her. He was amazing.

Even as the thought passed through her mind, warning bells began to ring. He was amazing. He was supportive. He was handsome. He was kind. He was protective. He was giving. In short, Richard Allington was everything she'd ever allowed herself to dream about.

Naturally, these dreams had been carefully controlled and usually came out of the box she kept them in only when she was at her lowest of low points, wanting a knight in shining armour to ride up on his white horse and rescue her from her horrible life. Then, when she'd come to her senses, she'd push those dreams back into their box, telling herself sternly that no man like that even existed, let alone would come to rescue her.

Keeping people—and especially men—at a distance was one of her specialities, but somehow in a short time Richard had pushed through those barriers, broken them down little by little. In a way it was wonderful, liberating, but Bergan also knew it would end. Richard would leave her, return to Paris to his former life, and soon he would have forgotten all about her. The thought made her want to hold on tighter to him now, to never let him go—but she knew she must, and the sooner, the better.

He was her dream man. Very real and very difficult to resist. The fact that she was coming to rely on him, that she felt exposed and vulnerable around him, that she'd even contemplated spending the rest of her life with him, was enough to turn the warning bells into a full-blown air-raid siren inside her head.

Danger! *Danger!* She had to get away from him as

quickly as possible, because if she didn't, when he left her—as she knew he would—she'd be the one with the broken heart.

CHAPTER TEN

EVEN AFTER THEY'D managed to remove the beam from Wendy's legs then stabilise her and move her carefully onto a stretcher, Bergan still hadn't been able to shake the feeling that she was swimming in uncharted waters.

They handed Wendy's care over to Reggie and Mackenzie, who both went with her in the ambulance.

'What's next?' Bergan asked Palmer once she and Richard were up top again.

'There's not much else you can do here now. From the numbers the police have given us, we've managed to get everyone else out. Most have been sent to the community centre, although quite a few have been taken immediately to Sunshine General.'

'OK, thanks, Palmer.'

Palmer looked from Richard back to Bergan and nodded. 'You two make a good team.' He held out his hand to Richard and shook it. 'Take care of her.'

Richard shook Palmer's hand, looking as though he had no clue what was happening. 'Bergan takes pretty good care of herself.'

Bergan glanced up at Richard, pleased he'd championed her. He truly believed in her. The knowledge warmed her heart and at the same time only made it more difficult for her to distance herself from him.

'What was that all about?' Richard asked as they both walked away from the rubble.

Bergan shrugged. 'Nothing much.'

'Has he tried to date you in the past?'

'He's asked me out a few times.'

'Ah. He wants to protect you, eh?' Richard nodded. 'That makes more sense.'

'What do you mean?'

Richard pushed his hands through his hair a few times, glad the hard hat was off his head as he tried to shake out the dust, which no doubt made him look almost grey. 'Most men want to protect the women they're interested in, especially when they abseil into unstable caverns.'

Bergan frowned. 'So you're saying I shouldn't have abseiled down to help you out?' Her tone was clipped and instantly defensive.

Richard was astonished and placed a hand on her arm to stop her from walking. 'No.' He looked down into her face, wanting to make sure he conveyed his point as clearly as possible. 'As I said to Palmer, you can take care of yourself. It's quite evident you've been taking care of yourself for most of your life. All I meant was that a lot of men want to protect the women they care about. It's been going on since caveman days.'

He smiled at her, that gorgeous heart-thumping smile that never failed to send Bergan's insides into overdrive. How was it he could defuse her temper so easily? One moment she was hot under the collar and the next she was melting simply because he'd smiled!

She closed her eyes for a moment and shook her head, and a small smattering of dust came loose. Richard coughed and she looked up at him. 'Sorry,' she murmured, as he reached out and brushed his fingers lightly over her hair. She'd wound the long plait into a bun at the nape of her neck when she'd changed into her retrieval overalls, but, even having worn the hard hat, there was still dust everywhere.

'We look like an old grey-haired couple with all this dust.' He coughed again then chuckled, resting his hands on her shoulders. Without another word he pulled her close into his arms and rested his chin on her head. Bergan found herself going willingly, wanting to be held by him, wanting to feel those big strong arms around her.

It was wonderful and she desperately wanted it to last for ever, to know that Richard would always be there, right by her side, but…that wasn't her life and she knew it. She'd known it for as long as she could remember. She was not the sort of woman who was destined to live a normal life.

'Richard?' she said after a few moments.

'Mmm?'

'Do *you* want to protect me?'

He eased back and looked at her, his arms still firmly around her body. He stared into her eyes for a long moment and Bergan began to wonder if he was ever going to answer her. Finally, he cleared his throat. 'Of course I do.' More than she could possibly know, but the last thing he wanted was to scare her, to make her feel as though he was trying to change her. She'd opened up to him, she'd allowed him into her inner sanctum, but he could also sense there was something jittery about her. Whether that had anything to do with Wendy's rescue or something Palmer might have said, he had no idea.

'Don't *you* want to protect *me*?' he asked her, and for some reason she seemed surprised by the question.

'Well, do you need protecting?'

His smile was slow, sensual and incredibly sexy. 'Everyone needs protecting from something, Bergan.'

'What do you need protecting from?'

'Right now? I need protecting from moving too fast, from wanting to capture your perfect lips in a perfect kiss—a kiss that has been a long time coming.' The last thing he wanted was to make a mistake, to do something that would spook Bergan, causing her to retreat.

'Why do you say things like that?' Bergan couldn't believe the slight tremble in her voice.

'Because I only want there to be truth between us.' He rubbed his hands gently on the small of her back, the touch causing a tingling warmth to burst forth within her, flooding her body with need, with wanting, with desperation.

It was what she wanted, too, so why was she hesitating? They'd been about to kiss before they'd been interrupted with the retrieval, so why, now that things were under control, did she hesitate? She didn't know. Sometimes she'd found it better to just jump into the deep end, to sink or swim.

Yes, she knew he would leave her and return to Paris. Yes, she knew he'd broken down far too many of her barriers. Yes, she knew she had to distance herself from him, and the sooner the better, but surely she couldn't deny herself this? This moment? This kiss? This synchronising of their hearts? Hadn't she earned it? All those bad relationships? That pain she'd lived through? Didn't she deserve some sort of reward, even if it was a temporary one?

Breathing in slowly, she held his gaze, ensuring her words and intentions were crystal clear.

'Richard?'

'Mmm?'

'Kiss me,' she whispered. 'Please?'

'You've said that to me once before, Bergan, and we ended up being interrupted by this emergency.' He glanced around at the emergency crews, still doing their job, still needing to continue cleaning up the damage well into the night. The sun was setting but the work would continue, and while he knew the day was far from over for both himself and Bergan, having these few selfish moments would definitely help him recharge his batteries.

'Then you should shut up and get on with it.'

Richard exhaled quickly at her words. 'You never fail to surprise me,' he murmured, his gaze dipping to take in her parted lips, ready, willing and waiting for him.

'Enough talk,' she grumbled impatiently as she laced her fingers into his hair and forced his head down, now almost bursting with need. She was happy that Richard hadn't pushed her, that he'd let her set the pace. She appreciated his chivalry and admired his patience and particularly after they'd been in such a precarious position not too long ago, caring for Wendy and working harmoniously alongside each other. Even she had to admit that enough was enough.

Back in her office, when they'd been standing so close, the need between them so powerful, she could have sworn Richard had been about to kiss her with all the restraint and tenderness he could muster, determined not to scare her, determined to woo her, to show her he cared. Now, though, after everything they'd endured, and with the fact that Bergan herself had very little patience or restraint left, when their mouths finally met, the kiss was hungry, hot and hard.

It was clear that Richard wanted her just as much as she wanted him, and Bergan was unable to fathom how she'd lost control over her desire for him. Here was a man who had been nothing but sweet and considerate to her, especially during the past few weeks. He'd shared his thoughts with her, he'd cuddled her, holding her close and making her feel as though finally she'd found someone she could truly trust.

As his mouth moved over hers, power and passion combined, both of them breathing unsteadily as they allowed themselves to be gathered up in the glorious sensations of a first kiss. While Richard may have felt like he'd waited an eternity for such a moment, his sluggish mind could at least acknowledge that any dreams or thoughts he'd had about kissing Bergan had been seriously underrated. The *real* Bergan was so much better than anything he'd ever contemplated, and his heart swelled with an emotion so huge he was almost too afraid to accept it. Almost…

To realise he was in love with Bergan was one thing, to *tell* her of his feelings was something completely different, especially as they were only just now sharing their first real and honest moment together.

He loved Bergan! Could it be possible? The realisation brought with it a thousand more questions, but, he decided, there was plenty of time for internalisation, and right now he wanted to concentrate on savouring every moment of her mouth moving perfectly against his own.

There was an uncontrollable need powering through them both, as though they'd been denying themselves for far too long and now that things had built to a frenzy, they were unable to quell it.

He gathered her closer, pressing their bodies close together, wishing they weren't dressed in retrieval overalls, as they were hardly the most romantic of outfits, but at the same time unable to really care.

As his mouth continued to create utter havoc with her senses, Bergan wanted nothing more than for the fire pulsing through them to take its natural course. Richard made her feel so...alive and she couldn't remember *ever* feeling this way.

That realisation should have been enough to scare her, to make her break off the kiss and to push free from his arms, and yet she found herself moaning with pleasure against his lips as she plunged her fingers once more into his hair. The action caused Richard to slow things down just a fraction, but somehow the intensity kept building.

The hunger was still there, but now his lips were more tender. Her heart rate continued to increase, and Bergan was sure that if she'd been hooked up to an ECG machine, she'd have broken it with her off-the-chart heartbeat. She leaned against him, unable to trust her own legs to hold her up. She knew Richard would hold her, that he would ensure she didn't fall—that was the level of trust she had in him—and this time warning bells did start to ring at the back of her mind. She ignored them.

Again and again his perfect and powerful mouth continued to bring forth a surprising and passionate response from her. How was it possible that with a masterful stroke of his tongue, gently caressing her lips, he was able to flood her body with tingles, make her go weak at the knees and cause her mind to stop working? Who was this man? Was he too good to be true?

Another warning bell began to ring, but once again Bergan ignored it.

When he broke his mouth from hers and started pressing a trail of fiery kisses across her cheek and down her neck, nuzzling near her ear, Bergan tilted her head to the side, eagerly allowing him access as she rapidly sucked air into her lungs.

'You are the most stunningly beautiful woman in the world,' he breathed, punctuating his words with little kisses, and she was pleased to note he was just as affected by the kiss as she was. His hands were splayed widely across her back, holding and supporting her, which was something she wanted him to go on doing for ever. Constant, unwavering support.

'For ever?' She whispered the words into the air surrounding them—and instantly wished she hadn't spoken out loud. Then again, it was difficult for her to control her thoughts when her mind had been turned to mush by Richard's masterful touch.

'Sorry?' He pressed more kisses to her neck, wishing her hair was loose, wishing they were somewhere that would afford them a bit more privacy. Although they weren't far from the accident site, Richard had managed to pull her off the main footpath, and now, thanks to the setting sun, they were safe from too many prying eyes, in the shadows of the night.

'Nothing,' she replied, carefully easing her hands from his hair. While he'd been kissing her, she hadn't wanted him to stop—ever. She'd wanted the moment to last for ever, to hear him say the words that would make all her crazy, silly dreams come true. That the two of them could be together...for ever.

Now, though, as her sluggish senses began to return to normal, she was acutely aware of their surroundings, of the number of people still working to clear the rubble, to put up fences and warning beacons to ensure the public's safety.

There were patients to see, a job to do, and she'd been indulging in the desire to finally have Richard's mouth against her own. She could rationalise and give the excuse that they'd been through so much medical trauma tonight they both deserved a few minutes to recharge and regroup, but she didn't like herself when she made excuses. She'd wanted Richard to kiss her. Pure and simple. An opportunity had presented itself and she'd taken it.

He was still bending down, brushing small kisses to her neck and jaw, as though savouring the sensations. Her eyelids fluttered closed as her mind zoomed in on the way his light and feathery kisses were still creating havoc with her equilibrium.

'Do you have any idea what you do to me?'

'Richard,' she breathed again, knowing she needed to put a stop to this. She slid her arms down from his neck, bringing them to rest at the top of his firm chest. 'We need to—'

'I'm so glad we waited until you were ready because I have to tell you, Bergan, I was not disappointed.'

She eased back a little. 'You weren't?' Why did she feel such an overwhelming sense of relief at this news? How was it he always seemed to know just what to say? In the back of her mind, while conscious they needed to stop what they were doing and concentrate on work, she had been wondering what he might be thinking, whether or not the kiss had meant as much to him as it had to her. The fact it had meant *a lot* to her set off another warning bell.

For now, she looked at the way he was smiling at her. 'No. The real Bergan is one hundred times better than any dreams I've had.'

'You dream about me?'

His smile increased. 'You don't dream about me?' There was a slight teasing note in his voice, and before she could say anything, he bent his head and pressed another firm but long and satisfying kiss to her mouth. 'Your lips are perfect for mine,' he murmured, then shifted his stance, marginally loosening his hold on her. 'And I'd like to request a repeat performance later on, once everything else is under control.'

'And you've finished your shift,' she pointed out, a tight pressure starting to wind itself around her heart. She wanted nothing more than to do as he asked, but at the same time being near Richard was starting to cause her to panic.

'Whatever you say, boss.' With great reluctance Richard dropped his arms and released her, before taking a step back. Bergan was surprised to find she felt both cold and bereft without his touch.

That wasn't right. She'd always been fiercely independent. She'd always been in control of her life, yet being here with Richard, wanting to hold him, kiss him and have him close to her at all times was wrong. It had to be wrong because the last thing she felt right now was in control.

She took a step back, putting some much-needed distance between them, rubbing her hands on her upper arms, trying to shake the sensation of returning to his arms...for ever.

'Are you all right?'

'Me? Sure. I'm fine. As fine as fine can be.' She started talking fast. 'I think we need to get back to work. To check and...to do things and find out what's happening with Wendy and see if we can be of assistance anywhere else.'

'Do you want to head to the hospital?' Richard asked.

'You go ahead.' She took another few steps away

from him and jerked her thumb over her shoulder. 'I'm going to go see how things are at the community centre.'

'But Palmer said Sunainah had things under control.'

'I know. I just want to check. She might need a break. To have a coffee or use the bathroom and she might not be able to if no one comes to relieve her. You know how busy a makeshift A and E can be.'

'I do. OK. I'll come with you.' He started to take a few steps towards her but she instantly put her hands up to stop him, making sure she didn't accidentally touch him in the process. She was having a difficult enough time controlling the way his nearness made her feel. Now that she knew how glorious it was to kiss Richard, she wanted to do it all the time.

'No. No. It's better that you go back to the hospital, make sure things are under control in A and E.'

'It won't take long to check the community centre,' he continued, clearly not able to take the hints she was dropping.

'Well, OK, then.' A slight edge came into her voice before she could stop it. 'You go to the community centre and I'll head back to A and E. That's probably the better option given it *is* my A and E department.' She gave a nervous laugh and pointed across the road, where she could see two paramedics finishing up securing their patient before leaving for the hospital. 'I'll hitch a ride with them.'

'Bergan?' Richard reached out, putting both hands on her shoulders. 'What's wrong?'

'Wrong? There's nothing wrong. I'm just trying to be efficient, ensure the patients are getting the best care. There's no point in us staying together, walking side by side like we're doing some sort of ward round.' She was talking faster again, trying not to succumb to the warmth of his hands on her shoulders, of the growing need she had to rest her head against his chest, to draw strength from him.

She didn't need his super-fantastic kindness right now. She didn't need his adorableness winding its way around her. She didn't need those hypnotic blue eyes that had the ability to make her forget anyone and everything as soon as she allowed herself to stare at them for more than a few seconds.

No. What she needed was distance, because even acknowledging she wanted nothing more than to be in his arms, feeling safe and secure, as though nothing bad would ever happen to her again, Bergan knew her childish fantasy would end in despair. It was best she kept herself safe, pull away from him sooner rather than later.

'I think Wendy's retrieval shook you up more than you realised,' he murmured, a small frown creasing his brow as though he really didn't understand her.

Bergan clutched at the excuse, using it willingly, even though she knew it wasn't necessarily true. 'You're probably right. We can only keep the professionalism in place for so long before the reality of the situations we see start to seep into our emotions.'

'Hmm.' He looked into her eyes for a moment. 'OK.' He relented, much to her relief. 'I'll check on how Sunainah is progressing at the community centre and you head back to the hospital.'

'OK.' Without another word she turned and all but sprinted over to the paramedics. 'Mind if I hitch a ride?' she asked, climbing into the back of the ambulance without being invited. 'I can care for the patient.'

'Thanks, Bergan,' they said, and within another few minutes she was on her way back to the hospital, away from Richard. Distance. She needed distance so she could think, to try and understand exactly what was going on between the two of them, because of one thing she was certain—that kiss had changed *everything*.

CHAPTER ELEVEN

IT WAS THE early hours of the morning before Bergan was able to finally make her way home. It had been a very long day, but she hadn't been able to leave the hospital until Wendy had come out of Theatre.

Bergan had stood by the bed in Recovery, looking at the woman who had been so brave, who had done everything they'd asked as the rescue crews had painstakingly removed rubble in order to get her out. She'd spoken to Wendy's family, explaining just how brave Wendy had been. Now, as she watched Wendy sleep, her body in an induced coma, Bergan knew exactly how her patient must have felt.

Wendy had had physical bricks and mortar closing her in. She herself, on the other hand, seemed to be buried beneath a mound of pain and hurt, repressed memories from her past and the inability to believe she could ever be truly happy.

The fact that Richard had broken down so many of her barriers was enough to cause her great anxiety. He was so wonderful and sweet and sexy and caring and... She sighed and closed her eyes, knowing the simple truth was that she didn't deserve a man like him. After everything she'd done in her past, even though she'd done her best to make amends, did she have the right to expect a man of Richard's calibre to sweep her off her feet and carry her off into the sunset?

'Hey. Here you are. I've been looking for you.'

She turned at the sound of his soft voice, her heart thumping with pure delight at the sight of him. Why did he have to be so...perfect? He looked at the information on the machines around Wendy's bed, nodding his head, pleased with the results. 'It's a miracle she's alive.'

'Yes.' Richard was standing just behind her, the warmth from his body surrounding her like a comforting blanket. Bergan closed her eyes for a moment, breathing in the scent of him, which always seemed to relax her. Her body tingled at his nearness and once more she found it difficult to concentrate.

At this time of the morning there were a few of the nursing staff around the place, but for the most part, as they stood by Wendy's bed, Bergan was only conscious of the two of them. Whenever Richard was near, it was as though the rest of the world melted away. She wanted to ease back a little, to lean against him, and before tonight she probably would have felt secure in doing that, but now...? Since that life-changing kiss? She just wasn't sure what was happening any more.

He was important to her. She liked him more than she could ever remember liking any man before, but the biggest thing that scared her more than anything was that she trusted him. She'd shared a very intimate and emotional part of her upbringing with him, she'd taken him to the drop-in centre, she'd experienced a moment of dreaded fear when Palmer had first told her that Richard was down in the cavern of rubble. What if something bad had happened to him? Even now, reflecting back, her heart was pierced with a pain she couldn't begin to fully comprehend.

It couldn't possibly be love. She didn't *do* love. Not the lifelong, happily-ever-after type of love that she'd occasionally witnessed. Mackenzie and her new husband John. Even Richard's parents, Helen and Thomas. It was clear that pure love *did* exist…but not for her.

As they stood there, Richard moved closer and draped his arm naturally around her shoulders. For the past few weeks, feeling his gentle, caring touch like this had filled her with delight, had helped her to let go of her stress, had relaxed her, but now, after the kiss, she wasn't sure what his touch meant.

Did it mean he wanted to leave and go somewhere else so they could continue kissing? Would he want *more* than kissing? When she'd been in his arms, she'd most certainly wanted to share more with him, but now…she wasn't so sure. It was as though he'd turned her world upside down and the sensation of falling, of ending up in a bottomless abyss, was enough to make her panic.

'You're so stiff and tense,' he murmured, and shifted behind her, resting both hands on her shoulders before tenderly massaging her trapezius. 'So tight, but I guess after the night we've had both at the retrieval site and in A and E, that's to be expected.' His words, his small chuckle, the warm breath on the back of her neck, the feel of his clever hands kneading away her stress made her feel light-headed. Bergan closed her eyes again, momentarily allowing him access to her, but the pain in her heart, the anxiety pulsing through her body would not be stilled.

'Uh…' She wriggled her shoulders and shifted away from him.

'Are you all right?' He instantly dropped his hands, looking at her quizzically.

'Uh…sure. Just tired and, well, you know, if you keep doing that, I might fall into a puddle at your feet.'

His smile was instant. 'Never mind. I'd pick you up and carry you home.'

Bergan sighed heavily and shook her head. 'Stop being so nice,' she whispered harshly, and then, seeing the surprised confusion in his eyes, she shook her head and walked away. She could almost feel him watching her, wondering what on earth he'd done wrong. Guilt swamped her. She shouldn't have snapped at him but… but… Her mind was spinning and she was unable to think straight, unable to put things into a neat and clear order.

Bergan stopped by her office, gathered what she needed, locked the door and headed to the car park, barely speaking to the security guard who walked her to her car. Driving home, she refused to think about anything except the small amount of traffic on the road. She found a radio station with a late-night talk show, glad of the mindless chatter in the background. It was far easier to listen to people debating the right amount of fertiliser to put on their vegetables in order to achieve award-winning status at local fairs than try and dissect the way she was feeling.

When she arrived home, she put all thoughts of Richard into a box and shoved it into the far recesses of her mind, before going through the motions of getting ready for bed. She was exhausted and yet, as she lay in her bed, tossing and turning and trying to get comfortable, the image of Richard, staring at her as though she'd just punched him in the solar plexus, refused to wipe itself from her memory.

She didn't want to hurt him, but she feared, in her quest for self-preservation, that she must. The sooner she broke things off with him, the less painful it would be. The fact that a connection had developed at all was her fault and she took complete responsibility for any fallout. Richard only had one more week here and then he would leave. Back to Paris. Back to his normal life… his normal life without her.

She pursed her lips at the thought, unable to stop her throat from thickening with sadness, unable to stop tears from springing to her eyes, unable to stop the pain piercing her heart. Richard would leave and he would forget about her. Once again she'd be alone, because that's the way it was supposed to be.

Turning her face into the pillow, Bergan began to weep. She curled into the foetal position, pulling the sheet tight around her as she allowed the pain and loss of the man who meant so much to her to bubble to the surface and overflow in a river of misery.

'Hi, Mum,' Richard said, answering his phone and lying back on the bed. It was his last day in Australia and he was avoiding getting out of bed, following the irrational theory that if he didn't get up, the day wouldn't start. Neither was he in the mood for chatting to his mother. There was only one person he wanted to talk to and *she* had been ignoring him.

In the days following the building collapse Bergan had put the brakes on and had made every effort to make herself completely unavailable to him. Every time he'd called to see when they were next going to get together, she'd make an excuse. He'd sent her text messages and not received an answer until the next day. She'd even gone as far as to change the roster at work, ensuring their shifts didn't overlap.

'All ready to head back to the northern hemisphere?' Helen asked.

'Sure.'

'Richard? You don't sound all that excited. I'd have thought, after travelling for such a long time, you'd be eager to get home.'

'I am, Mum. So, tell me about what you and Dad have been doing over the past few days,' he said, eager to change the subject, but it appeared Helen was having none of it.

'What's happened?' she asked.

'Nothing, Mum. Everything's fine.'

'Richard, I'm your mother. I know every tone in your voice. Now, I don't expect you to blurt everything out to me, you're a very private man, but I also won't have you insult my intelligence by lying to me when everything clearly isn't fine.'

'I have some things to sort through.'

'Regarding Bergan?'

Richard frowned at the phone. 'How do you figure that?'

Helen chuckled. 'I know every tone in your voice, remember. You may not have spoken much about her directly, but her name has come up quite a bit during our chats. It's not what you say but how you say it, darling.'

'I don't want to talk about it.'

'Mmm-hmm?'

Richard closed his eyes and shook his head. 'She's frustrating, Mum.'

'Mmm-hmm?'

'And annoying and exacerbating. She's driving me insane.'

'Mmm-hmm?'

'We only have a limited amount of time together and

over the last few days she's withdrawn from me, not taking my calls, not responding to my emails or text messages. I even wrote her a note and put it in her letterbox. Nothing. I'm leaving the country tonight, returning to Paris, and yet she hasn't wanted to spend time with me and we were…we were so good together. Or maybe it was only me who thought that.'

'Mmm-hmm?'

'Is she upset because I'm leaving? Is that it? If it is, it's ridiculous. She's known from the start that my time in Australia was limited, that I needed to return to Paris to present my findings.'

'Mmm-hmm?'

'Sure, in the beginning I wasn't sure what might happen when I returned to Paris, but that was before we kissed and now… I don't know how it's possible that a kiss can change things but it can—it did. We're perfect for each other and she was the one who showed me it was OK to take a chance, to try again. She's been knocked down so many times in her life, one thing after another, after another, after another and yet she always finds a way to get back on her feet, to persevere, to keep moving forward. She made me realise it was OK to hope again, to know that time would heal wounds and that I'd be able to love again. And I do. I love her but I know if I tell her, she'll run a mile.'

'Mmm-hmm?'

'Or has she already realised that I love her?' Richard opened his eyes and sat up in bed, this new realisation dawning on him. 'Is that why she's run? Perhaps she's realised that my feelings for her are intense and I'll bet hers are equally as intense and that's why she's put the brakes on. She doesn't *want* me to love her because she doesn't know if she can give me love in return.

'Maybe she's worried that when I return to Paris, I'll forget her. Not a chance of that happening. My heart beats out her name.' He shook his head.

'Mmm-hmm?'

'She's stubborn enough to believe that. Stubborn enough to lock herself away, ensuring she doesn't get hurt, and who can blame her, especially after everything she's been through? She doesn't know how to lean on others, how to believe they'll always be there for her. Doesn't she realise that my life is meaningless without her? Doesn't she know that it doesn't matter where I might be living, I'll only be half a person if she's not right there beside me?'

'Mmm-hmm?'

Richard was silent for a moment as everything he'd just been saying started sinking into some form of coherence in his mind. 'I need to speak to her.'

'Mmm-hmm?'

'But she's just finishing the night shift. She'll be tired and then sleeping. Oh, and I have that dinner tonight and as I'm the guest of honour, I have to go.' He growled in frustration. 'I'll leave early. Bergan is more important than any dinner. She's more important than the fellowship, more important than everything.'

'Mmm-hmm.'

'Thanks, Mum. It was great talking to you, but I've got to go. I've got a bit of planning to do.'

'Anytime, darling,' Helen chuckled.

Some of the A and E staff had organised a little farewell dinner for Richard. Bergan had declined to attend, preferring to head home to a quiet night of not thinking about him, knowing she didn't need to fear him casually dropping in.

When a loud knock came from her front door, Bergan almost jumped right out of her skin, gasping in surprise.

'Bergan?' Mackenzie's voice came from the other side of the door. 'Open up or I'll go and get my spare key.'

'I'm coming. I'm coming.' Bergan hurried to the door, checking first that her friend was alone before opening it.

'Hey. I thought you might have been at the dinner for Richard.'

'I was. He looks terrible.'

'He does?' Concern instantly flooded through her. 'Why? What's wrong?'

'You. You're what's wrong.' Mackenzie stormed into the house and turned to glare at her.

'What have I done now?' Bergan asked as she closed the front door then headed into the kitchen, knowing Mackenzie would follow.

'You know exactly what you've done. Why are you pushing Richard away?'

'What? He's leaving tonight. That's hardly pushing him away. The man has to return to Paris—to his *life* in Paris—and that's the end of it.'

'Is it? So…what? You've decided to push him away first? Self-preservation? You're an idiot.' Mackenzie was working herself up into a right rage. 'All those years you told me that if we worked hard, if we just believed, we could change our future. I believed you and *voilà*!' Mackenzie spread her arms wide. 'Look at me now. I'm *happy*. It wasn't always plain sailing, but from my first marriage came Ruthie and now I have John. It does happen, Bergan. Happiness *can* happen for people like us.'

'No. It happens for people like *you*.' Bergan walked to the fridge and opened it, stared inside for a moment before closing the door and turning to face her friend. 'I'm not meant to be happy.'

'Wha—?' Mackenzie stared at her, completely stunned. Bergan stood there, waiting for one of Mackenzie's optimistic tirades, but it didn't come. Instead, Mackenzie just shook her head, turned and walked to the front door. Bergan frowned. Mackenzie was walking out on her? That wasn't how things usually went.

She waited a moment, listening carefully, and when she heard the front door open, she rushed from the kitchen. 'Kenz! Wai—' She stopped when she saw Richard standing in the open doorway, Mackenzie pushing past him.

'Good luck.'

Had she just heard Mackenzie say that softly to Richard? Bergan's gaze took in the sight of the man of her dreams, standing before her. Her knees began to shake, her hands began to tremble and as she glanced at Mackenzie's retreating form, Bergan felt a surge of anger pulse through her. She wasn't sure whether she was more angry that after one look at Richard her body had betrayed her or that Mackenzie had been the betrayer.

'Did you set this up with her?' She stabbed a finger in the direction Mackenzie had gone.

Richard calmly came into her home, closing the door behind him, his voice quiet and controlled. 'You've been avoiding me, Bergan. I'm a desperate man and that means I needed to take desperate measures.'

She shook her head and turned on her heel, heading back into the kitchen. All she needed were a few seconds to regroup, to adjust to him being here, in her home, especially when she'd resigned herself to never seeing him face-to-face again.

When he sauntered casually into the kitchen, leaning against the doorjamb, his thumbs hooked into the back pockets of his jeans, Bergan's heart turned over. Didn't the man have any idea just how handsome he was? How sexy she found him? How she wanted nothing more than to throw herself into his arms and beg him to never let her go? She swallowed over the sudden dryness of her throat.

She shifted around to the other side of the kitchen table. The more obstacles they had between them the better. As she watched him, she realised he wasn't at all agitated, that he was cool, calm and collected. She tried to mimic his calmness and forced herself to cross to the sink and fill the kettle. 'Cup of tea?'

'Sure. Sounds great.'

So that was it? They were just going to chat politely to each other, drink tea and say goodbye? Was that all he wanted? Feeling as though she'd just had the rug pulled from under her, Bergan wasn't sure what was going to happen next. She took two cups from the cupboard and two teabags.

'How was the dinner?' When he didn't immediately answer, she turned and looked at him over her shoulder.

'I left early.'

Silence floated in the air between them, and from his relaxed, unhurried manner it was clear he wasn't going to make any effort to fill it.

'Oh? But you were the guest of honour.'

'I know.'

'Has that happened often at other hospitals you've visited? That you go out to dinner at the end of your placement?'

Another pause, then a shrug. 'Some.'

Bergan checked the kettle again, wishing it would hurry up and boil, thereby giving her something to do. She leaned against the kitchen cupboards and looked across at him, the uncomfortable tension mounting with each passing second.

'Good to see Wendy doing well.'

Richard nodded.

'Mackenzie said they had to amputate the right leg below the knee but have managed to save the other one.'

He nodded again.

'And Reggie said the bladder and intestinal ruptures are healing nicely.'

'So I've heard.'

Unable to take it any longer, Bergan spread her arms wide. 'What do you want, Richard?'

He raised his eyebrows and a slow smile began to sneak its way across his perfect mouth. 'That's a loaded question, especially coming from you.'

'Why?'

'Because I want you to marry me.' The words were delivered matter-of-factly and Bergan was relieved she was neither drinking nor holding anything in her hands because at those words her mind and body went completely numb.

Eventually, she managed to blink one long blink before staring at him and swallowing. 'M-m-marry?'

'Yes.' It was only then he slowly made his way around to where she was. Bergan felt like a deer caught in a car's headlights, unable to move or look away from this glorious, wonderful, scary man.

'This isn't the official proposal,' he said, coming to stand right next to her, invading her personal space and not seeming to care. 'When I propose, you'll know about it.'

'P-propose?'

His gorgeous smile was heart pounding and mind numbing at the same time. Richard placed his hands on her shoulders and looked down into her eyes. 'I'm in love with you, Bergan, and I have the sneakiest suspicion that you're in love with me.'

'Love?'

'And no doubt that scares the life out of you, which is why you've been incommunicado recently. I understand that, and I'm not going to rush you.'

'You're not?'

He shook his head. 'I'm flying out in a few hours' time and I wanted to spend as much of that time with you as I can.'

'Er...' The concern in her eyes matched the fear pulsing through her. What did that mean? What was she supposed to do? Say? She had wondered whether Richard might try and see her before he left, but she'd half expected him to be as mad as anything.

This calm acceptance of the situation wasn't what she'd mentally prepared for. She almost wished he'd yell at her, demand reasons why she'd shut him out, but perhaps...just perhaps he knew her better than she'd realised. If he pushed her, she'd get angry, making it easier for her to hate him and to walk away. Ooh, he was clever.

'I don't mind if we just snuggle up on the lounge, watch a bad movie, drink tea, eat popcorn, play a game of Scrabble.' He bent his head and brushed a small kiss on her cheek. 'I just want to be with you, Bergan.'

'Because you...lo—' She stopped and swallowed over the word.

'Love you?' He nodded. 'Yes.'

'And this…declaration isn't supposed to pressure me?'

'That wasn't my intention. I have two weeks of presenting my findings on the fellowship and then you'll fly to Paris to meet me.'

'I will?' The ground shifted beneath her feet yet again. There was disbelief in her tone and finally she started to regain some control over her mind and body. The kettle had switched itself off and as she stepped back Richard dropped his hands, watching as she poured boiling water into the cups. 'I thought you said you weren't going to rush me.'

'I'm also not completely stupid,' he returned. 'Besides, it's not rushing you, Bergan, it's more like giving you a gentle nudge in the right direction.'

'So I'm expected to take time off work away from my busy A and E department and fly off to Paris with barely a moment's notice.'

'Yes.'

'And who will look after A and E?'

'Mackenzie said she'd help organise that.'

'Oh, she did, did she? What else has Mackenzie volunteered for?'

Richard thought for a moment then shook his head. 'Nothing. Reggie is the one who's offered to pick you up and take you to the airport. I've given her the information for the flights that have been booked for you.'

'What?'

'I told you, Bergan. Desperate times call for desperate measures.'

'What about my home? My plants?'

'Mackenzie's daughter Ruthie has agreed to water them for you.'

'And Sunainah? What's her role in all this?' Bergan clattered the spoon roughly from side to side in the tea-cup, not caring what sort of noise she was making. Had her friends really agreed to gang up on her like this?

'She's going to be keeping you calm.' Richard watched as she threw the teaspoon into the sink then gripped the edge of the bench as she processed every-thing he was saying.

'So, because I haven't spoken to you all week long, you've turned my friends against me?'

'They love you, Bergan. You know that. They only want what's best for you.'

'Oh, and I suppose that's you?' She shook her head then turned and walked into the lounge room, not car-ing about the tea.

Richard instantly followed her and placed his arms around her, his chest pressed to her back. 'Yes, as a matter of fact it is. Bergan, I know this is difficult for you, but I can't let you go. You've brought brightness and sunshine back into my life. I love you.'

'And you're OK with that? With just forgetting your life with Chantelle and moving on?'

'I can't live in the past. I can't bring Chantelle back. She knew that. She told me that I needed to move for-ward and one day find someone else. And that someone else is you, Bergan. You are unique and kind and a little bit crazy, as well as passionate and faithful. And while, at times, you completely flabbergast and exasperate me, it doesn't change the fact that I am in love with you.'

'And how did you come to this conclusion, then?'

'When you started avoiding me, it made me really stop and think, really take stock of what was going on in my life. This past year, on the fellowship, my life hasn't been normal, and I honestly thought I needed to return to Paris, to finish the fellowship, to figure out who I was after a year of travelling, of having new experiences, and that's why I couldn't give you an answer whenever you asked me what might happen next between us.

'I knew you made me happy, happier than I've been in a very long time, but I wasn't sure how I'd feel when I returned to Europe.'

'And you do now?' She eased away. 'How can you possibly predict what might happen when you return? You can't. This…' she indicated the space between them '…thing between us is nothing more than some sort of holiday romance. When you get back and reality starts to seep into the imaginary world you've been living in, you'll see there's no room for me, no room for a woman with too much baggage to fit into your world.' She shook her head. 'We're better off apart, Richard.'

'Respectfully, Bergan, I completely disagree.'

'How, Richard?' She threw her arms up in the air, her control snapping. 'How can you possibly know that what we have here is something that can last for ever?'

'Because you frustrate me, because you drive me insane, because you perplex me.'

'Thanks a lot.' There was pain in her voice and she could feel tears starting to prick her eyes.

'You also excite me, challenge me, believe in me. My desire to be with you for the rest of my life isn't some whim, Bergan, and when I realised that, I knew it didn't matter whether I was in Paris or Australia or Timbuktu. Wherever I was, I didn't want to be without *you*.'

He closed the distance between them, slipped his arms around her waist and dipped his head to press his lips to hers, all in one swift movement. Anything she might have said disappeared into thin air as all she could focus on was the fact that Richard was kissing her. For days she had craved this, often waking up at night longing for his touch.

Unable to remain strong when he held her like this, when he created such havoc with her senses, she sighed into the embrace, leaning into him, showing him that although she was trying to push him away, she really wanted him as close as possible.

'Bergan,' he eventually said, drawing back slightly, 'you know me better than anyone else. I don't usually talk about Chantelle—to anyone. Of course my parents and my sisters supported me at the time of her death but grief has its own schedule, taking its sweet time to unravel. And that's exactly what I might have done had I not met you. I'd bottled my emotions up for so long, showing the world that I was coping just fine. I accepted the fellowship for two reasons. First, to force myself out of the life I'd boxed myself into. You know, home then hospital, home then hospital day after day after day.'

'Monotonous and lonely,' she stated, listening intently to every word he was saying and unable to stop her heart from being desperately affected by his words.

'Exactly. Second, I knew that when I was travelling, meeting new people, having to give lectures as well as working in different A and E departments in different countries, I could continue to hide, continue to portray that I really was OK.'

'But you weren't?'

'No, and I didn't realise I wasn't, not until I saw you at the Moon Lantern festival.'

'Really?'

'I looked across a crowd of thousands into your eyes and somehow felt as though I'd found my home.' He smiled in bemusement and shook his head. 'It sounds silly to say it out loud, but that's the way it was. I couldn't get you out of my mind, and then when I saw you at the hospital and found out you were not only my hospital contact but also my neighbour, I couldn't believe it. It's as though everything I'd been through in my life had been leading me towards meeting you, towards the time we've shared together, towards asking you to spend the rest of your life with me.'

Bergan started trembling again at his words. 'Is... *that* the propos—?'

'No. Again, you'll know when I'm properly proposing, but I want you to know my intentions are honourable. Old-fashioned, yes, but it's the truth. I love you, Bergan. Nothing will change that.'

She looked away as he said the words, unable to believe how vulnerable hearing them made her feel. Richard loved her. Could that be true? Richard wanted to marry her, to be with her for ever, to live the rest of his life with her. Was she really that worthy?

'Anyway, my real intention for coming here tonight was so I could spend the rest of the time I have in Australia with you.'

Bergan nodded, not trusting her voice because she was so choked up with emotion. Never had anyone made her feel so honoured, so cherished, so loved. Was it really possible for her to have a normal, happy relationship? Mackenzie seemed to think so, and so did Richard. He'd been through so much himself, grieving for his wife, battling loneliness, and yet here he was, standing before her, confessing his feelings, desperate to spend time with her.

Her heart turned over with love, and even though her first inclination was to discount the emotion, telling herself she didn't *do* love, she knew it was a lie. She couldn't, however, admit that to Richard, not yet. The fact that he'd come here to confess his feelings was all that was holding her together, knowing that *he* thought she was worthy of his love. If he'd left, returning to Paris without a word, as she'd expected, given her behaviour over the past few days, then anything he'd confessed wouldn't have had much impact.

He'd blown off his going-away dinner, leaving early even though he was the guest of honour, to come here and spend time with her. *With her!* He'd opened his heart, declared his intentions and was *showing* her exactly how he felt.

Until a few hours ago, she'd accepted her future existence: a life without Richard. Now, though, there were too many different possibilities that flooded through her mind, but in all of them she could picture him by her side, affirming her, encouraging her, believing in her.

With great reluctance he eased his hold on her and led her into the lounge, where they snuggled together, watching a movie and talking quietly as though this was an ordinary 'date' night rather than their last few hours together.

When it was time for him to leave, Richard held her tight in the circle of his arms before dipping his head and pressing slow, soft and sensual kisses to her mouth.

'I don't want you to go,' she whispered in his ear, her voice breaking, as she hugged him close. And when he finally released her, holding her hand until it was necessary to finally let go, he smiled and winked at her.

'That's a very good beginning.'

CHAPTER TWELVE

'You're jittery.' Drak sauntered over to where she was sitting at the desk in the drop-in centre.

'Hmm? Pardon?' Bergan looked up from where she'd been reading a document, the pen in her hand being tapped repeatedly on the desktop. Drak glanced pointedly at the pen and it was only then that Bergan seemed to realise she was moving it. 'Sorry.'

'Missing Richard?'

Bergan closed her eyes for a moment and shook her head. 'Not you, too. I get enough hounding from Mackenzie, Sunainah and Reggie.'

'Fine.' Drak held up his hands in surrender. 'I won't mention him.'

'I'd appreciate it.' She'd half expected Drak to walk away, to go and do something else—at least, that's what the *old* Drak would have done. This new Drak, the one who had changed into a responsible adult, pulled up a chair and sat down beside her.

'Whatcha working on?'

'Calendar of events for next year.'

'Need some ideas?'

'Sure. Fire away.' Anything to take her mind off her next big adventure.

Drak came up with several great suggestions and

some not so great. Some were far too silly and way out there to be considered, but they certainly made them both laugh.

'It's good to see you laughing. Haven't seen much of it these past few weeks.'

'No.'

'A lot on your mind, eh?'

She levelled a glare at him. 'Who's been talking to you?'

'Mackenzie. Sunainah. Reggie.'

'They shouldn't have. The last thing you need is to be burdened with my problems.'

'It's not a burden for true friends to be concerned about each other,' he pointed out. 'Besides, the three of them have been to visit Jammo in the rehab clinic, just like you. Jammo's so amazed at how much people *really* care about her.'

'She's a special girl.'

'You don't need to tell me.' Drak shook his head. 'That night…I think I aged a lifetime.'

Bergan smiled. 'Richard and I couldn't believe the way we literally watched you become a man.'

Drak rolled his eyes. 'Hey, don't get all mushy on me, OK? And speaking of Richard—'

'We weren't,' she interrupted, but he ignored her.

'Aren't you supposed to fly to Paris tomorrow?'

'Yes.'

'Are you going?'

'I don't know.'

'Why not?'

Bergan sighed then looked at him. 'Because I'm scared.' She spread her hands wide, not giving him the chance to say anything. 'You know my story. You know how difficult it is for people like us to trust again.'

'But you *do* trust Richard, don't you?'

'Yes.'

'Do you love him?'

Bergan sighed again, thinking of the video calls she'd shared with Richard during the past fortnight, how her heart rate had pounded out such an erratic rhythm the instant she'd seen his face on the screen and how her spirits had plummeted once it was all over.

She felt as though she was living from call to call and she could accept that, but to get on a plane to fly halfway around the world for a *man*? That was something she'd thought she'd never do. Yes, she trusted him. Yes, she loved him, at least she could admit that much now, but in getting on that plane tomorrow, wasn't that a declaration that she was willing to give up her inner self? To share the rest of her life with Richard, knowing he would always be there for her? That she would be there for him? That together they could really start making a different in this world?

'Do you love him?' Drak repeated.

'Yes.' There was a hint of annoyance in her tone at being pushed.

'Then what are you waiting for? Trusting and loving—those are the big things. Oh, and communicating. Jammo and I are working on that now. Making sure we talk to each other, tell each other when we're freaked out and stuff.'

'I'm really happy for you, Drak. I can't believe how only a few weeks ago you didn't want to carry that lantern.'

He laughed at the memory as he rubbed his fingers over a coffee stain on the wall next to him. 'How did you put up with me?'

She laughed back, teasing him. 'I have no idea!'

The smile slowly slid from Drak's face. 'You'll regret it if you don't go.'

'Yeah. I know. It's just…when I'm with Richard, everything is…magnified. I don't know how or why but it just is. Emotions are more powerful, time more precious, happiness more than I could ever imagine.'

'But?' he prompted.

'But what if I lose myself?'

Drak laughed, then quickly sobered. 'Oh, you're not joking. Bergan, I don't think you could ever lose the true person inside you. You're too strong for that.' He pointed to a coffee stain on the wall, one that had been there for as long as Bergan could remember. 'I've looked at this stain so many times over the years. I don't know who spilt their coffee one day but so many times, when I've just zoned out from what's been going on around me, I'd imagine being able to pick up a pen and turn this stain into a beautiful drawing.'

Bergan handed him a pen. 'Show me.'

Drak stared at her for a moment as though she'd lost her marbles, then took the pen from her. Within a matter of a few strokes his natural creativity had managed to change what had been splatters and splotches into two people riding on horses, side by side, off into the sunset. 'Perspective, Bergan. You taught me that. It's how you look at things and what you do with that knowledge that counts.'

Bergan stared at the beautiful drawing on the wall and was surprised when tears pricked her eyes. How could she not have realised how simple it all was? Yes, she considered she had a large stain on her life, but if she added Richard's love to that stain, she could change it into something beautiful.

'I'm going to Paris.' She whispered the words, as

though testing them out. She breathed in a deep, cleansing breath. 'I'm going to Paris.' She met Drak's gaze. He just rolled his eyes, but she could see he was trying hard not to smile, still needing to protect his 'tough guy' image. A grin touched her lips and she sat up a little straighter in her chair, thinking of seeing Richard face-to-face, being held in his arms, daring to make something new from the stain that was already on her life. The next time she spoke, her voice was filled with wonder, with excitement, with anticipated happiness. *'Je vais à Paris.'*

Drak nodded and stood up. 'Whatever. Just bring me back a croissant.'

Richard stood at airport arrivals, waiting impatiently. He tried not to pace up and down but wasn't all that successful. He tried sitting. He tried leaning. He tried having a coffee but ended up forgetting about it, letting it go cold. He'd arrived much earlier than necessary, just in case her flight time had changed.

He'd received a text message from Reggie saying she'd taken Bergan to the airport. 'She's eager to see you.' That's what the message had said, and since then, during the long twenty-two hours it took to fly from Brisbane to Paris, he'd been a wreck. Bergan was coming to him. A part of him had thought she might back out, but she hadn't. It only highlighted her inner strength, a strength he loved.

Richard checked the arrivals screen again and saw with great relief and delight that her flight had just landed. She was here. She was physically on the same side of the world as him, in the same country, in the same city, in the same airport. The time it took for her to disembark, pick up her luggage and go through immigration seemed to take an eternity but finally—*finally*—she was here.

He hadn't been quite sure what sort of reception he'd receive but what he had not mentally pictured was Bergan opening her arms wide and all but launching herself at him. With a happiness he hadn't thought he could feel, Richard caught her, instantly pressing his mouth to hers in a long-overdue kiss. He couldn't think right now, couldn't worry whether or not he was rushing her, because she was here. *His Bergan* was finally in his arms, her lips pressed against his.

'I've missed you,' she whispered the instant her lips left his.

'Really?' Richard eased her back a little, one arm still firmly around her waist, holding her in a fashion that was clearly possessive.

'Of course. Haven't you missed me, too?'

He swallowed at her words. 'More than you could possibly know.'

Bergan smiled and relaxed. She had two weeks' holiday booked and as it had been quite a while since she'd been to Paris, she was determined to enjoy herself, especially with Richard by her side.

As they headed for the taxi rank, Richard continued to have at least one arm about her, brushing small kisses to her cheeks and neck and lips. Bergan looked into his face and couldn't believe the love that seemed to flow freely from her heart. How…why had she ever tried to deny just how important this man was to her?

'How far is your apartment?' she asked.

'Twenty minutes. Not too bad.'

'Are your parents still here?'

He shook his head. 'They're staying at a hotel tonight and catching a very early train tomorrow morning. They're heading to Wales to see some family friends.'

'Oh. I'm sorry to have missed them.' Bergan smiled to herself as he hailed the taxi, wondering if Helen and Thomas hadn't been evicted from Richard's apartment simply because she was coming.

Richard hailed a taxi and after stowing her luggage in the boot sat with her in the back, his arms firmly around her. He kissed her slowly, carefully, not wanting anything to upset her but at the same time unable to keep his hands or lips off her.

'Don't you have any idea just how addictive you are?'

'Especially after so many weeks apart,' she murmured, equally interested in having his mouth firmly on hers. They were like a couple of teenagers, but neither of them cared, and when they finally arrived at his apartment, Richard insisting on carrying her suitcase up the two flights of stairs, Bergan entered the dark hallway and wandered through into the main living area, gasping in delight at the sight that greeted her.

Tealight candles seemed to be everywhere, their flames flickering perfectly, illuminating the area with a rosy glow.

'Richard?' She reached behind her for his hand but all he did was relieve her of her carry-on luggage. As she continued to look, noticing the mix of red and white rose petals scattered carefully around the furniture, she couldn't help but laugh in astonishment at the tealights on the table, arranged in a heart shape. 'How did you do all this?'

The scents of the candles mixed with the rose petals made a heady combination, and Bergan simply couldn't have removed the large smile from her face, even if someone had asked. She clutched her hands to her chest as she walked slowly and carefully around the place. It had to have been his mother who had set all this up. It was typical of Helen to want to help out, but how had Richard known? Was this as much of a surprise to him as it was to her?

'Richard?' she called again, and this time when she turned to look for him it was to find him holding out a perfect blue rose to her. 'Oh, my!' It wasn't until she reached out to take it from him that she realised her hands were trembling.

'H-how did you know?'

'Reggie. She was very forthcoming about the blue-rose theory, and I have to say you are unique and more beautiful than any flower, my Bergan.'

'Oh.' She swallowed over the lump that had formed in her throat at his heartfelt words. The instant she took the flower he pulled a small box from his pocket and went down on one knee, holding out his free hand to her.

'Bergan?'

The trembling was getting worse now, spreading from her fingers right through her entire body as she stepped forward and placed her hand in his.

'I told you that when I proposed, you'd know about it.'

'True. Very true.' She looked from him to the beautiful room then back again, gazing down at the man of her dreams, the one man, the most perfect man for her.

'Bergan.'

'Yes, Richard.'

'Will you do me the honour of becoming my wife?'

She bit her lip, her heart pounding so wildly against her ribs it was a wonder she could actually hear him speak. She swallowed once, twice, then smiled at him and nodded. 'Yes. A most definite *yes*.'

'Whew!' He chuckled then leaned forward and pressed a smooth kiss to her hand before opening the box. Inside, nestled on a soft blue velvet cushion, was a perfect pink diamond. 'You can choose the setting and the style of the ring. We'll have it made up.'

'Really?' He was letting her take control.

'Really.' He slowly rose to his feet, watching as she took the box from him, studying the perfectly cut stone.

'Richard. It's…' The enormity of the situation overcame her and to her utter surprise tears gathered behind her eyes. 'It's…perfect.' When she looked up at him, it was to find him staring down at her with the same sort of wonderment.

'You are. Most definitely perfect.' He wrapped his arms around her and drew her close. 'I love you so much, Bergan. I can't promise that our life together will always be smooth sailing, but I do promise to love and trust you for the rest of my days. We'll talk, we'll laugh, we'll cry and we'll do it *together.*'

'Yes.' She accepted his kisses and sighed against him, occasionally glancing down at the diamond—*her* diamond! 'How *did* you organise all of this? Was it your mother?'

'She lit the candles. I sent her a text when I was stowing your luggage in the taxi.'

'You fiend. And what if I'd been less than enthusiastic when I'd arrived at the airport? Or completely jet-lagged?'

'Then the plan would have changed, but as it was, with the way you all but launched yourself at me—'

'I did not!' she protested hotly as Richard led her to the soft sofa, pulling her onto his lap.

He kissed the tip of her nose. 'I beg to differ, but either way it gave me a clear indication that whatever had been holding you back had been resolved.'

'You gave me these two weeks to figure things out.' She nodded slowly. 'I did and I feel as though an enormous weight has been lifted from my shoulders.' Then she told him about the coffee stain and how Drak had drawn a perfect picture from it.

'Remind me to make Drak a groomsman at our wedding,' Richard said, and Bergan laughed.

'I doubt he'd see having to dress up in some suit as a reward.'

'Perhaps he'd make us a wedding lantern?'

'Good idea. One we can let go and have fly off into the night.'

'On the beach.'

'At dusk.'

'Perfect.' Bergan sighed against him, smiling happily.

'All this wedding talk isn't freaking you out?'

She shook her head. 'Nope. I'm right where I should be. It's been a long time coming but finally…' she snuggled closer, safe and secure in the protective circle of his arms '…I've found my home.'

EPILOGUE

'BUT WHY?' REGGIE protested.

'I thought you would have been happy to dress up in a pretty pink party dress, Reggie.' Bergan stood in the large white marquee reserved for the bride and her attendants, and smoothed a hand down her very simple, very plain, very elegant white wedding gown, staring at herself in the long mirror, unable to believe the woman looking back was actually her. It had happened. She'd found her Prince Charming and he'd made her the happiest princess on earth.

During the past four months, as Richard had relocated back to Australia and the Sunshine Coast, Bergan's love for him had increased every day. She was so proud, so happy to finally be a bride—a bride with a groom whom she loved and trusted with all her heart.

'I am but it's just…it makes me look about seventeen years old.'

'Oh, woe is you for having such a youthful complexion.' Bergan shook her head, small tendrils of auburn curls floating lightly at her neck, the rest of her hair pulled into a fancy arrangement on top of her head, which had taken the hairdresser almost an hour to achieve.

'Do you like the dress, Aunty Sunainah?' Ruthie,

the experienced flower girl who was wearing a dress identical to those of the rest of the bridesmaids, asked.

'I'll wear whatever it is my friend bids me wear on her wedding day, but I do have to say the style and colour perplexes me slightly.'

'Kenz? Care to explain?' Bergan asked as Mackenzie finished touching up the bride's lipstick.

'On the rare occasions, when we were in foster-care, that things actually were going smoothly, Bergan and I indulged our imaginations in planning her wedding.'

'Not your weddings?' Reggie asked.

Mackenzie shook her head. 'I would change mine almost every time, unable to choose exactly what I wanted, but Bergan had this crazy idea that all bridesmaid's dresses should be pink. Pink party dresses with tulle and lace. Fluffy and puffy.'

'So we're fulfilling a childhood fantasy?' Reggie checked.

'Exactly,' Bergan replied, smooching her lips together to blot the lipstick. Outside the marquee, the string quartet started to play and Ruthie started jumping up and down with excitement.

'It's starting. It's starting!'

'Yes,' Mackenzie told her daughter. 'So get your little basket of flowers and get ready because you go down first, remember.'

'I remember, Mummy,' Ruthie replied, her fingers sifting through the lovely blue rose petals in her basket. 'I have been a flower girl before, you know.'

Mackenzie only grinned at her daughter before turning to look at the blushing bride. 'Ready?'

Bergan smiled at her friend, then, before she picked up her bouquet of blue roses, held out her hands to her friends, Ruthie included. 'Thank you. I don't know what else to say, but without the three of you in my life, and for the last six years beautiful Ruthie as well, I wouldn't be here today. I don't *do* friendships easily, but you've stuck with me through so many different things—especially you, Kenz. So, yeah…' She laughed. 'Thanks.'

'Why do you brides always do this?' Reggie grumbled as she sniffed and blinked rapidly, carefully dabbing at her eyes with a tissue before picking up her bouquet of white roses. 'Why do you say these heartfelt words and then make us all want to cry when you know full well we can't because we'll smudge the make-up that took for ever to apply?'

Bergan laughed and nodded. 'I never thought I would, but then, I never thought I'd find that one true, perfect man for me.'

'But you did, and he's waiting, probably rather impatiently, for you now,' Sunainah said.

'I think Drak's probably more impatient than Richard,' Bergan added. 'Impatient to get out of that suit.' With John, Mackenzie's husband, and Thomas, his father, as his other groomsmen, that only left Helen, Richard's mother, on her own, so Bergan had asked a special favour of her future mother-in-law.

'Ready?' Helen asked, poking her head through the opening of the marquee. 'Oh, Bergan,' she gasped. 'You look breathtaking.'

'No crying!' Reggie demanded, holding out a hand towards Helen.

'Yes. Yes. Of course.' Helen sniffed. 'You're right.' She dragged in a deep breath and held out her hand to Bergan. 'It's time for me, not to give you away as happens to most brides on their wedding day, to walk you down the aisle, *accepting* you into our family.'

'Is it time *now*?' Ruthie demanded, and after everyone had taken a deep, cleansing breath and as the music rose to a beautiful crescendo, Bergan nodded.

'It's time.' And with the happiest smile on her face she started her walk towards the only man in the world for her—her Richard.

* * * * *

Look out for
Mills & Boon® TEMPTED™ 2-in-1s,
from September

*Fresh, contemporary romances
to tempt all lovers of
great stories*

A sneaky peek at next month...

Medical Romance™

CAPTIVATING MEDICAL DRAMA—WITH HEART

My wish list for next month's titles...

In stores from 6th September 2013:

Available at WHSmith, Tesco, Asda, Eason, Amazon and Apple

Just can't wait?

0813/03

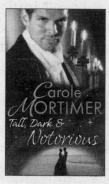
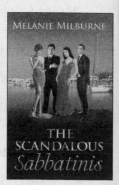